THE NIGHT HAWKS

ALSO BY ELLY GRIFFITHS

The Stranger Diaries
The Postscript Murders

THE RUTH GALLOWAY SERIES

The Crossing Places
The Janus Stone
The House at Sea's End
A Room Full of Bones
A Dying Fall
The Outcast Dead
The Ghost Fields
The Woman in Blue
The Chalk Pit
The Dark Angel
The Stone Circle
The Lantern Men

THE MAGIC MEN SERIES

The Zig Zag Girl
Smoke and Mirrors
The Blood Card
The Vanishing Box
Now You See Them

THE NIGHT HAWKS

A RUTH GALLOWAY MYSTERY

Elly Griffiths

MARINER

HarperCollins*Publishers*
Boston   New York

THE NIGHT HAWKS. Copyright © 2021 by Elly Griffiths. Excerpt from THE LOCKED
ROOM copyright © 2022 by Elly Griffiths. All rights reserved. Printed in the United
States of America. No part of this book may be used or reproduced in any manner
whatsoever without written permission except in the case of brief quotations
embodied in critical articles and reviews. For information, address HarperCollins
Publishers, 195 Broadway, New York, NY 10007.

HarperCollins books may be purchased for educational, business, or sales
promotional use. For information, please email the Special Markets Department
at SPsales@harpercollins.com.

Originally published as *The Night Hawks* in Great Britain in 2021 by Quercus.

First hardcover edition published in 2021 by Houghton Mifflin Harcourt.

FIRST MARINER BOOKS PAPERBACK EDITION PUBLISHED 2022

Library of Congress Cataloging-in-Publication Data has been applied for.

ISBN 978-0-358-69529-5

24 25 26 27 28 LBC 6 5 4 3 2

For Francesca, William and Robert –
who listened to my first series of stories

'They were the footprints of a gigantic hound!'

Arthur Conan Doyle,
The Hound of the Baskervilles

PROLOGUE

There's so much blood, that's what he always remembers. Even after the police and the ambulance have left, there's blood on the grass and even on the trees, dripping into the mud like some Old Testament plague. He follows his father who treads blood into the house and, when he leans heavily against the wall to take off his boots, a bloody handprint is outlined on the yellow wallpaper. His father goes into the sitting room, sits on his chair by the fire and opens the newspaper, almost as if nothing has happened, almost as if his hands aren't still stained with her blood.

He goes back out to the barn. The dog comes to him then, leans against him as if he understands. It's the only time the dog has shown him any affection and he supposes that he's grateful. But another part of him wonders if he'll ever feel any proper human emotion again. There's a flurry of action as the ambulance men manoeuvre the covered stretcher, sliding it into the vehicle – such an easy fluid movement. Then the wheels crunch away over the gravel and the birds rise up from the fields where they have been feasting on the scattered corn. And then, suddenly, everything is silent. Just the weathercock slowly turning on the roof. It's as if the house has retreated somehow and, from now on, no matter how much noise there is in the outside world, here it will always be silent.

Wednesday, 18 September 2019, 00.10

All along the coast on this very eastern edge of England, the tide is coming in. It rolls over dark sand at Holme, it crashes against the multicoloured cliffs at Hunstanton, it batters windows at Happisburgh, reminding home owners that this land is just on loan. And, on this spit of land jutting out into the North Sea, it approaches from all sides, turning streams into lagoons and lagoons into unfathomable lakes.

The Night Hawks are aware of the encroaching waters. This is dangerous territory, after all. But they are hunters and their blood is up. Iron Age coins have been discovered in the sand near Blakeney Point and there are rumours that they are part of something really big, perhaps even a hoard. The hawks spread out across the beach, their metal detectors glowing and humming. The sea rolls in, white waves on black water.

A young man with a torch like a third eye on his head calls, 'There's something here!' The other hawks converge on him, their machines picking up the message, the call of metal below the surface of the earth.

'Could be more coins.'

'Could be armour . . .'

'A metal torque. Arm rings . . .'

They start to dig. Someone sets up an arc light. It's not until there's a shout of 'Tide!' that they realise the waters are almost upon them. Then there's another cry, coming from Troy, a young hawk stationed at the mouth of one of the estuaries winding back inland. His comrades splash over to him, taking care to keep their machines above water.

'There's something . . .' says Troy. 'I almost fell over it.' He's very young, still a teenager, and his voice wavers and breaks.

Alan, an older detectorist, reaches out in the dark to touch his shoulder. 'What is it, lad?'

But another of the hawks is pointing his torch at the ground by Troy's feet. And they all see it, first some clothes swirling in the incoming tide, a movement that gives the appearance of life. But then, caught in a clump of sea grass, a dead body, its arm outstretched as if asking for their help.

1

Ruth parks in her usual spot under the lime tree and takes her usual route through the Natural Sciences department to the archaeology corridor. This route is so familiar to her that she almost stops at her old office, the place where she first met DCI Nelson twelve years ago. But, with only a slight hesitation, she continues on her way and heads to the last door, on which there is a new plaque: Dr Ruth Galloway, Head of Archaeology.

This corner office, which boasts two windows and has room for a sofa as well as a desk, chairs and a round table for meetings, was once occupied by Phil Trent, Ruth's old boss. But now Phil has taken early retirement and Ruth has the top job. Not that head of department at the University of North Norfolk is the toppest of top jobs (in fact Ruth's previous post as a senior lecturer at a Cambridge college was probably more prestigious) but on days like this, when she can see the ornamental lake glittering from her windows and the new freshers drifting across the campus, it does feel pretty special. I am in charge, thinks Ruth, putting her laptop on the desk and clicking onto the university intranet. It's a good feeling but she mustn't get too power hungry and start making her cat a senator or forcing the staff to call her Supreme Leader. It's still a medium job in a medium university. But at least she has her own coffee machine.

She's just about to have her first espresso of the morning when there's a perfunctory knock on the door. Before Ruth can say 'go away', the space in front of her is full of David Brown, the new archaeology lecturer. Her replacement, in fact.

'I've been thinking about our induction for new students,' says David, without even a 'Good morning, Supreme Leader'. 'It seems crazy that we don't have them digging as soon as possible. We give them all that crap about research methods but don't let them get down and dirty until the second semester.'

Ruth sighs. In principle she agrees. Digging, 'getting down and dirty', is one of the joys of archaeology. She would like her students to experience the thrill of discovery as soon as possible. But there are practical implications. Although Norfolk is one of the most archaeologically rich landscapes in the world, there are only ever a few digs running at one time and these could be ruined by over-eager first-years trampling all over the trenches. And the students themselves will be disappointed if, after a day in the bitter easterly winds, they only unearth a nail or a jubilee coin from 1977. Plus she despises the word semester. They're called *terms* in England, she tells David silently.

'We've thought about this before,' she says. *Before you came and disrupted everything* is the subtext. 'But there's not really a suitable dig at the moment. Caistor St Edmund needs Roman specialists and Sedgeford is only in the summer.'

'Then we should start our own dig.'

'We haven't got the funding,' says Ruth. She remembers how Phil used to irritate her with his constant talk of grants and funding, yet here she is playing the same tune. But the harsh reality is, they don't have the money or the person-power to start a new excavation, not unless another Bronze Age henge magically materialises on a Norfolk beach.

'Our induction programme is out of date,' says David. 'There's not enough on isotope analysis or DNA testing.'

Ruth, who updated the programme herself, glares at him but is distracted by her phone ringing. *Nelson* says the screen.

'Excuse me,' she says, 'I must take this call.'

David doesn't take the hint and leave but stands in front of her, blocking out the light.

'Ruth,' says Nelson. He, too, never bothers with niceties like 'Hallo'. 'I'm at Cley. A body's been washed up at Blakeney Point. I think you'd better come and see it.'

Ruth doesn't know quite how David Brown manages to come along too. It certainly isn't because she invited him. All she knows, as she climbs into her lime-spattered Renault, is that David is next to her, folding his long legs into the passenger seat and adjusting it without her permission. She can't really tell him to get out. Teaching hasn't started yet. The only official business of the day is the Meet and Greet with the freshers at five. She supposes that David has all the time in the world to inspect dead bodies.

'This might take a while,' she says, as she backs out of her space. 'I'm a special advisor to the north Norfolk police. They probably want me to look at the position of the body, provide some forensic analysis.'

All David says is, 'Mind the hedge,' as Ruth takes the corner too tightly. She grinds her teeth.

Ruth doesn't know quite why David annoys her so much. They have the same academic speciality, the prehistoric era, which doesn't help, but this is partly why Ruth employed David, to teach the courses that used to be her province. They even attended the same university, University College London, although David is four years older than Ruth so they didn't overlap. David then went to live and work in Sweden which is why he finds himself, aged fifty-five, applying for a job at UNN. But he was a good candidate and Ruth is lucky to have him on the team. It's just, why does he have to act as if he's all too aware of this?

It's a short drive to Cley and David is silent for most of it. Ruth is damned if she's going to make conversation, but she longs to point out the beauty of the landscape, the yellow grass and blue water, the flint cottages, the fishing boats in the harbour. Yet David hardly looks up from his phone. More fool him, thinks Ruth.

Nelson is waiting for them at the entrance to the car park. Ruth remembers meeting him, years ago, at Blakeney car park on their way to interview Cathbad in his caravan. Now Cathbad owns a charming cottage in nearby Wells, where he lives with his partner and three children. Everything changes, thinks Ruth, as she parks the car and gets out her wellingtons. She is wearing her best boots in honour of the Meet and Greet and she's not going to risk them getting wet. David watches her sardonically. He's wearing a trainer/shoe hybrid that will probably fare very badly in the mud and sand.

'What took you so long?' says Nelson, as soon as Ruth comes into speaking distance.

But some things never change.

'This is a colleague of mine, David Brown,' says Ruth, ignoring Nelson's comment. 'David, this is DCI Nelson.' She doesn't give Nelson's first name because no one in Norfolk, apart from his wife, calls Nelson 'Harry'.

Nelson nods at David and turns back to Ruth. 'The body's a little way along the beach. We'd better hurry because the tide's coming in.'

The only way to reach Blakeney Point is to take a boat or walk from Cley. By foot it is, by all accounts, an energetic four-mile trek. Ruth has never tried it herself. She has taken Kate on the boat trip though, to see the seals who loll on the sand bank like drunks who have been thrown out of a pub. She hopes that today's walk isn't going to be too arduous. It's a beautiful autumn day but she doesn't want to spend hours trudging along the shingle in her wellingtons. Nelson strides ahead and Ruth has to scurry to keep up with him. She's not going to trail behind the two men. Luckily David dawdles, taking pictures on his phone.

They walk along the beach, scrubby shingle on one side

and the sea on the other. Occasionally Ruth sees sea poppies and clumps of samphire. A yacht goes past, its sails very white against the blue. In the distance is a curious blue house like an upturned boat. Just as Ruth's legs start aching, Nelson turns inland. There are patches of still water here and, as they pass, the birds rise up in clouds. Eventually they reach a promontory where yellow police tape is fluttering gaily in the wind. Two figures in white coveralls are standing at the water's edge.

'Should we be suited up?' says Ruth.

'No,' says Nelson, 'we don't need to get that close.'

Ruth looks at him quizzically but says nothing. They climb the shingle bank so that they are looking down at the inlet. Here the water comes to a point and starts to trickle inland. On the higher ground a tent has been erected but, through the open flaps, Ruth can see the shape of a body.

'Male,' says Nelson. 'Young. Looks to be about twenty. We'll get his DNA, of course, but that'll only help if it matches someone on our records. My guess is that he's an illegal immigrant . . . a refugee,' he amends, looking at Ruth.

'Why do you think he's a migrant?' says David. 'Because he "looks foreign"?' He puts contemptuous quotes round the words.

'No,' says Nelson, scowling at him but keeping his voice even. 'But we've had reports of migrant boats coming this way. They're heading for Southwold because there's no coastguard there.'

Ruth looks across at the tent. She can see the head quite clearly, dark hair lifting in the breeze. A young man's body.

Has he really travelled hundreds of miles just to end up here, washed up on an unknown shore? She says what has been in her mind ever since she got Nelson's call. 'If you know who he is and why he's here, why do you need me?'

'Because his body was found by some archaeologists,' says Nelson. 'Metal detectorists. They call themselves the Night Hawks. And I think they've found something else too.'

2

'Nighthawks aren't archaeologists,' says Ruth.

'Why do you say that?' says Nelson. 'They looked pretty professional to me. Lots of equipment.' They've moved along the beach to a point where the earth is lying in huge mounds, as if a giant child has been building a sand-castle.

'They're not archaeologists,' says Ruth. 'They're amateurs who charge around looking for treasure. They've no idea how to excavate or how to read the context. They just dive in and dig up whatever looks shiny.'

'Wow,' says David. 'Elitism is alive and well and living in Norfolk.'

'What do you mean by that?' says Ruth.

'Archaeology isn't just the preserve of people with degrees,' says David. 'Detectorists are valid members of the community and these finds belong to the people.'

'Licensed metal detectorists are fine,' says Ruth. 'But Nelson called these people nighthawks.' She can hear her voice rising and takes a deep breath. She doesn't want

Nelson to hear her arguing with a colleague. Well, strictly speaking, an employee.

'It's what they called themselves,' says Nelson. 'Much as I hate to interrupt this academic discussion, as I was saying, the body was found by some metal detectorists who were looking for that.' He points at the mound.

'What is it?' says Ruth.

'It seems like a lot of old metal,' says Nelson. 'I thought you might like to have a look.'

Ruth feels her heart beating faster. This part of the coast is famous for buried treasure. There was the so-called jeweller's hoard at Snettisham, as if the contents of a Romano-British jewellery shop were just lying underground waiting to be discovered. Then there was the Sedgeford torc and the Iceni silver coins at Scole. Old metal, Nelson said, but he wouldn't know an Iron Age hoard from the contents of the slot machines on the Golden Mile in his beloved Blackpool.

'These metal detectorists,' Nelson is saying. 'They were here last night with their machines and lights and what have you. They found this and got all excited, then one of them, a young lad called Troy Evans, found the body. They called the police and two local PCs attended the scene. They called me first thing this morning.'

'We'll have to secure this site,' says Ruth. 'Stop anyone else trampling over it. Can you make it part of the crime scene, Nelson?'

She's half-joking but Nelson says, 'I suppose so as it was found at the same time as the body. Funny place to bury something, isn't it?'

'Not really,' says Ruth. 'Two thousand years ago it would have been well above the tide line.'

'But why bury something on the beach?'

'They could have been a votive offering,' says Ruth. 'An offering to the sea gods.' She looks at Nelson and knows that they are both thinking the same thing: bodies buried in the sand near here, murdered to placate nameless, vengeful gods. They have reached the hole – it can hardly be called a trench – and Ruth can see the dull gleam of greenish metal.

'Or sometimes you find escape hoards,' David cuts in. 'Warlords on the run, perhaps escaping back to Scandinavia. They buried their treasure, hoping they would come back for it.' He squats down to look. Ruth is rather pleased to see that his shoes and trousers are wet and spattered with sand. He leans closer and, when he speaks, his voice is different. Thick with excitement.

'Ruth! I think this is Bronze Age.'

Ruth comes forward to look. A Bronze Age hoard would be a find indeed. Rarer and older. Leaning in – uncomfortably close to David – she can see what looks like a fragment of a spear, shaped a bit like the club in a suit of cards.

'Broken spears,' says David. 'This could be Beaker.' Ruth knows that the Bronze Age, and the Beaker People specifically, is David's speciality.

Ruth has brought her excavation kit, a backpack containing trowel, brush and zip-lock bags. She brushes the sandy soil away from the metal and sees something else in the earth below, something smooth and off-white.

Nelson comes forward now.

'What's that?'

'I think it's a part of a skull,' says Ruth.

'There's a body there?' Ruth can sense Nelson's excitement, even without looking at him.

'I think so. We'll need to do a proper excavation.'

David has taken the trowel and widened the area around the bone. 'I think there's more here. Looks like we've got our dig.' He grins at her. It's the first time that Ruth has seen him smile and the effect is actually to make his face look even grimmer than before. She doesn't smile back. Someone is dead, after all. Two people, if you count the body lying amongst the Bronze Age spears. Which she does.

'Glad someone's happy,' says Nelson. 'It's an ill wind.' This too, suddenly sounds rather sinister, especially as the wind has been getting stronger in the last few minutes. Sand is rising from the beach in clouds, getting into Ruth's hair and her eyes. Ruth suspects that Nelson got this particular adage from his mother and it's never a good sign when he starts quoting Maureen.

When Ruth and her follower have trudged back to the car park, Nelson returns to the crime scene. The Forensics team are having to work quickly because of the incoming tide. Last night, the Night Hawks moved the body to higher ground. Normally Nelson would be cursing them for interfering but, in this case, it was the only thing to do. The tide was rising fast and, by the time that the police appeared, the body would have been lost to the water. It does mean that they can't gain any clues from the surrounding area, 'the context', Ruth would call it. And they need to move the dead man before the tide comes in again, at midday.

After exchanging a few words with the Forensics officers, Nelson heads back inland. There's nothing more for him to do here. He's not a fan of the north Norfolk coast, miles of sand and rocks and mangy looking vegetation. It whiffs to high heaven too, a horrible, rank, briny smell, not like the aroma of vinegar and chips which hovers over proper seaside resorts. As he treads carefully over the wet seaweed, he sees a woman coming towards him, dressed in a yellow raincoat. DI Judy Johnson always has the right gear for the climatic conditions. Cathbad, her partner, says it's because she is in tune with the weather gods.

'Hi, boss,' says Judy, when she gets closer. 'I saw Ruth leaving. Who was that with her?'

'Some dickhead from the university. And guess what? We've found another body.'

'Another body's been washed up?'

'No. Ruth thinks there's a skeleton buried with a pile of old metal higher up on the beach. That's what they were looking for, this Night Hawk gang. They call it a hoard. Of course, they didn't know there was a body there too.'

'Is that why you called Ruth?'

'No,' says Nelson, not looking at her. 'I didn't know about the skeleton. I just thought she'd be interested because some of her lot were involved. Though Ruth says that metal detectorists aren't proper archaeologists.'

'Cathbad goes out with the Night Hawks sometimes,' says Judy. 'He says that they're genuine questing souls.'

That figures, thinks Nelson. Cathbad is a druid. He also teaches meditation and once trained as an archaeologist. Nelson doubts that there's a single group of local eccentrics that Cathbad doesn't know about. And, if they go out at night and break a few laws along the way, that's right up his street. Questing souls indeed. He never knows quite what Judy, his best and most rational officer, makes of her partner's beliefs. She certainly manages to say this sort of thing with a straight face.

'We need to secure the archaeological site,' says Nelson. 'And inform the coroner. Even though the body will turn out to be thousands of years old.'

'It might not,' says Judy. 'Stranger things have happened.'

'They certainly have,' says Nelson. 'And mostly to us.'

'Do we know anything about the body washed up on the beach last night?' says Judy. 'Any identification on him?'

'No,' says Nelson. 'I think he must have come from a migrant boat. Have the coastguard reported anything?'

'No. I rang round all the stations this morning. Of course, they could have come ashore somewhere where there are no checks. Who attended the scene first?'

'PC Nathan Matthews and PC Mark Hammond. Local boys. Good coppers. I came across them in Cley last year.'

'I'll read their reports, but shall I get them to come in for the briefing later? Might be good to hear about it in their own words. Especially as we won't have forensics from the scene.'

'Good idea.'

'The tide's coming in,' says Judy as, on cue, a wave sneaks

over the shingle and breaks just in front of them. 'We need to move the body. I've got a private ambulance standing by.'

'I'll leave you to it,' says Nelson. 'Briefing at three. See you later.'

'Super Jo was looking for you,' says Judy, over her shoulder. 'I told her you were out.'

'Good work,' says Nelson. His boss, Superintendent Jo Archer, is always trying to make him have meetings with her. Avoiding her is his main form of exercise.

3

As soon as Ruth gets back to her office, she rings the coroner's office. She needs a licence before she can excavate the bones. In order to get the licence, she has to prove that excavating the remains will further historical and scientific understanding. She doesn't think that this will be difficult. If the weapons look to be Bronze Age, then it's reasonable to suppose that the skeleton must be too. Of course, there might not be a complete articulated skeleton – an animal could have deposited the bones there – but the presence of the swords makes Ruth think that this is a significant site of some kind and, in that case, it's quite likely that it's also a burial site. Bronze Age bodies are often found in burial mounds, typically surrounded by pottery and other grave goods. She remembers reading about a burial in Wiltshire – near Stonehenge, she thinks – where the body was surrounded by gold, like some Inca deity. What if they unearth something like that on Blakeney Point?

The encounter with Nelson had gone well, she thinks, perhaps helped by David's presence. Since she has returned to Norfolk, her relationship with Nelson has been cordial but slightly distant. She's aware that her feelings for him played a big part in the decision to return but she doesn't necessarily want him to know this. Nelson is the father of Ruth's child but he's still married and, whilst Ruth once might have overridden her conscience and ignored this fact, the arrival of baby George has made this impossible. She couldn't forgive herself if she took Nelson away from his three-year-old son, even assuming that he wanted to come. Nelson is a family man, first and foremost, and his family is his wife Michelle and their three children. Ruth thinks that there was a time when Nelson did consider leaving Michelle for her, but that time is firmly in the past. The trouble is that Ruth, as an archaeologist, feels more comfortable in the past. But, in the present, Ruth has her life with her daughter and her cat – and her work. She has to be content with that.

Her reverie is interrupted by David. If he knocked, she didn't hear him.

'You know, this is potentially a very exciting discovery,' he says.

'Come in,' says Ruth pointedly. She doesn't want David taking ownership of the find, something she suspects he is quite likely to do. He was only with her on Blakeney beach because she was too polite to tell him to get out of her car. Or was she just too feeble?

David looks around him, as if surprised to find himself in the room.

'I think it's a Beaker burial,' he says. 'You know I did my PhD research on the Beaker folk.'

'Yes,' says Ruth. She has read his CV, after all. The Beaker people are thought to have migrated to Central Europe from the Eurasian Steppe, continuing west until they eventually arrived in Britain around 4,400 years ago.

'As you know,' says David, 'just a few hundred years after the arrival of the Beakers, only ten per cent of the native population remained. Neolithic Britons were wiped out. It's my theory that it was a plague. A new virus brought by the Beakers from Central Europe. The native population had no immunity. Ninety per cent of them died. Their DNA just disappears.'

'A plague or genocide,' says Ruth.

'The Beakers were a peaceful people,' says David. 'They were interested in culture and pottery.' Ruth knows that the Beakers take their name from their distinctive bell-shaped pots, but she thinks that David is making some sweeping assumptions here.

'I was thinking,' says David. 'Once we've excavated our skeleton, we should get a facial reconstruction done. Beaker people were more likely to be blue-eyed and fair-skinned whereas the native Neolithic population were dark-skinned with brown eyes. It would make an interesting social point.'

Interesting, thinks Ruth, and potentially controversial. She doesn't want to feed into the idea that immigrants bring diseases which wipe out native populations. And she dreads to think of the sort of people who will crawl out of the woodwork complaining if they portray Neolithic Britons as people of colour. All the more reason to do it, of course. The real stumbling block is that facial reconstruction is very expensive. It's depressingly Phil-like to have to think in this way.

'We don't even know if there's a complete skeleton there yet,' she says.

'There is,' says David. 'I'm sure of it. I sense it.'

Ruth gives him a sharp look. Archaeology is divided between people like Phil, who love geophysics and technology, and those, like Ruth's old lecturer Erik, who rely on instinct and inspired guesswork. Before today, Ruth would have put David in the former camp. She likes to think that she is a mixture of the two.

'I've been talking to the coroner's office,' she says. 'We'll have to do a controlled excavation following IFA guidelines.' She can hear herself sounding more corporate by the second.

David sounds slightly chastened. Maybe it's the mention of the Institute for Archaeologists. Or the coroner.

'Of course,' he says. 'When we've excavated the body then maybe we can do a dig for the students. I've been talking to an old school friend of mine. He was actually one of the metal detectorists who found the body last night . . .'

'An old school friend?' says Ruth. 'Are you from Norfolk then?'

She remembers the Beakers from David's interview but she doesn't recall him ever saying that he was local. They had talked about UCL and David's years in Scandinavia but schooldays hadn't come up. Surely David should have mentioned that he knew the area well?

'It was a private prep school in West Runton,' he says now. 'Closed years ago, thank God. I was only there a short time.

Alan was a few years above me but he was kind to me, we were friends. I lost contact with him but we came across each other on a history forum a few years ago.'

No wonder David had been so quick to defend the Night Hawks.

'Anyway, Alan saw that there have been lots of discoveries along this part of the coast. Iron Age hoards but also Bronze Age burials. And there's the henge, of course. You were involved in excavating that, weren't you?'

A series of images flash across Ruth's brain: the timbers rising out of the sea, Erik falling to his knees in the henge circle, her then boyfriend Peter trapped on the quicksand with the tide rolling in, a little hand wearing a christening bracelet . . .

'Yes, I was involved,' she says. 'But it was a long time ago. I'll let you know when I've got the dig organised. Now, if you'll excuse me, I've got a lot of work to do before the Meet and Greet.'

The briefing room is full. The body on the beach isn't necessarily a case for the Serious Crimes Unit but any unexplained death has to be investigated. Nelson runs through the details: 'Deceased male, probably late teens or early twenties, found on Blakeney beach in the early hours of the morning. Death looks to be from drowning but we'll wait for the autopsy results to be sure. By the look of the body, the deceased had only been in the water for a few hours. The deceased . . .' He misses his former DS David Clough, now a DI, who would have given the dead man a name, probably taken from one of the *Godfather* films. The rest of his team are watching him intently. Judy, inscrutable, notebook in hand. Tanya, ever eager, hand hovering to be the first to ask a question. Tony, the new DS, trying to look mature with a newly grown beard and an expression of carefully cultivated nonchalance. Nathan and Mark, the PCs who first attended the 999 call, sitting awkwardly to one side. Nathan, in particular, looks nervous at finding himself in the CID lair. He is sweating profusely and has to keep wiping his forehead.

Mark Hammond takes the lead in reporting their part of the story. 'We got the call at one forty-five a.m.,' he says. 'We proceeded to Blakeney beach where we found four individuals beside the body of a deceased male. They stated that they had found the deceased while searching for buried treasure on the beach. They had moved the deceased to higher ground because the tide was coming in. We secured the site and took statements, then we allowed the witnesses to return home. Their names . . .' he consults his notebook, 'are Troy Evans, aged twenty-one, Alan White, aged fifty-eight, Neil Thomas, aged fifty-six, and Paul Noakes, aged thirty-one.'

'Do we know anything about these men?' asks Nelson.

'Alan White runs the Night Hawks,' says Judy, 'a local group of metal detectorists. They're a proper registered group. Alan is very respectable. Cathbad knows him. He's an ex-history teacher.'

Nelson nods but doesn't say anything. The words 'Cathbad' and 'respectable' don't exactly go together. And he'd like to know why Alan White left teaching. Once again, he misses Clough, who would certainly have been rolling his eyes.

'Did you get a look at the dead man?' Nelson asks the two PCs.

'We checked that he was dead,' says Nathan. His voice is hoarse and his hands are shaking slightly. Nelson wonders if he has the right temperament for a police officer. 'We also looked for any identifying documents but there was nothing in any of his pockets. He was wearing jeans and a check shirt. No shoes. They had probably come off in the water.'

'Anything that struck you as strange?' asks Nelson.

'He had a tattoo,' says Mark.

'Nothing so odd about that,' says Nelson. He has one himself. It says 'Seasiders', a reference to Blackpool FC, his beloved football club.

'This was a bit strange though,' says Mark. 'It was on his neck and it was a snake with sort of spikes on its back. Looked as if it was about to bite his ear off.'

Tony laughs and turns it into a cough. Tanya, who has a discreet dolphin tattoo on the inside of her wrist, says, 'Maybe it was some sort of gang insignia?'

'That's what I thought,' says Mark.

'An unusual tattoo might help with identification,' says Nelson. 'Thanks, boys. Looks like this poor lad was just unlucky. Maybe he took his own life or maybe he was in a ship that got into trouble. Anything from the coastguard, Judy?'

'A blank so far,' says Judy. 'No reports of any migrant boats last night but there are lots of places along the coast where ships could land unnoticed. Cathbad says that's why there used to be so much smuggling in the area.'

'There's still smuggling,' says Nelson, 'only now it's people, not barrels of rum. We're only about a hundred miles away from the Dutch ports. But let's not get fixed on the migrant idea. Our boy might just as well be local. We'll know more when we have his DNA. In the meantime, we'll make some enquiries. I don't want anything in the media just yet.' Super Jo will want to give a press conference. She's addicted to appearing in front of the cameras. Nelson, though, wants to avoid the world and its life partner claiming the boy as their own.

'Oh, and we've got another dead body,' he says. 'But don't get excited, it's probably a few thousand years old. These Night Hawks unearthed a lot of old metal and it looks like there's a skeleton there too.'

'Is Ruth going to excavate?' asks Tanya.

'Yes,' says Nelson. 'She was there today. I called her in because archaeology was involved.'

No one says anything. They all avoid mentioning archaeology in front of the boss.

When Phil was in charge, the Meet and Greet was one of Ruth's least favourite events of the year. Now, when it's her job to welcome the new students, the ordeal is even worse. The freshers stand in a nervous huddle close to the drinks, the staff are meant to circulate but often seem even more ill at ease than the students.

The Archaeology department at UNN is small. As well as Ruth and David it consists of Bob Bullmore, an anthropologist cruising towards retirement, Fiona Green, a newish recruit who still has a bit of idealism and energy, and Peter Llewelyn, who specialises in cultural heritage and rarely utters a word on social occasions. Also present are Ted Cross from the field archaeology team, who's only here for the beer, and several graduate research assistants circling the perimeter of the room.

Ruth stops to exchange a word with Ted, whom she knows from various digs.

'Congratulations on the new job,' says Ted, who is sticking mini pork pies together to make a more substantial whole.

'Thanks,' says Ruth. She got the job almost a year ago but had to work out her notice at Cambridge, and Phil was not going to be cheated out of a valedictory final term. She'd hoped that she could put off the move until her ten-year-old daughter, Kate, was at secondary school but has ended up moving Kate back to her old primary school for one last year. Kate has coped well and is clearly delighted to be back in their old cottage but it's one more thing to feel guilty about.

'We need a few more digs,' says Ted. Ruth eyes him suspiciously. It's natural for Ted to want more fieldwork, that's his department after all, but has he been talking to David? Has Ruth already lost an ally?

'A possible Bronze Age hoard has been found at Blakeney Point,' she says. 'Could be a really interesting excavation.'

'Good,' says Ted, rubbing his hands together. 'A bit of leprechaun gold.' Ted is often known as Irish Ted although he comes from Bolton and has no discernible Irish accent. Ruth thinks that he makes remarks like this just to add to the mystique.

'Looks like there are some bones there too,' says Ruth.

'Even better,' says Ted. 'That's your speciality. You're the Bones Lady.'

Bones are Ruth's speciality. She even has a life-size cut-out of Bones from *Star Trek* in her cottage, a present from some former students. She's not sure that she likes being described as the Bones Lady though.

David appears, holding a glass of wine in one hand and a mini kebab in the other. She hopes that he hasn't over-heard.

'Are you talking about our find?' he says.

There he goes again. *Our* find.

'We're talking about the possible Bronze Age hoard at Blakeney Point,' says Ruth.

'And there's a skeleton too,' says David. 'I'd like to get a facial reconstruction done.'

'They do wonders with that these days,' says Ted. 'Have you seen Oscar Nilsson's reconstructions at Brighton Museum?'

'Let's do the excavation first,' says Ruth. David looks as if he's about to argue so she grabs a fork and taps the side of her glass. The room goes silent. Ruth clears her throat. She doesn't mind public speaking – she's a lecturer, after all, and has even appeared on television – but there's something daunting about addressing the new students as head of department. She's conscious of David standing just behind her, no doubt looking deeply contemptuous. Ted raises his glass in a half-ironic salute.

'Welcome to archaeology,' says Ruth. 'I hope you'll have

an interesting and instructive three years with us. I'm Dr Ruth Galloway . . .'

Nelson is in his office looking at recent reports of migrant boats. A map of Sea Palling, a small Norfolk beach, was recently found in the possession of people smugglers arrested in the Netherlands. As Judy said, there are many stretches of the coast not covered by coastguards. He seems to remember though that there are some volunteer coast-watch groups set up in derelict coastguard huts. It might be worth getting in touch with some of them. They are probably all friends of Cathbad's.

He looks up and has to stifle an exclamation. Super Jo has materialised in front of him. How does she do that? Ruth's cat is the same. You're sitting there quietly on her sofa and suddenly that orange beast is in front of you, radiating waves of hatred.

Jo isn't radiating anything except friendliness. She's even holding two cups of takeaway coffee.

'Can I have a word, Nelson?'

'Of course,' he says, clearing a space on his already tidy desk.

He's not fooled. He knows what Jo wants to discuss and it's scarier than smuggling and skeletons put together.

Jo wants to talk about his retirement.

It's been in the air for a while now. Once, under a rule called A19, Nelson would have been forced to retire after thirty years of service. It would have seen him out of the door, clutching his silver carriage clock, at forty-eight. Now, it's up to the individual police force. Nelson can see where Jo's coming from. He has years of experience but he's expensive. If he retired, Jo could probably employ two new DCs and have some change to spare.

But Nelson is not going to go without a fight.

It's seven o'clock by the time Ruth gets into her car to go home. Kate is with her friend Tasha and won't be missing her mother, but Ruth doesn't want to impose too much on Tasha's parents. Tasha was Kate's best friend before the move to Cambridge and Ruth is delighted that the friendship seems intact. She supposes that social media has its uses. Nelson gave Kate a mobile phone for Christmas. Ruth had disapproved at the time but it has certainly helped Kate keep in contact with Tasha and this seems to have preserved their closeness. And Kate is good at friends, a nebulous skill that somehow seems essential for a successful and happy life. Ruth has no idea who she gets it from. Ruth has a few close friends but shies away from making new ones. She supposes that Judy and Cathbad are her best friends in Norfolk.

Ruth is just starting up her car when a face appears at her window. She actually jumps.

'Have you got a minute?' says David, when she lowers the window.

'Can it wait?' says Ruth. 'I need to collect my daughter.' She curses herself for giving the classic single-parent excuse but, then again, it's the truth.

'I didn't know you had a daughter,' says David. 'I do too.'

'How old is yours?' says Ruth, wondering when she can put the window up.

'Eleven,' says David.

'Mine too,' says Ruth. 'Well, she will be in November.' David says nothing but he has backed away slightly. Ruth seizes her chance. 'See you tomorrow,' she says, closing the window and starting the engine.

As she drives away, she sees David still standing in the car park, frowning after her.

4

Kate is high on sisterhood and e-numbers. She tells Ruth that she and Tasha watched a film and mimed to several pop songs. They also made cupcakes and iced them. Ruth takes her hat off to Nikki, Tasha's mum, although she's set a worryingly high standard for the return fixture.

'I found some buried treasure today,' she tells Kate as they take the turning for the Saltmarsh and their cottage.

'Real treasure,' says Kate warily, 'or just some old bones?' Poor Kate. The perils of being an archaeologist's daughter.

'There are some bones,' says Ruth. 'But also swords and daggers. Maybe some jewellery too. Necklaces and bracelets.'

'Do you get to keep the jewels?' says Kate. She has worry-ingly capitalist traits. Ruth blames her father.

'No,' says Ruth. 'It doesn't belong to me.' She thinks of David saying, 'These finds belong to the people.' He's not wrong but there's something annoying about the phrase all the same. Maybe it's the smug, slightly Stalinist tone of 'the people'.

It's almost dark by the time they reach their cottage but

there are still lights flickering on the marshes. Ruth thinks of the lantern men, mythical figures who are said to lead unwary travellers to their deaths. But these are more likely to be fishermen or even nighthawks searching for more leprechaun gold. The security light comes on as Ruth parks by the gate and it illuminates her cat, Flint, staring out of the sitting room window, managing to look both welcoming and disapproving.

'We're coming, Flint,' says Kate. 'Poor angel. He must have been worried.'

'He's just thinking about his supper,' says Ruth.

When she opens the door, Flint hurries towards them, weaving around their legs. If Kate is happy to be back in her old home, Flint is delighted. He didn't like the town house in Cambridge and, to Ruth's distress, became rather aloof and sullen. But, back in his old domain, he is his old demanding, affectionate self. Now he leads them into the kitchen and looks meaningfully at his bowl.

'You've still got some biscuits left,' Ruth tells him.

'He needs fresh food,' says Kate, getting out the packets of expensive cat food that is all Flint will contemplate eating. Feeding Flint is the only chore she is always happy to do.

Kate has already eaten and Ruth is full of mini pork pies so she makes them both hot chocolate and they watch an episode of *Friends*, something that feels like wholesome pre-bedtime viewing despite being full of sex references and men with anger problems. But, sitting on the sofa with Kate watching 'The One with All the Wedding Dresses', while Flint purrs noisily beside them, suddenly seems like the very pinnacle of earthly pleasure.

Joey is monologuing about 'I've gotta do what I've gotta do . . .' Ruth's attention drifts.

'Frank used to say "gotta",' says Kate.

'Yes, he did,' says Ruth. 'It was cool. Do you miss him?'

Ruth and Frank had lived together for nearly two years and, by and large, they had been peaceful, happy years. Ruth's decision to leave him and go back to Norfolk had been traumatic enough but having to mark time in Cambridge, living in a rented flat, dreading bumping into Frank on her way to and from college, had left Ruth in a constant state of tension and guilt. When she heard that Frank was going back to America, she had felt only relief. But now she finds that she does miss him. Which is probably why she's asking Kate the question.

'Sometimes,' says Kate. 'A bit. Not really.'

On the screen, Monica, Phoebe and Rachel are capering about in big, white dresses.

'You've never been a bride, have you, Mum?' says Kate.

'Never,' says Ruth. Frank asked her to marry him. She said no and that's when their relationship started to unravel.

'I won't either,' says Kate. 'I want to be an actress.'

'You can do both things,' says Ruth, refraining from adding 'or be a doctor'.

They watch *Friends* in silence for a while.

'Are you enjoying being in charge at work?' says Kate.

Ruth is touched that she has remembered. 'I think so,' she says. 'It will be better when teaching starts on Monday.'

'Dad says that he loves being in charge.'

'I can believe that,' says Ruth.

'I'm going to be in charge when I'm an actress,' says Kate.

'Acting is teamwork,' says Ruth. 'That's one of the best things about it.'

'But there's always someone in charge of the team,' says Kate.

Judy and Cathbad are in their garden. They have taken to sitting on the terrace in the evenings. Cathbad lights candles and has hung lanterns in the trees. Even in early autumn it's warm enough to sit outside although Judy has a blanket over her shoulders. Cathbad seems impervious to cold – or heat. Judy tells Cathbad about the body on the beach and the Bronze Age skeleton. Strictly speaking, this is still confidential, but she wants his take on the Night Hawks. Besides, Cathbad, though fond of gossip, can keep a secret.

'Blakeney's an odd place,' says Cathbad. 'The name means "black island". There's certainly lots of psychic energy around the place. Have you heard of the hyter sprites?'

'No,' says Judy. She hasn't heard of half the things that Cathbad talks about.

'They're little spider-like creatures that are said to live in tunnels underneath Blakeney. They kidnap children and take them out onto the marshes.'

'Charming,' says Judy, who is not fond of spiders. 'What do you know about Alan White? He's the leader of this metal detecting group.'

'Alan's a good man,' says Cathbad. 'I think he has suffered in his life. That's the impression I get, anyway. But he's a gentle soul.'

'Suffered? How?'

'I think he had a hard time at school. Then, like a lot of people who hated school themselves, he became a teacher. I think he's much happier now he has retired.'

'What about the Night Hawks? I told the boss they were legit.'

'They are. They're registered and they report anything they find. But I think archaeologists are suspicious of them because they always go out at night.'

'That does seem a bit odd.'

'I don't know. Sometimes you see more at night.' Cathbad's teeth gleam in the darkness as he grins. Judy knows that Cathbad's past included its share of night wandering, but she doesn't want to think about that now.

'Tell me about the dead man,' says Cathbad. 'Do you think he was an asylum seeker?'

'It's possible,' says Judy. 'I called the coastguard and they didn't see any suspicious vessels last night but that doesn't mean there weren't any.'

'The water's very deep in some of the coves,' says Cathbad. 'Weybourne, for example. That's why the area was popular with smugglers. You could get a big boat very close to the shore.'

'The dead man had an unusual tattoo,' says Judy. 'A snake with spikes down its back. Nelson thought it might be some gang insignia.'

'I wonder . . .' says Cathbad. At the end of the garden something, a fox maybe, is snuffling by the compost heap. Their dog, Thing, rushes out to bark at it.

'Wonder what?' says Judy, when the animal has quietened down.

'Well, the snake sounds a bit like the Norfolk Sea Serpent.'

'The what?' Judy is used to Cathbad coming up with pieces of arcane local knowledge but this is a new one.

'There have been a couple of sightings of a Sea Serpent in Norfolk. The last one was in Eccles-on-Sea before the war, I think. And it's meant to have spikes on its back. Like the Loch Ness Monster.'

'So, if our man has a Norfolk Sea Serpent tattoo . . .'

'He could be from Norfolk. Yes.'

5

Nelson's Thursday is spent attending a course on the issue of Challenging Gender Roles in Policing, as directed by Super Jo. The team are continuing to investigate the body on the beach and Judy has suggested some weird theory about the tattoo, courtesy of Cathbad, of course. Apparently, it could be something called the Norfolk Sea Serpent, which last popped up in 1936. Nelson tells Judy to continue to check with the coastguard and the volunteer coast-watch groups, just the same.

It's seven o'clock by the time Nelson gets home and is greeted by his German shepherd, Bruno, and his three-year-old son, George. Bruno comes racing along the hall, nails clattering, but stops just in front of Nelson and gazes at him adoringly. George shows no such restraint. Dressed in his pyjamas, he hurls himself at his father from the middle of the staircase. Nelson staggers but rights himself.

'Hallo, Georgie.'

Nelson's wife, Michelle, appears at the top of the stairs.

'Oh, Harry. I've just got him quiet for bedtime.'

'I'll put him to bed,' says Nelson, climbing the stairs with his son in his arms and his dog at his heels.

'Be calming,' says Michelle, as he passes her.

'I'm always calm,' says Nelson, leaning in for a kiss. Michelle kisses him on the cheek, her lips cool. She's still in her work clothes, a smart blue dress and chunky necklace, but she has swapped her heels for Ugg boots. She used to wear her hair up for work but, a year ago, she had it cut and now it just brushes her shoulders. It always looks good – blonde, high-lighted, layered – but Nelson misses her long hair. Michelle manages a hair salon in King's Lynn but she's part-time now and her work is flexible enough to allow her to collect George from nursery most days. Nelson and Michelle have two adult daughters; Laura, a primary school teacher who lives nearby, and Rebecca, who lives and works in Brighton. This third child was a surprise to both of them. They adore George but there's no doubt that his arrival has taken their lives in a different direction. Sometimes Nelson feels George has given him a new lease of life, at other times it feels more like a derailment.

Nelson means well but he can't resist playing a game where he is a hungry bear and George is his prey. Bruno encourages him with staccato barks. Michelle shouts up the stairs and Nelson reverts to the bedtime routine. But George is too excited to listen to a Thomas the Tank Engine story and Nelson's eyes are crossing with boredom as he reads. It's eight o'clock when George finally goes to sleep, then Bruno needs to be taken out for a walk, so it's past nine by the time that Nelson sits down in front of the TV with his heated-up supper on a tray.

'Good day?' asks Michelle, looking away from a programme which, inexplicably, appears to be about people
sewing.

'OK,' says Nelson, shovelling in cottage pie. 'Some poor
sod washed up on the beach. Probably an asylum seeker.'

'We should have stricter controls,' says Michelle, looking
back at the television.

Nelson wonders what Ruth would say to this, probably
something about looking after people in need. 'There's
plenty of money in the world,' she told him once, 'it's just
not shared out fairly.' He doesn't tell Michelle about the
hoard or the skeleton. He never mentions Ruth at home if
he can avoid it.

Michelle goes to bed at ten and Nelson isn't long after her.
They make love in an abstracted, but not untender, fashion
and Nelson falls asleep dreaming of buried treasure. He's
awoken by his work phone. It's ten minutes past midnight.

'Boss.' It's Judy. 'I'm at Black Dog Farm near Sheringham.
Gunshots and screams heard inside the house. I think you'd
better come.'

Nelson goes into the spare room and makes two more
calls, one to Jo and one to the Authorised Firearms team,
requesting their attendance at Black Dog Farm. It's not unusual to hear gunshots in rural areas, even at night when
poachers are around, but the presence of firearms inside a
house is another matter. If an officer has reason to suppose
that someone has access to a lethal weapon, then back up
is needed. Nelson gets dressed, quickly and quietly.

'Michelle? Love? I've been called out.'

'OK,' Michelle murmurs sleepily. He wonders if she'll remember in the morning.

As he descends the stairs, he can hear Bruno's tail beating against the wooden floor. The dog accompanies him to the front door.

'Sorry, mate,' says Nelson. 'This is work.'

Bruno recognises the tone and lies down, whining gently, as if reminding Nelson that he is descended from a long line of police dogs and would be a great help with whatever lies ahead in the farmhouse with the odd name. Nelson doesn't doubt it. He edges past Bruno and closes the door gently. It had been a mild day but the night is cold. Nelson can see his breath billowing as he unlocks his car. The cul-de-sac is dark and completely silent. But, as Nelson drives away, he thinks that he can still hear the soft whining of a dog.

It's about an hour's drive from King's Lynn to Sheringham but the roads are empty and Nelson drives fast. Super Jo once sent him on a speed awareness course but Nelson thinks that traffic rules are for other people. Judy has provided him with a postcode and his phone's satnav takes him on a bewildering route through shuttered villages and narrow tree-lined lanes. Nelson's headlights pick out abandoned petrol stations, pub signs creaking in the wind, the glassy eyes of a fox. God, how he loathes the countryside.

'You have arrived at your destination,' says his phone but, as far as Nelson can make out, he's still in the middle of bloody nowhere. He gets out of the car. He's in a lane with high hedges on either side. It's still pitch black but, when he turns his torch to the right, he sees a rotting gate propped open by a stone and a sign that says, uncompromisingly, 'To the farm'. He gets back in the car and proceeds along the long, pitted track, wincing at the thought of the damage to the suspension. Just when he's thinking that this can't possibly lead anywhere, a square house seems to appear out of the gloom. Several vehicles are parked nearby and he can see the bulky shapes of the Firearms team.

'Boss?' Judy appears at his window.

'What's going on?' says Nelson, getting out of the car.

'Shots reported at five past midnight. Since then, nothing. The AFOs are about to go in.'

As Nelson approaches the house, a security light comes on. The crouching figures are suddenly in the spotlight. One of them makes a gesture for him to step back. Nelson recognises her as the Operational Firearms Commander, Sara Bright.

Nelson goes to Sara's side.

'Take it gently,' he says. 'If someone inside the house is armed, we don't want them to become alarmed and start shooting.'

'Don't worry,' says Sara. 'I'm in touch with my TFC.'

The TFC is the Tactical Firearms Commander, who will be directing operations remotely. This is one reason why Nelson hates calling for the armed response team. He can't bear not being in control.

The armed officers spread out around the house, leaving Nelson, Sara and another officer by the front door. Sara knocks loudly. No answer. She shouts, 'Police! If you're in there, come out now and no one will get hurt.'

Her voice echoes against wood and stone. Nelson has a sense that, apart from the police, there's not another living soul for miles around.

'Armed police,' yells Sara. 'Come out of the address now or we're coming in.' Why the address and not the house? thinks Nelson inconsequentially. When did they all start speaking like this?

Sara looks at Nelson. He nods. The other officer kicks at the door. It opens easily; the wood must be as rotten as the gate.

'Let's go in,' says Nelson.

Nelson follows the two armed officers into the hall. His torch illuminates banisters, a grandfather clock, old-fashioned wallpaper.

'If there's anyone here,' he shouts, 'come out with your hands up.'

No answer except for the clock ticking. There are closed doors on the left and the right and one half-open straight ahead. The male officer kicks open the left-hand door. 'Nothing here.'

Nelson follows Sara through the open door. They're in a kitchen: pine units, Aga, tiles, hanging herbs, a strong smell of hot iron.

'On the floor,' says Sara.

Nelson lowers his torch and sees what's left of a face.

'Body here,' he says. 'Adult male. Deceased. Looks like he shot himself. Let's go upstairs,' he turns to Sara.

Judy is in the hallway. 'Wait outside,' says Nelson. He couldn't face Cathbad if anything happened to Judy. He's not sure that he could face himself, come to think of it.

At the top of the stairs they find a woman's body, face down, bullet wounds in her back. She too is dead. The firearms officers check the other rooms but they are all empty.

Back outside, Nelson calls the Forensics team and the coroner. The faintest tinge of daylight has started to silhouette the trees on the edge of the field. Nelson is dimly aware of birds singing.

'Murder-suicide?' says Judy.

'Looks like it. Any idea who they are?'

'Farm is owned by Dr Douglas Noakes and his wife Linda. That's all I know.'

'Who reported the shooting? It's not as if they have any neighbours.'

'A couple of men out walking in the fields.'

'Out walking? At midnight?'

'It's something they often do,' says Judy. 'They're metal detectorists.'

'Black Dog Farm,' says Tom Henty. 'That must be the Black Shuck. Sheringham, did you say? That's his patch, all right.'

Tom, the desk sergeant, has been at King's Lynn for as long as any of them can remember. He's also a fount of knowledge on Norfolk lore and customs. It's six a.m. and Judy and Nelson are drinking coffee in Tom's cubbyhole behind the reception desk. The early shift is starting to arrive. Nelson has called a briefing at seven.

'I think I've heard that name before,' says Nelson.

'The Black Shuck is famous round here,' says Judy,

who is also Norfolk born. 'It's a gigantic black dog who appears to people just before they die.'

'That's right,' says Tom cosily, offering a tin of biscuits. 'His eyes are made of hellfire and, if you see him, you die within the year.'

'Doesn't he have just one eye, like Cyclops?' says Judy.

'Sometimes,' says Tom. 'He appears all over Norfolk – and Suffolk too. You can see his claw marks on the church door in Bungay.'

'I heard that was the devil in dog form,' says Judy, 'not the Shuck at all.'

'Jesus wept,' says Nelson. 'What a lunatic bloody place this is. Don't tell me you believe in this Black Shack, do you?'

'Black Shuck,' says Judy. 'On stormy nights, you can hear him howling. Or you can hear him following you in the dark, his chain rattling behind him.'

'You've been living with Cathbad too long,' says Nelson. But, despite himself, he remembers Bruno whining as he left the house in the early hours of the morning, and the way that the sound had seemed to follow him as he drove through the dark streets. This place is finally getting to him. Maybe they should move back to Blackpool after all.

'Oh, Cathbad's seen the Black Shuck,' says Judy, 'and he's OK.'

'He's seen . . .' Nelson is temporarily speechless.

'Wonder if he's meant to haunt your farm,' says Tom. 'It's a funny name to give a place otherwise.'

'Well, he didn't bring the occupants much luck tonight,'

says Nelson, standing up. 'Come on, Judy. Let's get ready for this briefing.'

The briefing room is full. Even Super Jo is there. The double deaths and the presence of the Authorised Firearms team make this case a priority for everyone. Tanya is seething because she wasn't called out.

'We don't have a formal identification,' says Nelson, 'but we believe the deceased to be Dr Douglas Noakes, aged sixty, and his wife Linda, aged fifty-eight. Shots were heard coming from the farmhouse at approximately twelve midnight. Local police were called and they informed DI Johnson, who alerted me. I called the AFO who entered the house with me at 1.30 a.m. We found the body of a man in the kitchen who appeared to have been shot in the head. A handgun was beside him. A woman's body was at the top of the stairs. She had been shot several times in the back. Both victims were dead at the scene.'

Tanya's hand is up. 'Is it a murder-suicide?'

'Looks very much like it,' says Nelson, 'but let's not make assumptions until we have the coroner's report.' Once again, he misses Clough who would have classified this crime as DODI or 'Dead One Did It'.

He continues. 'Dr Noakes was a research scientist who worked in Cambridge, his wife was a retired primary school teacher. They have two adult children, Chloe and Paul. We're trying to trace them now.'

'Who reported the shots?' asks Tony Zhang.

'This is where it gets interesting,' says Nelson. 'The shots were reported by two metal detectorists who happened to be in the area. Their names are Alan White and Neil Thomas.'

'Weren't they two of the people who found the body yesterday?' says Tony.

'Yes,' says Nelson, pleased that he has remembered. 'And another of the detectorists, one of the so-called Night Hawks, is Paul Noakes, the son of Douglas and Linda.'

There's a murmur in the room. Nelson raises a hand. 'It could be just a coincidence but three bodies in two days certainly bears investigation. We'll be talking to all the Night Hawks today. Do you have anything to add, Superintendent Archer?' He says this because Jo has stood up in a meaningful way.

'We're making a statement to the press at nine a.m.,' says Jo. 'I want you to be there, Nelson, as well as DI Johnson and DC Zhang. I'll do the talking.'

I bet you will, thinks Nelson. He knows why she wants Judy and Tony – to show that the force isn't entirely male or of one ethnicity. Tanya will be furious.

6

By early afternoon Judy finds herself sinking into a dream-like lethargy. She is meant to be putting together a dossier on Douglas and Linda Noakes but in reality she's staring at the little letters as they rearrange themselves into different shapes and patterns. A line of Ns, slantwise on the screen, has her mesmerised for about ten minutes. She's too old to miss a night's sleep and still be able to function, she thinks. Although the boss, who is more than ten years older than her, seems unaffected. She can hear him barking orders in his office, which seems about a million miles away.

'Judy!'

Judy swims to the surface to find Leah, Nelson's PA, speaking to her.

'Your daughter's in reception.'

For a moment, Judy doesn't take this in. Her daughter, Miranda, aged five, is actually in the reception class at school. Why is Leah telling her this? Leah, a perceptive soul, must have noticed her confusion because she says, 'Your other daughter. The journalist.'

Ah, she must mean Maddie who is, strictly speaking, Cathbad's daughter and not hers. Judy isn't even her step-mother because she and Cathbad aren't married. Judy is fond of Maddie but she has no illusions about this visit. Maddie is after a story and she knows that saying she's Judy's daughter will get her an instant audience with the investigating team.

'Can you ask her to come up?' says Judy. 'Thank you, Leah.'

She must have got into another waking doze because, a few seconds later, Maddie materialises in front of her. Maddie is twenty-seven but looks a lot younger, small and slight with long blonde hair tied back in a ponytail. But Judy knows that Maddie's look of frailty is deceptive or, at least, only part of the picture. Maddie can be vulnerable at times. She has never really got over losing her half-sister, Scarlet, when she was a teenager. Scarlet was murdered – it was Judy's first case for the Serious Crimes Unit – and none of them have ever forgotten her. Ruth's daughter, Kate, has the middle name Scarlet. Judy sometimes thinks that Maddie's return to Norfolk, after university in Leeds, is part of her unrelenting search for her sister. But, despite all this, Maddie is also tough and determined, and an absolute terrier when on the trail of a story. She works for the local newspaper, the *Chronicle*.

'Hi, Judy,' says Maddie, taking the seat opposite her. 'You look tired.'

'Thanks. I was up all night.'

'Was that the Black Dog Farm shooting?'

'Yes.'

Jo's statement has been repeated on every news briefing since nine o'clock that morning. Judy is surprised it took Maddie so long to find her.

'So,' Maddie gets out her notebook, 'is it a murder-suicide?' She fixes Judy with her most compelling gaze. Maddie has remarkable eyes, green with flecks of gold. They must come from her mother, Delilah, because Cathbad's eyes are blue. Even though she's used to it, Judy blinks under the force of Maddie's stare.

'We can't be sure yet,' says Judy.

'Superintendent Archer said that two people were found dead at the house. Is that Douglas and Linda Noakes?'

Judy knows that Maddie has rather a crush on Super Jo. She, herself, had found the press conference a waste of time. What's the point of making a statement to say that you've nothing to say?

'Did Douglas kill Linda and then kill himself?' asks Maddie, pen poised.

'We don't know yet,' says Judy. 'We're still investigating. When we know something, I'll tell you.'

'Really? Can I have an exclusive?'

'I'll have to check it with the boss.'

'With Nelson? He'll say yes.' She's probably right. Maddie is friends with Nelson's daughters and he frequently treats her with the indulgence that he displays towards his family, and no one else.

'It's a funny place, Black Dog Farm,' says Maddie, settling back in her chair as if preparing for a long chat. Judy is starting to see black specks in front of her eyes.

'Do you know it, then?' asks Judy.

'I've heard stories about it,' says Maddie.

'The Black Shuck?'

'No,' says Maddie. 'You don't believe in that rubbish, do you? Is Cathbad getting to you at last?' Maddie almost always calls Cathbad by his adopted name, 'Dad' is reserved for her stepfather.

'I don't believe in it,' says Judy, slightly too sharply. 'But lots of people do.'

'People will believe anything,' says Maddie. 'It's the first thing you learn in journalism. No, I was thinking of something else. I think there was another murder there.'

Judy wakes up slightly. 'Let me know if you find anything out.'

'I will,' says Maddie, closing her book. 'And you let me know about the exclusive. Give my love to Cathbad and the kids.'

'You must come for supper one day,' says Judy. 'We'd all love to see you.'

When Nelson emerges from his office, he tells Judy to go home.

'Go and get some sleep,' he says. 'We need you at full strength in the morning.'

'Who's going to interview Alan White?' says Judy.

'Tanya can do it. She's well prepared.'

Judy bets that she is. But she's too tired to feel resentful. She gathers up her phone and car keys.

'Maddie was here earlier,' she says. 'She wants an exclusive.'

Nelson laughs, but quite benevolently. 'I'm not saying another word to the press. Not even to Maddie.'

Driving home, Judy thinks about her almost stepdaughter. Maddie lived with them for two years before moving out last year to share a flat in Lynn with two friends. At times Judy had been irritated by Maddie's presence – her erratic routine, her midnight raids on the fridge, her bedroom curtains drawn until midday – but now she misses her. She and Maddie had watched hours of trashy TV together (Cathbad thinks that televisions emit harmful rays) and it was fun to have a young adult about the place, someone to translate the mysteries of social media and to identify the celebrities on *Strictly Come Dancing*. It had been useful to have a built-in babysitter too; Michael and Miranda adore their half-sister.

Judy arrives home just as Cathbad is setting out to collect the kids from school.

'Come with me,' he says. 'Unless you want to go straight to bed. I could take them to the park so that you have a longer rest.'

'No, I'd like to come.' A brisk walk with Cathbad seems more invigorating than a nap and she suddenly has a visceral urge to see her children.

'It'll be a lovely surprise for them,' says Cathbad. 'We could take Thing too.'

Thing is their bull terrier. He normally accompanies Cathbad everywhere, but dogs aren't allowed in the school playground.

'OK,' says Judy. 'I'll look after him when you go in to

collect them.' Unlike Cathbad, who relishes every opportunity for human interaction, Judy doesn't enjoy mixing with the other parents. She can never remember people's names and, when she can, she worries that it's because she's recently arrested them. Michael is like her, serious and self-contained. Miranda is Cathbad reborn with fairy wings.

They walk by the sea wall, the boats clinking companionably from the water. It's another beautiful autumn day. Judy thinks of Black Dog Farm, its square, flint-lined walls, its air of total isolation. Well, it'll be full of people today: the scene-of-crime teams, local police, the press. She's already told Cathbad the basics on the phone but now she tells him about the farmhouse with the strange name.

'The Black Shuck,' says Cathbad immediately, 'the harbinger of death. Although he's not always evil. Sometimes he's just a travelling companion. Some legends link him to the black hound of Odin.'

Cathbad loves the Norse gods. Judy had to stop him telling stories about them at bedtime. The kids loved them; she was terrified.

'I told Nelson that you'd seen him,' she says.

Cathbad laughs. 'Now he'll think I'm crazier than ever. Actually, of course, deep down Nelson believes in it all. Just like, deep down, he's as devout a Catholic as his mother.'

Cathbad met Nelson's mother years ago and an unlikely friendship ensued. Maureen is planning to come to stay with Nelson and Michelle for Christmas. Only Cathbad is looking forward to the visit with unalloyed pleasure.

They turn inland and walk through the suburban streets,

Thing panting and grinning at every passer-by, most of whom draw back in horror. It's not easy being a devil dog.

'Tanya's interviewing your friend Alan White this afternoon,' says Judy.

'Because he reported the shots last night?' says Cathbad. Strictly speaking, Judy shouldn't have told him this but it's hard to keep secrets from Cathbad.

'Yes. And he was one of the people who found the body on the beach. You know what Nelson thinks about coincidence.'

'Coincidence is only another word for fate,' says Cathbad. 'But Alan has always struck me as a sincere soul. Maybe he was just guided to be there that night.'

'I can't see that excuse going down too well with Nelson,' says Judy. 'Or Tanya.'

They have reached the school. Cathbad goes into the playground to wait for Michael and Miranda. Judy sits on a nearby bench, holding Thing tightly. He loves children, which is sad because this love isn't always reciprocated.

'Judy! Hallo, Thing. Don't jump up, there's a good boy.'

It's Ruth, looking unusually smart in a black trouser suit.

'Hi, Ruth. Come to do the pick-up?'

'Yes. No students until Monday so I thought I'd give Sandra a break.' Sandra is Ruth's long-time childminder, a treasure in every sense.

'How's work?' says Judy. 'What's it like being in the hot seat?'

'OK,' says Ruth. 'Except that I've got a new lecturer who wants to tell me exactly how to do my job.'

'Tell me about it,' says Judy. 'Tanya's still snapping at my heels.'

'Were you involved with that shooting at Sheringham? I heard Super Jo talking about it on the radio.'

'Yes,' says Judy. 'I've been up all night, which is probably why I'm feeling a bit dopey now.'

'Did the man kill his wife and then kill himself? That's what it sounded like.'

'Looks that way but we can't be sure. I don't know why the super called a press conference just to say, "We can't tell you any more at the present time."'

'I bet Nelson wasn't keen.'

'He wasn't.'

Judy is conscious of the slight restraint they both feel whenever the boss's name is mentioned. Most people at the station know about Nelson and Ruth but the inner circle – Judy, Tanya and Clough before he left – avoid talking about it, even to each other.

'I'd better go in,' says Ruth. 'It's always manic on a Friday.'

'Is it Friday?' says Judy. 'I've lost track.'

'Yes. Term starts on Monday and I've got permission to excavate the Bronze Age site tomorrow. You should come along.'

'I will. Cathbad will be interested too.'

'Tell him to bring his trowel. We're always short of good diggers.' Cathbad seems to have lived many lives but in one of them he studied archaeology. Judy says that she'll pass it on. She's pretty sure that Cathbad will be on the beach at dawn.

Ruth goes through the gates and, a few minutes later, returns with a wildly excited Kate, dragging Michael along with her.

'We're going to the park and then to have pizza.'

'Is that OK?' says Cathbad, following along with Miranda and a pile of brightly coloured pictures, shedding glitter and sparkly stars. 'You could go home and rest if you want.'

'No, I'll come,' says Judy. The exhaustion has mutated into a rather pleasant dreaminess. She likes the idea of chatting with Cathbad and Ruth over pizza and a glass of wine. They walk towards the park, Cathbad in front with the children, Judy and Ruth following with the dog. Thing wants to be with his siblings, so he pants and pulls at the lead. Then, suddenly, he stops and turns round, hackles up.

'What up, Thing?' says Judy. Thing is growling, which is almost unheard of.

'Has he seen another dog?' says Ruth.

They both look back but the road, full of parents and children a few minutes ago, is now completely empty.

Tanya is finding Alan White an irritating interviewee. He's pleasant enough, offering coffee and home-made biscuits, chatting about the weather, but he keeps veering off into diversions about Iron Age settlements and something called a bulla, which turns out to be a kind of necklace. Tanya has no interest in history and is not surprised to learn that this was Alan's subject when he was a teacher.

'When did you retire?' asks Tanya.

'Three years ago,' says Alan. 'I was only fifty-five but I was burnt out. That's happening a lot in the profession these days.'

Tanya's wife, Petra, is a teacher but she always seems full of energy. Maybe a private school and small classes have something to do with this. Alan taught at Greenhill, the comprehensive in Sheringham.

'It was stressful,' he says. 'I had some fantastic pupils though. Lots of them went on to study history at university.'

'Tell me about the Night Hawks,' says Tanya. 'Do you go out at night looking for treasure?'

'That's a rather simplistic definition,' says Alan, sounding exactly like a history teacher. 'Nighthawking is the word used to describe the theft of historical artefacts from archaeological sites. It's a term of abuse. I thought I would try to redeem it. After all, hawks are beautiful creatures and I love watching birds at night. The Sheringham Night Hawks is a proper licensed metal detecting society, part of the Federation of Independent Detectorists. Any finds are reported to the Finds Liaison Officer immediately.'

'Why do you go out at night then?' says Tanya. 'Seems a bit dodgy, doesn't it?'

Alan sighs. He's rather bedraggled-looking, balding with a rim of grey fuzz, wearing a jumper that's unravelling at the edges. Tanya can just imagine what his pupils would have said about him.

'It's quieter at night,' he says. 'Fewer people around. And the younger members find it more exciting.'

'Tell me about finding the body on the beach,' says Tanya. 'Why were you there in the first place?'

'We knew that some coins had been found on the beach,' says Alan. 'We thought there might be a hoard there. And we were right. We'd just located it when Troy, one of our youngest members, shouted that he'd found a body. The tide was coming in so we pulled it – him – onto the rocks. Then I called the police. They came very quickly. Two nice young chaps. I'd taught them both.'

'And what about last night, at Black Dog Farm?'

'I was field walking with my friend Neil, another of the Night Hawks. There was once a Roman settlement near the farm so you can sometimes pick up nice bits of pottery, samian ware, you know. Anyway, we were walking along a lane and I heard a shot coming from the farmhouse, then a scream. It was really chilling. Then there was another shot and another. Three or four. I called the police. They came very quickly and took my name and details. Neil had gone home by then, but I waited in the lane outside the house. There were no more shots, in fact everything was totally silent. I saw the armed police go in and, much later, the bodies being brought out.'

'What did you do then?' asks Tanya. She thinks there's something creepy about Alan lurking outside the farmhouse until the bodies were brought out. She wonders if there was anyone at home to vouch for his return. She can't immediately deduce the presence of a partner in the house. They are sitting in Alan's kitchen which is tidy but not obsessively so, *Guardian* open on the table, a plastic bag labelled 'For Charity' by the back door.

She thinks that Alan hesitates slightly but then he says, 'I came home. I think I got in at about two a.m.'

'Does anyone live here with you?' asks Tanya.

'My wife died two years ago,' says Alan. 'Cancer.'

'I'm sorry,' says Tanya.

'We were looking forward to spending our retirement together,' says Alan. 'We never had children. We were going to travel, take up new hobbies. But it wasn't to be. That's probably why I'm a bit obsessive about my interests.'

This is said with a slight smile which Tanya finds rather touching. She senses that Alan knows exactly what kind of a figure he presents to the world. She asks him if he knew the Noakes family.

'Paul, their son, is one of the Night Hawks,' he says. 'He was also one my ex-pupils. I remember Dr Noakes and his wife from parents' evenings and the like. They seemed like perfectly pleasant people.'

Perfectly pleasant people. It sounds like the beginning of a Blur song.

'When did you last see Dr and Mrs Noakes?'

'Oh, it must have been more than ten years ago. When Paul was still at school. He must be about thirty now.'

Thirty-one, Tanya checks her notes. She wonders who will get the job of interviewing Paul Noakes.

'Have you got any idea what happened in Black Dog Farm last night?'

'I assumed ... from the police statement ... that Dr Noakes had killed his wife and then committed suicide.'

'Have you any idea why he might have done that?'

'No. As I say, I didn't really know them. But there are

secrets in every family, DS Fuller. You don't teach for thirty years without finding that out.'

'Secrets?' says Nelson. 'What does that mean?'

'I don't know,' says Tanya. 'I tried to get him to elaborate but he just kept going on about the Iron Age and the Romans.'

'Is Alan White a bit . . .' Nelson pauses, trying to think of an appropriate word. Super Jo is always telling him that he can't call people nutters.

'Mad?' says Tanya. 'I don't think so. Just eccentric and obsessed with history.'

Nelson thinks that this could just as easily apply to Cathbad. He looks round for Judy before remembering that he sent her home.

'We haven't got the forensics back yet,' he says. 'But this does look like a murder-suicide. Douglas Noakes appeared to have been shot in the head. We'll know more when we've got the detail on the angle of the bullet and whether his prints were on the gun. But it looks as if he shot his wife as she was running away from him up the stairs and then killed himself. All the same, it's worth getting as much information as we can on the family. Neil Thomas, the other metal detectorist, gave a statement today but I'd like you to go and see him, Tanya. See if he knows anything about Douglas and Linda Noakes. Take Tony with you.'

Tanya looks pleased. Tony less so. Tanya says, 'Have you spoken to the children? Paul and, what was her name, Chloe?'

'They're with the family liaison officer today,' says Nelson. 'But I'd like you or Judy to talk to them tomorrow.'

'Paul Noakes was one of Alan White's pupils,' says Tanya. 'That's a bit odd, isn't it?'

'It's a small place,' says Nelson. 'I suppose most people went to the same school. But it's a link, I admit.'

'Apparently the attending PCs were ex-pupils too.'

'He certainly seems to remember them all very well,' says Nelson. 'I wonder if there's anything sinister there. Can you speak to the school, Tanya?'

'Will do,' says Tanya. Nelson knows that she wants to be his number two on the case but that position rightfully belongs to Judy, who is a DI. Nelson is very keen on fairness. He thinks it comes from being the youngest in his family. He calls the meeting to an end and escapes into his office.

Nelson thinks of tiredness as something that only affects other people (ditto jet lag) but he has now been up since midnight and he does feel slightly strung out, all his senses on high alert. In the room next door Tony is whistling 'Heigh-ho, heigh-ho, it's off to work we go'. The notes feel as if they are being drilled into Nelson's head. He asks his PA, Leah, to make him a cup of coffee and, when she brings it, requests that she closes the door behind her. Tony is still whistling. That's a habit he has to break if he's going to carry on working for the Serious Crimes Unit. Nelson drinks the scalding liquid and thinks about the Black Dog Farm case. Should he chase the SOCO team for results? No, it's too soon for that. Maybe he should have another look through the crime-scene photos. He remembers the house: the patterned wallpaper, the ticking clock, the herbs hanging in the kitchen. Then the bodies, one on the floor, the other on the stairs. You never get used to the sight, not really.

He still doesn't have the post-mortem results on the body on the beach either. What was Tanya saying about the attending PCs being ex-pupils of Alan White? He opens the door to ask her but is told that DS Fuller and DC Zhang have just gone out. Maybe they've gone to interview Neil Thomas. It would be like Tanya not to waste any time and at least it means that the whistling has stopped. Maybe he should talk to the two constables again. Nelson rings Nathan's number and gets no answer. Then he tries Mark. The phone rings out and Nelson leaves a message. Mark rings him back almost immediately.

'DCI Nelson?' His voice sounds odd, as if he's a long way away.

'Yes, I just wanted to—'

'Haven't you heard about Nathan?'

'What about him?' says Nelson, irritated at being interrupted.

'He's dead.'

7

'What do you mean, he's dead?'

'I called for him yesterday morning,' says Mark, 'and there was no one home. He lives with his mum and dad. But a neighbour saw me leaving and she said that Nathan had been taken to hospital that night. I rang the hospital and they told me that he'd ... passed away.'

Nelson disapproves of the term 'passed away'. Death is death and it shouldn't be hidden behind a euphemism.

'How?' he says. 'What did he die of?'

'They don't know. He was feeling a bit crap on Wednesday. Sorry.' Even in his grief and distress, Mark apologises for his language when speaking to a senior officer.

'I thought he seemed like he had a cold,' says Nelson.

'Yes, that's all I thought it was. Plus, we'd been up all night. Nathan went home early but I thought he'd be fine by Thursday morning. And now he's dead.' There's a long pause and Nelson can hear Mark struggling to control his breathing. 'Sorry,' he says again. 'It's just ... It's a shock. Nathan and I have known each other since we were kids. We went to school together. He was saving up to get married.'

'I'm really sorry,' says Nelson. 'He was a good copper. Let me know if I can do anything.'

'I will. My sarge is heartbroken. I don't know how I can go into work on Monday.'

'Work helps sometimes,' says Nelson. 'Let me know about . . . about any arrangements.' It seems too soon to say the word 'funeral'. Only yesterday Nathan Matthews had sat in these offices, looking rather cold-ridden but otherwise healthy. And now he's dead, a young man in his – what? – mid-twenties? It doesn't make sense. He passes on the news to Jo who says all the right things about flowers and paying their respects.

'Maybe it was sudden adult death syndrome,' she says. 'That can happen to the healthiest people.'

Sudden adult death, thinks Nelson. That could refer to most murder victims. But Nathan wasn't murdered. This is simply a horrible human tragedy. Nelson looks at his watch. Nearly five. He won't stay late tonight. He suddenly longs to be at home with Georgie.

Nelson is right. Tanya and Tony are knocking on Neil Thomas's door. He lives just outside King's Lynn in what Tanya immediately perceives is a family house: large garage, bikes in the porch, a basketball net in the garden. Neil Thomas, who opens the door wearing tracksuit bottoms and a rugby top, says that he works from home as an IT consultant. He rises further in Tanya's esteem. IT, in her opinion, is a useful subject. Not like history.

While Neil makes them tea in the large, efficient-looking kitchen, two teenagers appear, grab some food, and disappear.

'Max and Megan,' says Neil. 'Home from school for a cheery chat with their dad.'

As neither adolescent said a single word, this is obviously meant to be ironical. Tanya asks what Neil's wife does, then regrets the way she has phrased the question. She and Petra have vowed never to use the word 'wife'. And Neil might just as easily be in a same-sex relationship.

Neil doesn't seem bothered by the W word. 'She's a solicitor,' he says. 'She works in Lynn. She won't be home for a few hours yet.'

'Can you tell us what happened last night at Black Dog Farm?' says Tanya.

'I was out field walking with Alan,' says Neil. 'I know that probably sounds odd, but I like walking at night. It's something the Night Hawks often do.' He pats a silver hawk badge which is pinned, rather incongruously, to the rugby shirt. 'I don't sleep well and there's something very peaceful about the countryside in the dark.'

'How do you know Alan?' asks Tanya.

'We used to teach together,' says Neil. 'I left about ten years ago. There's much more money in IT and you get to work in your pyjamas. What's not to like?'

He smiles but Tanya wonders if the freelance life is quite as rosy as it sounds. Neil is at home in his tracksuit bottoms (almost pyjamas) at five p.m., ignored by his kids and maybe also by his hard-working wife, not sleeping at night and roaming the countryside in the early hours. It doesn't exactly sound like having it all.

'So what happened last night?' says Tanya. 'When did you hear the shots?'

'I think it must have been about midnight,' says Neil. 'We were in the lane outside Black Dog Farm. We heard a gunshot, then a scream, then another two or three shots. We phoned the police immediately.'

'Who phoned?' says Tony. 'You or Alan?'

Tanya frowns at him for interrupting and Neil seems slightly thrown.

'Alan,' he says at last. 'Alan called the police. And he waited near the house for them to come.'

'Why didn't you wait with him?' asks Tanya.

'They told us to go home. Said it wasn't safe to approach the house. We gave them our names.'

'So why did Alan wait by the house?'

'Alan's a historian,' says Neil. 'He always wants to hear the end of the story. But I'd seen enough. I walked back to where I'd left my car and then I drove home.'

'What time did you get in?' asks Tanya.

'About twelve thirty,' says Neil. 'I remember looking at my phone when I plugged it in to charge. I slept in the spare room so as not to wake Emily.'

So no one can vouch for that return in the early hours, thinks Tanya. She asks if Neil had been to the farmhouse before.

'No,' says Neil, 'but Alan told me that Paul Noakes used

to live there. Paul's one of the Night Hawks. I taught him years ago. Bright boy.'

'Have you ever met Douglas or Linda Noakes?'

'Not to my knowledge. No.'

'Not when you used to teach Paul?'

'Paul didn't do IT for GCSE or A level and he wasn't in my form. There was no reason for them to see me.'

'The two police officers who attended the scene, Nathan Matthews and Mark Hammond, also went to Greenhill. Did you teach them?'

'I remember Mark. He was quite good at IT. Not sure about Nathan. After a bit the names and faces merge into one.'

Tanya imagines that this is true. After all, teachers must teach hundreds – thousands – of pupils. Does that make it stranger that Alan White appears to remember everyone so well? At any rate, there doesn't seem much more to be gained from Neil Thomas and, after a few more questions and a desultory chat about laptops, Tanya and Tony leave. In the car, Tanya says, 'Why did you ask that about the phone call?'

Tony blinks at her. He has an innocent face, round and rather childish. He's popular with the other officers because he takes his turn on the chocolate run and joins in the many running jokes, most of them as black as night, that circulate the police station. Tanya still doesn't quite trust him, mainly because he's known to be close to Judy and Tanya feels that Judy is her main rival at work. Tony answers her respectfully enough. 'It just struck me that they rang the local police, not 999. So whoever rang must already have their number.'

'Easy enough to find the number,' says Tanya. Even as she says it she realises this isn't quite true. Easy enough to google in the daylight but a different matter in the dark with a gunshot ringing in your ears. It's quite a good point but she's not going to tell Tony that.

8

Saturday is sunny but cold, a brisk wind is blowing through the reeds and ruffling the distant sea as Ruth drives to Cley for the excavation. It's early – just after six thirty – and the landscape has a pale, newly washed look, like a watercolour painting.

'Will we see the skeleton today?' says Kate.

Ruth is already having second thoughts about bringing Kate with her. But it's hard to find childcare at the weekend and Kate had begged to come. Even so, digging up human remains is hardly a wholesome mother/daughter activity. What if it traumatises Kate for life? It's more likely though that she'll be bored to tears. But, when Ruth texted Cathbad, he said that he'd be happy to keep an eye on Kate. 'Hecate can help dig,' he said. 'She'll love it.' It's a kindly offer so Ruth decides to ignore the fact that Cathbad, like Nelson, seems intent on renaming her daughter. Nelson calls her 'Katie', which is even worse.

'We might see some bones,' says Ruth. 'They probably won't look like a skeleton.'

'But the bones used to be a person.'

This is something that Ruth has to impress on her students. Skeletal matter, however long it has lain in the ground, once used to be a living, breathing creature. All remains should be treated with the utmost respect, excavated on one day if possible, numbered, recorded and otherwise acknowledged. Once a year there's a ceremony in the grounds of Norwich Castle to remember the 'outcast dead', bodies buried in unmarked graves, in unconsecrated ground, outside city walls. Ruth always tries to attend the service, despite being allergic to the religious element. It's always good to remember the dead.

'Yes,' she says now. 'These bones used to be a person. We won't know if it's a man or woman but there will be some clues from the bones. Women's pelvises are different and men's bones are usually longer.'

'What's a pelvis?' says Kate. Ruth starts to explain but Kate loses interest, which is probably just as well. She starts fiddling with her mobile phone, a new acquisition. Ruth hadn't wanted her to have one until she started secondary school next September. But Kate had put forward an impassioned case and, after some tense debate with Ruth, Nelson had bought her one for Christmas. Ruth doesn't like to see her daughter crouched over the little screen but she has to admit that it's comforting to think that she can contact Kate if she's at a sleepover or with Nelson. Just texting 'Night darling xx' makes Ruth feel less separate, that alarming feeling of amputation she has when Kate is out of physical contact.

Seeing Kate absorbed in her phone Ruth switches on the

radio and the soothing tones of Radio 4 fill the car. *Farming Today*, a programme Ruth loves despite knowing nothing about agriculture beyond what she gleans from *The Archers* (mostly information about silage, modern slavery and surrogate parenting).

'Can we listen to music?' says Kate.

They are singing along to Lady Gaga as they turn into the car park at Cley. Cathbad is already there and Kate squeals with delight when she sees that Michael is with him.

'Hope it's OK,' says Cathbad. 'I thought it might be more fun for Hecate to have a friend to play with. I thought they might have a go with this.'

He brandishes a metal detector. Ruth recoils as if it's a gun.

'Where did you get that?'

'It's an old one of Alan's. He lent it to me. He's coming along later.'

Ruth isn't surprised. Alan, too, probably regards the site as his own personal property. She will have to make sure that the dig is run according to her rules.

'Is Judy coming?' she asks. Police presence might also be helpful.

'Maybe later,' says Cathbad, 'but she's with the family of the couple killed at Black Dog Farm today.'

Ruth suspects that this oddly named place will not resemble anything in *Farming Today* or *The Archers*. She couldn't do Judy's job for a million pounds.

As they walk along the beach, the sand blows in their faces and turns Ruth's hair into a wild tangle. Kate and

Michael laugh excitedly as they carry the metal detector between them. Cathbad pulls up the hood of his anorak.

'I wish I'd brought my cloak,' he says.

'I'm glad you didn't,' says Ruth.

After a few minutes they see the police tape fluttering. The site is just above the tide line, in an area of sand and patchy sea kale. Ted is already there – Ruth spotted his van in the car park – and is measuring out a trench.

'We might need a second section,' says Ruth. 'But I don't think so. I think the body will be here. We can do a more extensive dig later with the students.'

They take off the tarpaulin, billowing wildly in the breeze, and there, exposed in the pale soil, are the metal fragments and the smooth skull bone.

'Is that the skeleton?' says Kate, peering under Ruth's arm.

'It's part of it,' says Ruth. 'Why don't you and Michael see if you can find some treasure further along the beach? Don't go too far, though.'

She watches them running along the sand and freezes when she sees two men approaching. They are both wearing dark jackets and look suddenly surreal, like faceless Magritte bankers on a sunny beach. Then she recognises one of them as David Brown, his scowl visible from a hundred metres away. She's pretty sure that the other man is Alan White. David stops to talk to the children and Ruth is surprised to hear laughter floating up from the group. Then the two men turn inland towards the trench.

'That your daughter, Ruth?' says David.

'Yes,' says Ruth. 'That's Kate. And Cathbad's son, Michael.' She's not about to apologise for bringing her daughter on the dig.

'Good to see them starting on metal detecting early,' says the other man. 'I'm Alan White, by the way. One of the Night Hawks.'

Why on earth did the detectorists give themselves that name? thinks Ruth. It predisposes her to think badly of them. Alan is even wearing a silver hawk badge on his padded gilet. Still, at least he's come prepared to help. Ruth greets Alan politely and turns to address the group.

'We've found some skeletal matter,' she says. 'And I think it's likely that there'll be more. We need to record the remains in situ, the position, direction and any archae-ological features. Then I'll excavate the bones and Ted will log them on the skeleton chart. Then I'll bag them up to be cleaned in the lab. We should take soil samples and log any other finds too. Any questions?'

She thinks that David will ask one for the sake of it, but he takes off his jacket and rolls up his sleeves.

'Let's get going,' he says.

Judy is sitting in a King's Lynn flat, with the sun streaming in through the windows, discussing suicide. Chloe Noakes is on the sofa opposite her, her brother Paul beside her. Chloe is a small woman with short brown hair and a busi-nesslike manner. She's a GP and Judy can just imagine her dispensing brisk medical advice in a way that manages to be sympathetic and efficient at the same time. Paul is a much less definite personality. He's tall with long arms and legs that still seem to come as a surprise to him. He's already knocked over his empty water glass twice. Both times Chloe righted it without looking at her brother. The flat is very tidy.

Yesterday, Chloe identified her parents' bodies at the morgue, attended by the family liaison officer, Maggie. Today's visit is really just so that Judy can establish a relationship with the siblings and let them know how the investigation is progressing.

'The scene-of-crime team are still at the house,' she says. 'But you should be able to go there tomorrow or Monday, if you'd like to.'

Paul looks at Chloe. 'I don't know if I could stand to see that place again.'

Chloe massages his arm, in a bracing yet comforting way. 'I think it might help. To see the . . . to see where it happened.'

Paul shudders. 'Were you there?' he asks Judy. 'Were you there when it happened?'

'I was one of the first on the scene,' says Judy. 'The call came through to the Serious Crimes Unit. Then we had to call for Authorised Firearms officers to attend, because a gunshot had been heard inside the house.'

'Did you go inside?' says Paul, wrapping his legs in a kind of knot. 'Did you see?'

'No,' says Judy gently. 'I didn't go in. My boss did though. DCI Nelson. You'll meet him soon.'

'I just can't believe it,' says Paul. 'Both of them just . . .

gone. I always thought there was something wrong about that house. Something bad.'

Judy thinks of Black Dog Farm, blank-faced and solid, even when all hell was breaking loose inside. She can imagine that it was a lonely place to grow up, but she'd like to know what Paul means by 'something bad'.

'Did you have any idea that your father might be troubled in some way?' asks Judy. 'Sorry. I know this is hard.'

'Are you sure that's what happened?' says Chloe. 'That he killed Mum and then he killed himself?' Her voice is calm and dispassionate but Judy notices that her hands are trembling. Paul must have noticed too because he takes his sister's hand in his own. So maybe the comforting goes both ways.

'We can't be sure until we have all the forensics and the post-mortem report,' says Judy. 'But it does look that way. I'm sorry.'

'Why though?' says Paul. 'Why would he do it?'

'Sometimes there isn't a reason,' says Chloe.

'But Dad . . . he's the last person I would have expected . . .'

'Dad was a strong character,' Chloe tells Judy. 'He never seemed to show weakness or doubt. That's why it's hard to imagine him taking his own life. But these things happen, I know. I've seen it in my own work.'

Chloe is drawing on her own professional experience, but Judy knows that this doesn't always help when the unthinkable happens, because you never expect it to happen to you.

'If I'd committed suicide,' says Paul. 'No one would be surprised. Typical Paul, they'd all say.'

It's a very odd thing to say. Chloe seems to realise this because she says, 'Neither of us know quite what to think or say, DI Johnson.'

'Judy, please. And I quite understand.'

She understands that, in extremis, people usually say exactly what they mean.

By the end of the day, Ruth has excavated a complete human skeleton and Kate has found several coins, a rusty nail and a key, the kind with a long shank and intricate-looking bit.

'The nail could be from a shipwreck,' says Alan, who has maintained a kindly interest in the children's activities. It doesn't surprise Ruth to learn that he'd been a history teacher.

'And the key could be for a treasure chest,' says Kate.

'Where's the chest then?' says Michael. He sounds uncharacteristically grumpy, maybe because Kate is taking all the credit for their joint finds.

'It's probably still buried in the sand,' says Alan. 'You should go on digging.'

Ruth shoots him a look. She suspects Alan of wanting to go on digging at the archaeological site. They have already found several broken spearheads, a pot and what looks like part of a bracelet but Alan keeps saying that 'there must be more'. How predictable, thinks Ruth. Treasure hunter.

The bones are now all numbered and bagged, ready to be taken to the laboratory. The skeleton was in a crouched position, typical of Bronze Age burials. What was less typical was the fact that it appeared to have a dagger in its hand.

From the look of the pelvis and the long bones, Ruth thinks the skeleton is that of a man. The skull also revealed surprisingly good teeth, which will help with aging. They will also be able to get isotope analysis done, which should tell them where the man grew up. Unlike bones, teeth don't renew themselves so they can provide a snapshot of the time of formation.

'He would have been a good-looker,' says Ted. 'Wonderful set of gnashers on him.'

'We'll know if we do a facial reconstruction,' says David who, Ruth is beginning to learn, never gives up.

Ruth has taken multiple soil samples, especially from the abdominal areas of the body where there are likely to be body fluids. Now they are packing up the sample bags and boxes to take them back to Ted's van.

'There might even be DNA,' says David. 'We could find out about whether he was carrying a virus. The virus that killed the Neolithic Britons.'

'DNA is hard to extract from articulated skeletons,' says Ruth. David should really know this stuff, she thinks. 'The process of putrefaction can destroy it. And we've no hair or soft tissue.' The first body she found on the Saltmarsh was buried in peat and so the hair, skin and nails were almost miraculously preserved. These remains, buried in sand, have not fared so well. But they will yield their secrets all the same. It's a good day's work, thinks Ruth, easing her aching back. All she wants now is to go home for a hot bath, a glass of wine and a helping of *The Young Montalbano*.

'Let's call it a day,' she says. 'Thanks so much, everyone. Great work.'

'We should wait until sunset and thank the gods,' says Cathbad. Ruth gives him an exasperated, but affectionate, look. Cathbad has been a real help all day, taking his turn with the excavation but also keeping an eye on the children. Even so, she's not going to sit around on the beach waiting for the sun to slip below the horizon.

'Can't you thank them now?' she says. 'So we can all get home.'

It's nearly sunset anyway. The wind has dropped and the sea is a smooth limpid blue. Everything around them is blue and gold, shot through with a strange, other-worldly light. Cathbad raises his hands. 'Mother Nature, we return thanks to you who sustain us. We return thanks for your light and your warmth and for the bounty of your earth. We return thanks for the moon and the stars, who give us light when the sun is gone. We ask you, Great Mother—'

'What's this?' says a voice. 'A séance?'

Of course, Nelson would have to appear when they've stopped working and seem to be taking part in some weird pagan ritual. Ruth will never hear the end of this.

'Dad!' shouts Kate, charging forwards. Ruth catches David's eye and looks away. He will obviously now have worked out Kate's parentage. Nelson swings Kate into the air. Ruth rubs her eyes.

'Sand in my eyes,' she explains to Cathbad, who is looking uncomfortably understanding.

'Carry on,' says Nelson. 'Don't mind me.'

Cathbad finishes his prayer, perhaps making fewer

references to Brother Sun and Sister Moon than he would otherwise have done. He finishes with a fervent 'Praise be', and then Ruth supervises the covering of the trench.

'Was it a successful dig?' asks Nelson.

'Yes,' says Ruth. 'We excavated a complete skeleton, probably a man, probably about four thousand years old. We'll know more when we get carbon-14 tests on the bones.'

'He's clutching a dagger,' says Cathbad. 'I think he could be a king, or a priest involved in a sacred rite.'

'A murder victim, more likely,' says Nelson. 'Or a murderer.' He looks at the group of people packing up boxes and equipment. 'You here again, Mr White?'

'I wanted to help with the excavation,' says Alan. He sounds defensive but talking to Nelson can do that to you.

'We might need to talk to you again about the events at Black Dog Farm,' says Nelson. 'Don't leave the country.'

Alan looks extremely nervous. Together with David, he picks up the boxes and they set off along the beach. Ted takes the geophysics equipment and Cathbad walks with Michael, carrying the metal detector. Ruth, Nelson and Kate bring up the rear, Kate hanging onto Nelson's arm.

The sand stretches out in front of them, now pockmarked with footprints. The marshes are darkening, starlings swirling like iron filings in the air.

'Murmuration,' says Nelson. 'I can't remember who taught me that word.'

'Probably Cathbad,' says Ruth.

'Probably. He seemed on good form today.'

'He's been a lot of help,' says Ruth.

They walk in silence for another minute.

'Good day?' says Nelson.

'Yes,' says Ruth. 'This could be an important find. Blakeney Point Man.'

'You probably know more about him than we do about our body,' says Nelson.

'No identification yet, then?'

'No, although he had a distinctive tattoo, which might help. Cathbad says it's the Norfolk Sea Serpent.'

'That's a new one,' says Ruth.

'I think he makes it up,' says Nelson. He raises his voice so that Cathbad can hear but Cathbad and Michael are now several metres ahead, Cathbad bending his head to listen to his son.

'I found lots of things on the beach,' says Kate. 'Money, a nail from a shipwreck and a key to a treasure chest.'

'You and Michael found them together,' says Ruth. She is still trying to push the notion of teamwork.

'I did most of it,' says Kate. 'Can we go to Redwings tomorrow, Dad?'

'We can't,' says Ruth. 'We're going to London to see Grandad.'

Although she tries to ignore it, Sunday gloom is already descending.

The slight feeling of depression grows stronger as the evening progresses. Ruth has always had a strained relationship with her parents. They were devout born-again Christians who disapproved of almost all of Ruth's life choices, from reading archaeology at university to having a child out of wedlock. Ruth's older brother Simon (wife, two children, any religious doubts politely suppressed) was their golden child. But, when Ruth's mother died four years ago, Ruth found herself missing her to a surprising degree. Her life felt untethered and precarious without Jean's certainty in the background. She found herself inventing her mother's responses to events, taking comfort in Jean's uncompromising attitude, even from beyond the grave. 'No point crying over spilt milk, Ruth, he's not going to leave his wife.' 'You wanted that job, no use moaning about it now.'

Ruth and Simon embarked on a programme of looking after their father, Arthur. Simon, who lives nearby, in south London, visited every week. Ruth made the journey from Norfolk to Eltham about once a month. At first, Ruth found it very hard. The drive was long and boring, and she couldn't get used to not seeing her mother at the end of it. The house didn't seem the same without Jean. Arthur didn't fill it in the same way and, in the weeks after Jean's death, he seemed to close in on himself, existing in a few rooms, moving in an apologetic way as if embarrassed to find himself the surviving partner. Jean would have flourished as a widow; Arthur was clearly not designed for the single life.

And so it proved. When Arthur started up a friendship with Gloria, a woman from the Bereaved Support Group at his church, Ruth and Simon had been relieved. It meant that they wouldn't feel so responsible for their father, a duty that rested heavily on Simon's shoulders. But when Arthur and Gloria moved in together, Simon hadn't been so impressed.

'It's an insult to Mum,' he said to Ruth, during one of their infrequent phone conversations. 'She's probably after his money.' 'He hasn't got any money,' Ruth countered. 'He's got a house in London,' said Simon, 'and that makes him a millionaire.'

But Ruth is pleased with the new arrangement. She likes Gloria, who is a widow with four grown-up children and six grandchildren. Arthur is obviously happiest as part of a couple and the fact that Gloria is a woman of colour means that he is less prone to making alarmingly crypto-racist statements. What's more, Gloria seems to expand to fill the little house. She cooks, she wears bright colours, she laughs readily and often. Simon says that he hates to see Gloria in 'Mum's kitchen', but Ruth finds that Gloria's presence makes her notice her mother's absence less. Besides, Gloria is always very nice to Kate and Kate seems to enjoy their Sundays in Eltham. On their last visit Ruth and Kate met Gloria's son, Ambrose, and his two daughters. Kate had been delighted to acquire two almost-relatives, especially cool London teenagers with iPhones and dangly earrings.

Even so, Ruth finds herself feeling low once Kate is finally in bed and she is alone looking at photographs of the dig, human bones lying next to measuring rods. Or is the feeling really all about Nelson? What will he be doing tomorrow? Will he and Michelle visit a garden centre, that haven for married couples? Perhaps they'll have Sunday lunch in a pub somewhere, watching George rampage around the soft play area and laughing softly over their roast beef with all the trimmings?

No, she tells herself, Nelson loathes gardens and family-friendly pubs. Besides, he'll be busy with his dead body and with the shooting at the farmhouse. Michelle will probably be left to entertain George on her own, unless Laura comes over. It's not an easy life, being married to a police officer. It probably only works if you're Cathbad, full of inner resources and slightly magical into the bargain. Ruth is lucky to live on her own, accountable to no one. She sighs and goes back to her skeleton.

9

'We found a body on the beach. He had a dagger in his hand and he was probably murdered,' says Kate.

'Oh, my Lord.' Gloria puts her hand to her heart as if the dagger is in her own chest.

'A body?' quavers Arthur. 'That's not a suitable thing for a child to see.'

Ruth sighs. Does her father really think that she would let Kate pull dead bodies from the water, like some Victorian scavenger child? And Gloria looks as if she's about to faint into the roast beef.

'It's an archaeological dig,' she says. 'The body is just a skeleton and it's probably about four thousand years old.'

'Four thousand?' queries Arthur. 'Was he a cave man?'

Ruth hopes that her father has not become one of those Christians who believe that the earth is only ten thousand years old and that dinosaurs are fakes invented by cunning atheists. She also dislikes the term 'cave man', not least because it excludes women.

'We think our skeleton is from the Bronze Age,' she says,

'which starts around three thousand years BC. It's a really interesting find, actually.'

'Where did you find it?' says Gloria, passing the gravy. She sounds as if the skeleton was a lost wallet, but Ruth appreciates that she's trying to show some interest. And she has cooked a splendid Sunday lunch.

'On the beach at Blakeney Point,' says Ruth. 'The skeleton was surrounded by broken swords. That's how we know it's Bronze Age.'

Arthur looks bemused, and rather revolted, at the thought of the weapons.

'Funny place to find a load of swords,' he says, 'just lying about on the beach. Isn't that a bit dangerous?'

'It wouldn't have been a beach then,' says Ruth, trying vainly to keep the conversation going. 'In the Bronze Age Blakeney Point would probably have been marshland. The weapons may have been grave goods, offerings to the gods.' Arthur and Gloria exchange looks. They like to pretend that pagan gods didn't exist and that prehistoric people were C of E really.

'I found some coins,' says Kate. 'And the key to a treasure chest.'

Arthur and Gloria smile at Kate. They both dote on her, which is just as well really. All the same, Arthur manages to look reprovingly at Ruth, as if reminding her that swords – even if four thousand years old – are not suitable for children.

It's a shame because the day had been going well so far. Ruth accomplished the journey without encountering too

much traffic. Gloria and Arthur had given them a big welcome and Kate had regaled the company with a description
of her school's Christmas play.

'It's *Scrooge* which is *A Christmas Carol* really. I'm Scrooge,
which is the best part.'

Kate only found this out on Friday. Ruth noted that Kate
still does not wholly subscribe to the 'drama as teamwork'
idea. She's also very proud of her.

'Isn't Scrooge a man?' said Arthur. 'You don't want to
play a man.'

'I do because it's the best part,' explained Kate patiently.

'I can help with making costumes,' said Gloria. 'Doesn't
Scrooge wear chains?'

'That's Jacob Marley,' said Kate, 'but thank you,' she
added, catching Ruth's eye.

'That's really kind of you,' said Ruth. 'I can't sew at all.'

'Your mother did try to teach you,' said Arthur, 'but you
didn't have the patience.'

I had enough patience to study for my A levels, thought
Ruth, and get a first-class honours degree. I've got enough
patience to excavate a site, layer by layer, sifting each sieve-
full of soil by hand. But there didn't seem much point in
saying any of this. Ruth knows that Arthur is proud of her,
in his own way, but she also knows that she's a mystery to
him. Her mother had understood Ruth better although she
hadn't exactly approved of her. Although Jean would, Ruth
thought suddenly, have been impressed by the corner office
and Ruth's name on the door.

But now, over lunch, the conversation seems to have run

dry. Ruth thinks that Arthur and Gloria are just horrified at the thought of the skeleton on the beach, but it turns out that they have their own announcement to make. They wait until Ruth and Kate have eaten their treacle tart and ice cream. Ruth is longing for coffee, but Gloria thinks that caffeine is a poison.

'Gloria and I,' says Arthur, 'have something to tell you.' He pauses awkwardly but that could be because he has treacle tart stuck to his dentures.

'Is it something nice?' says Ruth, wanting to help him along.

'I think so,' says Arthur hoarsely. 'Very nice. Gloria and I are getting married.'

'Wow,' says Ruth. 'That's . . . that's great! When?' There are many other things she wants to ask. Have you told Simon? Has Gloria told her family? *What about Mum who died only four years ago?*

'We thought a Christmas wedding would be nice,' says Gloria.

'Can I be a bridesmaid?' says Kate.

Perhaps because this is the first genuinely positive response, both Arthur and Gloria become misty-eyed. Gloria hurries round the table to hug Kate.

'Of course you can, darling.'

'Christmas?' says Ruth. 'That's quite soon.' It's mid-September now. Surely weddings take years to arrange? But Ruth wouldn't know because she's never been a bride.

'We just want a simple ceremony,' says Arthur. 'A service at our church and perhaps a meal afterwards. Just family. And the church elders, of course.'

Of course.

'Have you told anyone else?' says Ruth. She means Simon.

'Just my daughters,' says Gloria. 'I'm going to tell Ambrose and Christopher this week.'

'I thought that we might go over to Simon's this afternoon,' says Arthur. 'We could tell him together. And Kate would like to see Jack and George.'

'I would like to see them,' Kate agrees.

'That's decided then,' says Arthur. He tries to look cheerful, but Ruth knows dread when she sees it.

'You are joking. Tell me that you're joking.'

They're sitting in Simon's conservatory, the afternoon sun uncomfortably hot. Simon's wife Cathy has produced tea for the adults and orange juice for Kate. Despite Arthur's promise, neither of the boys are present. Nineteen-year-old George is at university in Sheffield and seventeen-year-old Jack hasn't yet emerged from his room.

Arthur's announcement, blurted out in an almost defiant way, has not gone down well.

'Of course I'm not joking,' he says. 'Gloria and I are getting married.'

'Mum's barely cold in her grave.'

'Your mother's been dead for four years,' says Arthur, with dignity. But Ruth sees that his hands are shaking. She feels a pang for him. Her father suddenly looks very vulnerable in his cardigan and slacks, teamed as usual with a shirt and tie. He's not as painfully thin as he was, though, which must be thanks to Gloria's cooking.

'Katie, love,' says Cathy. 'Do you want to see Jack?' She holds out her hand. Ruth feels rather irritated. Not only has Cathy decided to distort Kate's name (as Nelson always does) but she's making the unilateral decision that this conversation is unsuitable for her. But, on the other hand, it probably *is* unsuitable.

Kate follows her aunt out of the room, leaving father and children together. Ruth suspects that Cathy was also looking for a way to escape.

Simon paces the little glass room. There's no shade apart from a large rubber plant; Ruth tries to shift her wicker chair under its leaves. Simon stops in front of his father. 'You hardly know Gloria,' he says. 'We hardly know her.'

'I've known her for years,' says Arthur. 'She's a member of the church. I knew her when Jean and Ted – Gloria's husband – were alive. She's a good friend.'

'She's a bit more than a friend now, though, isn't she?' says Simon. There's a sneering note in his voice that Ruth hasn't heard before. When they were children Simon tended to sulk, to withdraw – he wasn't one for confrontation or answering back. Ruth used to argue with her parents but Simon, though he often agreed with her, never backed her up. But he's definitely feeling confrontational now.

'How old is Gloria?' asks Simon.

'She's seventy-two,' says Arthur. 'I know she looks younger,' he adds, with rather touching pride.

'I just wonder why she wants to get married,' says Simon. 'Doesn't she have a house of her own?'

'We're in love,' says Arthur, ignoring this. 'I loved your

mother and I didn't think I'd experience that feeling again but I have. That's all.'

Ruth finds it almost shocking to hear her father talking about being 'in love'. She assumed that her parents loved each other but she never heard either of them mention the fact. And now Arthur is experiencing *that feeling* with someone else. She has to fight her instinctive reaction that this is disloyal to Jean. After all, Ruth herself is in love with a married man and, if anything happened to Michelle . . . But she can't let herself think that way.

'That's lovely, Dad,' she says.

'I don't think it's lovely at all.' Simon shoots Ruth a look.

'Why can't you be happy for me?' says Arthur, looking up at his son. He sounds querulous and every day of his eighty-one years.

Simon sits down. 'I want you to be happy,' he says, in a slightly more conciliatory tone. 'I just don't want you to rush into anything.'

'Why not wait a bit?' says Ruth. 'Why not wait until the spring?' Spring, renewal and rebirth, the dead rising again. She can hear Cathbad's voice in her head, which is always disconcerting.

Her father does not seem enamoured of the season of rebirth. 'No,' he says. 'We've set a date. December the fifteenth.'

This is the first Ruth has heard of an actual date. Simon, too, looks taken aback.

'Well, I won't be going to the wedding,' he says.

Arthur looks shocked and even Simon seems surprised

at what he's said. They both look at Ruth, which makes her feel very nervous.

'Let's not make any rash decisions now,' she says, trying for a soothing tone.

'Dad's making a pretty rash decision,' says Simon.

'I'm not being rash,' says Arthur. 'I just want to spend the rest of my life with Gloria. I've probably only got about ten years left. Don't you want them to be happy?'

This is fairly unanswerable and Ruth can sense Simon weakening. A shame, then, that Arthur follows it up with, 'And I don't want to spend my final years without sex, either.'

10

Nelson looks up at Black Dog Farm. The building is as solid and impenetrable as ever, as square as a child's drawing, two windows above, two windows below. Even though the Forensics teams have been swarming over it all weekend and have erected a canopy over the front door and a plastic sheeted corridor leading to the back of the house, it still retains its air of mystery. There's a weathervane on the roof with a black cockerel on it. It's not moving today as if it, too, is waiting. Douglas and Linda Noakes weren't farmers, so why on earth did they live here in the middle of nowhere? There's not another house as far as the eye can see, just flat fields with a few trees and wind-blown shrubs. Nelson is due to meet the Noakes children, Paul and Chloe, at the house. He wants to ask them what it was like to grow up here, so far from their friends and everyday pleasures like cinemas and swimming pools. He often worries about Katie, living in that godforsaken cottage. OK, she loves it now but how will she feel when she's sixteen and wants to go into Lynn with her friends? Nelson spent his daughters' teenage years as an unpaid, and often unacknowledged, taxi service. Will Ruth be prepared to do the same? He doubts it sometimes.

Mike Halloran, who's in charge of the SOCO team, emerges from behind the plastic sheets. He's in a white hazmat suit and walks with the ponderous deliberation of a polar bear.

'Anything I should know about?' says Nelson.

Mike lowers his mask. 'I think we've got a suicide note,' he says.

'Really?' This is news. A note will go a long way towards proving the murder-suicide theory, though they will still have to wait for the forensic tests on the bodies and the guns.

'Where was it?' asks Nelson.

'In what looks like Dr Douglas's study. It was in the tray of the printer.'

'The printer? It was typewritten?'

'Yes.'

This is unusual but then suicide notes are fairly unusual in themselves. Nelson has often been surprised by the way that people seem to take this final, irrevocable step without leaving behind an explanation. But then, maybe, it can't be explained. Not in words, anyway.

'Can I see?' says Nelson.

'You'll have to put on a suit.'

'If I have to.' Nelson is nostalgic for the days when the police galloped all over a crime scene, perhaps – if they were very conscientious – pausing to tuck their ties into shirt fronts. Now policemen don't wear ties and they aren't allowed onto the scene until the experts have swept, tested and otherwise decoded it. Nelson knows that this is progress, and forensics have helped him catch many criminals over the years, but he still hates putting on paper coveralls.

'Will you have the scene clear by the time the family gets here?' he asks. Paul and Chloe Noakes are due any minute. Judy reported that they seemed conflicted about visiting the site of their parents' deaths, but Nelson wants them to come. He wants to see the house through their eyes.

'We're almost finished,' says Mike. 'The study will have to be sealed, though.'

Dressed in a voluminous white suit that crackles as he walks, Nelson follows Mike through the awning. Inside, a plastic walkway has been laid down and Nelson can see numbers on the floor indicating places where the SOCO teams have seized objects or taken samples. He thinks of the last time he entered the farmhouse: the firearms officer kicking down the door, Sara breathing heavily as she raised her gun, the clock ticking, the smell of blood, the shattered face on the floor. The bodies have been taken away but everywhere he looks there's evidence of the dead couple: gumboots by the front door, the local paper on the mat, a coat hanging on the end of the banisters, a laundry bag on the top landing. Douglas and Linda had been going for walks, reading the papers, doing their washing. What had happened to make their lives stop so suddenly?

'Before we go upstairs,' says Mike. 'There's something you should see.'

He pushes open a door to the left of the hall, not touching

it with his hands even though he's wearing gloves. They are in a white-walled room with a desk, two chairs, a sink and what looks like a hospital bed, covered with plastic sheeting. There are also two filing cabinets that look very locked.

Nelson sniffs the air. There's an antiseptic smell that reminds him, morbidly, of the mortuary.

'Well,' says Mike. 'What do you think?'

'It's like a doctor's surgery,' says Nelson. 'Douglas Noakes wasn't a GP, was he?'

'No, he was a research scientist. But this looks very like a place where you'd see patients.'

Nelson looks at the bed. He hasn't been to the doctor for years, but he remembers accompanying Michelle for scans when she was pregnant. Well, he was there for most of them, he thinks, defensive even to himself. He remembers thinking at the time about the indignities that women have to go through. The plastic-covered bed reminds him of that.

Mike leads the way out of the room and they climb the stairs. There's still a bloody handprint on the wall where Linda had breathed her last. Nelson and Mike edge past, crabwise. Mike opens a door off the landing, again using his elbow to push down the handle. They are in a small room, very tidy, just a desk and a chair, a bookcase full of scientific-looking tomes, a large metal filing cabinet. A closed laptop lies on the desk and, next to it, there's a printer. A piece of paper lies where it was spewed out by the machine. By twisting his head, Nelson is able to read the few lines at the top of the page. He wishes that he could put his glasses on.

It's just impossible to go on. I'm sorry for all the things I've said and done. For the body in the garden and all of it. I've been a bad father but I hope that, when all this is over, my scientific work will still be taken into account. My family knows how I feel about them.

Douglas Noakes

'Jesus.' Nelson looks at Mike.

'Yes.'

Nelson glances at the window which looks out over a large and overgrown garden.

'The body in the garden?'

'I thought you'd like that bit,' says Mike.

'We need to get digging,' says Nelson. 'We need a forensic archaeologist. We need Ruth.'

Paul and Chloe Noakes are waiting outside. Judy is with them, keeping just the right distance away. Judy is excellent with families, she knows exactly when to speak and when to be quiet, when to coax and when to drop back. Not for the first time, Nelson prays that she's not looking for DI jobs elsewhere.

Chloe Noakes is a small, slight woman, dressed in jeans and a padded jacket. Paul is thin too but he's very tall, perhaps a foot taller than his sister. They must look very odd in family photos. Nelson tries to remember if he saw any such photos in the house. There were none in the study, that's for certain. The walls had been bare.

Nelson approaches the group.

'I'm DCI Nelson. I'm sorry for your loss.'

Chloe looks taken aback. Perhaps it's the suit.

'I was told we could go in the house,' she says.

'You can,' says Nelson. 'We're just waiting for the Forensics team to finish.' As he speaks, the awning is coming down. Nelson moves away to climb out of his suit. Impossible to do this sort of thing with any dignity. He can hear Judy explain about the scene-of-crime work. 'They're very careful, very respectful. They won't miss a thing.' Mike always says that every contact leaves a trace. 'You could leave this room,' he tells them in briefings, 'and I could tell you exactly where you were all sitting.'

'We'll have to be careful not to touch anything in the house,' Nelson says now. 'And some things will be distressing for you. I'm sorry.'

Chloe takes her brother's arm. 'Come on, Paul.' The small woman leads the tall man into the house. Nelson and Judy follow them. Chloe leads the way into the kitchen. There's a newspaper still open on the table. *The Times*, Nelson thinks. A Guide Dogs for the Blind calendar is on the wall, a chocolate Labrador for September. But what they all see immediately is the brown stain on the yellow linoleum. Paul gasps. Chloe puts her hand on his arm. Chloe seems remarkably composed. She was the one who identified her parents' bodies in the morgue. Nelson is pretty sure that Chloe will cope. He's less sure about Paul.

'Is this where Dad . . .?' says Paul.

'Dr Noakes was found here,' says Nelson. 'He had been

shot in the head and a gun was beside him. Did your father own a handgun?'

'No,' says Paul. 'I don't think so. He had a shotgun though. He used to shoot rabbits sometimes.'

'Keeping the population down,' says Chloe, her voice even. 'That's what he said.'

'Are you sure ...' Paul's voice is quavering, 'are you sure ... that he killed himself?'

'We can't be certain until we see the forensics results,' says Nelson, 'but it does look that way.'

They walk back through the hallway with its brown and yellow geometric wallpaper. Nelson is hardly an expert in contemporary interior design but even to him it seems very old-fashioned – from the sixties or seventies, perhaps? The grandfather clock is older and has more gravitas. It continues its ponderous ticking.

'I want to show you something,' says Nelson. He pushes open the door to the small room with the smell of antiseptic.

This time it's Chloe who gasps.

'Was this room open? He kept it locked ...'

'As far as I know it was open,' says Nelson. 'Did your father see patients here?'

'He wasn't a GP,' says Chloe, who is one herself, of course. 'He was a scientist. He owned a research company in Cambridge.'

Nelson notes that Chloe has no problem referring to her father in the past tense.

'So you've no idea what this was used for?' He points to the plastic-covered bed.

'No,' says Paul. 'Can we leave now?'

They go back into the hall. Paul looks up at the stairs. Nelson hopes that he can't see the handprint.

'Is this where ... where Mum was found?'

'Mrs Noakes was at the top of the stairs,' says Nelson.

Paul turns away, sobbing, almost retching. Chloe says, 'Did it look as if she was running away from him?'

'It did,' says Nelson, 'yes.'

'I need to get out,' says Paul. He stumbles out through the front door. The others follow him. Paul is standing with his back to the house, looking out at the fields. Chloe goes up to him and puts her hand on his arm. Judy says, 'Do you need a moment? We could talk back at the station if you prefer. I know this must be very hard.'

'It's all right,' says Chloe. 'It's just ... seeing where it happened.'

Nelson says, 'You should know that we've found a piece of paper that looks like a suicide note. I can't show you the letter itself yet but here's a photograph.' He hands Chloe his phone and the siblings lean in to look at it. Judy raises her eyebrows at Nelson. It's the first she's heard of the note.

'Does that read like something your father would have written?' says Nelson.

'Yes,' says Chloe, 'it does. He was always keen on getting his due recognition. His work was everything to him.'

'Do you know what he means by the body in the garden?'

'Dad used to say that there was a dead body in the garden,' says Paul. 'He said that, if we didn't behave, it would rise up out of the ground and kill us.'

This is said in an absolutely flat voice but, for the first time in his life, Nelson feels the hairs standing up on the back of his neck. The house is behind him and suddenly he wants to turn to check that it hasn't moved, that it isn't watching them.

Chloe says, 'Just so that you know, Paul and I hate this place and we hated our father. We're glad he's dead.'

11

By midday, Ruth is beginning to admit, cautiously, that the first day of lectures is going well. She had the first slot, with An Introduction to Archaeology, and she was pleased that the students seemed engaged and asked interested questions. She didn't sit in on the other sessions because she thought that would be off-putting for the lecturers but she hovered in the corridor and coffee area and was half-pleased, half-irritated to hear the freshers coming out full of praise for David's talk on the Neolithic era.

'That guy is sick,' says someone. Ruth is pretty sure this is a compliment. She knows that she should be pleased that her new appointee is proving popular, but she worries that this will make David more arrogant than ever. She also can't help hoping that the students will still like her best.

She goes back to her office to prepare for her first tutorials and sees that she has a missed call from Nelson. What can he want? He's not due to see Kate until the weekend. Maybe it's about the body on the beach but Nelson said on Saturday that they didn't have an identification yet.

Maybe he wants to ask how Sunday went. Unlikely but possible. She rings him back.

'Ruth.' No pleasantries, as ever. 'Can you come to Black Dog Farm?'

'Black Dog Farm?' The name rings a faint, and rather ominous, bell.

'It's near Sheringham,' says Nelson.

'Is that the place where those people were found dead the other day?'

'That's right. Can you come?'

'Nelson,' says Ruth. 'I'm working. I can't come racing over to Sheringham at a moment's notice.'

Nelson never really believes in anyone else's work. It's one of the many infuriating things about him. Unfortunately, knowing this doesn't make Ruth feel any differently about him.

'Can you come later?' he says. 'When you've finished.'

'I'm not finished until four and then I've got to collect Kate from the childminder.'

'Bring Katie too. She doesn't need to go inside.'

'Go inside where?'

'The farmhouse. It's the garden I want you to look at.'

'The garden?'

'I'll explain when you get here. It won't take long and it's on your way home.'

'No, it isn't.'

'I think you'd find it interesting.' Should Ruth wait until he says 'please'? But, in that case, she might be waiting for a very long time.

'I can't stay long,' she says.

'That's fine. I'll meet you there. About five?'

'OK,' says Ruth, agreeing, as she had always known she would.

'He was abusive,' says Chloe. 'I'm sure you've heard this sort of thing before.'

They are sitting at a wooden table with bench seats attached, the kind found in the beer gardens of pubs. This one looks out onto the back of Black Dog Farm, an overgrown space vaguely bordered by rockery stones and some half-hearted shrubs. Nelson tries to look at it with Ruth's eyes. What did she say about nettles being a sign of human presence, maybe even a body? Well there are plenty of nettles here as well as brambles and knotweed and some prettier weeds with white flowers. It's an unloved garden but, in the autumn sunshine, it's not an entirely unpleasant place.

Paul and Chloe sit on one side of the bench, Judy and Nelson on the other. Chloe is telling them about her father, her voice level and dispassionate. A doctor's voice. Paul sits beside her, picking at the skin around his fingernails.

'It wasn't really physical, though he did hit us. It was mental cruelty. If we liked something, a book or a TV programme, he'd ban us from reading or watching it. He even stopped us watching *Blue Peter*, for God's sake. He wouldn't let us have friends over or listen to music. It was about power and control, of course. All we were allowed to do was work. He wanted us to study and become scientists, preferably doctors.' She laughs, without humour. 'Well, I followed his instructions to the letter.'

'I didn't,' says Paul. 'He was furious when I decided to study history at university. He hasn't even got my graduation picture up. Only yours.'

'Remember what he said to your history teacher?' says Chloe.

'You're corrupting my son.' Paul adopts a deep voice that's obviously meant to be his father. 'You're a disgrace to the profession.'

'Your history teacher,' says Nelson, 'was that Alan White?'

'Yes,' says Paul. 'Alan supported me. He's still a good friend.'

'You were with him and the Night Hawks when a man's body was found on the beach on Wednesday night, weren't you?' says Nelson.

'Yes. I gave a statement to the police.'

'Did any of your teachers suspect that your father was ill-treating you?' says Judy. 'Did you ever try to tell anyone?'

'No,' says Chloe. 'Dad presented this ultra respectable front to the outside world, renowned scientist, all that crap. And he was always polite to our teachers. Except that one time.'

'The body buried in the garden,' says Nelson. 'Do you know if that has any basis in truth? Did your father ever say who was buried there?'

'I assumed he made it up,' says Chloe. 'He had a dark imagination but even I never suspected Dad of murder.'

'He murdered Mum, didn't he?' says Paul, his voice rising.

'Yes,' says Chloe, 'he did.'

'Have you any idea why he would have done such a thing?' asks Judy.

'No,' says Chloe. 'Dad was such a narcissist, he's the last person I would have thought would commit suicide.'

'When did you last see your parents?' says Judy.

'A few months ago,' says Chloe. 'I dropped in because I needed them to sign some papers.'

'I saw them last week,' says Paul. 'I called in to see Mum on Monday night. I tried to come at times when Dad was out. I thought he'd be at bridge club, but he came home early. He was his usual charming self, talking about how I'd wasted my life in my dead-end job.'

Paul Noakes is a teacher at a sixth form college, Nelson remembers. Most parents would consider this a success.

'How did your mum seem?' asks Judy.

'The usual. Scared, placatory, not standing up to him,' says Paul. 'But not standing up for me either.'

He sounds like a hurt child, thinks Nelson. There's a silence and then Chloe says, 'You know what really surprises me about the note? It's the fact that he said sorry.'

It's past five by the time that Ruth arrives at Black Dog Farm. Nelson is standing waiting for her at a sign saying, 'To the farm'. To Kate's delight, he gets into the back seat for the drive along the rough track to the building itself.

'You're late,' he says.

'There was lots of traffic,' says Ruth. And then curses herself for offering an excuse.

'Have you ever sat in the back of a car before, Dad?' says Kate.

'Very rarely,' says Nelson, wincing – unnecessarily, in Ruth's opinion – as the car judders forwards.

There are dense hedges on either side of the track so that, when the house appears, it does so with surprising suddenness. It's a square, flint-lined building, surrounded by outhouses bordering a concrete yard. Nelson's white Mercedes is parked there beside another car, a red Toyota Yaris. As soon as Ruth stops, Nelson gets out and strides over to this vehicle and speaks to the two people inside. After a few words from him, the driver performs a three-point turn and departs.

'Reporters,' says Nelson. 'Vultures circling.'

'I suppose people are always fascinated by this sort of story,' says Ruth.

'Yeah,' says Nelson. 'Spooky house. Dysfunctional family. It's got it all. I've got Maddie Henderson – Cathbad's daughter – nagging me for an exclusive. She's not the worst but I can just imagine the sort of thing she'll write.'

Ruth looks up at the house. It has a dour, closed face, curtains drawn, door firmly shut, boarded up, police tape across it. A rook caws loudly from the roof.

'Is this where . . .?' Ruth looks at Kate, who is watching the rabbits in the next-door field.

'Yes,' says Nelson. 'This is where the bodies where found. I want to show you the back garden, though.'

Calling Kate, Ruth follows Nelson round the house to a fenced-off garden. It's very overgrown but there are signs that someone must have tended it once: the remains of a rockery, the ropes of a swing hanging from a tree. They sit at a wooden bench and Ruth offers Kate a carton of juice that she has brought with her. Kate sips it unenthusiastically.

'How was Sunday?' says Nelson. 'Did you see your dad?'

'Yes,' says Ruth. 'And, over lunch, he announced that he wants to marry his girlfriend.'

'I'm going to be a bridesmaid,' says Kate.

'You'll be a beautiful bridesmaid,' says Nelson. Kate seems satisfied with this response and, a few minutes later, wanders off to explore the garden.

'How do you feel about it?' Nelson asks Ruth.

'OK, I suppose. I mean I want Dad to be happy and Gloria seems really nice. Simon – my brother – is finding it a bit hard to deal with.'

'I can understand that,' says Nelson. 'I can't imagine what I would have felt if my mother had married again after my dad died.'

'Did your mother ever think of marrying again?'

'God, no!' Nelson sounds so shocked that Ruth lets it drop. Honestly, what is it about men and their mothers? Time to change the subject.

'Well,' she says. 'Why did you want me to come here?'

'You know that there was a shooting here last week. We think that one of the inhabitants of the house, Douglas Noakes, killed his wife and then killed himself.'

'How awful.'

'Yes,' says Nelson. 'These sorts of crime scenes are always very distressing. We've had the SOCO team in the house since Friday and today they've found what looked to be a suicide note from Dr Noakes. In it he mentions "the body buried in the garden".'

Ruth looks over towards Kate but, thankfully, she is at the very end of the garden. Even so, Ruth suddenly wants to shout out to her to be careful. Two more rooks are watching them from the branches of an elm.

'"The body buried in the garden"? My God, do you think there's someone buried here?'

'I don't know but I think we have to dig it up. That's why I called you.'

'We'll need diggers,' says Ruth. 'And geophysics equipment. A resistivity metre, maybe a magnetometer.'

'You can arrange that, can't you?'

'Yes, but it might take several days.'

'I was thinking about something you once said,' says Nelson, 'about nettles.'

'Nice to know that you listen,' says Ruth.

'I always listen,' says Nelson. 'You said once that, if there were nettles, it meant that there might be a body.'

'It means there's been human activity,' says Ruth. 'That could just mean that someone once had a pee in the garden.'

'Or a body could be buried here.'

'It could, I suppose.'

'Well,' Nelson stands up. 'Let's get a dig organised. Get Irish Ted on the job.'

'He'll be delighted.'

'What about that man who was with you when we first found the body?' says Nelson. 'Will he be involved?'

'David?' says Ruth, feeling defensive, though she couldn't have said why. 'He's a new lecturer. I hired him in the summer. He wouldn't be involved with this.'

'He struck me as the kind of bloke who wants to be involved with everything. He was there on Saturday, wasn't he?'

What is Nelson getting at? 'He'll do what I tell him,' says Ruth.

'Ha.' Nelson gives a bark of laughter. 'That's my girl.'

Ruth wants to tell him not to call her a girl, to tell him that she's not his girl, not in any sense. Instead she says, 'What do you know about the people who lived here?'

'Douglas Noakes, Dr Douglas Noakes, was an eminent scientist, involved with some sort of research in Cambridge. And, by his children's account, he was a nasty piece of work. His wife Linda was a retired primary school teacher. Sounds as if she was completely dominated by her husband.'

'And he killed her and then killed himself?'

'It looks that way, yes.'

Ruth looks up at the house. The back is as stark as the front. Four sash windows, all the same size and shape. Two sloping attic windows. Curtains drawn, eyes closed.

'I wouldn't like to live here,' she says.

'Why? You live in the middle of nowhere.'

'There's a difference,' says Ruth. 'I live near the sea. You can see the edges. Here you feel completely hemmed in.'

'I think the Noakes children, Paul and Chloe, felt the same,' says Nelson. While they have been speaking, the light has just begun to fade. The rooks fly into the air, calling spectrally. Ruth thinks of Nelson's comment. *Vultures circling.*

'Come on, Katie,' says Nelson. 'Let's go.'

'Yes, come on, *Kate*,' says Ruth. She will never stop trying to educate him about their daughter's name.

As Ruth bumps along the track that leads to the gate, Kate tells her about rehearsals for *Scrooge*.

'And then I have to be really angry and throw a book at Bob Cratchit. Miss Walker says that I'm really good at being angry.'

This too must be something she has inherited from Nelson.

'And then I tell him that he can't have Christmas Eve off and then . . . Mum!'

But Ruth has seen it too. She slams on the brakes. Behind them, Nelson hoots impatiently.

'What was that?' says Kate, slightly breathless.

'I don't know. Maybe a deer.'

The animal had appeared from the hedgerow and had seemed to look at them before disappearing back into the darkness.

'It looked like a dog,' says Kate, 'a dog with red eyes.'

'It was too big for a dog,' says Ruth. She starts the car again, ignoring Nelson's pantomime of frustration in the car behind.

12

Ruth can't get the image of the strange animal out of her mind. Back home, after Kate has gone to bed, she does what she always does when faced with the mystical and fantastical. She rings Cathbad.

'Hallo, Ruth.'

'Hi. Is it too late to ring?'

She has just realised that it's past ten. Kate seems to go to sleep later and later these days. Even if Ruth starts the process in good time, her daughter now lies in bed reading or listening to music for hours. Is she in training for being a teenager? Ruth remembers reading in bed – Georgette Heyer and Jilly Cooper as well as school books – in her little room in Eltham. What will happen to that bedroom when Gloria and Arthur get married? Maybe Gloria will turn it into her sewing room.

'It's not too late,' says Cathbad. 'Judy and I were just sitting in the garden. It's beautiful at night.'

Just for a second, this image makes Ruth feel so jealous that she can hardly breathe. Cathbad and Judy, their children in bed, sitting in their night-scented garden, chatting and drinking tea. She stamps on this emotion as hard as she can. Living with a man is not all it's cracked up to be. If she was sharing a house with Nelson, they would probably argue all the time. In the evenings they would certainly not be admiring the beauties of nature. Nelson would almost definitely be watching the football.

'I was at Black Dog Farm today,' says Ruth.

'Judy's been telling me about the place. It has a very bad energy.'

'It's certainly a bit creepy,' says Ruth, thinking of the shuttered house, the rooks in the garden. 'But I was thinking about the name. Do you think it's linked to the Black Shuck?' She has lived in Norfolk long enough to know about the spectral dog.

'I think it must be,' says Cathbad. 'The legend is very strong around Sheringham way. Funnily enough, though, there have been quite a few sightings near Black Dog Farm. Recent sightings, I mean.'

'How do you know?'

'A friend of mine does a lot of field walking around there. He's a bit of an amateur archaeologist.'

Cogs turn in Ruth's mind. Surely this is a sign of the great web at its knottiest?

'This friend,' she says. 'Is it Alan White?'

'Yes.'

'The Alan White who just turned up at the dig on Saturday?'

'That's right. He's interested in archaeology. And he's a nice man. You saw how good he was with Hecate.'

'Her name's Kate. I just think it's a bit sinister the way this Alan keeps popping up everywhere.'

'He's a questing soul,' says Cathbad. It sounds as if he's said this before. There's more to this than meets the eye but it's not Ruth's job to investigate links between the two deaths. It's Nelson's, and she's fairly sure that he won't have missed the connection.

'The thing is,' she says. 'When I was driving away from the farm today, I saw something that looked like a big black dog.'

Cathbad draws in his breath. 'Ruth, you've seen the Black Shuck.'

'That's bad, right? Aren't I about to drop dead?' She can't stop herself touching the wood of her desk as she says this. Nelson, a lapsed Catholic, would have crossed himself.

'Not necessarily,' says Cathbad. 'As I said to Judy, the Black Shuck can just be a travelling companion. I've seen him twice. Once when I was walking near Beeston Bump. I saw the shadow of a large dog walking beside me. It was comforting.'

'When was the other time?'

'Just before Tim died.'

'That's less comforting.' Tim, a police officer on Nelson's team, died in tragic circumstances four years ago.

'The Shuck can warn of a death,' says Cathbad. 'Not necessarily the death of the person who sees him.'

'Well, he arrived at Black Dog Farm a bit late,' says Ruth. 'There have already been two deaths.'

'Two deaths so far,' says Cathbad.

He sounds remarkably upbeat about it.

*

The next morning, Ruth is reading about the Black Shuck in her office when David gives a perfunctory knock and barges in.

'Any news on our skeleton?' he says.

'The lab only got the samples late on Saturday,' says Ruth. 'They won't have any results for us yet.'

'This could be big, Ruth,' says David. 'We could have a display at the museum with a reconstruction and everything. We could tell the story about how the deadly virus came to England.'

'The deadly virus is just a theory,' says Ruth. *Your* theory, she adds silently. 'I don't think *our* skeleton will help prove or disprove it.'

'Scientists have found the hepatitis virus in fossilised bird bones,' says David. 'It's not impossible.'

'We'll have to wait and see,' says Ruth, sounding Phil-ish again. 'In the meantime, I've got another excavation to do for the police. At Black Dog Farm.' She doesn't know why she tells him this. Perhaps to show that she's got better things to do than speculate on prehistoric viruses. Perhaps she is just showing off – a rather lowering thought.

'Black Dog Farm?' echoes David. His face changes but Ruth is not quite sure how.

'Yes. The police are conducting an excavation there.'

'Two people were found dead there last week,' says David. 'Alan told me. He says it was a murder-suicide.'

'Alan seems to know more than the police,' says Ruth. 'I don't think they're sure what happened.'

'If they're not sure, they'll make it up,' says David, with

a return to his arrogant manner. 'But Black Dog Farm is a bad place.'

Ruth sees the square house in the middle of the fields, watching her out of the drooping eyelids of its curtained windows. She sees the overgrown garden, the nettles, the hanging swing. Then she sees the dog running across their path, the flash of its red eyes. *The Shuck can warn of a death, not necessarily the death of the person who sees him.*

'What do you mean, a bad place?'

'Bad things have happened there,' says David. 'Places don't forget.'

Now he sounds like Ruth's old lecturer, Erik, who believed that landscape held memories and could, in itself, be cursed or sacred.

'Are you talking about the Black Shuck?' she says, trying for a lighter tone.

'The Black Shuck,' David laughs, a harsh, humourless noise. 'The devil dog. That's just a story. The Matron at West Runton used to be full of Norfolk ghost stories. The Black Shuck, the ghostly coach and horses at Hedenham, the bride of White Woman Lane, the green children of Woolpit. I liked the Sheringham mermaid best – I liked the way she came up from the sea to listen to the service in the church. Though if the vicar was anything like Reverend Peters in my day, she would have been better off staying in the water.'

David seems to have drifted off down a memory lane full of ghosts. Ruth doesn't like to ask any more about West Runton. She doesn't know who sounds more sinister, Matron or Reverend Peters. Instead she says, 'Norfolk is full of stories. I think it's because people seem to live here for a long time. Generations staying in the same area. These legends get passed down.'

'Norfolk's been occupied for a long time,' says David. 'That's why this Bronze Age reconstruction could be so exciting. We could even get some DNA from the skeleton. Imagine if there was a match with some local people.'

'I am imagining it,' says Ruth. She took part in a similar study once, with dramatic results.

'Just be careful at Black Dog Farm,' says David. 'I'd hate anything to happen to you.'

Is this solicitude or a threat? thinks Ruth. With David Brown it's hard to tell.

13

Two interesting pieces of information greet Nelson when he arrives at his desk. One, the body on the beach has been identified as being that of twenty-five-year-old Jem Taylor. Far from being an illegal immigrant, Taylor was born in Cromer and was recently released from prison in Norwich. The second email is a preliminary forensics report from Black Dog Farm. It confirms that Douglas Noakes's prints were on the gun. This, together with the note, makes the murder-suicide theory more likely. Nelson thinks of the house, its sullen, shuttered air, the birds calling from the elm tree, and he looks at the report again. *Dad used to say that there was a dead body in the garden. He said that, if we didn't behave, it would rise up out of the ground and kill us.*

Nelson makes a phone call to Chloe Noakes.

The briefing is at nine. By now Tanya has prepared a short dossier on Jem Taylor. Born 1994 in Sheringham, attended a comprehensive school in Cromer, and worked as an apprentice plumber before being sent to a young offenders' unit for burglary. He had recently completed a prison sentence for robbery with violence.

'Was he at the school where Alan White used to teach?' asks Nelson.

'No,' says Tanya. 'That was Greenhill. Neil Thomas taught there too.'

'And Paul Noakes was a pupil there,' says Nelson. 'But Jem went to a different school which is probably why no one recognised the body. Not even with a very distinctive tattoo.'

'Jem's mother and stepfather are coming to identify the body later today,' says Judy. 'They might be able to tell us some more.'

'Poor lad,' says Nelson. 'He doesn't seem to have had many lucky breaks in life.' He always identifies with young men who have drifted into crime. Not that he was ever tempted – his mother would never have let him stray off the straight and narrow – but he's seen it happen many times. Even Cloughie sailed pretty close to the wind as a boy.

Nelson then goes through the forensics report.

'Dr Noakes's prints were on the gun but I double-checked with his daughter. The prints on the gun are from his right hand. Douglas Noakes was left-handed.'

'Are they different then?' says Tony and then looks as if he wishes he hadn't spoken. Nelson, though, is glad that someone has raised this.

'Yes, all fingerprints are unique and we have different prints on our left and right hands. I checked because I remembered a mug in the kitchen saying, "Leftie and proud".'

'So Douglas Noakes might not have killed himself. Or his wife,' says Judy.

'That's right,' says Nelson. 'Although that could still be the case. Plenty of people can use their left and right hands equally well. But I think we should still treat this as a possible murder investigation. We need to look into the Noakes family. The son and daughter both said the father was abusive.'

'Do you think one of them could have killed their parents?' says Tony. He looks shocked. Tony often talks about his family and they sound very close. This will be unthinkable to the young DC but, Nelson tells him silently, it's a police officer's job to think of the unthinkable.

'We have to keep an open mind,' says Nelson, 'but it's possible. I've applied to the Noakeses' solicitor for a copy of their will. If the property is left to Paul and Chloe, then that's a motive.'

'Is the farm worth much, though?' says Judy. 'It's very run-down and in the middle of nowhere.'

'It's worth something,' says Nelson, 'and money is always a motive.'

'What about the suicide note?' says Judy.

Nelson still has the picture on his phone and, with some help from Judy, he projects this onto the big screen.

It's just impossible to go on. I'm sorry for all the things I've said and done. For the body in the garden and all of it. I've been a bad father but I hope that, when all this is over, my scientific work will still be taken into account. My family knows how I feel about them.

    Douglas Noakes

'"The body in the garden",' says Tanya. 'What does that mean?'

'I don't know,' says Nelson. 'But I've asked Ruth to do an excavation.'

He notices Judy and Tanya exchange glances. Tony is oblivious.

'The tone of the letter is very cold,' says Tanya. 'Hoping his work will be taken into account ... signing himself Douglas Noakes, just like it was a business letter.'

'Chloe Noakes said the note sounded typical of her father,' says Judy, 'though she was surprised he said sorry. She said that he was very concerned with his scientific reputation. She said that he was abusive to her and Paul, both physically and emotionally. She said that they were glad he was dead.'

'But they seemed upset about the mother,' says Nelson. 'I can see Chloe or Paul killing their father but not their mother too. Paul was very distressed at the scene.'

'That could have been a sign of guilt,' says Judy. 'Paul was quite odd when I first spoke to him. Said that he couldn't believe his father committed suicide but, if it had been him, no one would have been surprised.'

'That is a bit strange,' says Nelson. 'Maybe we need to look into Paul's medical history. I know ...' He raises his hand to stop Judy telling him not to stigmatise mental illness. 'Being depressed isn't a sign that you're about to kill someone. But we should talk to Chloe and Paul again. Judy, you're the number two on this.' He doesn't look at Tanya. 'We need to talk to their friends, their colleagues, other members of the family. We need to find out where they both were on

Thursday night. We might have a double murder on our hands.'

He hopes that his team don't catch the note of excitement in his voice.

Back in his office, Nelson looks at the picture of Jem Taylor. It's a prison mugshot so he doesn't look his best but he's a good-looking young man, strong-featured with dark hair pulled back into a ponytail, the tattoo just visible beneath his left ear. He looks like a man who is used to looking after himself. Why had Taylor ended up dead on the beach that night? He's a local and distinctive-looking. Surely someone should have recognised him. Who were the four Night Hawks who discovered the body? Nelson looks back through his notes. Alan White, Neil Thomas, Paul Noakes and Troy Evans, aged twenty-one. Troy is not far in age from Jem. Nelson goes back through the files and finds a number. He rings but there's no answer. He leaves a message and, a few minutes later, there's a call back.

'Did you just call this number?'

'Yes. This is DCI Nelson from the Serious Crimes Squad. Is that Troy Evans? I've just got a few additional questions.'

'I can't talk now,' says Troy. 'Can you meet me at Wells Harbour at one?'

'All right,' says Nelson. He'll have to avoid Super Jo as he passes her office. He doesn't want to explain why he's conducting interviews himself. Or have another chat about retirement.

14

Troy Evans is a fisherman, a job that, to Nelson, seems to belong to fairy stories or the Bible. *Follow me and I will make you fishers of men.* Troy's boat, a good-sized vessel painted blue and white, is lying beached on the sand. It's hung round with rubber fenders and what look like flags made from bin liners, black and curiously sinister.

'It's so we can see where we put the crab nets,' says Troy. He's sitting on the harbour wall eating some chips. Nelson's stomach rumbles. Michelle is on one of her health kicks again and makes him a salad to take to work every morning. Nelson keeps finding them weeks later, in his desk drawers, covered in slime and mould. He usually has a Tesco's Meal Deal: sandwich, crisps, fizzy drink. A properly balanced lunch.

'How long have you been a fisherman?'

'Since leaving school. It's in the family, you see. My dad was a longshoreman and my granddad before him. That's the way it is in these parts. All the family are fishermen. Except my uncle. He's the black sheep.'

'What does he do?' says Nelson.

'He's a policeman,' says Troy.

Nelson doesn't know if this is a joke or not. He asks Troy if his uncle is with the local force.

'He was but he's retired now.'

That word again.

'Do you work all year round?' Nelson asks Troy. He can see the appeal on a day like this, the open sea and the blue sky, but he imagines that it's a different story in midwinter.

'Yes. We fish for crabs in the summer and harvest mussels in the winter. It's hard work but I like the freedom. Six miles out from land, you lose your mobile phone signal. No one can get at you.'

An interesting way to put it, thinks Nelson, but he knows what Troy means. Nelson keeps his phone switched on all the time – in case work or his family needs him – but there's no denying that it's a tyranny of sorts.

'I understand you're interested in archaeology too,' he says.

'Yes,' says Troy, hoovering up salt with a moistened finger. 'Mr White taught me history at school. He made it all sound so real. The Iceni fighting the Romans. The Viking raiders. The what-do-you-call-them, the Beakers, coming here and killing everyone off. Then, when I learnt that you could actually find stuff from those times, just lying on the beach. Axe-heads and coins and bits of pottery. I was hooked.'

'And you joined the Night Hawks?'

'Yes.'

'Do you normally do your metal detecting at night?'

'Sometimes,' says Troy. He drops a chip and three sea-gulls fall on it, arguing furiously. Nelson knows how they feel. 'It's more exciting at night, especially when the tide's coming in. Plus, it's quieter. Not so many civilians – members of the public – around.'

'Can you tell me what happened last Wednesday? I know you've already spoken to my officers. I'm just curious about a couple of points.'

Troy looks at him suspiciously for a minute but he takes up the story readily enough.

'We were on Blakeney Point. It's dangerous there because you can get cut off by the tide, so I was on tide watch. It can come in so quickly you have to know the markers. I was watching one of the old pill boxes, you know, from the war. The other Hawks were further down on the beach. They'd found something and they were setting up lights and stuff. I was watching them, so I wasn't concentrating for a minute. When I looked back, the pill box was submerged. I was looking at the water and I saw something white. I real-ised it was some material. Then, when I got closer, I saw it was a body.'

'What did you do next?'

'I shouted for the others. They came over. The body was still in the water. Mr White . . . Alan . . . said that we had to get it on higher ground or it'd be taken by the tide. So we pulled it . . . him . . . onto the rocks. Alan took his pulse and said he was dead. Then we called the police.'

'Who called them?'

'Alan. The others took the equipment and went home.

I waited though because Alan said the police would want to speak to me. Neil and Paul waited too.'

'Neil Thomas and Paul Noakes?'

'That's right.'

'Do you know them well?'

'Not really. Just as members of the group.'

'Did anyone else touch the dead body? Just you and Alan?'

'I think so. When the police came, one of them examined him.'

Nathan Matthews, thinks Nelson. Who is now dead.

'Did you recognise the dead man?' asks Nelson.

Troy looks surprised. 'No. I assumed he was one of those illegal immigrants.'

'No. He was born and bred in Sheringham. He went to Cromer Comprehensive.'

'You're kidding.'

'You went to Greenhill, didn't you? You said Alan White used to teach you.'

'That's right.'

'What about Neil Thomas? He taught IT.'

'I don't remember him at school.'

Tanya said that Neil left Greenhill ten years ago. Troy is only twenty-one. It's possible that they wouldn't have overlapped.

'Does the name Jem Taylor mean anything to you?' asks Nelson.

'Jem Taylor? I don't know. I think the name's a bit familiar. Was he the dead body?'

Yes, he was the dead body, thinks Nelson. But, before that,

he was a living and breathing young man, only four years older than Troy.

'The man found dead on the beach has been identified as Jem Taylor,' says Nelson. 'Details haven't been revealed to the press yet so if you could keep this to yourself for the time being.'

'Of course,' says Troy, looking slightly scared by the change of tone.

'Did you notice Jem's tattoo?' says Nelson. 'It was quite distinctive.'

'A snake, wasn't it?'

'That's right,' says Nelson. 'Someone has suggested that it could be something called the Norfolk Sea Serpent.'

'I hadn't thought of that,' says Troy. 'It could be the serpent, I suppose. I thought the tattoo was different though. More exotic.' Codeword for foreign, thinks Nelson. He notes the familiarity with which Troy refers to 'the serpent'.

'You've heard of the sea serpent then? It was a new one on me.'

'Everyone round here's heard of her. You see strange things sometimes, when you're far out to sea. When you get back to shore, you wonder if it was all a dream. That you actually saw what you saw.'

Troy's voice has taken on a dreamy quality. Nelson is particularly struck by the fact that the sea serpent is obviously female.

'Ah, Harry. I was looking for you.'

Of course, Super Jo would be lurking on the back stairs just as Nelson gets back to the station.

'Just following a lead,' he says.

Jo's nose wrinkles. 'I smell chips,' she says.

'Do you?'

'Can I have a quick word? In my office?'

Nelson dumps the chip wrappers in a nearby bin and follows Jo into her sanctum. His heart sinks when he sees that she's rising and falling gently. It always makes him nervous when Jo sits on her yoga ball.

'Just wondered if you'd given a thought to what we discussed last week, Harry.'

Up and down. Up and down. It's enough to give you motion sickness.

'What was that?'

'Your retirement.'

Now Nelson really does feel sick.

'I've thought about it,' he says. 'And I don't want to retire.'

Jo puts her head on one side, vibrating gently. 'What does Michelle think?'

'She agrees with me.' That's to say, Michelle had nodded in a resigned fashion, when Nelson swore that he'd never retire, that they'd have to bring him out of King's Lynn CID boots first.

'She wouldn't want me at home anyway.' Nelson tries for humour. 'Getting under her feet all the time.'

Jo nods as if she understands this.

'It's worth thinking about though. You're in your fifties.'

'I'm fifty-one.' Jo's own age is a closely guarded secret. Clough once launched a competition to find out the year of her birth. Nelson misses Clough.

'You've been in the police for . . . how long? Thirty years?'

'Thirty-three.' Nelson joined the police as a cadet at eighteen. He has honestly never wanted to do another job. This is who he is.

'You've done your bit,' says Jo. 'No one would blame you if you wanted to stand down. Spend more time with your family. Maybe go back to . . . to the north.'

'I've got a good few years left in me yet,' says Nelson. 'Now, if you'll excuse me, I'd better get on with my work.'

Judy is with Jem Taylor. Or rather, she's with his body. His face is all that's on view, the sheet folded back across his neck. This is because of the post-mortem and Judy hopes she won't have to warn the parents not to lift the sheet.

But Jem's mother, Cheryl, is only looking at her son's face.

'That's him,' she says. And reaches out to touch his cheek.

Jem's stepfather, Graham, pats his wife's shoulder. 'He looks peaceful,' he says.

'Yes,' says Judy. 'He does.' The mortician has done a good job. Jem looks peaceful and rather majestic, his black hair combed back from his forehead, eyes shut. He looks, thinks Judy, a bit like a Viking warrior laid to rest. Then she thinks: I've been living with Cathbad for too long.

'Just for the record,' says Judy. 'This is your son Jeremy, Jem?'

'Yes.' Cheryl touches the dark hair. 'This is Jem.'

'I'm so sorry,' says Judy.

'He was no angel,' says Graham. 'But he was a good lad.

He loved his mum.' He stops because he's crying. Cheryl, though, is dry-eyed, still stroking her son's hair.

'I'll give you a few minutes,' says Judy. 'I'll just be in the next room.'

In the waiting room – lilac walls, purple curtains, large box of tissues on the table – Judy fills in the paperwork. Cheryl and Graham join her a few minutes later. Cheryl is an attractive blonde woman in her late forties. Jem must have inherited his distinctive dark looks from his father. Graham is slightly older, bald and nervous-looking.

'I know this is hard,' says Judy. 'But we are investigating Jem's death. Can you think of any reason why he might have died in this way?'

'It wasn't suicide,' says Cheryl, understanding immediately. 'Jem would never do that. He was in a good place. Getting his life back together.'

The good place. That's how some people describe heaven, thinks Judy. She doesn't know if Cheryl and Graham have any religious convictions or where they think their son is now. Somewhere good, she hopes.

'Where was Jem living?' she asks.

'In a hostel in King's Lynn,' says Cheryl. 'His probation officer was hoping to find him work. Jem completed his plumbing course in prison. People always want plumbers.'

But do people want plumbers – tradespeople who come right into their houses – who have been in prison? thinks Judy. She still can't quite forgive Cathbad for employing a gardener who did time for armed robbery.

'Do you have any idea how he came to be in the sea?' says

Judy. 'Did he ever swim at night? Or go fishing?' Cathbad enjoys night swimming although he thinks that fishing is cruel.

'Jem?' Cheryl laughs, a painful sound that turns into a cough. 'He couldn't swim. He was terrified of water.'

The coastguard think that Jem's body might have floated from Wells or Holme-next-the-Sea. Dr Chris Stephenson, the pathologist, thought that he had been dead for about two hours when he was discovered on Blakeney Point. Wells is a small fishing port. Could Jem have been in a boat despite his fear of water? Judy asks about Jem's friends. Did he keep in touch with many people? She means, after being in prison.

'There was his girlfriend, Summer. They've been together since they were fifteen. She stood by him through thick and thin. And he still kept up with friends from school. Everyone loved Jem.' Cheryl's voice wobbles and Graham pats her arm, though he looks as stricken as his wife.

'I'd like to speak to Summer,' says Judy. 'If that's all right.'

'I'll give you her number,' says Cheryl. 'She's heart-broken. She's a lovely girl. I'd hoped . . .' She waves a hand as if fighting away the memories, but Judy knows what she means. Cheryl had hoped that Summer and Jem would settle down and maybe, one day, give her grandchildren. Judy had married her childhood boyfriend and her parents, too, had been delighted. But then she'd met Cathbad.

'How did Jem seem when you saw him last?' says Judy.

'Good,' says Graham. 'He came over last Monday and fixed our leaking tap. He seemed in high spirits, talking about going on holiday with Summer in a few weeks.'

'He didn't mention anything that was bothering him?'

'No. Except . . .' Graham looks at Cheryl.

'Except?' Judy prompts.

'Except he had a bit of a cold,' says Cheryl. 'Which wasn't like him. I said he should take some vitamin C and he said, "I can't. They told me not to."'

'They told me not to? Do you know what he meant by that?'

'No, but he seemed odd when he said it. Secretive, which wasn't like Jem at all.'

Graham laughs sadly. 'Jem wasn't one to keep a secret.'

But maybe he's keeping one now, thinks Judy.

15

Back in his office, Nelson thinks about retirement for about eight seconds and then dismisses the idea. The force needs his experience and know-how. There are some things you can only learn from years of actually doing the job. Recently, though, he has begun to be aware of a faint muttering among the younger officers. He imagines the conversations. 'When is he going to go?' 'How old is he again?' 'You'd think he'd take his pension and run.' No one would ever dare say this to his face but a couple of times he has been asked if he has any plans for retirement. 'None,' he always replies briskly. Nelson is a DCI; that is who he is. He literally can't imagine waking up one morning to find that he's plain Mr Nelson.

The mutterings don't come from his team, of course, but sometimes he does worry that his mere presence is holding them back. Judy is a DI now. She should be in charge of her own department which, unless he retires, means that she has to leave Norfolk, where she has lived all her life. Clough has already left to work as a DI in Cambridgeshire. It's not far away but Nelson misses his protégé. Really, he wants everything to stay exactly as it was. He was the same when his daughters were growing up.

He thinks about ringing Ruth to distract himself from these gloomy thoughts and is still staring at his phone when her name flashes up. Cathbad would have something to say about that.

'Hallo, Ruth. What's up? Is it Katie?'

'*Kate* is fine. I was just ringing because ... well, it might be nothing ... but, you know when we were leaving the farm yesterday, I thought I saw something running across the path. Remember I braked suddenly?'

'Yes. I nearly went into the back of you.'

'I thought I saw an animal, too big to be a dog, but like a dog. I told Cathbad and he said ...'

'Don't tell me, he said it was the bloody Black Shuck. The omen of death. And you believed him? I'm surprised at you, Ruth.'

'I know what I saw,' says Ruth, sounding irritated. 'Kate saw him too.'

Nelson's hand hovers in an instinctive sign of the cross. He does not want Katie to have seen the Black Shuck.

'Probably a deer,' he says. 'There are loads round there.'

'Probably,' says Ruth. 'But Cathbad said that there had been a few sightings of the Shuck recently. He'd heard it from Alan White. You know, the metal detectorist?'

'I know Mr White.'

'Well, I was thinking, if someone is spreading the rumour that the Black Shuck is haunting the farm, I wonder what they want to hide?'

Now that is a good question, thinks Nelson. The world is officially sane again.

Ruth clicks off her phone, feeling irritated. Now Nelson will think that she's gone completely mad. But she can't quite get yesterday's image out of her mind. The darkening sky, the birds circling like some sort of omen, and then the creature emerging from the hedge, as tall as a deer but without that animal's legginess, shaggy and feral-looking, moving with a loping, wolfish stride. There are always rumours in Norfolk about big cats escaping from various zoos but this didn't look cat-like either. It had looked, she has to admit, like a very large dog, a wolfhound or something similar. Had she seen the Black Shuck or, rather, had she seen what people see when they think they've seen the spectral hound?

Did she call Nelson just to hear his voice? She can't quite acquit herself of this. But, she tells herself defensively, it could be important that both David and Cathbad know Alan White and that White has been reporting sightings of the Black Shuck. She thought that Nelson seemed to register her last point, that the ghost stories could be spread by someone with something to hide. But she has to stop playing detective. That has got her into trouble before. Besides, she has enough real work to do.

Ruth turns back to her notes. *Palaeopathological Diagnosis and Interpretation.* She has given this lecture many times before but there are always new developments and if any of the other lecturers – well, David – are listening then she wants to show them that the head of department keeps up to date with the latest thinking. It's unusual for the head of department to do so much lecturing – Phil did hardly any – but Ruth loves teaching and doesn't want to give it up completely. It does mean that she has even less time for her own research which is a worry because, apparently, one reason she got the job was because she had 'an international research profile'. Ruth doesn't know how this can be the case when, barring an ill-starred trip to Italy, she hadn't been abroad for years.

When there's a knock on the door she thinks at first that it must be David with some new ideas on how she could do her job better. But her visitor is waiting patiently for permission to enter so it can't possibly be him.

'Come in.'

'Hallo, Ruth. I thought at first you were too important to see me now.'

Shona. Ruth's best friend at the university and Phil's partner. Ruth feels guilty because she *has* been too busy to see much of Shona recently.

'It's lovely to see you,' she says, getting up and giving her friend a hug.

It *is* lovely and makes Ruth realise how much she has missed Shona. Just seeing her there, in Ruth's posh corner office, the sun glinting on her red-gold hair, lifts the spirits. Shona teaches English Literature but she's part-time since having her son and rarely ventures over to the Natural Sciences Block.

'Have you got a few minutes?' says Shona.

'Of course. I've got a lecture in half an hour though.'

'I just wanted to say hallo. Seems like ages since I saw you.'

'Let's have a coffee,' says Ruth. 'I've got my own espresso machine.'

'Fancy. That's new since Phil's day.'

Ruth wonders if this is said with a slight edge. She hasn't really altered the office at all, beyond adding the coffee machine (bought with her own money) and her poster of Indiana Jones but maybe Shona thinks that Ruth is set on eradicating all traces of her predecessor.

'How's Phil?' she asks, just to show that she hasn't forgotten him.

'Really well. Retirement suits him. We've got an allotment and he's growing all sorts of vegetables. And he's loving spending so much time with Louis. He's even joined the PTA.'

Shona and Phil's son Louis is a little younger than Kate. Ruth wonders if she should suggest that they all get together one day. The trouble is that Kate doesn't really like Louis and, unlike Ruth, will not be embarrassed to admit this.

'We're thinking of doing a round-the-world trip next year. Backpacking. We could take Louis out of school. He won't miss much. Travelling with his parents will be more of an education.'

In theory Ruth agrees with this but she can't imagine herself taking Kate out of school just when she's about to start her secondary education. She can't imagine herself backpacking round the world either. The thought depresses her slightly.

'How are you enjoying the top job?' says Shona. There's a definite edge now.

'It's OK,' says Ruth. 'Lots of paperwork. Lots of HR stuff. Lots of meetings. I can see what Phil meant about the meetings now.'

'Universities have far too many meetings,' says Shona. 'Humanities is the same. I met one of your new lecturers in the canteen the other day.'

'Who?' says Ruth, although there's really only one person it could be.

'David Brown. We had a good old chat. I thought he was quite dishy.'

I bet you did, thinks Ruth. She's not going to ask if David mentioned her.

'He mentioned you,' says Shona. 'Said that you seemed really overworked.'

'Did he?'

'Yes. I reminded him that you were still getting used to being HoD. He said that you were involved in some police case.'

This must be another reason for Shona's visit. She's incorrigibly nosy about Ruth's forensic work.

'A body was washed up on Blakeney Point,' says Ruth. 'Some metal detectorists found it when they were looking for treasure. They found the treasure too. A Bronze Age skeleton surrounded by grave goods.'

'Phil's horrible about metal detectorists. I've always wondered why. It looks a fun hobby to me.'

Once again, Ruth finds herself silently siding with Phil. This really has to stop.

'Licensed detectorists are fine,' she says. 'This lot seem

to be OK. Although they do go out at night, which is rather suspicious.'

'I thought that David said something about Black Dog Farm. Where there was that shooting the other day.'

This is interesting. David was talking about Black Dog Farm before Ruth told him about the excavation.

'I was there yesterday,' says Ruth, evasively. 'Advising the police.'

'The police? Nelson?'

'He was there too.'

'Be careful, Ruth.'

'What do you mean?'

'This is how it always starts. Nelson asks for your advice and, the next thing you know, you're involved in some horrible murder case, being chased by some madman.'

Ruth wants to argue, to say that Shona is overdramatising everything (she teaches English, hyperbole is her speciality) but, though Ruth does not like to admit it, Shona's words have a certain truth to them. She has been involved in some dangerous cases over the past ten years and Shona herself has been caught up in a few of them.

'I'll be careful,' she says.

'Good,' says Shona. 'We're not getting any younger, after all. It's not the time to take risks.'

'Says the woman who's planning to backpack round the world.'

'That's different. We'll be having experiences.'

'I'm having experiences.'

'Not good ones, though. What's Black Dog Farm like?

It sounds very spooky. I thought I saw the Black Shuck on Hunstanton beach once. Phil said it was a donkey.'

Summer Mulhearn is a beautician. Usually, when she's with someone from the beauty industry, Judy becomes self-conscious about her nails and hair, but she can tell immediately that Summer, although very pretty, isn't the sort of person who makes you feel bad about yourself. She's more like those hairdressers who spend so much time telling you that your hair is lovely and long that you let them cut most of it off.

Summer works from home but the sign in her window – 'Summer Beauty' – now has a sticker saying, 'Closed until further notice'. Summer lives with her parents but they have given her their big front room to use as a salon. It looks very professional, with a treatment table, hair dryers and multiple mirrors. Summer's overalls are hanging on the back of her door and there are numerous framed certificates attesting to her prowess at lash techniques, eyebrow-threading and facials. But Summer herself, dark hair pulled back into a ponytail, eyes puffy, doesn't look as if she is ready to put on her pink overall any time soon.

'I still can't believe it,' she says. 'I just keep expecting him to walk through that door.'

Summer points to the door and in the direction of a large photograph of the couple cheek-to-cheek. They look incredibly glamourous, as if they are modelling a lifestyle too idyllic to be true. But Jem was hardly the perfect boyfriend. He must have spent a good part of their relationship in prison.

'I'm so sad for Cheryl too,' says Summer. 'She's been like a second mum to me.'

'Cheryl said that you and Jem have been together a long time,' says Judy.

'Yes, we met at school when we were fifteen. Jem was the boy everyone fancied.' Summer smiles at the memory. 'I don't know why he chose me. I was a shy little thing in those days. But he did.'

He chose me. Jem was a career criminal and Summer a successful businesswoman, but she still seems grateful that the class heart-throb picked her as his girlfriend.

'When did you last see Jem?' asks Judy.

'Last Tuesday,' says Summer. 'He came over here and we watched a film together.'

'When did he leave?' asks Judy. By the early hours of Wednesday morning Jem's body was lying lifeless on the beach.

'About ten o'clock.'

'Did he say if he was going on anywhere else?'

'I assumed he was going back to the hostel. They've got a curfew, you see.'

'And how did he seem, in himself?'

'Happy.' Summers eyes fill with tears. 'Really happy. He was getting himself together. We were going on holiday in a few weeks.'

'Where were you going?'

'St Lucia.'

Judy thinks, St Lucia is expensive. She knows because she once looked up holidays there although Cathbad now refuses to fly because of the damage to the planet. Summer's business is apparently doing well but Jem had only just got out of prison.

'Who was paying for the holiday?' she asks.

'Jem.'

There's a silence and then Judy says, gently, 'How?'

'He was doing some work.' Summer looks away, picking at her pristine nail varnish.

'What sort of work?'

'Don't tell his mum,' says Summer, in a rush.

'Was it something illegal?'

'No. It was all above board. It's just that Jem knew his mum wouldn't like it. He was doing some medical trials, you see.'

'Medical trials?'

'Yes. For this place in Cambridge. He was trialling a vaccine. They paid good money.'

'Do you know the name of the place?'

'No, but the logo had a dog on it. A black dog.'

And Judy hears Cathbad's voice, 'The Black Shuck, the harbinger of death.'

16

Kate has drama club after school so Ruth doesn't drive to Sandra's to collect her. Instead she parks at the Cley visitor centre and takes the path through the long grasses to the beach. It's a beautiful evening and the marshes are full of birds, swooping down to the inland pools and rising up in clouds, wheeling and turning. Ruth passes the thatched hides, knowing that they will contain birdwatchers, silent and devout, watching through binoculars. She hopes, though, that the beach is empty. She wants to look at the excavation site again. She walks along the shingle thinking of Cathbad's story about the dog who had walked beside him. It's tempting now to imagine that other footsteps follow hers, that she can see a shadow, large and misshapen, falling on the shallow water. What is the third who walks beside you? Christ on the road to Emmaus. She remembers Cathbad telling her once that, in extreme stress, we often imagine that we are accompanied by another person, a companion or a protector. This might explain stories from the First World War of soldiers sensing an unknown presence, often described as an angel, marching beside them through the mud and the horror. But today there's only Ruth. She moves quickly, stepping firmly over the shifting ground.

As she rounds the cove, she sees the cruciform shape of a huge bird, its wings dark against the low evening sun. A buzzard? A kestrel? An eagle? Ruth is vague about ornithology, despite living for over twenty years in one of the richest bird-life habitats in the world. She is lost in her own thoughts and so doesn't notice, until she is almost at the site, that there are two other figures silhouetted against the sea. One very tall, the other smaller and squatter. Birdwatchers? No, she recognises the smaller man, his flyaway grey hair and unravelling jumper. Alan White.

'Hallo, Ruth,' Alan greets her. 'Beautiful evening, isn't it?'

'Hallo,' says Ruth. 'Out for a stroll?'

She means this to be ironical. The men have clearly been looking into the trench. The other man is even holding a trowel.

'Taking a look at the site,' says Alan. 'Oh, this is Paul. A friend of mine.'

Paul. The name sounds vaguely familiar to Ruth. She assumes the tall man is another of the wretched Night Hawks.

'The site shouldn't really be disturbed,' says Ruth. 'Especially since human remains were found here.'

'Oh no,' Alan assures her. 'We were just looking.'

Ruth thinks that 'just looking' is the opposite of the Night Hawks' motto. The man called Paul, though, looks rather uncomfortable.

'Human remains?' he says.

'We found a skeleton here,' says Ruth. 'Probably Bronze Age. We'll know more when we get the test results back.'

'Do you know when that will be?' says Alan, bouncing on his toes to show his eagerness.

'By the end of this week, I hope.'

'It's very interesting,' Alan tells his friend. 'David. My old school friend, David Brown. He's a renowned archaeologist and he was telling me that Bronze Age people carried a virus that effectively wiped out the native population.'

Paul now looks positively terrified. 'A virus?' he repeats.

'A deadly virus,' says Alan. 'They brought it with them from Central Europe. The natives had no immunity, you see.'

Ruth knows she's being irrational, but she's irritated by this. For one thing, David Brown is hardly a renowned archaeologist – she's the one who's written three books and appeared on TV, for God's sake. And for another, she's fed up with the virus narrative being put forward as fact.

'David's told me his theory,' she says. 'He works for me at the university.'

'He's a great admirer of yours,' says Alan, which mollifies Ruth slightly.

'That's nice,' she says. 'Well, I'll leave you to your walk.'

She doesn't think that they'll dare disturb the trench again. Besides, it's getting dark and the wind is getting stronger. Her last view is of the tarpaulin rising and falling like a sail on a sea of sand.

*

'This must be the firm,' says Judy, staring at her computer screen. 'It's the only one with a black dog on it.'

The dog, its mouth open in a bark, reminds Judy of pictures she has seen of a mosaic at Pompeii. *Cave Canem*. She must persuade Cathbad to let them fly to Italy for a holiday.

'"Cambridge Bioresearch,"' reads Nelson aloud over her shoulder. '"Directors: Dr Douglas Noakes, Dr Claudia Albertini." I think we need to talk to this Dr Albertini.'

'Summer said that the drugs trial was all above board. It's legal to pay people for this sort of thing.'

'It might be legal but there's something odd going on. For one thing, one of the directors is dead. Possibly murdered. To say nothing of the fact that there could be another body buried in his back garden. Sounds a tiny bit dodgy to me.'

It's always a bad sign when the boss tries to do irony.

'Is Ruth going to dig up the garden?' Judy asks.

'Yes. I'm hoping she can do it tomorrow or the next day.'

'Tanya's spoken to Paul and Chloe Noakes again,' says Judy. 'They both say they don't know anything about their father's work.'

'Chloe must know something. She's a doctor, for God's sake. Get Tanya to interview her again. No, you talk to her. I'm sure the family are hiding something.'

'Yes, boss,' says Judy. She's thinking that she'll have to move very carefully to avoid ruffling Tanya's feathers.

When Nelson has departed, in a hurry as usual, Judy gathers up her things and prepares to leave. On the way home, she thinks of the company with the dog on its logo and of Jem's mother saying, 'He couldn't swim. He was terrified of water.'

When she gets in Michael is playing the piano, Cathbad is cooking supper and Miranda is trying to teach Thing to dance.

'It's for *Britain's Got Talent*. We're doing it at school for poor children.'

Judy thinks that the charity would probably rather have a direct debit. She hugs her daughter and Thing takes advantage of his trainer's distraction to escape into the garden.

'Good day?' says Cathbad, leaning over to give her a kiss. He smells of lemongrass.

'OK. I had to see some bereaved parents. That's always tough.'

'You need to put a protective circle around yourself,' says Cathbad, turning back to the food. 'I'll show you how.'

'Thanks,' says Judy. Cathbad has shown her before and she sometimes tries to chant a protective mantra under her breath. It never seems to work, though.

Cathbad puts the lid on the saucepan and opens the fridge door.

'Glass of wine?' he says, his face lit by the blue glow.

'Yes, please.' They try not to drink in the week but, Judy tells herself, in the absence of a protective circle, alcohol will take the edge off the day.

Cathbad pours them both glasses of Winbirri white. Through the French windows they can see Miranda polkaing with Thing in the garden.

'Ruth's going to excavate the garden at Black Dog Farm tomorrow,' says Judy.

'It's the feast of Our Lady of Walsingham today,' says Cathbad. 'A good omen.'

'If you say so,' says Judy. She hasn't forgotten the events that happened in Walsingham a few years ago. She takes a deep swig of wine.

'I heard from Alan White this afternoon,' says Cathbad.

'What did he want?'

'The Hawks are going out on Thursday night. He invited me to join them.'

'Where are they going?'

'Blakeney Point. They want to see if there are any other Bronze Age relics. Alan is sure that there must be more, maybe even some more bodies.'

'Ruth won't like that,' says Judy. 'Are you going to go?'

'I think so, if it's OK with you. For one thing, I can stop them damaging the original site. For another . . .'

He pauses, looking out into the garden, where Thing is now barking at a seagull.

'What?'

'Alan said that he wanted to talk to me about something. He said he couldn't tell me on the phone.'

'Have you any idea what it could be?'

'He said something about telling the police. Asked me whether he could trust them.'

'I hope you said yes.'

'I said that you and DCI Nelson were both eminently trustworthy.'

This is probably as good as she can expect. Cathbad is no fan of the police in general and, sometimes, looking at events around the world, Judy agrees with him.

'Do you have any idea why he was asking?' she says.

'I think he's scared. He said, "I think I've heard the Black Shuck barking."'

Despite the cosy kitchen, the piano music and the scent of lemongrass, Judy feels her skin crawl.

'What do you think he meant by that?'

'I think he's had a premonition of his own death,' says Cathbad calmly. 'I've a feeling that's why he's asked me to go along. For protection.'

Protection again. For such a benign concept, thinks Judy, the word has a very sinister sound.

17

It's a misty morning when Ruth starts the dig at Black Dog Farm. As she bumps along the track to the house, she can only see a few feet in front of her. It's like driving into grey, swirling nothingness. If the weather doesn't clear, they may have to postpone the excavation. She's meeting Ted at the house and has booked a mechanical digger for the afternoon. It will be a real pain if she has to reschedule.

The house appears windows first, like the Cheshire Cat's grin. She sees the dark frames, sinister in their very symmetry, then the door, then the roof with the weathercock, invisible but creaking gently. The mist blows around the farm buildings like smoke. There are two other cars parked in the yard and Ruth is surprised to see that Nelson is already there, talking to Ted.

'Nice day for it,' Nelson greets her.

'Do you think it'll clear?' Ruth addresses her question to Ted who includes weather divination as one of his many skills.

'Bound to. It's just a sea fret blown inland.'

They walk round to the back garden. Here the mist is low-lying, leaving the trees floating and the broken swing hanging in mid-air.

'Where do we start?' says Ted.

'There are some nettles right in the middle.'

'The middle it is, then.'

Ted is accompanied by Steve, another field archaeologist. Together they get the equipment from their van including a resistivity metre, two poles attached to a metal bar with prongs at either end.

'What's that?' says Nelson. 'A metal detector? I thought you didn't approve of them.'

Sometimes Ruth wonders if he does it just to annoy her.

'It measures electrical resistance,' she tells him. 'Burials create a pattern of resistance, if a hole has been dug here then there'll be a higher water content in the soil. The resistivity metre helps us plot this.'

Ted cuts the nettles and long grass with a scythe, allowing Steve to insert the metal prongs into the earth at regular intervals. Ruth plots their progress on a data log. She thinks how much Phil would have enjoyed this. He loves geophysics, the more technical equipment needed the better. She has a feeling that David, with his professed liking for getting 'down and dirty', would disapprove.

The mist is dispersing now and the rooks watch them from the elm tree.

Nelson watches them for a few minutes, but it always irritates him to be a spectator. He knows that Jo would think it a waste of his highly paid time to be present at the excavation. It's a DC's job, if that. But Nelson had felt drawn back to the house. He's sure that there is something buried in the strange, oppressive garden. And, if he's honest with himself, he wanted to see Ruth. It always fascinated him to see her at work, so calm and composed, able – it seems – to see beneath the earth itself. Electrical resistance, high water content, it's all meaningless to him. What matters is that Ruth can tell where the bodies are buried. He's seen her do it before.

But he can't stand around all morning. Nelson walks round to the front of the house, wondering whether to go back to the station. He can always drop in again later in the day. In the meantime, young Tony can keep an eye on things. As he approaches his car, he sees another vehicle bumping along the uneven track, a smart jeep-like affair being driven with extreme care. Nelson recognises the driver and starts to smile.

'Well, if it's not DI Dave Clough.'

Clough emerges from his vehicle, brushing imaginary specks from his leather jacket. Since his promotion and move to Cambridge, he has begun dressing in a way that is both fashionable and, in Nelson's opinion, far too young for him. But maybe the fault lies with Clough's wife Cassandra, a glamorous ex-actress who used to criticise Clough for 'looking like a policeman'. This, in Nelson's book, is not an insult but he's pleased to see his ex-sergeant, ridiculous jacket or not.

'Lost your motorbike?' he says.

'Can't believe that thing's still running.' Clough points at Nelson's Mercedes.

'It's a classic. It'll keep running for ever.'

'You or the car?'

They shake hands. Clough looks well, Nelson thinks. He also can't imagine why on earth he's here.

'Thought I'd come to see your murder scene,' says Clough, as if Nelson had asked the question.

'How did you know I was here?'

'Judy said that Ruth was digging up the garden.'

There's no need for either of them to say more.

'Creepy-looking house,' says Clough. 'Murder-suicide wasn't it? DODI?'

'Possibly,' says Nelson. 'It's possible there's also a body buried in the garden.'

Clough gives a low whistle. 'Interesting. Guy who owned this place worked in Cambridge. Ran a scientific research place.'

'I know. Judy's there today.'

Clough looks down, scuffing the concrete with his trendy looking trainers. Nelson waits.

'It's him I've come to talk to you about,' says Clough. 'Douglas Noakes. Dr Noakes.'

'Yes?'

By mutual consent they come to lean against Nelson's car. Clough says, 'You remember my brother Mark?'

Whatever Nelson expected, it wasn't this. Nelson doesn't know Mark Clough personally. He thinks he's seen him twice, once at Clough's wedding and once when he was seriously ill in hospital. He does know that Mark was once a petty criminal. It was Mark's encounter with a sympathetic policeman that had inspired his younger brother Dave in his career.

'Mark's straight now,' says Clough, sounding slightly defensive. 'But he still hears things. He still knows people. You know what I mean.'

Nelson knows.

'Well, he's heard a few things about Dr Noakes.'

'What sort of things?'

'That he was paying ex-cons to test drugs for him.'

'Where did Mark hear this?' says Nelson.

'He wouldn't say but I could lean on him a bit. Mark knew the lad who was found on the beach. Jem something. Said he was a good kid at heart. He wanted to make some money to take his girlfriend on holiday. Noakes got him to do a drugs trial. Next thing, he's dead. What did the post mortem say?'

'Got the results today. No water in his lungs.'

'So he was dead before he went into the water?'

'Looks that way.'

'Anything odd in his blood?'

'There's nothing in the report but I suppose they weren't looking. The girlfriend knew about the drugs trial but she thought it was all above board. There's something dodgy going on though. Douglas Noakes left a suicide note. It said something about a body in the garden.'

'That's why Ruth is digging?'

'That's why.'

'If he left a note,' says Clough, 'that points to suicide.'

'It does. And Noakes's prints were on the gun. Unfortunately, they were from his right hand and he was left-handed.'

'Bloody hell. So it could be a double murder.'

'It could.'

There's a silence broken by Ruth appearing from the garden, rather muddy and bramble-scratched.

'Nelson— Oh, hi, Clough. Nelson, we've found something.'

Cambridge Bioresearch is a discreet-looking building on the outskirts of Cambridge. Judy visited Ruth a few times when she was teaching at St Jude's and had always felt overawed by the town of Cambridge, by the general sense of privacy and scholarship and signs saying 'don't walk on the grass'. This is just a unit in an industrial estate, identifiable only by the barking dog logo. Judy waits in a reception area that gives no hint of the work that the company might do: pink walls, grey sofas, bland watercolours of mountain scenery, a coffee table devoid of any reading matter, water cooler humming gently. The receptionist tells her that Dr Albertini will be with her 'directly', a word that seems to offer much but mean very little. Judy gazes at the nearest mountaintop and tries not to fiddle with her phone.

'DI Johnson?'

The woman seems to have materialised while Judy was lost in the Alps.

Claudia Albertini is tall and elegant, wearing a white coat with her name embroidered on the chest pocket. Her dark hair is drawn back into a ponytail and she's wearing those narrow, gold-rimmed glasses that automatically make Judy feel intellectually inferior.

'So sorry to keep you waiting.'

There's a slight accent. Italian perhaps? Cathbad speaks Italian and has been teaching Judy and the kids. Should she try a few words or would that seem incredibly presumptuous?

'It's very good of you to see me,' says Judy. 'I'm sure you're very busy.'

Claudia makes a gesture that seems half resignation, half frustration. 'It's been a very difficult few days.'

'Dr Noakes's death must have been a terrible shock for you.'

'Yes,' says Claudia. 'We have worked together for a long time. Shall we?'

They take the lift to the second floor and Claudia shows Judy into her office, another bland room with more mountain peaks.

'Coffee? Tea?'

'No, thank you.' You're meant to accept refreshments from interviewees but Judy doesn't want to take up too much of the doctor's time. Already she can see her foot, shod in an expensive-looking loafer, tapping under the table.

'How long have you worked with Douglas Noakes?' asks Judy.

'Ten years,' says Claudia. 'We set up this company together. Douglas was working at another company in Cambridge and I was doing research in Zurich.'

Ah, she's Swiss. That explains the mountains – and the accent.

'What sort of work is it that you do?'

'We're an early stage contract research organisation,' says Claudia. She must have registered the lack of comprehension in Judy's face because she shifts into a lower gear. 'We support the pharmaceutical, biotechnical and medical industries by outsourcing research. Specifically, we develop new medicines and drugs and test them both in *vitro* and in *vivo*.'

'*In vitro* is test tubes?'

'Yes. And in *vivo* is in living subjects.'

'Humans?'

'And animals. Yes.'

'Do you advertise for people to take part in clinical trials?'

'Sometimes, yes.'

'Could you tell me if someone called Jeremy – Jem – Taylor took part in a trial recently?'

Claudia opens a laptop on her desk, so slim and discreet that Judy had not noticed it before. She taps for a few seconds, making no sound. Her fingernails must be as short as a piano player's. Michael's piano teacher, Mrs Mazzini, is always going on about nails.

'There's no one of that name on our lists.'

'Is there any way he could have taken part in a trial without being on the list?'

'No. Definitely not. Before you start a trial here you have to speak to the registration team on the phone, then come into our clinic to have a full medical check. It's all logged into the system. We have to be very thorough, as I'm sure you'll understand.'

So, if Jem Taylor did take part in a trial, it was on an unofficial basis, thinks Judy.

'What was Douglas like to work with?' she asks, going for a relaxed tone.

Claudia hesitates for a second but, under the desk, her foot is still tapping out distress signals. 'He was very professional,' she says at last.

That's hardly a ringing personal accolade, thinks Judy.

'How did Douglas seem in recent weeks?' she says. 'Did he seem to be worried about anything?'

'He was the same as ever,' says Claudia. 'He wasn't one to bring his home life to work.'

'Did you know his family?' asks Judy. 'His wife and children?'

'I met Linda several times,' says Claudia. 'I thought she was a very nice woman. I never met the son but I knew the daughter, Chloe, quite well.'

'Really?'

'Yes. She came here on work experience. Bright girl. Woman, I should say.'

'What did she do while she was here on work experience?'

'Just general office duties, answering the phone, filing, that sort of thing. I let her help with some of the pharmaceutical work too because she was planning on studying medicine.'

'Did you keep in touch with Chloe afterwards?'

Is it Judy's imagination or does Claudia hesitate slightly? 'Not really. I think she sent a thank-you card and I sent a good luck card and that was it. I wondered whether I should get in touch after . . . after what happened last week.'

'Were you surprised when you found out?'

Claudia pushes back her glasses and meets Judy's gaze squarely. 'Of *course* I was surprised! It's not something you ever expect to happen. Not to someone you know. And Douglas . . . well, I would have said that Douglas was the last person in the world to commit suicide.'

'Really? Why?'

'Douglas was very absorbed in his work and we were making some real breakthroughs. I can't imagine him wanting to die before we had our results. But the human brain is a strange thing, as I'm sure you know, DI Johnson.'

You can say that again, thinks Judy, as she descends in the noiseless lift. She notes that Claudia was surprised that Douglas committed suicide, not that he killed his wife.

'We've found some bones,' says Ruth. Nelson, following her into the garden, is amazed at the progress the team has made in such a short time. The grass has all been scythed and, in the middle of what was once the lawn, is a large hole, as neat as only archaeologists can make it, the sides as straight as if drawn with a ruler. The trench is not very deep yet, but Nelson can already see something yellowy white in the dark earth.

'Is it human?' he says.

'I don't think so but it's hard to tell at first,' says Ruth. 'I've seen wild pig bones confused with human ones before. But this is a vertebra and human vertebrae tend to be quite distinctive. They modified as we evolved to walk on two legs.'

'Some of us anyway,' murmurs Clough in the background.

Steve is brushing soil away from another bone. 'Here's a femur,' he says.

Ruth leans over to look and beckons Nelson forward. 'Look, the femoral head is a different shape and there's no marked linea aspera down the back of the shaft.'

'If you say so,' says Nelson. 'It looks similar to a human bone to me.'

'Animal bones tend to have a more rugged appearance,' says Ruth, 'and the shaft isn't as straight.'

'This is a pretty long bone though,' says Ted. Holding his scythe, he temporarily blocks out the hazy sun.

'Yes, it is long,' says Ruth.

'Is it a farm animal?' says Nelson. 'After all, this was a farm once.'

'Maybe,' says Ruth. 'We need to find the skull really.'

'Some of the bones are broken up,' says Steve. 'Maybe with a spade or even a mechanical digger.'

'The femur could be human,' says Ted. 'It's about the right size.'

Now Ruth is working away with her trowel. She can never resist the chance to dig and, unlike Michelle and most women Nelson knows, never seems to worry about the effect on her hands and clothes.

'Here's the mandible,' she says. 'It's not human. You can tell by the teeth.'

'What is it?' says Steve. 'A sheep? It looks too big.'

'I think it's a dog,' says Ruth, looking at Nelson. 'A very big one.'

18

'Bloody hell, Ruth,' says Clough. 'You've found the Black Shuck.'

Ted and Steve both laugh but Nelson says, on a note of asperity, 'Don't tell me you know that ridiculous story too, Cloughie.'

'Of course,' says Clough. 'Norfolk born and bred, me. I know people who've seen the Shuck. It chased Mark home from the pub once.'

Everyone laughs, sending the birds skirling into the air. Ruth lifts another bone out of the soil.

'Here's another part of the skull. The orbital bone, I think.'

'The eye socket,' says Ted. 'Of course, by rights, it should be full of hellfire.'

'It's certainly a big dog,' says Steve, who is laying the bones out on the tarpaulin.

The atmosphere has changed now that the bones are definitely not human, thinks Ruth. Ted and Clough are joking about pubs where the hell hound might be mistaken for one of the regulars. Steve is continuing to arrange the skeleton but he's not taking the care that he would with human remains, even raising the jawbone to his mouth and making snapping gestures with it. Nelson is looking at something on his phone.

But Ruth doesn't feel reassured. She's still convinced that something is hidden in this sad patch of ground. And, even if the bones are canine, there's still a mystery here. A dog's bones at Black Dog Farm. Is this what Douglas Noakes meant in his note?

Ruth continues to dust the soil from the remains.

I'm sorry for all the things I've said and done. For the body in the garden and all of it.

Nelson is looking at an encrypted email from Judy. She has been to Cambridge Bioresearch and is now on her way to the school where Linda Noakes was a teacher. Judy's notes are brief: *No Jem Taylor on the records. Chloe Noakes did work experience here!* Something is obviously going on at Cambridge Bioresearch. And there's something else too. Something involving Jem Taylor and PC Nathan Matthews. It's niggling away at Nelson, like a bit of apple core caught in his teeth, but he can't quite locate it.

There's now a raucous atmosphere to the excavation. Cloughie and Irish Ted are wise-cracking away and the other archaeologist is joining in. Only Ruth is continuing to work. Nelson approves. Murder is no laughing matter, and this is a house where two people died.

He should be getting back to work. Super Jo will be breathing fire like the Shuck itself – or the Norfolk Sea

Serpent – and muttering about retirement. He'll send Tony over to the house to supervise the rest of the dig.

'I'm off,' he announces to the group at large.

'See you, boss,' says Cloughie. Old habits die hard.

Ruth says nothing.

Nelson walks round to the front of the house and gets in his car. He drives slowly down the track, thinking of the elderly car ('It's a classic,' he tells Clough in his head) and half-distracted by trying to plug his phone in. When a figure suddenly appears in front of him, he swears and brakes violently. The figure, an elderly bearded man, then proceeds to stand in front of the car, staring at him. Resisting the temptation to yell, 'Get out of my way,' Nelson winds down his window.

The man approaches, maddeningly slowly.

'You with the police?' He has a strong Norfolk accent, something that is increasingly rare, even in rural areas.

'Yes,' says Nelson.

'You here about the murder?'

That's an interesting way of putting it, thinks Nelson.

'I'm here about the shooting last week,' he says. 'Do you live nearby?'

He almost says, 'Are you a neighbour?' but there are no other houses as far as the eye can see.

'Yes,' says the man. He continues to stare at Nelson out of milky blue eyes. He looks about a hundred but living in the countryside can do that to you. Nelson switches off the engine and waits.

'I knew this place when it was a real farm,' says the ancient.

'How long ago was that?'

'Thirty, forty year back. Course, it wasn't called Black Dog Farm then.'

'Wasn't it?'

'No, that was his idea. Noakes. This was North End Farm in those days.'

'Did you know Douglas Noakes?'

'Just to say hallo to. He kept himself to himself. I heard things sometimes, though.'

'What sort of things?'

'Screaming, crying. Coming from the house. And I heard him howling at night. The Black Shuck.'

Nelson's heart sinks. 'The Black Shuck?'

'Don't you believe in the Shuck?' The man grins, revealing a mouth that showcases a single, yellow tooth. 'I've seen him as clear I see you. He haunts this place, you know.'

'Really?'

'He comes back for blood, because blood was spilt here. There's a curse on the house, you know.'

It just gets better, thinks Nelson.

'A farmer called Manning, he killed his wife here, years ago. The Shuck doesn't forget.'

Before Nelson can reply, the man touches his cap and, moving surprisingly quickly, disappears into the tree-lined lane.

Linda Noakes taught at a Sheringham school called St Luke's. Judy arrives at three o'clock and is slightly surprised to find that it's the end of the school day. When you're at school, last lesson feels like the evening, the best of the day is over by the time you get home. But, in the adult world, school ends just after lunchtime. At the station they would be arguing about whose turn it was to do the chocolate run.

Judy watches the parents collecting their children and walking away carrying school bags and sundry pieces of artwork. She remembers Miranda flying out of school last Friday, leaving a trail of glitter behind her. It had been nice to go with Cathbad to collect the children but she's still glad that she doesn't have to do it every day. Just seeing the mothers with their four-by-fours and designer sunglasses makes her feel nervous.

In a remarkably short space of time, the playground is empty apart from a caretaker gloomily picking up rubbish and two children waiting anxiously with their teacher. 'Mum will be here soon,' the teacher is saying. 'It's hard to get away when you've got patients to see.' That would be Michael and Miranda's fate if Judy was a single mother. She silently thanks the goddess for Cathbad as she goes up to the desk and asks for Selina Spencer, the headteacher.

Judy has noticed that authority figures are starting to look young to her, so she's reassured to see that Selina has grey hair and is wearing a sensible wine-coloured trouser suit. She has a round, cheerful face that doesn't seem suited to her sombre expression when she mentions Linda.

'I'll miss her a lot,' she says. 'We were the two oldies, counting down the days until retirement. We used to joke about it.'

Linda Noakes was fifty-eight, Selina doesn't look much

older but maybe teachers, like police officers, retire early. There are always rumours that the boss is planning to retire but Judy will believe that when she sees it.

'How long had Linda worked here?' asks Judy.

'Twelve years,' says Selina. 'She came back to work when the children left home. She was part-time, a job share in Year Four. Parents always complain about job shares but actually they work very well in primary schools. It gives the children two experienced teachers for the price of one.'

'I'm sorry to ask,' says Judy, 'but we're obviously looking into the circumstances of Linda's death. Had she ever given any indication that things were difficult at home?'

'No,' says Selina. 'We were all so shocked when we heard. Linda was a private person, she didn't talk about her home life much, but I think – I hope – that I would have picked up if something was wrong. She always seemed very cheerful, very sensible and down-to-earth. As I say, we used to joke about being the older generation. We've got a lot of young teachers here. There was only me, Linda and Bryan in the oldies' club.'

'Did Linda ever talk about her children, Chloe and Paul?'

'Sometimes. They came here, you know, so we always had an interest in them. Linda was so proud when Chloe became a doctor.'

'And Paul? Was she proud of him too?'

'Of course.' But there seems to be a slight hesitation. Surely Linda, a teacher herself, would approve of Paul's career choice.

'Did you know Douglas Noakes at all?'

'I just met him once, at a summer fete. He seemed rather distant, rather cold, quite a contrast to Linda. But I certainly never thought . . .'

You never thought that he'd kill his wife, thinks Judy. But you're not that surprised either.

By the afternoon, the digger has reduced the garden to churned mud. Ruth has found several pieces of what look like medieval pottery, a Victorian glass bottle and a collection of coins. Yet the only bones are those of the dog, now arranged in anatomically correct position on the blue tarpaulin. Ruth is muddy, tired and extremely hungry. She's also annoyed to find herself hoping that Nelson might come back. Tony, the new young DC, turned up at lunchtime and has just left. He's pleasant and very keen – actually getting into the trench himself at one point – but, for Ruth, he's no substitute for Nelson or even for Judy and Clough, the double act from the old days. Clough left shortly after Nelson. It had been good to see him again but disconcerting that he seems to be getting younger with each passing year.

The digger driver has gone, taking Steve with him, and now there's only Ruth and Ted, bagging the bones and marking them on a skeleton chart, more for form's sake than anything else. Ruth has also collected some soil samples and recorded all the finds. Now she's thinking of home and a hot bath. She's picking Kate up from Sandra's at five and it's nearly four. She is, therefore, not delighted when a tall shadow falls across her log book.

'Just thought I'd drop in. The policeman outside said it was OK.'

'Hallo, David.'

'What did you find?'

'Just some dog bones.' Ruth indicates the box containing the sample bags. 'And a few pieces of pottery.'

'Anything old?'

He's hoping for some Beaker pots, Ruth thinks.

'Not prehistoric. They look medieval.'

'Bottle could be interesting,' says David. 'Could be from an apothecary.'

'Maybe,' says Ruth. Old glass, she remembers, was one of Phil's specialities.

'But no body in the garden?'

'Unless you count the dog, no.'

There are only a few bones remaining on the tarpaulin, but they are enough to show the size of the animal. It was, in Ted's words, 'as big as a pony'.

'You were talking about the Black Shuck,' says David, 'and here it is.' He lifts up one of the bones and, for a weird moment, Ruth thinks that he's going to kiss it. Instead, David holds the fragment up to the sun so that it's almost translucent.

'"The good is oft interred with their bones",' he says. 'We did Julius Caesar at school. I was Mark Anthony.'

'Was that when you were at school with Alan White?' says Ruth. She distrusts people who quote Shakespeare. Shona's always doing it.

'Yes. West Runton Prep. It's a good play for an all-boys

school. Alan was Cassius. Or Casca. One of the conspirators anyway.'

'I saw Alan yesterday. He was at the Bronze Age site with a friend. I hope he isn't planning to do any digging.'

David laughs. 'You do like to be in charge, Ruth, don't you?'

Ruth ignores this. *I am in charge* she tells David in her head. Ted puts the last bone in its paper evidence bag and Ruth marks it on the chart. *Thoracic Vertebrae.* She straightens up. Her back is aching like hell.

David is staring up at the house. Suddenly he lets out an exclamation.

'What is it?' says Ruth.

'Nothing,' says David. 'Just ... I thought I saw something ... someone ... at the window.'

Ruth follows his gaze. She's glad of the solid presence of Ted behind her. The house stares back at her, the windows reflecting the late afternoon sun so that, for a second, it looks as if there's a fire burning somewhere inside.

'It's just the light,' says Ted. 'You get dramatic sunsets around here.'

'Yes,' says David. 'It must have been a trick of the light.'

Ted lifts up the box of bones while Ruth takes the box containing the finds. After a moment's hesitation, David takes the scythe and resistivity metre. They walk round to the front of the house and load the equipment and the boxes into Ted's van. Ruth sees David's car, a vintage Citroën, next to her six-year-old Renault. She's irritated with him for having such an Instagrammable car.

'Shall I take the bones to the lab?' says Ted.

'Yes. The police might still want to examine them. I suppose they might have fingerprints or DNA on them.'

From the condition and the objects found in the context – coins and building rubble – Ruth thinks that the bones have been in the soil for about thirty years. She's not sure though. It's usually easy enough to tell newly buried bones, but, without carbon-14 testing, it's possible to confuse fifty-year-old bones with ancient ones. Ruth can't see the police paying for C14 tests on dog bones.

Ted drives off and Ruth gets into her car with a sigh of pleasure. The driving seat feels wonderfully supportive for her back. She's just searching for her water bottle when David says, 'What's that?'

Why does he keep seeing things? It's making Ruth nervous. This time, David is pointing towards the outbuildings. Rather reluctantly, Ruth looks. And sees a black shape disappearing behind a wall.

'What was that?' she says.

'Looked like a dog,' says David. He glances at her with that odd, uneven smile. 'Shall we investigate?'

'I need to collect my daughter.'

'Won't take a second.'

Ruth doesn't want to follow him. It's still daylight although the shadows are lengthening. The farm suddenly seems very quiet. Even the birds have stopped singing. There's not a breath of air and the sky is a strange yellowy colour. She thinks a storm is on its way.

'Come on,' says David. 'Don't be chicken.'

That does it. Ruth gets out of her car.

'This way,' says David. 'I think he went into the barn.' Ruth follows David across the yard. The barn is almost directly opposite the house, a dark, windowless building with huge doors, bolted shut. But, as they approach, they see that there's another entrance, a smaller door at the side. It's ajar.

'Anyone there?' David kicks the door open.

'Be careful,' says Ruth.

'Are you afraid of the Black Shuck?'

Yes, Ruth wants to say. Anyone with any sense would be afraid of a wild dog the size of a pony. But she joins David at the open door.

It's pitch-black inside the barn but Ruth gets the sense of a vast, empty space. David shines his phone torch into the void. It highlights rafters, a ladder, an old dinghy. And a dog's bed and feeding bowl. The latter licked shining clean.

The storm breaks just as Ruth and Kate get home. Ruth feels as if it's been chasing her across the marshes, the wind buffeting her little car from side to side as they negotiate the high, exposed road with ditches at each side. One false move and she and Kate will be plunged into darkness. The sky is purple now with a yellow line across the horizon. Ruth and Kate run into the house and, as they shut the door, the rain hits the windows as if a wave has risen up and swallowed the flat landscape. There's an explosion of thunder and the dark house is lit by lightning. Kate gives an excited scream. Ruth turns on the lights and goes to look for Flint. After an anxious few minutes, he is eventually discovered on

Kate's bed, disguised as a teddy bear. As Kate cuddles the disapproving cat, lightning illuminates the row of dusty Sylvanians on her window ledge.

'We'd better bring Flint downstairs,' says Kate. 'He's scared of thunder.'

He's not the only one, thinks Ruth. She's had a few nasty experiences with storms herself but, in front of Kate, she puts on a jolly façade of 'Isn't nature wonderful, aren't we lucky to be all cosy inside?' Kate agrees but she sits very close to Ruth on the sofa as they eat their pasta. Flint sits directly in front of them, trying to make them feel guilty for monopolising his preferred nap spot.

The storm lasts all evening. They count the seconds between lightning flashes and thunderclaps and, for a long time, it seems as if it is acting out its tantrum right over the house. Ruth's cottage is one of a group of three but both sets of neighbours are away at the moment. It's just Ruth, Kate and Flint in the middle of the marshes with the wind howling – as locals always like to tell you – all the way from Siberia. Ruth thinks of Black Dog Farm, of David looking up at the windows, of the red light flickering behind the glass, of the strange animal disappearing into the shadows. When Kate is finally in bed, she rings Nelson.

'What's up?' He doesn't ask about Kate, which makes Ruth think that Michelle is listening.

'It's probably nothing,' she says, 'but David Brown turned up after you left.'

'That man seems to get everywhere.'

Ruth ignores this. 'He just came to help with the dig, but

it was almost finished. He helped us clear up and, when we were getting into our cars, we saw something.'

'What?' Ruth can hear the television in the background. Has she interrupted a cosy evening in front of *MasterChef*?

'We thought we saw a dog . . .'

'Not the bloody Shuck again.'

'No,' says Ruth. 'An actual real-life dog. We followed it into the barn and saw its actual real-life feeding bowl and basket.'

'Well, well, well,' says Nelson. 'That is interesting. So someone at the farm was keeping a dog.'

'It looks like it.'

'Thanks for letting me know, Ruth. Is the weather bad out your way? I don't like to think of you out there in the middle of nowhere.'

'It's fine,' says Ruth. 'I like thunder.'

Outside, the storm rages.

19

'It was a dog,' says Tony. 'A dog the size of an elephant.'

'An elephant, Tony?' says Judy. 'Really?' She usually finds Tony's enthusiasm endearing but sometimes he sounds like a schoolboy in the back of a bus describing how he saw a spider *that big* in the bath.

'A baby elephant,' says Tony.

'And that was all they found in the garden?' says Tanya, who is making rather ostentatious notes.

'Apart from a few bits of rubble,' says Tony. 'I actually got in the trench. Must be great fun to be an archaeologist.'

'It's more like a lot of hard work,' says Judy, thinking of the times that she's seen Ruth on an excavation, meticulously trowelling and sifting and recording.

'So, when Douglas Noakes said, "the body in the garden",' says Tanya, 'he could have been talking about a dog?'

'I suppose so,' says Judy. 'Let's ask Paul and Chloe when we talk to them today. Oh, and the boss rang me last night to say that Ruth had found a dog bowl and bed in one of the outhouses. She thought she saw a dog too, a big one.'

'Maybe that was the Black Whatsit,' says Tony. 'The ghost dog.'

'The Black Shuck,' says Judy. 'Honestly, you went to UEA, I would have thought that you would have known all the local legends.'

'We did do a ghost tour of Norwich once,' says Tony. 'I got locked in the park by the Cow Tower.'

'So maybe they had a dog and buried it in the garden,' says Tanya, in a 'summing up' voice. 'And maybe they had another dog and kept it in an outhouse. I don't see that gets us anywhere.'

'It tells us something about the Noakes family though,' says Judy. 'Neither of the children mentioned a dog so why would Douglas and Linda be keeping one secretly? And there's something odd going on at the research company. Jem Taylor's girlfriend said he did a drugs trial for them but he's not on the books. Plus, Chloe Noakes did work experience there and forgot to mention it. Do you want to talk to her, Tanya, and I'll take Paul?' She's aware that she's placating Tanya by offering her the more interesting sibling.

'What shall I do?' says Tony.

'Stay here and go through the witness statements,' says Judy. 'See if there's anything we've missed. And brief the boss when he gets back.'

'Where is he?' says Tanya.

'He's at the funeral of that PC who died,' says Judy.

*

Nathan's funeral brings back horrible memories of Tim's. The coffin covered in the Union flag, the lines of uniformed police officers, the sobbing relatives, the scent of flowers and candles. Of course, Tim had died a hero's death and Nathan had succumbed to an illness, apparently described on the death certificate as pneumonia. There's no press interest this time, no crowds of spectators outside the church, half prurient, half respectful. But the Norfolk police force has turned out to honour one of their own. Nelson sits with Jo in a row of dark blue uniforms. Jo is in uniform too, which rather suits her. Nelson is wearing a black suit and what he thinks of as his funeral tie. He can see Mark Hammond two rows in front; occasionally he drops his head and his neighbour pats his shoulder. It's a terrible thing to lose a partner and Mark and Nathan had known each other all their lives. Nathan's family are in the front row, mother, father and siblings. There's also a blonde woman who might be the fiancée. Hadn't Mark said that Nathan was saving up to get married?

The service passes in a blur of readings and hymns and heart-rending tributes to the deceased. Nathan's brother describes him as his best friend. Mark stumbles up to the lectern to say that he knew Nathan 'since we were spotty schoolboys together'. His face crumples as he concludes, 'I'll never forget you, buddy.' Nathan's fiancée is sobbing in the front row. When the last hymn – 'Thine Be The Glory' – starts up, Nelson finds himself rubbing his eyes. Jo puts her hand on his arm but says nothing. Nelson is oddly touched by this.

Outside, the coffin is borne away to a 'private interment'. The police contingent stands on the steps watching the hearse drive away with autumn leaves swirling up around it like funeral confetti. It's a cold, squally day, the remnants of last night's storm. Jo is talking to her fellow high-ups. Nelson finds himself next to Mark Hammond.

'I'm sorry,' he says, again. 'This must be very hard for you. Are you back at work?'

'I'm still on compassionate leave,' says Mark. 'I think I'm going to volunteer to be a dog handler,' he continues, in a hard, bright voice. 'I don't think I could face having another human partner. Animals never let you down.'

Nathan didn't let anyone down, except by dying, but Nelson knows what Mark means. And, in Nelson's experience, dog handlers get every bit as involved with their canine companions. He knows Jan Adams, the senior police dog handler in Norfolk, very well. Bruno is a distant relative of her dog, Barney.

'You did well to speak in church,' he says. 'I'm sure it was a comfort to Nathan's parents.'

'I don't think anything will comfort them,' says Mark. 'Or Faye, Nathan's fiancée. They were planning to get married next year.'

These words run through Nelson's mind as he walks back to the police station. This is what has been niggling away at him. Nathan was saving to get married. Jem Taylor had been saving for a holiday. Was it possible that they had both turned to Cambridge Bioresearch as a way of making some extra money?

At the station, there's only young Tony, looking very conscientious with a pile of reports in front of him.

'How was the funeral?' he asks, and then blushes. 'I mean . . . I know it must have been awful . . .'

'It was as good as it could have been,' says Nelson. 'A proper police send-off.' He sometimes finds himself wondering, rather morbidly, what his own funeral will be like. Will Jo make a speech? Will Cloughie cry? His mother has planned her own funeral right down to all the hymns. Maybe he should do the same.

'How did you find Black Dog Farm?' he asks Tony.

Tony swivels his chair round. Nelson has noticed before that the new recruit is always keen to chat.

'Pretty creepy. It was fascinating watching Dr Galloway work though. She knew exactly how old the bones were, just from what was buried alongside them.'

'Hmm.' Does Tony really not know about Nelson and Ruth? Surely Tanya will have told him by now. He assumes that everyone in Norfolk Police knows.

'Do me a favour, Tony,' says Nelson, 'and look up the land registry for the farm. It used to be called North End. Find out if a family called Manning used to live there.'

He goes into his office and looks up Cambridge Bio-research. Ten minutes later, Tony is tapping on the door.

'Terry and Geraldine Manning-Brown lived in North End Farm from 1963 to 1980,' says Tony. 'And I found this in the EDP archives.'

Nelson looks at the printout from the *Eastern Daily Press*.

It is dated 3 June 1976.

HORROR ACCIDENT AT FARM

> In what police described as a horrific accident,
> Mrs Geraldine Manning-Brown, aged 39, was killed
> when she fell into a combine harvester at North
> End Farm, Sheringham. Her husband, Terry, aged
> 50, who found her body was said to be in shock
> today. The Manning-Browns have owned the farm
> for several generations and were described by
> neighbours as 'pillars of the community'.

Hadn't the Noakes family been described in the same
way? The article is accompanied by a picture of an unsmiling
couple standing in front of the familiar, square house.

At the man's side is a large black dog.

20

Paul Noakes teaches at a sixth-form college on the outskirts of King's Lynn. Judy didn't attend this school herself but it's enough like her alma mater to make her feel slightly panicky. She did well enough at school but couldn't wait to leave at eighteen and join the police force, even though her A levels were good enough for university. She can't understand people like Ruth and Shona who voluntarily stay in academic establishments all their lives. Even Cathbad had been working at a university when she first met him. Libraries and common rooms don't make Cathbad feel nervous, in fact they probably energise him because they offer two of his favourite things: people and books.

King's Lynn Sixth Form is not exactly an ivory tower. It's a modern building, square and featureless, with bars on the downstairs windows like a prison. Paul meets her in the history common room, which doesn't seem to contain a single book. He's friendly enough, making coffee and searching for biscuits in an old Quality Street tin, but he also seems nervous, running his hands through his (thinning) hair and moving around in that odd, uncoordinated way. He seems even taller indoors.

Paul hands Judy a cup stained brown inside from years of instant coffee. Ruth would have recoiled in horror but Judy is made of sterner stuff. Paul folds his long limbs into a chair and starts jiggling one foot in a way that reminds Judy, unexpectedly, of Claudia Albertini.

Judy takes a sip of coffee. Luckily, it's too hot to taste of anything much.

'This is great,' she says. 'Thanks.'

'I'm trying to cut down on coffee,' says Paul. 'It makes me too hyper.' Jiggle, jiggle, jiggle.

'Me too,' says Judy. 'But I never manage it.'

She takes another molten sip. Paul seems to have finished his already.

'As you know,' she says, 'we had a team of forensic archaeologists digging at Black Dog Farm yesterday.'

'Did they find anything?' Paul seems to notice his leg twitching and stops, with an obvious effort.

'No human bones,' says Judy. She thinks it's important to say this quickly. 'But we did find a skeleton that looks like a dog. A very large dog.'

She watches Paul as she says these words but isn't prepared for the look of dawning realisation – and something else, anger? – that crosses his face.

'So it *was* there,' he says. 'The old bastard was right.'

Ruth is in a meeting about Virtual Learning Environments. It's very dull and rather depressing. Steven, the head of

technical support, is telling them that soon they will be able
to communicate remotely with their students via something
called Zoom.

'You won't have to see your students at all,' he says with
a cheery smile, 'except on the computer screen.'

It sounds like a nightmare to Ruth. She frequently complains about her students – though not aloud now that she's
department head – but, in truth, interacting with them is
one of the best things about the job. No intake is ever the
same, which is why teaching stays so interesting. She gets
a lot of satisfaction when a student, so shy in the first term
that they can't speak, suddenly becomes obsessed with Iron
Age burials in the third and won't stop talking about them.
How will this manifest itself via this Zoom thingy? A song
of the same name by Fat Larry's Band comes into her head
and, unfortunately, stays there.

It's lunchtime when the meeting ends. Ruth walks over
to the cafeteria, planning to take a sandwich back to her
office, but finds herself queuing behind David.

'I've just had a great session on Palaeolithic artefacts,' he
tells her. 'The students were really engaged.'

'That's great,' says Ruth. He's trying to impress her, she
notes with slight surprise. She remembers saying similar
things to Phil in the early days, before she realised that he
was only interested in Arts Council grants and appearing
on television.

'Shall we sit on the terrace?' says David, when they've
both collected their sandwiches – and cake, in Ruth's case.
He seems to assume that they'll sit together so Ruth feels

that it would look unsociable to go back to her office now. Besides, the sun is out and it would be nice to sit outside.

It's sunny but there's a cold wind so they have the terrace almost to themselves. From here they can see all the way across the campus. Last night's storm has stripped the trees of some of their leaves and the statue of Elizabeth Fry is still wearing its freshers' week traffic cone but otherwise the place is looking its best, the ornamental lake ruffled like chiffon.

'I like this university,' says David. 'It has good energy.'

This sounds very much like Cathbad. Ruth remembers many happy lunches here with Cathbad, in the days when he was a lab assistant.

'Better than Uppsala?' she says, teasingly because the Swedish university is far more prestigious than UNN.

'Different,' says David.

They talk about Sweden for a while. It turns out that David's ex-wife, Signe, is Swedish and that she and his daughter, Maja, live in Stockholm although they are currently in the UK visiting relatives.

'Maja is coming to me at the weekend,' says David. 'It'll be the first time that she's seen my cottage. I hope she likes it.'

This is the most human statement Ruth has ever heard from David. She knows that he lives in Stiffkey, another charming north Norfolk village.

'I'm sure she will,' she says. 'Kids love the seaside.'

'I hope it's sunny enough to go to the beach,' says David. 'Otherwise I might be a bit stuck.'

Ruth has heard similar things from other separated fathers – though never from Nelson, to be fair. She stops herself from offering a list of child-friendly local attractions.

'You'll have a great time,' she says firmly.

'You're a single parent, aren't you?' says David. 'I met your daughter last weekend.'

'Yes, you did,' says Ruth tightly. She doesn't want to discuss Kate or her parentage. David saw Nelson with Kate last Saturday and will have drawn his own conclusions.

'Must be tough,' says David. 'Signe says it is anyway.'

'I cope,' says Ruth in a tone which – she hopes – puts an end to the conversation.

They have finished their sandwiches and Ruth is wondering whether to save her cake for later. Two seagulls are watching closely from the balustrade as if they know of her internal struggle. Suddenly, David appears to be sunk in gloom.

'I sometimes wonder if I was right to come back to Norfolk,' he says.

'Why did you?' Ruth starts to pick at the cellophane around her lemon drizzle.

'I missed it,' says David, after a slight pause. 'I was at school here and the place just got to me.'

'Was that West Runton?' asks Ruth. 'I thought that you didn't have a very good time there.'

There's another pause. David drains the last of his coffee.

'It was hell,' he says. 'Freezing cold, sadistic teachers, inedible food. I was a sad child anyway. My mother died when I was quite young and my dad . . . well, he was a cold fish. Home was unbearable but school was even worse.'

'It sounds awful,' says Ruth. 'Poor you.' David is a very grown-up-looking man, perhaps it's the height, but suddenly she sees him as a child, gangly and awkward, unwanted at home and unhappy at school.

'But, on Sundays,' says David, his voice dreamy, 'we used to go on a walk to the sea. That coast almost made up for everything.'

'It is beautiful,' says Ruth. 'I came here to do a dig twenty years ago and never left.'

'Was that the henge?' says David. 'You mentioned it the other day.'

'Yes,' says Ruth. 'It was an incredible discovery.'

'Alan says that the timbers are in King's Lynn museum. I must visit them.'

'You should. They've done it really well.' Cathbad, of course, thinks the wood should have been left where it was, prey to time and tide, ebb and flow, life and death.

'Alan and the Night Hawks are going out tonight,' says David.

'Where?' says Ruth. 'If they're going to Blakeney Point I hope they leave the trench alone. It's a burial site. It should be treated with respect.'

'I'm going with them,' says David. 'I'll keep an eye on things.'

Ruth is so irritated that she eats her cake.

'What do you mean?' says Judy. 'Who was right?'

'My father,' says Paul. His leg is vibrating again. He looks around, as if searching for escape.

'Your father?' prompts Judy.

'You know I told you he used to say that there was a dead body in the garden,' says Paul. 'And, if we didn't behave, it would rise up out of the ground and kill us.'

'Yes,' says Judy. She's not likely to forget.

'Well, he was right, wasn't he? There was a body buried there.'

Paul says this as if his father has won again. It makes Judy feel quite sad.

'But it wasn't a human,' she says. 'It was a dog.'

'He used to talk about the Black Shuck a lot,' says Paul. 'He said that he haunted the house. You know the legend? It's this giant dog, jet black with red eyes. If you see it, you die with a week.'

'I've heard the story. I was born in Norfolk.'

'Well, maybe the Black Shuck was buried in our garden.'

He says it with a slight smile, but Judy doesn't think that it's really a joke. The way Paul talks about his father is utterly chilling. Judy has heard stories of abusive parents before but there's something about using a local legend to terrify children that strikes her as especially evil.

'Have you talked about your childhood with anyone?' she asks. It occurs to her that some therapy might not be a bad thing.

'Only with Chloe. It makes you close, having parents . . . a father . . . like that. I used to go into Chloe's room at night when he was shouting.'

'Who was he shouting at, your mother?'

'Sometimes. Sometimes he was just ranting at something

he saw on the telly. Any little thing could set him off. A contestant getting a science question wrong on a quiz programme, a scientist who wasn't him being asked for their opinion. We lived in constant terror of getting something wrong. And it was worse for Chloe.'

'You could still talk to someone about it,' says Judy. 'It's not too late. Therapy can really help with supressed memories.'

'I haven't suppressed them,' says Paul. 'That's the problem.'

Judy judges that it's time to let the matter drop although she thinks she might bring it up again.

'What about the bones in the garden?' she says. 'Do you have any idea whose dog it might have been? Did your parents have a pet?'

'No. Dad didn't believe in pets.' He says it like not believing in Father Christmas. Judy is ready to bet that Santa didn't play a big part in the Noakes children's lives.

'We found a dog's bed and feeding bowl in one of the outhouses,' says Judy. 'Do you know anything about that?'

'A dog's bed?' says Paul. 'That can't be right. We never had a pet. I used to beg for one. My mother bought me a hamster once, but Dad made her take it back.'

His voice breaks slightly, and Judy sees the boy inside the tall, awkward man. She asks if Paul has a pet now.

'A hamster,' he says with a slight smile. 'I'd like to have a dog, but I couldn't leave it alone all day.'

'We used to have two hamsters called Sonny and Fredo,' says Judy. 'They died last year. I was surprised how upset I was.'

'I'll be devastated when Daphne dies,' says Paul.

Across the town, in The Crossroads GP Practice, Tanya is hearing a similar story from Dr Chloe Noakes.

'He used to tell us stories about the Black Shuck,' says Chloe, sitting in her surgery framed by a large poster of a waterfall advertising antibacterial handwash. 'I used to imagine it rising up in the night, its eyes red, prowling into the house and up the stairs. I was so scared I used to wet the bed. And got punished for it, of course.'

'And you had no idea that an actual dog was buried there?'

'No. I thought the body in the garden must be a human. Or maybe I just got mixed up. When I got older, I just assumed Dad had made up these stories as a way of controlling us. He liked the legend of the Black Shuck though. That's why he changed the name of the farm.'

'It was North End Farm before?'

'That's right. Apparently one of the previous owners fell into a combine harvester and died. I used to have nightmares about that too.'

Chloe gives Tanya a tight smile. She's a small woman, neat and contained in all her movements but, although very thin – underweight, in Tanya's opinion – she's not insubstantial. Chloe has a presence, though this is probably helped by the fact that she's a doctor sitting in her own surgery.

'How involved were you with your dad's company, Cambridge Bioresearch?' asks Tanya.

Chloe seems to tighten still further. 'Not at all involved.'

'But you did work experience there.'

'When I was eighteen and applying to medical school. You have to have something to put on your personal statement.'

'But it must have interested you. I mean, you're a scientist.' Tanya studied sports science at university and considers herself very much on this side of the fence.

'Look.' Chloe leans forward. Tanya can see the tiny lines around her mouth and eyes. At thirty-three Chloe should not have these lines. Maybe she's a smoker? 'Look, I'm a doctor, I'm a GP. Dad was a research scientist. They are very different jobs. I want to help people, Dad wanted . . .' She stops.

'What did he want?' asks Tanya. It strikes her that this would be very useful information.

'Knowledge,' says Chloe. 'Control. He was interested in science for its own sake, not for what it could do for people. Claudia is a bit different.'

'Claudia Albertini?'

'Yes, Dad's partner in the business. She's a scientist, a pharmacologist, but she wants to make the world a better place. She and Dad used to argue all the time.'

'About what?'

'About animal testing, for one thing. Claudia wanted to stop it, or at least make sure it was as ethical as possible. Dad didn't care.'

'What about human testing? Dr Albertini told my colleague that the company does a lot of drugs tests.'

'Yes,' says Chloe. 'All drugs companies do. It's perfectly legal.'

'Did your dad and Dr Albertini argue about the drugs tests? Maybe Claudia thought that your dad was taking some shortcuts?'

'What are you getting at?'

'It's just a line of enquiry.'

Chloe takes a visible breath. 'I really don't know anything about the business. I haven't even heard from Claudia in years.'

Tanya looks at her notes. 'You said that you last saw your parents a few months ago when you asked them to sign some papers. What was that about?'

'I was remortgaging my house,' says Chloe. 'Dad was my guarantor.'

Is it usual to have your father as a guarantor when you're in your thirties and, presumably, pretty well paid? Tanya doesn't know. Her parents have never even owned their own house. And Tanya has a good, if healthily distant, relationship with her family. But Chloe hated her father. Why had she ever accepted his financial help?

'Why were you remortgaging?'

'I don't see how that's relevant.'

But finances are always relevant, thinks Tanya. Why would Chloe need to remortgage? As far as Tanya knows, she lives on her own with no dependents, which is quite unusual in itself at thirty-three, she thinks. Most of Tanya's schoolfriends were married or in relationships by then. Is Chloe gay? Tanya doesn't think so and, over the years, she's become good at picking up the signals. But, then again, maybe Chloe is gay and doesn't know it yet. Tanya was still dating men in her late twenties. Until she met Petra, in fact.

Tanya decides to drop the subject. For now, anyway.

'Did your parents own a dog?' she asks.

'What? Is this a joke? I told you about the Black Shuck.'

'We found dog accessories in one of the barns.' As soon as Tanya says this, she realises how weird it sounds. What are dog accessories? Designer poo bags? Little necklaces with bones on?

Chloe is not about to let her get away with this. 'Dog accessories? What are you talking about?'

Tanya gives the doctor a hard stare. A joke's a joke but Tanya's a police officer on duty and she's not going to let anyone laugh at her.

'Did your parents own a dog?'

'No,' says Chloe. 'Like I said, Dad hated all animals.'

Cathbad is tempted to walk to Cley. At night, it would only take about two and a half hours. Cathbad loves walking, which is why, years ago, at a rather directionless time in his life, he became a postman. But, somehow, when you have a house and a life partner and three children, you can't just walk all night, stopping to sleep in a hedgerow if the mood takes you. Cathbad misses the freedom of the wandering years, although he is honest enough to admit that it was also an anxious and sometimes lonely time. He's much happier now, in his little cottage with Judy and the children and Thing. But he would like the occasional midnight walk.

So he drives to Cley and waits in the car park for the Night Hawks. They arrive in cars and vans, unloading their metal detectors and a worrying array of equipment, arc lights, shovels, even fishing rods and nets. Cathbad doesn't believe in disturbing nature, often at its busiest during the hours of darkness, and this looks rather too invasive for him.

It's hard to recognise people in the dark. Cathbad can't hear Alan's voice but thinks he identifies people whom he met on previous excursions: the IT guy, Neil, and the historian, Paul. A younger man, who appears on a bike without headlights, is hailed as Troy by the others. No one speaks to Cathbad and he assumes that, in his camouflage jacket and woolly hat, he blends into the background. Another middle-aged thrill-seeker looking for treasure.

'Where's Al?' asks someone.

'Maybe he's already on the beach,' says someone else.

'His car's here,' says a third voice.

'We can't wait for him,' says a voice Cathbad recognises. David Brown. Cathbad remembers him from the dig with Ruth. Now there's an edge of anger to his voice that wasn't there the other day.

'Has anyone heard from him?' says Paul.

Now would be the time for Cathbad to speak up but, by now, he thinks that it would be more prudent to remain silent. He will be the Other, the Visitor, the Third, the one who walks beside you, unheard and unseen. The Night Hawks make their way down to the beach, making enough noise and light, with their boots and equipment and torches, to scare away all the wildlife for miles around. A line from the Good Friday service, and his Irish Catholic upbringing, comes back to Cathbad. Judas goes to meet Jesus in the Garden of Gethsemane, preparing to betray him. Judas is accompanied by a gang of soldiers and temple police, 'all with lanterns and torches and weapons'. It's never a good sign when men go out armed at night, even if it's only with metal detectors.

Cathbad doesn't need a torch. He knows the coastal path very well and has often made this journey, by day and night. He walks by the water's edge, his walking boots are waterproof and he likes the way the waves break over his feet. On the higher ground, he can hear the Hawks talking. They have the original GPS location for the place where the skeleton and the grave goods were found. Cathbad knows that Alan wants to scour the area looking for more Bronze Age treasure. Cathbad has appointed himself guardian of the dead man, the possible priest who was buried with a dagger in his hand. He will defend him from the temple police.

Paul is obviously still worried about Alan, but David Brown says that Alan can take care of himself. 'I know him better than you do,' Cathbad hears him say. Interesting, he thinks, splashing along in the shallows. He remembers the sea serpent. He has looked up the reports from 1936, when the creature was spotted by no less a personage than the Mayor of Norwich, who described it as moving swiftly and silently through the water. Is the Norfolk Nessie out there in the darkness somewhere, sleeping in the depths for hundreds of years, only to rise again when the omens are right? Cathbad sends it a peaceful salutation, just in case.

They turn inland and the torches reflect the still waters of pools and lagoons. A night bird flies overhead and there's an answering call from the saltmarsh. Cathbad can hear the tarpaulin flapping long before they reach the trench. Someone shouts, 'The cover is off.'

David says, 'Alan must have got here already.'

'There's no sign of Alan,' says someone.

A confusion of lights and voices and then a shout, hoarse and terrified. 'Oh my God.'

'What?'

'What is it?'

'Bring the arc light over here.'

'Jesus Christ.'

Cathbad moves into the light just as it shines into the uncovered trench. He can see the chalky soil, the gleam of quartz and the dead body of Alan White, face down in the earth.

Once again, Nelson is roused from his sleep. Blearily, he looks at his phone. Cathbad. Why the hell is Cathbad calling him in the middle of the night?

'This had better be good,' says Nelson.

'I don't know about good,' says Cathbad. 'But I think Alan White has been murdered.'

'What? Where are you?'

'On the beach near Blakeney Point with the Night Hawks. Alan's body was in the trench. The one where we found the Bronze Age skeleton.'

'Jesus. Don't let anyone move it or touch it.'

'I won't.'

Nelson gets up and reaches wearily for his clothes. Michelle doesn't stir.

'Don't touch the body,' says Cathbad, turning back to the group.

They seem to register his existence for the first time. David says, 'Who the hell are you?'

'I'm a friend of Alan's,' says Cathbad. 'He asked me to come along tonight.'

'I know who you are,' says David. 'You're the chap who was here with Ruth the other day. Cathbad.'

'Cathbad?' Paul raises his head. He was the first person to see the body and had climbed into the trench to check for a pulse. He is now squatting on the ground, looking as if he might be sick. Some of the Hawks have rigged up the arc light which gives the whole scene a strange, theatrical atmosphere.

'Cathbad?' says Paul. 'I've heard Alan mention you. You're a druid, aren't you?'

'That's right,' says Cathbad.

'We need the police,' says someone. 'Not a bloody druid.'

'I've called the police,' says Cathbad.

'I've already rung them,' says Neil, coming into the circle of light.

'I contacted the Serious Crimes Squad,' says Cathbad. 'DCI Nelson.'

'Why would you do that?' says David. 'Alan obviously fell into the trench. It's an awful accident. That's all.'

'I don't know,' says Paul, his voice wavering. 'There's blood on his . . . on his head.'

'Don't touch anything,' says Cathbad. 'The murder weapon could be nearby.'

'Murder weapon?' says David. 'What are you talking about?' Cathbad can see his aura now, dark and smoky.

'Let's just wait for DCI Nelson,' says Cathbad.

'I can't believe there's another body,' says the young man called Troy. 'Right where we found the first one.'

'This is a liminal zone,' says Cathbad. 'A sacred realm between life and death.'

'Alan was right about you,' says David. 'He said you were completely mad.'

'That's nice,' says Cathbad. And he sits on the coarse grass to await the police.

22

Nelson drives fast through the dark streets. His headlights illuminate signposts, scurrying foxes and, once, a deer nibbling at a hedgerow but, as he crosses the marshes, there is only blackness. He arrives at the car park by Cley beach just as the squad car is drawing up. Nelson half expects to see Mark Hammond but, of course, he's still on leave after his partner's death. Jesus, was Nathan's funeral only that morning? Yesterday morning now. Nelson doesn't recognise the two uniformed constables but introduces himself briefly and leads the way to the shore. It feels strange to be the one who knows the way in this godforsaken place, eerier than ever in the night, with the sea on one side and the whispering grasses on the other.

Before long, though, he sees lights and hears voices. A group of people are huddled around a tarpaulin. An arc light casts strange shadows on the motley crew, some of them carrying metal detectors and other equipment. And just outside the circle sits a familiar figure, cross-legged on the grass. Nelson knows, just by looking at him, that Cathbad is meditating.

'Wakey, wakey,' says Nelson, approaching him. 'Time to come back to the real world.'

'I never left it,' says Cathbad, standing up.

'What happened?' says Nelson. Cathbad might be a new-age nutter but Nelson trusts him to tell a story calmly, with the events in the right order. He has sometimes even thought that Cathbad would have made a good police officer.

'Alan White invited me to join the Night Hawks on an outing,' says Cathbad. 'But, when I arrived, he wasn't here. We walked to the site and Paul discovered his body face-down in the trench.'

'Paul?'

'Paul Noakes.'

'I see. Did you see the body?'

'Yes, and I would say that Alan had been hit on the head by a heavy object. Possibly a rock or a piece of flint. I'm praying for his soul.'

'You keep doing that,' says Nelson, and he strides away to the group around the trench. The PCs are taking names and addresses. Nelson shines his torch into the hole. He sees the body, which is on its side, the head ruined and bloody. Briefly he remembers the body on the kitchen floor of Black Dog Farm. Douglas Noakes, his head blown off.

'Did anyone touch the body?' he asks. Cathbad had said that Alan was 'face down' in the trench but now he's lying on his side.

'I did,' says Paul. 'Just to check . . . you know . . . just to check if he was breathing.'

Even in the dark, Nelson can see that Paul looks dreadful,

white and shaking. He supposes that Paul, too, was reminded of the deaths at Black Dog Farm. And now he has lost the man who, unlike his father, was a positive paternal influence. No wonder he looks as if he's about to be sick.

'We need to get SOCO here immediately,' Nelson tells the uniforms. 'All these others can go as soon as you've got their details. Mr Noakes, can you wait a minute?'

'What do you want with Paul?' says one of the Hawks, a tall man in glasses that, rather disconcertingly, have turned dark in the glare of the lights.

'I need to ask Mr Noakes a few more questions,' says Nelson. 'And you are?'

'David Brown. I work with Ruth Galloway. We met the other day.'

'Oh yes. I remember. Well, if you've given your contact details to my colleagues, Mr Brown, there's no need for you to stay.'

Even Ruth's irritating lecturer can hardly ignore this dismissal. He turns and walks away, looking back once or twice as he does so.

'That man has a very hostile energy,' says a voice in Nelson's ear.

Nelson arrives at King's Lynn police station just as dawn is breaking. The night sergeant is preparing to go home but he makes Nelson a cup of coffee which he takes upstairs to his office. Nelson is tempted to try to get a few hours' sleep in his chair, but he doesn't fancy being caught napping by the team when they come thundering in at nine. There is, of course, a sofa in Jo's office but being woken up by Jo in her early morning jogging kit would be worse than the squad barging in. So Nelson drinks his coffee and makes notes while the scene on Cley beach is still fresh in his mind.

Paul Noakes said that Alan had been dead when he found him, the body cold. Even from a cursory glance it was obvious that Alan had been hit over the head with a heavy object and – Cathbad had been right – a blood-stained rock had been found by SOCO a few metres away. Alan had then fallen, or been pushed, into the trench. Ruth, he thinks wryly, would be almost more shocked about this than the murder. He wonders if David Bloody Brown will tell her the story when she gets into work this morning.

They don't have a time of death yet, but the body hadn't been stiff which makes Nelson think that the murder occurred less than an hour before the Night Hawks arrived. Alan had told Cathbad to meet him in the car park at midnight, a rendezvous he hadn't been able to keep. Alan had also, apparently, been worried about something. 'I think he wanted my protection,' said Cathbad. 'He must have been desperate then,' Nelson had replied.

Alan had been scared and now Alan is dead. Alan had been there when Jem Taylor's body was found, he had been outside the farmhouse when Douglas and Linda had died. Somehow the history teacher, the mild-mannered man with his metal detector, had taken centre stage. Had someone arranged to meet Alan before the Night Hawks had convened in the car park, hit him over the head and pushed him in the trench? Why? Was it linked to the treasure itself, to Black Dog Farm, to Cambridge Bioresearch? Nelson doesn't know and he has to find out.

Words and voices are starting to swim through his head.

They could have been a votive offering. An offering to the sea gods.

Armed police. We're coming in.

A couple of men out walking in the fields.

His eyes are made of hellfire and, if you see him, you die within the year.

I thought he'd be fine by Thursday morning. And now he's dead.

You see strange things sometimes, when you're far out to sea.

Dad used to say that there was a dead body in the garden.

We hated our father. We're glad he's dead.

The next thing he knows, Leah is standing in front of him.

'I've made you some coffee.'

'Thank you.' Nelson rubs his eyes. 'Sorry. I must have fallen asleep.' His head feels thick and muzzy. He shakes it.

'At first I thought you were late,' says Leah, 'but then I saw your car was in the car park.'

'I've been here since four a.m.,' says Nelson. 'I was called out in the night.' He takes a gulp of coffee. It's as if it's a molten stream cutting through the moss in his brain. He looks at his watch. Eight thirty. 'Is everyone here?'

'Tanya's here. Judy's on her way up, I think.'

'Grand. Tell them there's a briefing at nine. And Leah?'

'Yes?'

'Any chance of a bacon butty?'

Leah often pretends not to understand him when he's being Northern, but she sighs and says she'll see what she can do.

*

Ruth is preparing for her first lecture of the day when David appears at her door. She gathers up her papers to show that she doesn't have time to chat.

'Have you heard?' says David, ignoring the hint.

'Heard what?'

'Alan White's dead. We found his body in the trench.'

'*What?*'

David seems pleased with the sensation he has caused. He leans against her door with his arms crossed.

'You found him in the trench?'

'Yes. Remember I told you I was going out with the Night Hawks? Alan wasn't at the meeting place but, when we got to the trench, there he was.'

'Murdered?' Ruth realises that she's whispering.

'That's what your friend thinks. The druid bloke. Cathbad.'

'Cathbad was there?'

'Yes. And he called your other friend. DCI Nelson. Seems that he has him on speed dial.'

'Jesus.' Ruth had stood up when she heard the news. Now she sits down again, heavily. 'What did Nelson say?'

'He did all the officious police stuff. Asked for names and addresses. Cleared the site. Except for Paul.'

'Paul?'

'Paul Noakes. He was the one who found the body.'

The name rings a faint bell somewhere in Ruth's brain. Paul, the man she saw with Alan by the trench. The other Night Hawk. Then she remembers Nelson talking about 'the Noakes children, Chloe and Paul'.

'How did Alan die?' she asked.

'Cathbad seemed to think he might have been hit over the head with a rock. He's quite the detective.'

There's a definite sneer this time. David really doesn't like the police, or even amateur sleuths.

'So he was definitely murdered then?'

'I thought it was an accident at first,' says David, sounding more human suddenly. 'Poor Alan. I just can't believe it. He loved that beach.'

So do you, thinks Ruth. And so does she. Yet there's no doubt that something very dark is happening along this stretch of beautiful coastline. She hears her father's voice. *A load of swords just lying about on the beach. Isn't that a bit dangerous?*

'I'm sorry,' she says to David. 'This must be a terrible shock for you. Do you want to take the day off?'

'No, thanks,' says David. 'I think I'm better off here at work. It stops me thinking about it.'

David looks terrible, thinks Ruth, observing him properly for the first time. He's cadaverous anyway but now it's as if you can see the bones beneath the skin. Of course, he has probably stayed up all night. Ruth bets that Alan's ridiculous dig started at midnight.

'Do you have any idea what happened?' she asks.

But the tired human has gone, and the irritating smirk is back.

'Are you a detective now, Ruth?'

No, I'm your head of department, Ruth wants to say. But she doesn't want to argue with David when he has just lost his friend.

'Take it easy today,' she says. 'Maybe go home early.'

It's a dismissal of sorts, however gently phrased, and David takes the hint. As soon as her office door shuts behind him, Ruth rings Cathbad. He sounds remarkably chirpy although he too has been up all night.

'I knew something was going to happen,' he says. 'Alan did too. He told me that he'd heard the Black Shuck barking.'

'*What?*'

'Alan was worried. He must have had a premonition of his own death. He mentioned the Black Shuck, the omen of death.'

'You said he wasn't always a bad omen.'

'Not always but, in this case, he was the harbinger of death.'

You can't really argue with that, Ruth supposes. 'Did Alan say what he was worried about?'

'No. He said that he wanted to talk to me about something, but he couldn't tell me on the phone.'

'Do you know what it could have been?'

'No, but I think it had to do with the deaths at Black Dog Farm. There are lots of links between the Night Hawks and the farm. You know that Paul Noakes actually found the body?'

'Yes, David told me.'

'Ah yes. David Brown. He's a strange man, isn't he? He has a very hostile energy. I said as much to Nelson.'

'What did he say to that?'

'He took it in, I think.'

'David said that Alan's body was actually found in the trench. *Our* trench.'

'That's right. I keep thinking about what Nelson said the day we did our dig on the beach. You remember I said that I thought our man – our skeleton – might have been a priest involved in some sort of sacred rite or sacrifice, or a king because of the knife in his hand. And Nelson said, "A murder victim, most likely."'

Ruth remembers. '"Or a murderer",' she says.

23

The bacon butty does the trick and Nelson finds a new surge of energy for the briefing. He tells the team that Alan White's body was found at the archaeological site on Cley beach last night. He appeared to have been beaten about the head with a heavy stone. His body was found at approximately twenty past midnight and reported to the police five minutes later. Initial examination seemed to suggest that Alan was killed about an hour earlier. SOCO were currently on site.

'Alan White's car is parked in the car park near the beach,' says Nelson. 'There's no CCTV there but he might have been picked up by a speed camera on his way from his home in Sheringham. I want us to go door-to-door today, talk to his neighbours. Time of death will be very important.'

'Who actually found the body?' asks Tanya, who has her notebook out.

'Paul Noakes,' says Nelson, pausing to let the name sink in. 'You know how I feel about coincidence. Judy, Cathbad was at the dig – did he think that Noakes was acting oddly?'

'He thought he seemed nervous,' says Judy. 'But apparently he's rather a nervous man.'

'Noakes could have killed Alan earlier and then joined the Night Hawks for the dig,' says Tanya. 'It seems rather suspicious that he was the one to find the body. Gives him an excuse when we find his DNA all over it.'

'Exactly,' says Nelson.

'But why would Paul kill him?' says Judy. 'I thought they had a good relationship. Alan White was Paul's history teacher, he inspired him to study history at university.'

'Do you remember what Douglas Noakes is meant to have said to Alan White at some parents' evening?' says Nelson.

Judy flicks back through her notes. '"You're corrupting my son,"' she reads. '"You're a disgrace to the profession."' She looks at Nelson. 'Do you think that Alan White could have been abusing Paul Noakes?'

'I don't know,' says Nelson. 'But it's a line of enquiry. Tanya, did you speak to the school where Alan White taught, Greenhill?'

'Yes,' says Tanya. 'The head, Steph Brice, said that Alan White was a much-loved teacher. There were never any safeguarding issues.'

'Much-loved,' says Nelson. 'I'm always suspicious of teachers who want their pupils to love them. Go and talk to them, Tanya. Maybe we need to dig a little.'

'What about the link to Black Dog Farm?' says Tony. 'Alan White was on the scene of the murders there, he was the one who reported hearing the shots.'

'That's right,' says Nelson, pleased that the new recruit is thinking this way. 'Alan White and Neil Thomas, who was also on the excursion last night. Tanya, what did you make of Thomas when you interviewed him?'

'He seemed a little stressed,' says Tanya. 'Said he didn't sleep well. That's why he was out walking with Alan that night.'

'Neil Thomas taught with Alan White,' says Tony. 'He might know more about his relationship with Paul Noakes.'

'Good point,' says Nelson. 'Let's speak to him again. We need to interview all the so-called Night Hawks who were out last night. Ruth's colleague, David Brown, was one of them.'

'He turned up at the Black Dog Farm excavation,' says Tony. 'He arrived just as I was leaving.'

'Yes, he was with Ruth when they found the dog's bed and stuff. Did Chloe and Paul have anything to say about that?'

'Paul said they'd never had a pet,' says Judy. 'His mother bought him a hamster once, but his father made her take it back.'

'Yes,' says Tanya. 'Chloe said that her father hated animals.'

And Nelson sees that kitchen again: the Aga, the swinging herbs, the smell of blood, the open newspaper. And the calendar hanging by a nail from the wall. A calendar made by the charity supporting Guide Dogs for the Blind.

Ruth is teaching all morning and so doesn't get Nelson's text until lunchtime.

Call Me. N.

How long would it take to type 'please'? Ruth thinks. And why sign off N when she knows it's him? But she's given up trying to reform Nelson's texting habits. It can't be that urgent, anyway, otherwise he would have left a voicemail. Ruth gets a sandwich from the cafeteria and takes it back to her office. Then she rings N.

'Where have you been?' says Nelson. 'I called over an hour ago.'

'Teaching,' says Ruth, wondering how many times they've had this exchange. Fifty times? A hundred?

'Have you heard about last night?' says Nelson.

'Alan White's body being found? Yes. David told me first thing.'

'I saw him last night. Bad-tempered bloke, isn't he?'

'He reminds me of you.'

'You're joking.' Nelson sounds positively appalled. Clearly, Ruth has hit a nerve.

'What do you want, Nelson?'

'Could you meet me at Black Dog Farm after work?'

'I have to pick up Kate.'

'I thought she had a rehearsal after school. For *Scrooge*.' Why has Nelson chosen today to remember Kate's schedule? And why does he want her to go to the spooky farmhouse again?

'I just want you to show me where you saw the dog stuff,' says Nelson. 'It's not a big deal. It'll just be you and me.'

'I can't stay long,' says Ruth.

Tanya decides to drive straight to Greenhill Comprehensive School. She's irritated by the thought that she might have missed something when she spoke to the headteacher the first time. She'd liked Steph Brice over the phone, had thought she sounded organised and no-nonsense. Is it possible that she let this cloud her judgment?

Greenhill is a large collection of low-lying buildings linked by walkways. It reminds Tanya of the UEA campus where she has sometimes attended classes and meetings. She thinks the university was built in the sixties and this has the same air of having been modern and cutting-edge once. Now these buildings look distinctly the worse for wear. There are boarded-up windows and places where ornamental tiles have fallen off, leaving patches of exposed brick. The car park reveals a number of potholes and the flowers optimistically planted in the window boxes all seem to be dead.

Steph meets Tanya in reception and leads the way to her office. On the way they pass displays of students' work, posters for plays and sporting events, even the odd trophy or two. The infrastructure may be failing, thinks Tanya, but the school isn't. Marriage to Petra has taught her a little about these things.

The head's office is a comfortable and welcoming place. Tanya can't imagine pupils being scared of being sent to Ms Brice. Not that she's a pushover, though. In person she seems very much as she did on the phone, friendly but professional. She's about Tanya's age, mid-thirties, which seems young to be a headteacher.

'I heard about Alan,' says Steph as they sit down. 'What an awful thing to happen.'

'Did you work with Alan?' asks Tanya. 'I think you said you did.'

'Yes. I've been here five years. Alan retired three years ago. As I said on the phone, he was a popular teacher. We had a big party when he left. Lots of former students sent messages and cards.'

'Paul Noakes was one of his ex-pupils, wasn't he?'

'He was. I looked him up when you mentioned him. Alan taught Paul for GCSE and A level history. Paul was one of Alan's best pupils, I understand. He went on to study history at Bristol.'

'And there was never any suggestion that Alan had an inappropriate relationship with Paul?'

Steph sounds irritated now, a teacher whose class had tried her patience too far.

'As I told you when you asked before, there was never any allegation of inappropriate conduct. Our safeguarding procedures are very strict. Alan was a popular teacher and a responsible one. If he formed friendships with former pupils after they left school, that's a very different matter.'

'It's a bit unusual though, isn't it?'

'Maybe,' says Steph. 'But I understand that Alan and Paul mostly socialised through their mutual interest in archaeology.'

'And what about Neil Thomas? Did you work with him too?'

'No. Neil had left before I started.' Steph's voice, so warm when talking about Alan, cools several degrees. 'He left for medical reasons.'

'Medical reasons?'

'Some sort of breakdown, I believe. I think there was also some suggestion that he had let his pupils down academically. Taught them the wrong coursework. Something like that. As I say, it was before my time.'

And you don't want to talk about it, thinks Tanya. She remembers Neil in his posh kitchen, being ignored by his kids. She can imagine him getting his coursework muddled up.

'What about Nathan Matthews and Mark Hammond?' she says. 'I mentioned them on the phone too. Did Alan teach them?'

'The two police officers? Yes, I looked through the records. Alan taught both of them. They were in the same year and very close friends, apparently.'

'Did they know Paul Noakes? He was in the year above, wasn't he?'

'I asked Barry McNair, one of our older staff members, who remembers all three boys,' says Steph. 'Nathan and Mark weren't friends with Paul as far as he knew. In fact, he remembered that Mark and Paul had once had a fight.'

'Really?' says Tanya. 'What did they fight about?'

'Barry couldn't quite remember but he thought it was about a girl.'

It usually is, thinks Tanya.

24

Ruth thinks that Nelson looks tired. She supposes that he was called out in the middle of the night when Alan White's body was found. According to David, Cathbad 'had him on speed dial'. Why is David so hostile to Cathbad? And to Nelson too, for that matter.

For all his tiredness, Nelson still seems full of energy. He's pacing around the yard when Ruth turns up. It's a windy day and leaves are blowing across the concrete. On the roof of the house, the black weather vane is spinning.

'What's going to happen to the house now?' says Ruth.

'It's left to the children, Paul and Chloe. I suppose they'll sell it. I can't imagine either of them wanting to live here.'

'No, I can understand that. I suppose it might be hard to sell though if people associate it with a murder.'

'There was a suspicious death here before that,' says Nelson. 'A woman fell into a combine harvester. There were rumours that her husband pushed her.'

'Jesus,' says Ruth, 'no wonder the place has an atmosphere.'

'I've got a picture of the combine harvester couple,' says Nelson. 'They owned a large dog.'

Ruth looks at him. 'Do you think that could be the dog that's buried in the garden?'

'It's a possibility, wouldn't you say? The dog looks to be a Doberman, a big one. Can you identify the dog breed from the skeleton?'

'I could ask a zoo-archaeologist. Or a vet.'

'Could you? I'd like to know.'

'Shall I show you where we saw the dog the other day?'

'Yes, but I want to check something in the house first. Do you mind?'

It's strictly a rhetorical question because Nelson has already headed off towards the house. Ruth follows him. She doesn't want to go inside but she doesn't want to be outside on her own either.

The front door has been boarded up. Ruth wonders whether police had to break it down when they first entered the house. Police tape forms a forbidding X. Nelson, though, goes to a side entrance. He opens the door with a key. It's on his own fob which Ruth knows has a picture of his daughters attached to it. His two older daughters. It's one of the things that never fails to give her a stab of pain.

The door leads directly into a kitchen. It's one of the most depressing rooms that Ruth has ever seen: yellow lino, old pine cabinets, walls discoloured with grease. Yet it could be a charming country kitchen with a little effort – there are beams, a scarred oak table, an Aga. Maybe whoever buys the house will give it a makeover. At the moment, though, it's not just the outdated furnishings, it's the sense of sadness and dread that hangs over the space, floating in the dust motes and hovering in the air that smells of old cooking and something far more sinister. There's a brownish stain on the floor. Ruth hopes that it isn't blood. Even more chilling are the signs of recent habitation, a newspaper left open on the table and a cup beside it, now full of mould. Ruth supposes that the SOCO team will have examined these and then left them in place. She wonders whether Paul and Chloe have been into this room.

But Nelson doesn't seem to notice any of this. He strides over to a noticeboard where a Guide Dogs calendar hangs by a pin.

'Bingo,' he says.

'What?'

'We think that Jem Taylor, our body on the beach, may have been doing illegal drugs trials for Douglas Noakes. He wasn't on the records at Noakes's research company but he's here on the calendar. "J. Taylor Tuesday 17th 2pm." Jesus, that was probably the day he died. His body was found in the early hours on Wednesday. And look what's below him. "N. Matthews 8pm." That was the young policeman who died suddenly. He died on the Thursday.'

'And you think they died because the drugs trials went wrong?'

'It's certainly a possibility. There's a room in this house that's all done up like a doctor's surgery. Creepiest thing you've ever seen. I think Douglas Noakes was seeing his guinea pigs here. Funny, really, because he didn't let his children have guinea pigs. His daughter said he hated animals.'

'Then why did he have a calendar with dogs on it?'

'Very good, Ruth. I'll make a police officer of you yet.'

There are many replies that Ruth could make to this but, typically, Nelson doesn't wait to hear them. Nelson takes the calendar off the wall, folds it and puts it in his pocket. Obviously he's having no truck with keeping it sterile. Then he heads for the door without looking round. Ruth has no choice but to follow him. It's a relief to breathe in the gusty air after the fetid staleness of the kitchen.

'Now,' says Nelson, almost sniffing the air like a bloodhound. 'Where did you see this dog stuff?'

'In the barn at the front of the house.'

'Let's go, then.'

The double doors are still bolted shut but, as they skirt the wooden building, they see the back door propped open by a bucket.

'Was this there last time?' says Nelson, kicking it to one side.

'I don't know. Maybe. I can't remember.'

All she remembers is that she and David had left the barn very hastily. They had gone straight to their cars and driven away. She had almost been too scared to look in her driving mirror.

Now, with Nelson, she feels safer. He has a proper torch with him, not just a phone, and it sweeps the gloomy space like a searchlight. Ruth sees the ladder, the dinghy and the dog's bed and feeding bowl. This time there's food in the bowl.

'Looks like we're expecting company,' says Nelson.

Ruth looks around. Is that something moving in the shadows? She realises that she has moved closer to Nelson. He looks down at her. 'Don't worry, Ruth. I won't let the Black Shuck get you.'

'I'm not worried,' says Ruth. But she is, slightly. She likes dogs but she has never owned one. Deep down, she prefers cats. She doesn't want to face a devil hound with red eyes.

Nelson has moved across to the dinghy.

'Was this here last time?'

'Yes. I think so.'

Nelson squats down. 'There's seaweed on it. Did you notice if it was there last week? It's dry but it doesn't look brittle.'

'I didn't notice.' In all honesty, Ruth had only given the boat a cursory glance. But now she understands what Nelson is thinking.

'Do you think that the man on the beach . . . Jem . . . died here and his body was taken out to sea?'

'I don't know,' says Nelson, who is taking pictures of the boat. 'But I'd like to know how old this seaweed is.'

'My mum used to say that you could tell the weather from seaweed,' says Ruth, remembering. Her mother hadn't actually explained how the algae had managed to perform this trick. It was, like so many of her mother's statements, inexplicable and unanswerable.

'That sounds like the sort of thing my mum would say,' says Nelson.

Having met Maureen, Ruth can believe this. Kate says that

Nelson's mother is coming for Christmas. She doesn't seem to realise that this mythical being is also her only living grandmother.

Ruth is about to say something about mothers, grandmothers and their sayings when she hears a noise outside. Nelson has heard it too. He comes to her side.

There's a snuffling sound by the door and, a minute later, a large black shape enters the barn. At the same time, a gust of wind bangs the door shut.

They are locked in with the devil dog.

Nelson steps towards the creature, which strikes Ruth as very foolhardy.

'Hi there, fella.'

It's a large animal, jet black except for brown bits around its muzzle. A Doberman? A Rottweiler? Ruth is vague about dog breeds. It turns towards them – she's relieved to see that its eyes are brown not red – in a way that suggests puzzlement rather than aggression.

'Good boy,' says Nelson encouragingly.

The dog is clearly torn between wanting its food and suspicion of the strangers. Nelson is trying to skirt past the animal to get to the door. Ruth sticks close to him. Nelson reaches for the door handle. The dog growls.

'It's OK, boy.'

The dog watches as Nelson tries the door but, when he aims a kick at the wood, the animal bares its teeth.

'OK, OK.' Nelson backs away. He turns to Ruth. 'It's locked. The latch must have come down on the other side. It was held open with a bucket. Did I push it out of the way, do you remember?'

'I think so.'

'The wind must have swung the door shut. I could probably charge it but I don't want to upset our friend here.' He gestures towards the dog whose hackles are still up.

'Please don't,' says Ruth.

The dog is now edging towards its food. Nelson gestures at Ruth to stand still. She is only too happy to do so. She watches as the dog sniffs at the bowl, gives one last superstitious look towards the humans and then starts gobbling the food. There's a flash of light when Nelson takes a photo, but the animal doesn't seem to notice. Nelson reaches out a hand to Ruth, she takes it and they move slowly towards the door. Nelson rattles the handle again and squats down to try to see through the slats. Ruth keeps an eye on the dog who is still scoffing away noisily. Funny how it's endearing to hear animals eating loudly but horrific when it's humans.

Nelson looks round at her.

'The wood looks fairly rotten. I'm going to try and kick it down.'

'What about the dog?' Ruth hopes she doesn't sound as scared as she feels.

'He's busy eating at the moment.'

Nelson aims a kick at the door. The dog looks up, ears pricked. Nelson kicks again and the wood starts to give way. But the dog is growling. Nelson shoulder barges the door and the dog jumps forward. Moving incredibly quickly, Nelson shields Ruth with his body.

The dog is now facing them, crouched, ready to spring.

'Steady on, lad,' says Nelson.

The dog lies down, still watchful but, it seems to Ruth, less angry. Nelson and the dog stare at each other for a long moment.

Ruth hasn't been this close to Nelson in ages and, even at this moment, she notices. She can smell his aftershave and the fabric conditioner that someone – probably Michelle – puts on his shirts. She can feel him breathing, remarkably calmly. Her arms slide round his waist. She feels him catch his breath. Then, suddenly, they are framed in light as the door behind them opens.

'Who's there?' says a woman's voice.

The dog sees its chance and darts for freedom. Ruth lets go of Nelson and turns to see a small shape silhouetted in the doorway. Nelson seems to recognise it.

'Chloe,' he says.

'DCI Nelson,' says the woman. 'What are you doing here?'

'Checking out your devil dog,' says Nelson.

He moves towards the door and Ruth follows, embarrassed though she couldn't say why. In the open air, she looks around for the dog but he's nowhere to be seen. The wind is still whipping the trees into a frenzy and the weathervane continues to spin.

'I just came to look at the house,' says the woman. Chloe. 'To see what needs to be done before selling it.'

So this must be Chloe Noakes, one of the dead couple's children. Ruth thinks it's interesting that she feels she needs to explain herself to Nelson.

'This is Dr Ruth Galloway,' Nelson is saying.

'Hallo.' Chloe holds out her hand, unsmiling. 'You're the forensic archaeologist, aren't you? The one that excavated the garden.'

'That's right,' says Ruth. Chloe has a very direct manner. Not unfriendly, exactly, but rather challenging. She's small, a good few inches shorter than Ruth and much slighter, but she's still rather intimidating.

'Talking of dogs,' says Nelson, who does not seem intimidated, 'we've met the dog your parents kept in the barn. Seems that someone's still feeding him.'

'My parents didn't have any pets,' says Chloe. 'I told that to DS Fuller.'

'Come and see,' says Nelson. He leads the way back into the barn and shines his torch on the feeding bowl, now licked clean again, and the basket.

'You saw the dog just now. It ran straight past you. A Doberman cross, I would say. Nice animal.'

How Nelson can say this is beyond Ruth. It's as if he and the dog have been out for a male-bonding session at the pub.

'I've never seen that dog before,' says Chloe, sounding exasperated now.

'Not when you visited your parents?'

'I've told you. I visited them as little as possible.'

Nelson directs the torch towards the opposite end of the barn.

'Have you seen that boat before?'

'We went out in it sometimes when we were children,' says Chloe. 'Paul was keener on it than I was.'

'Do you know if anyone has used it recently?'

'No,' says Chloe. 'Why?'

Nelson doesn't answer and the three of them troop out into the light again. Chloe now seems preoccupied. She kicks at a pile of fallen leaves, her slight frame suddenly childlike.

'I heard about Alan,' she says at last. 'Paul told me. Do you know how he died?'

'It's an ongoing investigation,' says Nelson, at his most policeman-like.

There's another brief silence and then Chloe says, as if they are detaining her. 'If you'll excuse me. I've got things to do.' And she strides off towards the house. Nelson watches her go, looking thoughtful. Ruth checks her phone. Nearly six o'clock.

'I must go,' she says. 'I need to collect Kate.'

'It's been grand,' says Nelson. 'We must do this again.'

'Maybe without the mad dog,' says Ruth. But she thinks about this remark all the way back to her car.

25

Even though it's Saturday, the briefing room is full. Alan White's death is now officially a murder investigation and Nelson is increasingly convinced that Douglas and Linda Noakes were also killed by person or persons unknown. The Serious Crimes Unit is at full strength, with civilian officers seconded from other forces. Tanya, ever alert, sits at the front. Tony has one of those reusable coffee cups in front of him. And a yoghurt! Jesus wept. Once again, Nelson misses Clough, who would definitely have brought a McDonald's breakfast muffin.

Nelson asks Judy, as his number two, to update him on the previous day's interviews.

'We've spoken to all the Night Hawks,' says Judy. 'There were eight people there on Thursday night.' The names flash up on the screen.

David Brown
Darren Carter
Troy Evans

Ed Fitzherbert
Michael Malone (Cathbad)
Paul Noakes
Neil Thomas
Bryan Walker

Nelson's lips twitch at 'Michael Malone'. He doesn't think anyone ever calls Cathbad by his given name. Certainly, Judy doesn't. But she's right to put her partner on the list. He was an important witness.

Judy continues. 'Everyone we spoke to claimed to have got to the car park at midnight, the agreed meeting time. Everyone was in cars – except Troy Evans who was on a bike – so we might be able to trace them. All were members of the Night Hawks, except David Brown who was invited by Alan White. And Cathbad, of course.'

'What did you make of David Brown?' asks Nelson. 'He seemed quite hostile when I arrived at the scene.'

'He was polite enough to Tony and me,' says Judy. 'We spoke to him at the university. He said that he'd been at school with Alan. He seemed quite shaken at his death, kept saying that it must be an accident.'

'Not much hope of that,' says Nelson. The post-mortem has confirmed that Alan died from wounds consistent with blunt force trauma, i.e. being hit over the head with a heavy object.

'What about Neil Thomas?' says Nelson. 'He's another one who's been at the scene of the crime a few too many times.'

'He was obviously quite distressed,' says Judy. 'We spoke to him at his house. He said that he left for Cley at eleven forty p.m. and his wife can vouch for this. He also says that he spoke to Alan White that morning and that he seemed worried about something. Cathbad says the same. Alan asked him to come along on Thursday night for protection.'

Nelson recalls Cathbad saying something similar to him. 'He didn't say what he needed protecting from?'

'No.'

'I spoke to Steph Brice, the headteacher at Greenhill,' says Tanya. 'She said that Neil Thomas left the school after a mental breakdown. She also said that there'd been an issue with Neil teaching the wrong coursework, or something like that.'

'That doesn't make him a murderer,' says Judy.

'I didn't say it did,' says Tanya.

Nelson feels that he should step in. 'Neil Thomas was present, or close by, for all three deaths. I think we should keep an eye on him. Anything else from the Night Hawks, Judy? What about Troy Evans?'

'He arrived at the car park by bike at a few minutes to midnight,' says Judy. 'He lives with his parents although they were apparently both in bed when he left. He says that he hadn't seen Alan since the night they found Jem Taylor's body.'

'Did Troy know the Noakes family?' asks Nelson.

'Not as far as I know,' says Judy. 'Why?'

'Well, he's a fisherman and there's a boat in the Noakes's barn. I saw it there yesterday. I just wondered if Jem Taylor could have died at the farm and then his body taken out to sea. Troy was a similar age to Jem. There might be a link there.'

'I'll look into it,' says Judy.

'And get someone from SOCO to look at the boat,' says Nelson. 'There's seaweed on it. I'm sure there's a seaweed expert somewhere if we look hard enough.'

'Cathbad eats a lot of seaweed,' says Judy. 'He says it's a good source of protective antioxidants.'

'You don't surprise me,' says Nelson. 'I had a look at the calendar in the kitchen at Black Dog Farm. Douglas Noakes had appointments with Jem Taylor and Nathan Matthews. There are other names on the calendar too. Tony, you can go through and check them out. It'll take your mind off eating yoghurt. And we need to make a proper search of that room, the one done up like a doctor's surgery. There's a filing cabinet and a safe. We need to look inside. Clough says the word on the street is that Noakes was paying ex-cons to do illegal drugs trials for him. If that's true, then we need to talk to everyone involved. I'm going to talk to Nathan Matthew's fiancée this afternoon.'

'Do you want me to talk to her?' says Judy. 'I talked to Jem's girlfriend.'

'I'll do it,' says Nelson. 'I can be sensitive too, you know.'

No one contradicts him but Judy exchanges a look with Tanya, something that only happens on the rarest of occasions.

Ruth is having a relaxing Saturday. When Kate was younger, Ruth used to fill the day with activities: swimming, soft-play centres, the cinema. She supposes that she was trying to make up for the wholesome, two-parent family life that she believed Kate was missing. And, also, weekends can be very lonely when you're a single parent, with no one to share a bottle of wine with on Friday evening, or order a takeway on Saturday night. Now things are a little different. On Saturdays Kate usually has an invitation to a party or a playdate and just requires a chauffeur service there and back. Ruth passes the time in between drinking coffee in cafés or browsing the shelves at Waterstones in King's Lynn. And the evenings aren't so lonely because Kate stays up and shares the take-away with her. They usually watch a film on Saturday night and spend Sunday variously doing homework. Ruth is finding the head of department paperwork quite daunting.

This Saturday morning Ruth is at Lynn museum. She remembers telling David Brown that he should visit the place and rather hopes that he won't decide to do so today. The museum has an unprepossessing exterior, situated on the outskirts of a concrete shopping mall, but, inside, the seahenge display is magical, with huge photographs of the marshes in all their glory. The timbers themselves are behind glass. Given pride of place is the upside-down tree stump found in the centre of the circle, thought by some – including Cathbad – to be a reference to the Norse legend of the World Tree, Yggdrasil. Here it looks almost like the tail of some vast sea-creature, or perhaps a mermaid, disappearing beneath the water. Ruth remembers Cathbad talking about the Norfolk Sea Serpent, that Friday when they went for a pizza. Maybe this is what's represented here?

Ruth goes to sit in the story-telling area where there's a reconstruction of the central tree. She looks at it dreamily, thinking about the significance of the henge in her life. It was the archaeological dig that brought her to Norfolk, that introduced her to Cathbad and, later, to Nelson. Without these timbers – these sacred pieces of bog oak – she would never have had her beloved daughter, would probably not have her job in the university, might even now be living in some soulless city somewhere.

She jumps when her phone buzzes. Maybe Kate has been hurt – she's at a wall-climbing party – or maybe Ruth's father is ill. But the name David Brown flashes ominously onto the screen. What is he doing invading her space again?

'Hallo, David.'

'Hi, Ruth. What are you doing?'

Ruth is tempted to make something up. 'Can't talk now, I'm white-water rafting.' 'Better be quick. I'm attending a black mass and they've just got to the human sacrifice . . .'

Instead she says, 'I'm at Lynn museum.' Let David think she's at a high-level meeting with the curator if he wants.

This is clearly not what he thinks. 'Is Kate with you?'

Ruth is surprised that he has remembered her daughter's name. 'I'm just about to pick her up,' she says.

'It's just . . .' David hesitates so long that she wonders if the connection is lost. But no, he's still there. 'I've got Maja with me. She really loves the cottage. I was thinking of taking her to see the seals at Blakeney Point.'

'Good idea,' says Ruth, hearing herself sounding bracing. A boat trip to the seals is a great way to spend the afternoon though she does wonder why David would want to go near a place where, only yesterday, he saw the dead body of his friend.

'The thing is,' says David, 'would you and Kate like to come too? It'll be more fun for Maja with another child her age.'

While David is talking, Ruth is heading towards the exit. She doesn't want to be late for pick-up, a heinous crime in motherland. Now she stops in the middle of the gift shop, staring at a plastic replica of the henge, encased in a snow globe.

'Please, Ruth.'

Why on earth does David want their company so much? Ruth is not very keen on boats, having once had a terrifying experience on the friendly Norfolk Broads. She had planned to take Kate for a pizza and then head home. But, on the other hand, Kate does love the seals.

'OK,' she says. 'Meet you at Blakeney Harbour in an hour.'

26

David is waiting for them by a jetty with a sign for Evans Boats. He's accompanied by a very blonde child, slightly smaller than Kate, and dressed in jeans and a yellow waterproof jacket.

Kate tugs at Ruth's sleeve. 'Mum, what if she doesn't speak English? Do you speak Swedish?'

'She will,' says Ruth. She's always embarrassed by the fluency of her Scandinavian colleagues. She doesn't speak any language other than English, despite having an A level in French.

David is looking at his phone but Ruth decides not to condemn him for bad parenting. Not yet, anyhow. He looks up when they approach, crunching over the pebbles.

'Ruth! Hi, Kate. This is Maja.'

'Hallo,' says Maja. 'I can't wait to see the seals.' She speaks perfect English with only a trace of an accent. And she's only ten! Ruth feels inadequate all over again.

'Want to watch a TikTok video on my phone?' says Kate to Maja. It's not quite the wholesome outdoor activity that

Ruth had in mind but she's pleased to see the dark and fair heads bent together over the screen. David, too, smiles almost benignly.

'Thanks for coming, Ruth,' he says. 'It's so much easier with other people.'

What's so much easier? wonders Ruth. Spending time with his own child? But, all the same, she thinks she knows what he means. It's exhausting being the only adult, even if you're used to it. It's exhausting playing games or pretending to like TikTok videos. It's exhausting thinking of meals and activities, being the one who knows all the timetables and schedules, who makes the packed lunches and books the tickets. This reminds her that she hasn't paid for the boat excursion.

'It's OK,' says David. 'The boat belongs to a friend of mine.'

Ruth notices, for the first time, that there are queues at the jetties belonging to other boat companies, but not at the Evans sign.

'Troy's taking us out privately,' says David. 'It's not one of his official trips.'

Troy. Where has Ruth heard that name before? Oh yes, he's one of the Night Hawks. The one who first found the body on the beach.

As he's speaking, a young man sprints along the jetty and jumps lightly into the boat. Ruth notices the vessel's name for the first time, *The Sheringham Mermaid*. Didn't David say something about this mythical creature once? Something about her coming out of the sea to listen to a sermon? But there's no time to ask now. Troy hands out lifejackets to the four of them. Ruth helps Kate tie hers up, remembering that mantra from inflight safety demonstrations, 'make sure your own oxygen mask is securely fitted before helping children.' But surely it's only natural to make sure your child is safe before you are? Maja is fitting hers efficiently, without needing help from David.

When they're onboard, Troy issues brisk instructions ('keep one hand on the boat at all times') and takes the tiller. The boat glides out of the harbour and starts to skirt the sandbanks. The sea, which looked millpond smooth from the land, is choppier here and occasionally waves break over the sides of the boat, delighting both the girls. Ruth, who is dressed for museum visiting and not seafaring, soon finds her jacket quite soaked.

In the distance, Ruth can see the blue lifeboat house at Blakeney Point. She remembers walking there with David, the day Jem Taylor's body was found, the islands of sand and seagrass linked by lagoons of blue water, the birds rising into the air at their approach. It's a beautiful landscape, but a slightly eerie one, home to countless sea creatures, somehow inhospitable to humans.

'Seals,' says Troy. 'Over there.'

Ruth realises that the grey rocks at the water's edge are, in fact, seals, sunning themselves on the sand. Kate and Maja squeal with delight.

'The grey seals are larger and have speckles on them,' says Troy. 'The common seals have rounder heads. Grey seals are actually more common than the common seals.' It sounds as if this is part of his official spiel.

'Are there any baby seals?' asks Kate.

'Not yet,' says Troy. 'Pups are mainly born between November and January. The western end of the point is sealed off then.'

Ruth tries to take a picture but it's hard to capture the charm of the bulky grey shapes with their strangely smiling faces. David is standing beside Troy at the tiller. Ruth is suddenly aware of the two men talking in lowered voices.

'. . . asking about Alan's death . . .'

'. . . two of them . . .'

'. . . Judy Johnson . . .'

'. . . didn't tell them anything, did you?'

Ruth's antennae are immediately on alert. Why is David checking that Troy didn't tell the police anything? What is there to tell? She looks back at the expanse of blue-green water between them and the shore. She and Kate are on a boat with two men they hardly know. Why has David lured them here? And what about Troy, who suddenly looks burly and threatening rather than muscular and competent? Troy found the first body, the man Nelson initially thought was an asylum seeker. Could he be linked with this second death? There must be something sinister going on, otherwise why would the two men be talking about hiding information from the police?

Instinctively, Ruth clutches hold of Kate, who wriggles free. Maja and Kate are excitedly taking pictures, running from side to side, snapping wildly with their phones.

'Be careful, girls,' says David. His voice sounds so exactly normal, a father worried about his child's safety – as Nelson always is – that Ruth finds herself feeling soothed.

David comes to stand next to her. 'OK, Ruth?'

Troy is pointing out a couple of seals flopping into the sea. The ungainly creatures transform themselves into sleek water nymphs. Maybe this is where the myth of the Sheringham mermaid comes from, thinks Ruth.

'I'm OK,' says Ruth.

'Quite something, isn't it?' says David.

And Ruth, eyes stinging from sea spray and from the sight of the wondrous amphibious animals, agrees that it is quite something.

Judy is talking to a seaweed expert. More specifically, she is talking to Sumaira Smith, a bioscientist at UNN, a contact given to her by Ruth.

'I've looked at the photographs,' says Sumaira, 'and the seaweed on your boat is rhodophyta and chlorophyta, both found in profusion on the north Norfolk coast. The chlorophyta is sometimes known as gutweed. It's got a very strong scent.'

Judy remembers the boss moaning about the smell of the beach at Blakeney Point.

'Can you tell how old it is?' she asks.

'Not with any accuracy. From the picture it looks quite fresh, it hasn't dried out completely.'

'What about the barnacles?'

'Barnacles take at least three days to become attached to a seaborne object,' says Sumaira. 'So these might have been there a while. They do prove that the boat was in salt water, though, rather than fresh.'

'Is there anything else?' says Judy. 'I appreciate that you can't tell much from a few photographs.'

'Only that these types of seaweed are usually found close to the shore, which means that the boat didn't go very far out or that it was moored on the beach for some time.'

'Thank you,' says Judy. 'You've been very helpful.'

'No problem. Give my regards to Ruth.'

This means that the boat in the barn at Black Dog Farm had definitely been in the sea fairly recently. That's something, thinks Judy, though it wouldn't get them very far with the CPS. What next? She looks at her list of the Night Hawks.

David Brown
Darren Carter
Troy Evans
Ed Fitzherbert
Michael Malone (Cathbad)
Paul Noakes
Neil Thomas
Bryan Walker

David is a lecturer at the university, Darren is a carpenter and Troy a fisherman. Ed, Paul and Bryan are all teachers and Neil is an IT consultant. Is there anything else that this group have in common? The men range in age from Ed at fifty-eight to Troy at twenty-one. They are all local to the area. Troy, Paul and Darren are ex-pupils of Alan's, Ed and Neil were his colleagues. Where does Bryan teach?

Judy looks back through her notes. Bryan Walker teaches at St Luke's Primary. And Judy sees a school playground and Selina Spencer, a smiling figure in her wine-coloured trouser suit. *There was only me, Linda and Bryan in the oldies club.*

She has her link.

Ruth's legs feel quite wobbly when she steps out onto the jetty. She's only been at sea for an hour and already she's forgotten how to walk. How on earth do round-the-world sailors manage it? Kate and Maja run ahead, unaffected by seasickness. The two girls seem to have developed a friendship in that miraculous way that children do sometimes. Ruth turns around to thank Troy for the trip but he's already striding away across the beach.

'Thank you!' Ruth shouts after him. Troy raises his hand in a laconic salute.

'Did you enjoy it?' asks David. Ruth stumbles on the pebbles and David steadies her.

'Very much,' says Ruth, extracting herself. She doesn't want to be helped along like an old lady. 'It was kind of Troy to take us. I hope it wasn't too upsetting after yesterday.'

She's fishing but without a boat.

'Poor Alan,' says David. He's frowning in a way that's now familiar. Ruth thinks he's going to say more but, suddenly, his face clears. 'Fancy some fish and chips?' he says.

It's only three o'clock. Ruth should go home and do some work. She's still disturbed by the comment she overheard on the boat. But Kate and Maja have come to halt by a small café with a giant plastic crab in front of it. The blue and white awning flaps in the breeze and a delicious smell of frying batter floats towards them.

'Oh, all right then,' says Ruth.

Despite his claims of sensitivity, Nelson is finding the interview with Nathan's fiancée hard going. Faye Wilson meets him at the shoe shop where she works. Her sympathetic employer allows them to talk in the stockroom, which smells of leather. Shoeboxes surround them, all apparently named after girls: Nancy, Jessica, Emily and Tara. Faye sits on a low stool and weeps when she talks about Nathan. Nelson is used to tears – he has three daughters, after all – but now he can't do the bracing 'cheer up, love' routine that works at home. All he can do is pass Faye tissues and hope that the tide turns soon.

'Nathan always wanted to be a policeman,' says Faye, pressing a tissue against her eyes.

'Me too,' says Nelson. 'But it doesn't pay that well, does it? Not in the early days.' He thinks again of Jo calculating how many new recruits she could snaffle for the cost of one aging DCI.

'No,' says Faye, sniffing.

'Is that why Nathan did the drugs trials at Black Dog Farm?' asks Nelson, as gently as possible.

Faye looks at him, wide-eyed. 'How did you . . .?'

'We're looking into recent events at the farm,' says Nelson. 'Including the appointments at the surgery.'

'Of course,' says Faye. 'That's where the shooting was. I've hardly looked at the news recently.'

'I don't blame you,' says Nelson. 'Can you tell me anything about the drugs trial?'

'It was all above-board,' says Faye. 'It was with a proper doctor and everything. Nathan just didn't tell his parents about it because they'd worry. And also because he got to hear of it from a man he'd arrested.'

'Jem Taylor?'

'I can't remember the name. This man said that he'd been doing these trials for weeks. You just had to have an injection and make of note of how you felt. And it paid really good money. We were saving ... we were saving to get married.' And the tears fall again.

'Can you remember what this trial was about?'

'No,' says Faye. 'But it wasn't anything serious. The flu, Nathan says. And you can't die of flu, can you?'

You can, thinks Nelson, and Nathan did. But he just thanks Faye for her time and stands up to leave. Faye remains sitting, surrounded by Nancy, Jessica, Emily and the rest of the girls.

Ruth likes the café. There's vinegar on the tables and ketchup in tomato-shaped bottles. The fish and chips come in pretend newspaper and there are framed seaside postcards on the walls. Depressingly sexist, of course, but in keeping with the retro feel.

The girls talk about school. Kate is thrilled at the thought of summer camp and asks Ruth if she can go to one.

'I don't think they have them in England,' says Ruth. 'Not unless you're a Girl Guide or something.'

'Can I be a Girl Guide then?'

'If you like.' Ruth's mother was a Guider. Ruth remembers a picture of her in uniform, bristling with badges. Well, maybe it's different these days. Less bowing to the Queen, more feminism.

'I was a Boy Scout for a while,' says David. 'It was more or less compulsory at West Runton.' His face falls again, as it always does when he mentions the past. Or perhaps he's thinking about Alan White, his old schoolfriend.

'My mother was keen on the Guides,' says Ruth, 'but then she was keen on religion too. I suppose the two are linked in my mind.'

'You're not religious then?' says David, shaking vinegar onto his chips.

'No,' says Ruth. 'I'm glad my parents had the comfort of it though. And the church helped my dad a lot after my mum died.'

'Granddad's getting married at Christmas,' says Kate. 'I'm going to be a bridesmaid.'

Maja asks what a bridesmaid is, and Kate explains at length.

'My father married again after my mother died,' says David. 'I remember thinking: I just hope it makes him happier. And it did, I think.'

'Is your father still alive?' asks Ruth. She realised recently that this is now her first question when people of her age mention their parents.

'Yes,' says David. 'He lives in Ireland. His second wife is much younger and so my half-brothers are only in their early twenties. They're nice enough but I don't feel as if they've got much to do with me.'

David is a loner, thinks Ruth. There's something about him that reminds her of Cathbad, even though Cathbad is now moored by a partner and family. But, in David, you can see the traces of the lonely child, even now when he's laughing and relaxed, in the company of his daughter.

When they've finished eating, David and Maja walk Ruth and Kate to their car.

'What are you going to do tonight?' David asks Ruth.

'Work,' says Ruth. 'I always thought Phil was exaggerating about the paperwork but he wasn't.'

'Phil was your predecessor?'

'That's right. Phil Trent. I think you met his wife, Shona, the other day. She teaches English at UNN.'

'The beautiful redhead? Yes, I remember.'

This description irritates Ruth although it is the literal truth.

'We're going to play Monopoly tonight,' says Maja.

'It's not much of a game with two,' says David.

For a moment Ruth thinks he's going to ask them to join them and hastily starts to formulate excuses, starting with work and ending up with 'I don't trust you because you're hiding something from the police.'

'Goodbye,' she says, in a tone which she hopes combines friendliness with finality. 'Thank you for asking us.' David looks as if he's going to say something but in the end just raises his hand.

'Bye, Ruth.'

The girls are promising to keep in touch. They are still waving when Ruth puts the car into gear and drives away.

It's a beautiful early evening, the marshes glittering with secret water, birds rising up out of the grass, practising their migratory manoeuvres. Back at the cottage, Kate wanders off to find Flint, and Ruth opens her laptop. She clicks onto the latest NSS student experience surveys but these always make her depressed, even if they are broadly positive. She's sure that the correspondent who said they had 'no contact time' must be lying but she'll still be held responsible if this puts her course below the university average. She should look at student numbers for 2020, but instead she googles 'The Sheringham Mermaid'. She finds an article from the *Eastern Daily Press* entitled 'Weird Norfolk'.

The 5th-century pews in the 900-year-old church of All Saints in Upper Sheringham tell the fishy tale of an unusual visitor to the village who has left her mark on this corner of north Norfolk for all to see.

There, on the bench end of the pew closest to the north door, is a not-so-little mermaid, a formidable-looking siren of the sea immortalised in carved wood.

Legend has it that the mermaid was drawn to the church from more than a mile away by the sound of heavenly singing and, despite the encumbrance of a tail, dragged herself laboriously from beach to churchyard.

With the service still in full swing, the church beadle unceremoniously slammed the door in the face of the sea princess, leaving her floundering outside.

'Git yew arn out, we carn't have noo marmeards in 'are,' the Beadle hissed.

But mermaids are made of stern stuff and a mile and a half is too far to slither without a sit-down – as soon as she was able, she crept into the back of the church and can still be found there today.

Ruth thinks of the seals today, so awkward on land, so lithe and graceful in the water. She thinks of the Sheringham mermaid dragging herself up from the beach with her 'encumbrance of a tail'. She remembers reading somewhere that *The Little Mermaid* by Hans Christian Andersen is an allegory about puberty. When the mermaid develops legs, every step is like 'walking on knives'. She has no voice either, Ruth seems to remember, having traded her tongue for legs. Of course, in the stories, mermaids are meant to enjoy singing, hence the Sheringham sea princess being so enchanted by the church choir. Erik had many tales about sea sprites whose unearthly music lured men to their deaths. Maybe those were also warnings about avoiding the dangerous sexuality of women. Unlike the Disney version, there's no happy ending for Andersen's mermaid. She dies and becomes sea foam, a kind of purgatory, neither life nor death.

Ruth thinks again about the conversation she heard between Alan and Troy, the skipper of *The Sheringham Mermaid*. Then she gets out her phone and rings Nelson.

'Ruth,' says Nelson loudly. It sounds like he's in the car. He always thinks that he has to shout when on the hands-free setting. 'What the matter?'

'Nothing's the matter,' says Ruth, wondering if this is true. 'Kate and I have just been to Blakeney Point to see the seals.'

'That bloody place,' says Nelson. 'I'd be happy never to go there again.'

'Kate likes the seals,' says Ruth, 'as you know. Anyway, we went with David Brown, my colleague from the university. He's got a daughter Kate's age.'

'I didn't know you were so chummy with him,' says Nelson.

'I'm not chummy with him,' says Ruth. She tells herself not to be defensive. She can spend her Saturdays any way she likes. She takes a calming breath. 'David suggested it. He wanted some company for Maja, his daughter. Anyway, that's not the point. The point is that we went out on a boat owned by a man called Troy Evans. He's one of the Night Hawks. You know, the ones who go around at night trampling on archaeological sites.'

'I know Evans,' says Nelson.

'It's probably nothing but I heard Troy and David talking. They said something about being interviewed by the police and David said, "You didn't tell them anything, did you?"'

'Interesting,' says Nelson. 'Very interesting.'

'Like I say, it's probably nothing,' says Ruth.

'But it might be something,' says Nelson. 'Thank you for letting me know. Can I say hallo to Katie?'

'I'll get her. She's upstairs with Flint.'

'I think she prefers that bloody cat to me.'

And, if she does, sometimes Ruth doesn't blame her.

*

After a lively chat with Katie about seals and cats, Nelson thinks about David Brown for the rest of the way home. He'd disliked him from the start, had thought him the sort of bespectacled smart Alec who writes letters to the *Guardian* about police incompetence but calls them in pretty quickly if his second home gets burgled. Ruth had seemed to find David irritating that day, but she'd probably thought the same about him when they first met and look where that led to. But that's not the important thing here. He wrenches his thoughts away with an effort. No, the important thing is that David talked to Troy about potentially concealing evidence. Is this linked to Alan White's death or to the events at Black Dog Farm? Do either of the men know about the illegal drugs trials that potentially killed Jem Taylor and Nathan Matthews? Either way, the Night Hawks clearly have something to hide.

It's six o'clock when Nelson reaches the cul-de-sac. He hears voices from the garden and finds his wife and daughter drinking Prosecco on the patio. George is playing on his trampoline, watched anxiously by Bruno.

'We never had a trampoline,' says Laura, by way of greeting.

'No one had trampolines then,' says Nelson, bending to kiss her. 'You and Rebecca had a treehouse. I remember putting it up.' He'd put his back out, he recalls, and missed a five-a-side football tournament. Frank bought Katie a trampoline last year. Nelson had been furious at the time but now Frank is back in America, where he belongs, and the trampoline is in Ruth's tiny back garden, taking up all the lawn.

'How's school?' Nelson asks, pulling a chair next to Laura's sunlounger. Michelle brings him a beer. Suddenly all is right in his world.

'OK,' says Laura. She teaches at a primary school in Lynn. It's hard work but she seems to love it. Nelson often worries about his oldest daughter. Is she happy? Is she too thin? Is she seeing an unsuitable man? But, at present, Laura seems content with her job and her flatmates. There's no man on the horizon and her legs, in faded blue jeans, look slim rather than skinny. Laura is the daughter who looks most like Michelle, with long blonde hair, now in a careless pony-tail, and the same effortless elegance. Rebecca is dark but she, too, favours her mother. Katie is probably the only one who looks like him. Much prettier though.

Laura and Rebecca know about Katie and see her often but, by tacit agreement, they don't talk about her at home.

'Mum says you've got a murder case,' says Laura. She's also the only member of his family who is really interested in his work.

'Yes,' says Nelson, taking a long swig of beer. 'Man found on the beach at Blakeney Point.'

'Blakeney Point! I used to love going to see the seals there. Remember, Mum?'

'I remember that time it was rough and your dad was sick.'

'That was something I ate,' says Nelson. But the truth is that he – like Ruth – is not a fan of boats.

'What about the other case?' says Laura. 'The couple found in the farmhouse? Was that murder?'

'It's still an ongoing investigation,' says Nelson.

'That means yes,' says Laura. 'I went to that house once.'

'What?' Nelson turns so violently that he knocks his beer over. Bruno barks reprovingly. 'You went to that house? When?'

'When I was at school. A whole group of us went to a party there. I think the parents were away. It was a bloody spooky place.'

Nelson turns to Michelle. 'Did you know about this?'

'I don't remember it,' says Michelle. 'Laura went to so many parties. How old would you have been, Laura?'

'About sixteen. It was when I was going out with Lee.'

'Whose party was it?' says Nelson. 'Paul's?'

Paul Noakes is thirty-one. Laura – incredibly – is twenty-eight. It's not impossible that they knew each other at school.

'No, it was his sister,' says Laura. 'Chloe, I think her name was. She was older and at university. I remember there had been some scandal at school because she was having an affair with a teacher.'

'Her history teacher?' says Nelson, thinking of Douglas Noakes's words to Alan White. *You're corrupting my son. You're a disgrace to the profession.* Maybe it was his daughter that Alan was corrupting.

'No,' says Laura. 'IT, I think. One of those subjects anyway.'

27

'Neil Thomas?' says Judy. 'He was having an affair with Chloe Noakes?'

'It's a definite possibility,' says Nelson. 'Laura said it was an IT teacher.'

'There are probably lots of IT teachers at Greenhill,' says Tanya. 'It's a big school.'

'All the same,' says Nelson. 'It's worth checking. Do you want to talk to him again, Tanya, as he knows you?'

'OK,' says Tanya. 'I wouldn't say we exactly hit it off, though.'

'I'll talk to Chloe,' says Judy. 'I've spoken to her a few times although I wouldn't say we'd built up a rapport either, exactly.'

'She was at the farm the other day,' says Nelson. 'She wants to put the place on the market.'

'That's fair enough, I suppose,' says Judy.

'Yes,' says Nelson, 'but remember what Chloe said to Tanya about remortgaging? I wonder if she's short of money. Might be worth trying to find out. We can't look at her accounts without an information order, but we could ask a few questions.'

'Was the farm left equally to Paul and Chloe?' asks Tony.

'Yes,' says Nelson. 'We've had a copy of the will. Douglas and Linda left everything to each other but, in the event of them both dying, the house and the share of the firm are left to Paul and Chloe.'

'The shares must be worth something,' says Judy. 'Cambridge Bioresearch seemed to be a thriving business.'

'Yes,' says Nelson. 'Maybe you should go back and talk to the director again. What was her name? Something Italian?'

'Claudia Albertini,' says Judy. 'And she's Swiss.'

'Check to see if Paul and Chloe had any dealings with the firm that we don't know about,' says Nelson. 'We know that Chloe did work experience there, but it might be interesting if either of them paid attention to the company accounts, for example.'

'Are they serious suspects then?' says Tony. He's sitting up very straight, notebook and reusable coffee mug in front of him. Nelson can tell he's enjoying every minute.

'Everyone's a suspect,' says Nelson. 'We've taken Chloe and Paul's fingerprints – officially to eliminate them from the scene – and it will be interesting to see where they crop up around the house. And there's no denying that they do have a motive, whether it's money or revenge for childhood ill-treatment.'

'Neither of them has an alibi,' says Judy. 'Both claim to have been alone in their respective houses on the night of their parents' deaths.'

'We need to talk to them again,' says Nelson. 'And I've also heard something suspicious about two of the Night Hawks, David Brown and Troy Evans.' He tells them the conversation that Ruth overheard. He watches Judy and Tanya when he says Ruth's name but neither of them reacts. Judy is writing in her notebook and Tanya has her intense 'super sleuth' face on.

'We can't say who gave us this information,' says Nelson. 'But I think it's worth talking to these characters again. Tony, you talk to Troy. He might respond to another youngster.'

'I'm twenty-five,' says Tony, sounding hurt.

'Exactly,' says Nelson.

'I think I've found another link,' says Judy. 'Bryan Walker – one of the Night Hawks who was there the other night – taught at the same school as Linda Noakes. He's got no connection to Black Dog Farm that I can see but it's a bit of a coincidence.'

'It is indeed,' says Nelson. 'Maybe we've been thinking too much about Douglas and ignoring Linda.'

'Sounds as if everyone did that when they were alive too,' says Judy.

'Go and see this Bryan Walker again, Judy,' says Nelson. 'See what he can tell us about Linda. But for today let's concentrate on Neil Thomas and Chloe Noakes. And I think I'll have a little chat with David Brown.'

He's looking forward to it.

'It's Sunday,' says Neil Thomas, as Tanya approaches. And Neil is engaged in that most Sunday-ish of activities, washing his car. He's making a proper job of it, with hose and sponges and a portable hoover for the inside. When she was young, Tanya's father used to give her two pounds for washing his car, but she can't imagine that the two spoilt teenagers she glimpsed last time are so easily bought.

'I've just got a few questions,' says Tanya. 'Is there somewhere private that we can talk?'

Neil shoots her a look that could be irritation or could be fear.

'It's not a good time,' he says. 'Alison's cooking lunch.'

A traditional family. Mummy cooking Sunday roast, Daddy washing the car. It's like a Ladybird book, or a David Lynch film. Something sinister anyway.

'It'll only take a few minutes,' says Tanya.

Neil leads her into the house, past the kitchen, which is wafting rather wonderful roast beef vapours, and into a study bristling with technology. Tanya sits between the wide screen TV and the drum deck. Neil takes what looks like a gaming chair with lumbar support for those long hours at Grand Theft Auto.

'Mr Thomas,' says Tanya. 'What exactly was your relationship with Chloe Noakes?'

One look at his face is enough.

'It's not what you think,' says Chloe Noakes.

Judy knows better than to react to this. They are sitting in Chloe's quayside apartment in King's Lynn. Water reflections ripple on the ceiling.

'I'd left school,' says Chloe. 'There was nothing illegal

about it. We didn't get together until the summer after A levels.'

This doesn't change the fact that Neil Thomas was married with two children and had, just a few months earlier, been one of Chloe's teachers. But Judy stays quiet.

'He was so different from my other boyfriends,' says Chloe. 'They were schoolboys, all spotty and jealous. Neil was cool. Or so he seemed to me.'

'How long did your relationship continue?' asks Judy.

'Just for that summer,' says Chloe. 'It petered out when I went to university in Manchester.'

'Did you stay in touch?' asks Judy.

'Not really. We didn't have WhatsApp and all that stuff then.'

But you had email, thinks Judy, and Facebook. Plenty of ways to maintain an illicit relationship. She should know. She remembers how, when she was married to Darren, her heart used to jump when she saw a text or an email from Cathbad. And Cathbad has since told her that he used to gaze for hours at the Google Maps image of Judy and Darren's house.

'You didn't mention this relationship when we asked you about Neil Thomas before,' says Judy.

'Of course not!' says Chloe. 'Paul was there. He didn't know anything about it.'

Judy wouldn't be too sure about that. After all, Laura Nelson knew and she was five years younger and at a different school. These things get out. She wonders if the rumours had anything to do with Neil's early retirement from teaching. All the same, she thinks it's interesting that Chloe still wants the affair kept from her brother.

'Have you seen Neil recently?' she asks.

'No,' says Chloe. 'He's happy with his wife and two point four kids.'

There's definitely some bitterness there, thinks Judy. She decides to push a little further.

'Neil Thomas was near Black Dog Farm the night your parents were killed,' she says.

'He had an alibi,' says Chloe. 'He was with Alan White.'

Judy thinks of something the boss said once. *Who needs alibis? Guilty people.*

Nelson is not sure what he's expecting when he drives into Stiffkey looking for David Brown's house. A mansion? A slum? But what he finds is a tiny, terraced cottage, flint-faced with a low tiled roof. The front gate leads into a sunny patio and there sits Brown himself, reading the *Observer*, and a blonde girl, about Katie's age, busy with a sketchbook.

Nelson had known about the daughter but the sight of her brings him up short. Brown looks up from his paper.

'DCI Nelson,' he says. 'What are you doing here?'

'Can I have a quick word?' says Nelson.

David Brown stands up. Nelson is conscious of the unusual sensation of feeling slightly in the wrong. David Brown is enjoying a quiet morning with his daughter. There's no real reason why Nelson's questions can't wait until Monday. Brown is looking very belligerent. He's also slightly taller than Nelson, which doesn't happen often.

'No, you can't have a word,' says Brown, moving towards him. 'This is police harassment.'

'I'm conducting a murder inquiry,' says Nelson, not budging. The girl looks up at the word 'murder' which, again, makes him feel a little guilty.

'I'm not talking to you without my lawyer present,' says Brown. And he goes back to his chair and picks up his paper, shaking it with a flourish.

There's nothing Nelson can do but retreat. When he looks back Brown is hidden behind the *Observer* but the girl gives him a timid, tentative wave.

28

When Ruth gets into work on Monday, she finds some interesting emails waiting for her: the results of the carbon-14 and isotope tests on the Blakeney Point skeleton. The C14 dating puts the bones between three thousand five hundred and four thousand years old. Ruth smiles when she thinks how unsatisfactory Nelson would find this margin but radiocarbon dating can be skewed by all sorts of things, including solar flares and sunspots. The important thing is that these results place the skeleton firmly in the Bronze Age. Even more interesting is the isotope analysis which seems to show that the bones belonged to someone who grew up somewhere in central Europe.

She must tell David. This fits with his Beaker invader theory. She forwards the emails and, a few minutes later, a dark shape appears in the glass panel of her door. It's only at this moment that Ruth remembers her call to Nelson on Saturday, after the seal trip. At the time she had told herself that Nelson needed to know about the conversation on the boat. Now she feels like a traitor. Will her suspicions have been enough to send Nelson to David's door? If so, she hopes he kept her name out of it.

'David,' she says, with unnecessary heartiness. 'Did you see the lab results?'

'Yes,' he says, with his lopsided grin. 'I told you that he was a Beaker.'

'They think he was a he too,' says Ruth. The lab had examined five points on the head and come to the conclusion that the skeleton was eighty per cent likely to be male. But Ruth had already made up her own mind about this. From the long bones, pelvis and shape of the skull, she is sure that their skeleton is a man and a tall, handsome one at that.

'It's interesting too that he was found with weapons around him,' she says. 'That's unusual for a Bronze Age burial. I wonder if Cathbad was right about him being someone high status like a king or a priest.'

'Is Cathbad an archaeologist?' This is said with a definite edge. Hostile energy again.

'He studied archaeology,' she says. 'He's actually very knowledgeable. Have you looked at the isotope analysis?'

'Strontium isotope levels point to him being from as far east as Poland,' says David. 'Incredible to think that he had travelled all this way.'

'Only to die on a Norfolk beach,' says Ruth. She thinks of her feelings when she first saw the body of the young man discovered by the Night Hawks. That was when they had thought he was an 'illegal immigrant', to use Nelson's words. How sad, she'd thought, to come all these miles in search of a better life, only to end up lying dead on foreign sand. She thinks the same about their Bronze Age man.

'We should give him a name,' says David. 'What about Erik?'

'No!' says Ruth, too sharply. Does David know about her association with Erik Anderssen? It wouldn't be too hard to discover that he'd been her tutor at Southampton.

'Erik is too much of a Viking name,' she says now. 'What about something Polish? Stanislaw?'

'Stan for short,' says David. 'Have you told your friend Nelson about the test results?'

'No,' says Ruth, wary again. 'Why?'

'I thought he might be interested, seeing as he was there when we discovered Stan,' says David. Ruth thinks how having a name changes everything. As Kate said, the bones used to be a person and now that person is called Stan.

David adds, in what seems to be an elaborately casual tone, 'You know, he came to see me yesterday.'

'Who?' says Ruth. Though she can guess.

'DCI Nelson. He came barging in just when I was sitting in the front garden with Maja. He was very aggressive. Had the cheek to say he was conducting a murder inquiry.'

'Well, he is, I suppose.'

'I said I wouldn't talk to him without my lawyer.'

Ruth can't imagine that this went down well with Nelson.

'Did he say what he wanted specifically?' she asks.

'No,' says David. He fiddles with his phone for a few minutes before asking, 'Do you know what's going on with the investigation?'

'No,' says Ruth, meeting his eyes squarely. 'I've no idea. I'm not involved in the investigation at all. You probably know more than I do.' *Because you were there when the body was found*, she adds silently. *Because you have something you want to hide from the police.*

'Is Nelson always so charmless?'

'People usually describe him as tough but fair.'

'Do they? Well I think he's trying to frame me for something. I get the distinct impression that DCI Nelson dislikes me.'

'Why would he dislike you?'

'Because I work with you. Because we're becoming friends.'

Is this what's happening? Are they becoming friends? Ruth hopes that she's not blushing.

'Nelson's Kate's dad, isn't he?'

'Yes,' says Ruth. She's damned if she'd going to explain further. 'But Nelson's very professional. He wouldn't let his private feelings get in the way of an investigation.'

'If you say so,' says David. He sounds unconvinced and Ruth is relieved when, after a few minutes' chat about Stan, David stalks away to prepare for a lecture.

Judy is, once again, at the offices of Cambridge Bioresearch. This time Claudia Albertini is not quite so gracious.

'I'm rather busy,' is the first thing she says. They are in Claudia's office with the tasteful Alpine scenes. Claudia has her discreet laptop in front of her and now she taps at it as if to show how little time she's got to spare.

'It won't take long,' says Judy. 'We've had a copy of Douglas Noakes's will. He left everything to his wife but, because she died too, everything goes to Paul and Chloe, including the shares in this company.'

'I'm aware of that,' says Claudia.

'Can you tell me how much those shares are worth?'

'It's hard to tell,' says Claudia. 'Our products go through a rigorous, costly, and time-consuming testing process before potentially obtaining approval from NICE. This means that investors may wait for years before knowing whether a drug under development will pay off.'

'But potentially they could be worth quite a lot.'

'Potentially, yes.'

'Do you think Paul and Chloe were aware of this? Did either of them ever show any interest in the company accounts, for example?'

'None of the family ever showed any interest in the accounts,' says Claudia. 'Even Douglas. It was hard enough to get him to attend shareholders' meetings. He was only interested in the research for its own sake.'

She says this like it's a bad thing.

'Douglas wanted knowledge and he wanted power,' Claudia goes on. 'He wasn't really interested in what our research could do for people. Or in whether we made money.'

Chloe had said something similar when Tanya interviewed her, Judy seems to remember. She wishes she had the notes in front of her. She thinks of Black Dog Farm. It certainly doesn't seem like the home of someone who cared about money or possessions.

'Dr Albertini,' she says. 'We've found evidence that suggests that Dr Noakes was performing illegal drugs trials. Did you ever suspect that this was going on?'

She has the satisfaction of seeing real shock flicker across the scientist's composed features.

'Illegal drugs trials?' What do you mean?'

'Dr Noakes was conducting drugs trials at his home. We suspect that at least one of these trials might have gone wrong, resulting in a man's death.'

Now Claudia puts her hand to her mouth. 'I can't believe it.'

'You said that Douglas Noakes wanted knowledge and power. Can you think of any reason why he would have been conducting these unofficial tests?'

Claudia is silent for a minute, her fingers playing a scale on the edge of her desk.

'We did have a conversation once about bio-hacking,' she says.

'Bio-hacking?' repeats Judy. 'What's that?'

'It's when people inject themselves with untested gene therapies, genes to prevent cell death or boost muscle growth, for example. There are even bio-hacking conferences in the States, where people get together to experiment on themselves. The aims are very lofty – to cure disease, prevent aging, that sort of thing – but it's incredibly dangerous. The participants have no training in medicine or genetic engineering. I said how foolish it was but Douglas said maybe this was the only way to make progress. He always got very impatient waiting for approval for tests.'

'And you think that's what he might have been doing at Black Dog Farm? Injecting people with untested drugs?'

'I've no idea. It's just a theory. Hard to imagine that Douglas could be so foolhardy but, then again, I'm coming to the conclusion that I never really knew him very well.'

Nobody really knew Douglas Noakes, Judy thinks. Except, perhaps, his wife. And now she's dead too.

'Have you had any contact with Paul and Chloe Noakes recently?' she asks. 'Have either of them visited the offices?'

'I told you,' says Claudia, with a return to her haughty manner. 'I haven't seen either of them for years.'

'Do you mind if I look through your visitors' book?'

'Be my guest,' says Claudia. 'My secretary will show it to you downstairs.'

In the bland reception area, Judy rifles through the pages of the visitors' book. Drugs rep, drugs rep, someone to mend the photocopier, drugs rep. Ah, this is more interesting.

Monday 16th September. David Brown. University of North Norfolk.

'David Brown?' says Nelson. 'Now that *is* interesting. I knew the bastard was dodgy. We should bring him in for questioning.'

'Is it enough, though?' says Judy. She's in her car, on the way to interview Bryan Walker, the Night Hawk who taught with Linda Noakes. Nelson is in his office, trying not to have a meeting with Jo.

'It'll shake him up a bit,' says Nelson. 'We know he's got something to hide, because of the conversation Ruth overheard. I'll give him a ring and ask him to come in this afternoon. Let him get a lawyer if he wants one.'

'OK,' says Judy. 'I'll be back in an hour or two.'

But before Nelson can call David Brown and initiate the shaking-up process, a call comes through on his phone. It's from Mark Hammond.

'There's been a break-in at Black Dog Farm. I thought you'd like to know. I'm there now.'

Anything to escape from the office. Nelson grabs his phone, tells Leah that he's going out and is in his car before she can remind him about the afternoon's meetings. Nelson races through the Monday morning traffic (though what are they all doing, still on the road at ten o'clock?), feeling the familiar sense of well-being that he gets when on the trail of a case. He could never give this up, no matter how much Jo nags him to retire.

The journey is now all too familiar. The broken gate, the uneven track, the square house with the black weather-cock spinning gently. There's a squad car outside and Mark Hammond, still looking diminished without his partner, is standing beside it.

Nelson gets out of the car and strides over to him. 'Hi, Mark. How are you doing?'

'Better now that I'm back at work.'

You see, Nelson tells Jo in his head, work is good for you.

'What's going on here?' Nelson asks.

'We're keeping an eye on the house,' says Mark, 'making it part of our daily rounds. I drove past about half an hour ago and I saw a van coming out of the turning. Thought that was a bit odd, so I came up here and . . .' He points to the front door. It had been boarded up after the shooting – Nelson remembers standing outside with the firearms squad listening to the rotten wood giving way – but now the door is ajar. Nelson can see boot marks on the thin planks. It wouldn't have been hard to break down.

'Have you been in?' he asks.

'No,' says Mark. 'I thought I should wait for you.'

'Did you get the number of the van?'

'No.' Mark looks slightly shamefaced. 'I assumed it might be one of you lot. Or the SOCO team.'

'OK,' says Nelson. 'Let's have a look inside.'

It's like the first time. The dust motes in the air, the grandfather clock ticking. Why is it still working? Nelson wonders. Don't those things have to be wound up every few days? Instinctively, Nelson looks up at the staircase where Linda Noakes's body was found. The handprint is still on the wallpaper. It strikes him that the hallway is slightly lighter than usual, and he realises this is because a door is open. There's a shaft of sunlight and a faint smell of antiseptic. It's the private surgery, the room that Douglas Noakes kept locked at all times. A specialist team is due at the farm that afternoon, to clear this room and examine all the evidence. It looks as if someone has got there first.

'Bloody hell,' says Mark. Of course, it's the first time he's seen the secret room.

The drawers of the filing cabinets are open, their contents strewn over the floor. A chair has been knocked over and it looks as if someone has tried to jemmy the desk open.

'They didn't try to hide their tracks,' says Nelson.

'Maybe they were in a hurry,' says Mark. He's still looking rather dazed.

'Better get SOCO back here,' says Nelson, aware that he has already contaminated the scene. In for a penny ... He leans over the papers on the floor. They are alphabetical files. A–C. D–F. He can't see M to O, which would contain Nathan Matthews's file, but he doesn't like to say this in front of Mark.

'Maybe they were looking for drugs,' says Mark. 'People round here must know that a doctor lived here.'

A research scientist would have no reason to keep drugs in the house, thinks Nelson, but he's pretty sure that Douglas Noakes had a generous supply.

'Maybe,' says Nelson. 'And maybe they were just thrill seekers, wanting to be in the house where there's been a murder.'

'I can't imagine anyone wanting to come here,' says Mark. 'And there are no neighbours for miles around.'

'That's true,' says Nelson. 'But the house has been in the papers quite a lot. Maybe someone made a special trip.'

'This is probably where the drugs are.' Mark points at a safe on the wall. It's still closed but there are jemmy marks on it and a dent as if someone has thrown something heavy at the metal door. Kicking the door in, battering the safe. The intruders obviously weren't the stealthy sort, thinks Nelson. They are obviously not dealing with the Secret

Shadow here. He moves closer to the safe and, as he does so, spots something that glints on the floor.

'Look at this,' he says, taking a quick picture on his phone.

Mark comes over. 'What is it?'

'It's a badge. I saw Alan White once wearing something very similar.' It's a bird with wings outspread, made of silver or pewter. Nelson thinks back to the day of Ruth's excavation on the beach, Cathbad raising his arms and spouting some nonsense about Mother Earth, Alan watching, wearing a gilet adorned with this pin.

'I think it's a Night Hawk badge,' says Nelson.

'A nighthawk? Oh, you mean the metal detectorists.'

'Yes,' says Nelson. 'The question is, what's it doing here? Seems very careless to have dropped it. Maybe it's a message of some kind.'

'A message? Who from?'

'That's the question. We need SOCO to have a good look at it. Come on, let's get out of here.'

They back out of the room. Nelson is turning to check that the front door is secured when he hears Mark give an exclamation. He's pointing towards the field at the side of the house. Racing through the yellowing autumn grass is a large black dog.

Judy arrives at St Luke's school at first break. This time the playground is full of children, some playing hopscotch, some skipping. A group of older girls are sitting on the climbing frame, deep in discussion, as serious as politicians. Two little boys with coats over their heads are zooming around causing mayhem. The sound that rises from the space, laughter and raucous shouts, takes Judy right back to her own childhood and the joy of simply running around. Michael will be going to secondary school the year after next and she dreads him leaving this safe primary-coloured world for the wild west of the local comprehensive. At least, if Kate's going there too, she'll keep an eye on him. That is, if Nelson doesn't persuade Ruth to send Kate to the private school attended by his older daughters. Judy doesn't think this is likely, but the boss can be persuasive when he wants.

Bryan Walker is waiting for her in an empty classroom. There are poems about seashells on the walls and spaceships made from silver foil hanging from the ceiling.

'I'll miss all this when I retire next year,' says Bryan. 'I love all the creative stuff but it's all literacy and numeracy now.'

Cathbad would agree but Judy doesn't think there's anything wrong with knowing how to read and count.

Judy remembers Selina Spencer talking about 'the oldies club' but Bryan doesn't look as if he's near retirement age. He's a small man, thin and tanned with hair that's still more brown than grey. He tells Judy that he's fifty-five.

'Early retirement,' he says. 'My wife and I want to travel. We've got this plan that involves me visiting archaeological sites and Sue visiting beaches.'

'You're interested in archaeology, then? I know you're a member of the Night Hawks.'

'I actually studied archaeology at university, but jobs were hard to find – and very badly paid. I sort of drifted into teaching when our first child was born. But I grew to love it.'

'Were you a friend of Alan White's?'

Bryan's face clouds. 'Yes. Poor Alan. Such an awful thing to happen. I met him at an NUT meeting and he mentioned his metal detecting club. I went once and was hooked.'

'Like I said on the phone,' says Judy, 'I'm interested in the fact that you knew Linda Noakes too. I know that she taught here. Can you tell me anything about her? She's been rather a shadowy figure in our investigations so far.'

'She was a nice woman. Rather quiet and reserved but she had a sense of humour too. The children liked her a lot and they have a sixth sense about who to trust. We were all really shocked when we heard what had happened.'

'Did you ever meet her husband, Douglas?'

'No, but that's not unusual. Partners tend to avoid social gatherings, too much jargon and too many in-jokes. I bet it's the same with the police.'

'It is,' says Judy. 'I should tell you that we've had reports that Douglas Noakes was abusive to his children. Did you ever hear anything like that? Or suspect anything?'

Bryan rubs his eyes. 'No. Never. Linda didn't talk about her children much. Like I say, she was very private. But I got the impression that she was proud of them. The daughter was a doctor and the son was a teacher.'

Put like that, Chloe and Paul do sound the epitome of respectability.

Judy says, 'Did Linda ever say that she was worried about anything? Anything at all?'

'I don't think so,' says Bryan. 'There's not much time for talking about worries when you're a primary school teacher. There was just one thing once . . .'

'What?' Judy is instantly alert, sitting on her uncomfortable children's chair.

'She said that her daughter, Chloe, had an unsuitable boyfriend.'

'Unsuitable? Did she say why?'

'I think she said that he was very possessive. I said that one of my daughters – I've got three of them – had a boyfriend like that and we were pleased when they split up. Linda said that she'd be pleased when this chap was out of the picture.'

'She didn't say what his name was?'

'No.'

'Did you know that Chloe and Neil Thomas once had an affair?'

'Neil Thomas. The Night Hawk? But he's miles older than her. He must be about my age.'

Exactly Bryan's age, according to Judy's records. Bryan looks quite revolted at the thought of the two of them together.

'Neil used to be Chloe's teacher,' she says.

'My God,' says Bryan. 'That's awful.' He looks around the room as if seeking assurance that he exists in a better, kinder world. The silver spacecrafts twinkle back at them.

Cathbad is walking by the harbour at Wells. He has taken the children to school and now he and Thing are enjoying the autumn sunshine. Cathbad is teaching a meditation class at eleven but there's time for some healing breaths of sea air. The last few days have been rather disturbing to the equilibrium, even though Cathbad has taken the usual precautions – casting a protective circle, drinking turmeric tea and reciting the serenity prayer. But, even so, he can't altogether banish the image of Alan White's body lying in the open grave. He's also haunted by the thought that Alan had been scared and had reached out to Cathbad for support. Should he have done more? If he had done more, would Alan be alive today? But such thoughts do no good and, if not directed into a more positive stream, are in danger of spiralling downwards. Gazing at the sea will help restore the balance.

Cathbad loves watching the sea. There's always something new to see, an unusual bird, a foreign ship with Cyrillic script on its bows, some flotsam brought in by the tide. Even the water changes every day, sometimes white with chalk, at other times as clear and green as the Mediterranean. There are plenty of ghosts in Wells too. An old lady in Victorian costume is meant to haunt the distant sandbank, disappearing into the sea if approached. Cathbad hasn't seen her yet but he lives in hope.

He sits on the wall and gets Thing's bowl out of his rucksack. He fills the bowl with water from a flask and then gets out a second flask full of turmeric tea. He takes a sip of the aromatic liquid and then shuts his eyes and lets the sun warm his face.

'It's Cathbad, isn't it?'

Cathbad opens his eyes. It's the young Night Hawk. What's his name? Something classical. Hector?

'It's Troy. Troy Evans.'

'Hallo, Troy.'

'Do you live in Wells?'

'Yes,' says Cathbad, 'in one of the old fisherman's cottages.' It doesn't take druidical powers to guess Troy's occupation. He's dressed like all the local fishermen, in waders and a flat cap.

'You were a friend of Alan's, weren't you?'

'Yes,' says Cathbad. 'Do you want some turmeric tea?'

Troy shudders. 'No thanks. You know that policeman too, don't you? DCI Nelson.'

'Yes,' says Cathbad. He assumes that Troy will get to the point sooner or later.

But Troy is looking out at the water. The tide is coming in and the boats are rising up, coming to life again.

'There was a shipwreck here once,' says Troy. 'Before the First World War. My granddad told me about it. He had it from his dad. The SS *Heathfield* it was called. Ran aground on the sandbank at Sheringham. Eleven men were washed up in Wells harbour. They're buried in St Nicholas's church-yard.'

'I've seen the graves,' says Cathbad. The inscription on the plaque reads 'God will wipe away tears from all faces.' It never fails to move Cathbad to tears.

'The sea can be treacherous,' says Troy. 'People don't realise that.'

'"They that go down to the sea in ships, that do business

in the deep waters, these see the work of the Lord and his wonders in the deep."'

'Where's that from?'

'The Bible. It's a psalm, I think.'

'My granddad was one for church,' says Troy. 'I'm not. You're a druid, aren't you?'

Cathbad agrees modestly that he is.

'I think that's how he died,' says Troy. 'I think he was in a boat with someone who didn't understand the sea.'

'Who?' says Cathbad. 'Alan?'

'No.' Troy looks at him as if he's mad. 'Jem. Jem Taylor.'

29

The dog is getting closer. Nelson can see its eyes and lolling tongue. There's a fence between the field and the yard but the dog squeezes under it easily. It's definitely the same animal that Nelson saw with Ruth, a large Doberman, possibly crossed with something even bigger.

'Hi, boy,' says Nelson.

The dog pauses, head on one side. Then he turns, as if he has heard something. Now Nelson hears it too. A car approaching. The next minute, a new-looking jeep appears. For a moment, Nelson thinks it's Clough. But then he recognises the driver. Paul Noakes.

The car stops and Noakes gets out. The dog runs over to him, tail wagging. Paul ignores it.

'The police called me,' he says, addressing himself to Mark. 'Apparently there's been a break-in.'

'Yes,' says Mark. 'Someone has broken the door down. We don't know if anything's been stolen yet. Could just be kids. Could be people looking for drugs.'

'Do you know that dog?' says Nelson.

'No,' says Paul. The dog thinks otherwise. It is sitting at Paul's feet, looking up at him expectantly.

'Looks like it knows you,' says Nelson.

'I've never seen it before in my life,' says Paul. 'Shoo,' he says to the dog, who wags its tail.

'It's been living in that barn,' says Nelson. 'Want to look inside?'

Without waiting for an answer, he walks towards the outbuildings. The humans all follow but the dog is quickest. It bounds past Nelson and shimmies through the half-open side door. Nelson flings the door wide and turns on his torch.

'Someone's feeding that animal,' he says, pointing at the dog, who is now gulping down food from its bowl.

'I don't know who that could be,' says Paul. At the sound of his voice, the dog looks up and wags its tail again.

Nelson is shining his torch around the cavernous barn, remembering the last time he was here, with Ruth. What would have happened if Chloe hadn't come in when she did?

'Whose is the boat?' he asks.

'My father's,' says Paul.

'Your sister says that you like boating,' says Nelson.

'Only messing about on the river,' says Paul. 'Nothing serious.'

The dinghy did not acquire its seaweed decorations on the river, thinks Nelson. Judy's expert has confirmed as much.

The dog has now come up to Paul and is looking up at him once more.

'Do you want to take him home with you?' says Nelson. 'Just until his real owner turns up?'

Mark Hammond laughs and turns it into a cough. Paul looks awkward, his hands hanging down at his side. The dog is obviously all for the idea.

'I can't,' says Paul at last. 'I'm out at work all day.'

But Paul isn't at work now, thinks Nelson. Why not?

'I'll take charge of the dog,' says Mark.

He looks quite cheerful about it. Nelson remembers Mark saying that he wanted to be a police dog handler. This could be the start of a whole new career.

Nelson drives back to the station in a thoughtful frame of mind. The dog knew Paul Noakes. No question about it. And Paul, unlike his sister, was a fairly frequent visitor to his parents' house. Could he have met the dog there and was he the one still feeding and caring for it? If so, why keep this a secret? And he was obviously lying about the boat too. Nelson remembers what Chloe had said about sailing. *Paul was keener on it than me.* Is it possible that Paul was his father's assistant in whatever shady dealings were taking place at Black Dog Farm? Did Paul help his father dispose of Jem Taylor's body? Was it Paul who ransacked the filing cabinets to dispose of the relevant evidence?

And what about the badge? Is it the same one Alan White was wearing or did all the Hawks sport this insignia? If so, did this mean that the intruder was a Night Hawk? That includes Paul Noakes, of course. Also Neil Thomas and Troy Evans. Was it one of these men who ransacked the doctor's office?

So many questions and, by the time he reaches King's Lynn, Nelson hasn't found any answers. Tanya and Tony are in the briefing room, both busy at their computers. Jo's door is shut and Nelson can hear the murmur of her voice on the phone. Is she on the phone to head office, planning to get rid of Nelson and all the other dinosaurs? But this is no time to get paranoid. Nelson slides into his office and switches on his computer. Leah – God bless her – brings him a coffee. He clicks through various boring admin emails and is just sinking into a torpor when Judy knocks on his door.

'Hi, boss,' she says. 'I went to see Bryan Walker. You know, the Night Hawk who knew Linda Noakes.'

'Oh yes?' Nelson cheers up immediately. 'Get anything interesting?'

'He did say one interesting thing. Apparently, Linda was very quiet and reserved and didn't talk about her family much, but she once said that Chloe had an unsuitable boyfriend.'

'Neil Thomas?'

'Maybe. Linda said that he was possessive. That sounds a bit like a man with a younger girlfriend. Thomas is married but that might not stop him being jealous about Chloe.'

'We should talk to this Neil again,' says Nelson. 'He was there at both deaths. And Tanya said that he seemed nervous.'

'Tanya would make anyone nervous,' says Judy. 'But I think we should talk to him. And I've been thinking about Chloe Noakes's finances. I rang a Lynn estate agency on the off-chance and Chloe put her flat on the market three months ago. She's just withdrawn it.'

'Good work,' says Nelson. 'I've been visiting our favourite farmhouse.'

'Black Dog Farm? Why?'

Nelson tells her about the break-in and about the sudden appearance of the dog.

'That dog knew Paul Noakes,' he says. 'I'm sure of it. You can tell a dog with their master. Bruno's the same with me. He's a one-man dog.' He tries not to sound too smug about it.

'That's like Thing with Cathbad,' says Judy. 'Do you think Paul's been looking after this dog then? Does that mean he was helping his father?'

'I think it's a definite possibility,' says Nelson. 'I think he might have been using the boat too.'

'To dispose of Jem Taylor's body?'

'Possibly. Look what else I found.' Nelson shows Judy the picture of the hawk badge.

'I saw Alan wearing a badge like this once,' he says. 'Do you think all the Night Hawks have them?'

'Maybe,' says Judy. 'I don't think I noticed any when I did the interviews after Alan's murder and I talked to all the Night Hawks. It seems a bit odd to have found it at the scene. It's not the sort of thing that would drop off by accident. Was it some sort of message, do you think?'

'I don't know,' says Nelson. 'We'll have to see if there are any prints on it.'

He glances at his computer. An email has popped up on his screen. *Forensic Report No. C580. Classified.* It's the final report from Black Dog Farm. Nelson beckons to Judy to read it with him. He scrolls through, conscious of the fact that she probably reads faster than him. Most of the information he knows already. But then he stops at the section headed 'Fingerprint evidence'.

Fingerprints taken from Item K1 (gun) were examined and compared to those of family members. Two sets of prints were found on the gun.

    Dr Douglas Noakes

    Dr Chloe Noakes

'Chloe's prints are on the gun,' says Judy, seconds before he gets there.

'Yes,' says Nelson. 'It's time to talk to Dr Chloe Noakes again.'

30

There's not enough evidence to arrest Chloe but Nelson decides to interview her under caution. He asks Tanya and Tony to bring her in later that afternoon. He toys with the idea of sending a squad car to the university to pick up David Brown but decides – regretfully – that this would be unnecessarily provocative. Instead, he makes a call.

'David Brown.'

'Hallo, Mr Brown. This is DCI Nelson.'

'What do you want?'

'Could you come into the station, Mr Brown? I've got a few questions for you.'

'I've told you. I'm not talking to you without a solicitor present.'

'You are very welcome to bring a solicitor with you.'

There's a pause. Nelson says, 'Can you make two o'clock this afternoon?' It's nearly midday now but this will give them time to prepare an interview strategy.

'I've got a lecture at two.'

'When are you free?'

'My lecture finishes at four.'

'See you at four thirty then. Bye now.'

Nelson ends the call, aware that he's smiling like a Bond villain.

Ruth's phone buzzes throughout her meeting on recruitment. When she's finally free, she checks her missed calls. Four from David Brown. One from Cathbad. She buys a sandwich from the cafeteria and takes it to her office. Then she rings David. She'll save Cathbad as a treat.

'That Neanderthal Nelson. Do you know what he's done?'

Ruth does not remind David that archaeologists now think that Neanderthals had a rather sophisticated society, possibly even burying their dead with ritual, surrounded by garlands of flowers. Nor that all humans, outside Africa, have some Neanderthal DNA.

'What's he done?'

'He wants to talk to me. He said to bring a lawyer.'

'Gosh.' It's an inadequate response, she knows. She tries so hard not to swear in front of Kate that her vocabulary sometimes sounds like a 1950s children's book.

'Have you got a lawyer?' she asks.

'Someone has recommended a solicitor. Nirupa Khan.'

Ruth has a feeling that Nelson knows – and dislikes – Nirupa.

'Do you know why he wants to speak to you?' she asks. Nelson must be acting on more than the comments she overheard yesterday. Again, she hopes that he doesn't mention her name.

'He's trying to pin Alan's murder on me. That's what I think. That's what the police are like.'

Once, Ruth might have agreed with him but Nelson, she knows, is obsessive in his quest for justice. And he would never frame an innocent man. *Is* David innocent?

'I'll do my lecture,' says David, 'and then leave at four.'

'Are you sure?' says Ruth. She runs through workload allocations in her head. 'I could cover for you.'

'It's fine,' says David. 'I think the students are looking forward to hearing what I have to say.'

'Good luck,' says Ruth.

Just when she's feeling friendly towards David, he has to come up with something like this. She's so eaten up with irritation and curiosity that she almost forgets to eat her sandwich. She has completely forgotten Cathbad until he rings again, just before her two o'clock tutorial.

'Ruth. Did you get my message?'

'Sorry. No.' She sees now that she has an answerphone notification.

'It's probably not a big deal but it's about David Brown.'

'Oh yes?'

'I was doing my meditation class and I suddenly remembered something Alan said, when he asked me to come on the midnight dig. He said that something was worrying him, something he couldn't tell me on the phone. I said something light-hearted about the Black Shuck and he said, "It's not black, it's brown." I thought he was talking about the dog but now I think that he meant Brown with a capital B. David Brown. I think he was scared of David Brown. I saw his aura the night that Alan was killed. It was dark and cloudy, as if he had something to hide.'

'Have you told Nelson? Not about the aura but about what Alan said?'

'No. Do you think I should?'

'Nelson's asked David to go into the station for questioning. He's taking a solicitor with him.'

'I was right then.' Cathbad seems overawed at his own powers of perspicacity. 'I knew there was something malign about that man.'

'You might be right. I went on a boat trip with David on Saturday. I heard him talking to the boatman – Troy – saying something about not telling the police.'

'Did *you* tell Nelson?'

'Yes.'

'No wonder Nelson doesn't like him.'

Ruth doesn't like to ask what this means.

'I think you should tell Nelson what Alan said to you,' she says.

'I will,' says Cathbad. 'The unconscious mind is a wonderful thing, isn't it?'

'Dr Noakes,' says Tanya. 'Did you ever handle your father's gun?'

'His gun?' says Chloe. 'No. We didn't even know he had a handgun.'

Chloe seems superficially calm despite being left in the waiting room for a judicious half hour before being ushered into an interview room and faced with two detectives and a tape recorder. Nelson, watching through the two-way mirror, sees Chloe raise a paper cup of water to her lips with a hand that seems remarkably steady. Of course, you need steady hands to be a doctor. Or to fire a gun.

'Your prints were on the gun found beside your father's body,' says Tanya.

Nelson watches as Chloe takes another sip of water. Playing for time, he thinks.

'When did you last visit your parents?'

'About two months ago.'

'Was that when you asked your father to guarantee your remortgage payments?' says Tanya.

Chloe gives her an icy glance. 'Probably.'

'Must be tough being a GP today,' says Tony. 'Are you a partner in your practice?'

It's well done. Tony sounds genuinely sympathetic. Subtly Chloe shifts her weight away from Tanya and towards him.

'Yes, I'm a partner,' she says.

'So you're personally liable for any losses,' says Tanya. 'Especially if the practice isn't doing too well.'

'The practice is doing fine, thanks,' says Chloe.

'Did you ask your father for a loan?' says Tanya. 'Did he say no?'

'He agreed to be a guarantor,' says Chloe.

'Must have been hard, asking him for help,' says Tony. 'My parents are pretty strict. I'm still scared of them, even as an adult.'

Nelson doesn't believe this is true. Tony's mother still knits him sweaters. It seems to work though because Chloe seems to relax slightly.

'You didn't get on with your dad, did you?' says Tanya.

Chloe stiffens immediately. 'No,' she says. 'But I didn't kill him.'

It's too early for this to be out in the open. Chloe is taking charge of the situation. Nelson stands up to relieve his frustration. There's a knock on the door.

It's Tom Henty. 'Nirupa Khan and a client to see you, DCI Nelson.'

Nelson groans inwardly.

'What grounds have you got for asking to see my client?' says Nirupa Khan. She's small and slight but so, Nelson often thinks, is a piranha fish.

'Mr Brown,' says Judy. 'Did you visit Cambridge Bioresearch on Monday the sixteenth of September?'

'You don't have to answer,' Nirupa tells David.

Judy says, for the tape, 'I'm showing Mr Brown a photocopy of a page from the visitors' book at Cambridge Bioresearch. Is that your handwriting, Mr Brown?'

David says nothing. Nelson adds, 'There's plenty of CCTV at the company. We can easily call it in.'

'OK,' says David. 'I was there.'

'Want to tell us why?' says Nelson.

David sighs again. 'I'm interested in their work. I'm sure you know, DCI Nelson, that my academic speciality is the Bronze Age.'

This is said in a very nasty tone. Nelson says nothing. He can never remember whether the Bronze Age comes before or after the Iron Age.

'How is that relevant?' says Judy.

'It's my theory that, when the Beaker people invaded Britain, they brought with them a deadly virus that wiped out the native population. I wanted to talk to a scientist about this theory, so I made an appointment to see Dr Noakes.'

'Was he helpful?' asks Judy.

'Yes,' says David. 'He knew a great deal about viruses and how they spread.'

'Were you aware that Dr Noakes was conducting illegal drugs trials?' says Nelson.

'What? No.'

'Were you involved in those trials?'

'Categorically not.'

'Then what was the information that you asked Troy Evans to withhold from the police?'

For the first time, David looks shaken. 'Ruth told you,' he says. 'She told you that. She must have overheard on the boat.'

Nelson says nothing. He feels uncomfortable enough about using the information acquired from Ruth.

'What was the secret you wanted Troy to keep?' says Judy.

'No comment,' says David.

*

In the end, they have to let David Brown go. They've nothing on him apart from a perfectly legal visit to a research company and a slightly suspicious conversation, relayed at second hand. Nelson reflects grimly that all today has achieved is to give David a burning sense of grievance which might be fanned by Nirupa Khan into a full-on complaint.

Jo would love that, he thinks. It would give her the chance to mention the R word again. 'Policing has changed since your day, Nelson. You can't go around intimidating people. Perhaps it's time to think about . . .'

And, to make matters worse, Cathbad has just rung with a lunatic theory about David Brown and the Black Shuck. 'Thanks, Cathbad,' said Nelson, 'let me know if anything else comes to you when you're meditating.'

'I will,' said Cathbad, not seeming to notice the sarcasm.

Now the team are gathered in the briefing room. The names are all up on the board: Chloe Noakes, Paul Noakes, Alan White, Neil Thomas, Troy Evans, David Brown.

'So, what do we think about Chloe Noakes?' says Nelson.

They have released Chloe too. She now knows that she's a 'person of interest' in their inquiry, which might make her panic and confess, but Nelson doubts it somehow. Unless they can prove that she was in the farmhouse on the night her parents died, they can't charge her with anything.

'She's hiding something,' says Tanya.

'I agree,' says Nelson. 'But what?'

'I think she was in the house when her parents were killed,' says Tanya. 'Her prints were on the gun and she doesn't have an alibi.'

'We shouldn't forget David Brown,' says Nelson. 'He's also obviously hiding something too. Remember what he said to Troy Evans. And Brown visited Cambridge Bioresearch. That's suspicious, in my book. I don't buy all that crap about research into the Bronze Age.'

'But there's no link between Chloe and David,' objects

Judy. 'I think we should look at Neil Thomas. He could still be having an affair with Chloe. Maybe they did it together.'

'It's more likely to be Paul and Chloe,' says Tanya. 'And Paul's obviously a more frequent visitor to the house than he let on originally.'

'Maybe,' says Judy. 'Paul and Chloe do seem very close, very protective of each other. Chloe didn't want Paul to know about her affair with Neil.'

'Paul has clearly been feeding the dog,' says Nelson. 'The dog that both siblings swore didn't exist.'

'"Dad hated all animals." That's what Chloe said to me,' says Tanya. 'So why would they be secretly keeping a dog?'

'To keep people away,' says Tony. 'Maybe that's why their father made such a thing about the legend of the Black Shuck, changing the house's name and everything. Having a big black dog running around stopped anyone from getting too close.'

'Because Douglas Noakes was doing human experiments in that creepy surgery,' says Judy.

'Chloe was in financial difficulties,' says Tanya. 'She put her flat on the market. That was a motive to kill her parents. Now she and Paul have the farm and shares in the business.'

'And revenge on their parents,' says Judy.

'It's a good theory,' says Nelson. And he means it. The team are working well together. 'We just have to prove it.'

Nelson drives home in a thoughtful frame of mind. He senses that they are close to a solution but, without more evidence, they can't charge anyone. He hates this situation, when it seems as if the perpetrator is going to get away with it. It goes against all his instincts as a policeman. The famous instincts which, as he keeps telling Jo, are worth his inflated salary.

The traffic has stopped again. Nelson grinds his teeth. He'd love to put his siren on but thinks this would not go down well with Jo, if she got to hear about it. Instead he twists and turns through the backstreets of Lynn, trying to avoid the main roads. He has his radio switched on and can hear the crackly instructions issuing from control. A broken-down car on the London Road, drunk driver arrested on Wootton Road, a break-in on North End Lane. Hang on, North End Lane is the road leading to the accursed Black Dog Farm. Two break-ins in one day? That's more than coincidence. He performs a multi-point turn and heads in the direction of Sheringham. Now he can legitimately put his siren on, and he enjoys the sensation of actually doing something, of making ground, zigzagging in and out of the gridlocked traffic, shooting through red lights. It's dark by the time that he reaches the outskirts of Sheringham. Nearly October now. Soon it will be November – Katie's birthday and his own – and then Christmas and his mum coming to stay. Well, no time to think of any of that now. Nelson presses his foot down on the accelerator.

There are lights by the entrance to the farm. They look very bright in the dark lane, reflecting the high hedges and the broken white gate. As Nelson gets nearer, he sees that there are also bollards across the road and a 'Police Incident' sign. How have the traffic police got here so quickly? Nelson stops his car and gets out. There's a white van parked by the sign for the farm. Nelson walks towards it.

'What's going on?'

The van door opens and a man gets out. He's wearing a ski mask which startles Nelson so much that he doesn't, at first, notice the gun in the man's hand.

Even when the gun goes off, Nelson's first reaction is surprise.

And then, nothingness.

31

Ruth is glad when the day is over. Earlier in the afternoon she watched from her window as David Brown drove away, presumably to his interview with Nelson. The whole situation makes her twitchy. Is David an actual suspect for Alan White's murder or is Nelson just after him because of the comment overheard by Ruth? She doesn't know which scenario makes her more nervous. She finishes her last lecture on autopilot, then fires off some emails and prepares to go home.

She doesn't have to rush because Kate is having a sleepover with Tasha. This is unusual for a weekday but it's Tasha's birthday and she wants her two best friends to stay the night, as a pre-celebration before the lavish party planned for Saturday. Ruth is glad that Kate has retained her status as one of the best friends, but she is rather dreading the party and already feels slightly intimidated by Tasha, who has pierced ears and her own rose gold iPhone. Still, it means that Ruth can watch reruns of *Time Team* all evening and have a long bath with a glass of red wine.

As she contemplates this, while loading her book bag into the car, she suddenly, for the first time in ages, misses Frank. He would have run the bath for her and poured the wine. He was a considerate partner, always understanding her need for space and privacy, commodities that are much easier to achieve when there are two adults, co-parenting. Frank was a good man in every sense and Ruth was very fond of him. Not fond enough to become Mrs Frank Barker though. No, she is Dr Ruth Galloway for ever. The thought cheers her up. It's like a mantra that runs through her head as she drives slowly through the university grounds. Dr Ruth Galloway for ever. *You've never been a bride, have you, Mum?*

She's almost at the turn-off for the Saltmarsh when her phone beeps. She considers ignoring it – she's nearly home, after all – but the Paranoid Mother voice in her head says: what if it's Kate? What if she's had an allergic reaction to Tasha's birthday cake? What if a masked gunman has burst in and shot them all? She pulls over, into the forecourt of a boarded-up pub, and gets out her phone.

It's a message from Nelson.

Can you meet me at Black Dog Farm? Might have discovered something important x

She rings back but the phone is switched off. Typical Nelson, to demand her presence and then go incommunicado. She considers ignoring the message, going home and putting on the History channel. But Nelson needs her and, says another voice in her head – definitely not the Mother this time – she has the whole evening free. Potentially the whole night.

Ruth turns her car in the opposite direction. Away from home.

Michelle is preparing supper. She doesn't know when Harry will be home, but she's trying to eat at regular times to maintain her post-baby weight loss. George, no longer a baby, watches her from the kitchen table where he's playing with his cars. Bruno is lying by the door, looking martyred. He wants his master, his food and a walk. Probably in that order.

'Police,' says George. 'Nee naw, nee naw.' Why is he making that noise when sirens now have a transatlantic whine? It's like T for Train in his alphabet book, which shows a steam train puffing smoke. When did trains last look like that? Even the Telephone on the same page is a landline version when, to most children, a phone is that little rectangular object buzzing in Mum's handbag. It irritates Michelle that George is playing police cars.

It's been a strange time, the first three years of George's life. If Michelle were to describe it in one word she'd say, 'Becalmed,' remembering her mother's description of sailing boats at Fleetwood Yacht Club. She and Harry are still afloat, and their little craft now contains George, as well as Laura and Rebecca. They are bobbing gently on a tranquil sea but are they going anywhere? She knows that Nelson was in love with Ruth – still might be – and she was, if not in love with Tim, then in *something* with him. But now Tim is dead, and Harry has obviously decided to stay with her for the sake of the family, for George in particular. And it's fine. They get on well, they still have sex sometimes and it's wonderful to share the surprising gift of a late baby. But they don't really talk; about Ruth, about Tim, about Katie, even about what will happen when Maureen comes for Christmas. They just float on, looking after George and Bruno, taking one day at a time.

'Phone,' says George. The little rectangular object is buzzing in Michelle's bag. She wipes her hands and goes to retrieve it. It's Harry, probably saying he's working late again.

Can you meet me at Black Dog Farm? I need your help x

Michelle looks at the message feeling mingled irritation, pleasure and curiosity. Harry needs her help. *Her* help, not the assistance of Dr Know-all Galloway. This must be a first. Typical of him not to say more. She rings back but his phone is switched off. This, too, is typical.

'Nee naw, nee naw,' says George. Bruno whines softly.

Michelle clicks onto Laura's number. 'Sweetheart, do you think you could babysit for an hour?'

32

It's dark by the time that Ruth reaches Black Dog Farm but a full moon casts a silvery, diffuse light on the treetops. As Ruth bumps along the track with the louring hedges on both sides, she's aware of feeling anxious, her chest tightening as she gets nearer and nearer the house. When she finally turns into the yard and sees Nelson's Mercedes parked at an angle, she exhales with relief. It's OK. Nelson is here.

Ruth gets out of the car.

'Nelson?' she calls. There's no answer. The weathercock creaks from the roof. She can hear the wind in the trees and, faint and far away, a dog barking. The front door is boarded up but open, there's a dent in the wood as if it's been kicked. Ruth approaches, her phone torch held in front of her like a shield. A light comes on and she stops in her tracks. But it's only a security light. Nelson insisted that she install one outside her cottage but, when it's activated by foxes in the middle of the night, Ruth finds it scarier than darkness. She doesn't want to go inside the house with its grease-stained walls and stench of death. But that's where Nelson is.

She pushes open the door. She can hear a grandfather clock ticking and another noise, something that makes her skin crawl and all her senses start to send out alarm signals.

She takes another step inside the house.

And darkness falls.

Michelle practically growls with irritation when she sees Ruth's car parked next to Harry's. Really, she tells him silently. Really? Does he really think that she won't recognise Ruth's car? She knows everything about Ruth. She knows her mobile phone number, her email address, her star sign, her parents' names. She has looked up Ruth's books on Amazon. *The Tomb of the Raven King*. *The Shadow Fields*. *The Devil's Number*. She knows the few reviews almost by heart. She would stalk Ruth on Facebook if Ruth could be bothered to have an account. So yes, Harry, I do recognise her car.

Michelle marches up to the open front door. It's only when she's inside the hall, a gloomy place with hideous wallpaper, that she feels the first glimmer of unease. Where is Harry? Where is Ruth? There's a faint noise coming from one of the inner rooms, a sort of slithery, clanking sound. Michelle moves towards it.

The house is silent when Judy gets home. Cathbad is collecting Michael from his piano lesson and he must have taken Thing with him, as well as Miranda. Mrs Mazzini will not be impressed. But the peace is wonderful. Judy goes into the kitchen and sits at the table without turning on the lights. Outside, the moon is riding across the cloudy sky. A full moon, which means high tides and, anecdotally amongst the police, a rise in violent crime. Lunacy, as Cathbad is fond of saying, simply means affected by the moon.

Judy sits, lit by this strange satellite, and thinks about the Black Dog Farm case. They haven't charged Chloe Noakes with her parents' murder but there's no doubt that there's a case against her. She had a motive, both financial and emotional, she has no real alibi and her fingerprints were on the gun. Judy thinks back over her encounters with the GP. When she first met Chloe Noakes, she'd thought her character rather closed and self-contained, but not abnormally so. According to the FLO, Chloe had been calm when identifying her parents' bodies, but she hadn't been unaffected. Judy remembers Chloe saying, when she first spoke to her on the phone, 'I'm glad Paul didn't see them like this.' Was Chloe's motivation a desire to protect her brother? She thinks of the siblings sitting side by side in Chloe's flat, Chloe righting her brother's upturned glass. She sees them entering their childhood home, when the SOCO teams had finished, the tall man and the small woman. It had been clear who was protecting whom. 'Paul and I hate this place,' Chloe had said, 'and we hated our father. We're glad he's dead.'

Had Chloe Noakes killed her parents? Had she shot her mother and then her father, calmly pressing her father's dead hand to the gun? But surely, if so, she wouldn't have used the wrong hand? And she would have been careful to wipe her own fingerprints off. Could the siblings have acted together? Or did Chloe have another accomplice?

Judy tries to picture Chloe Noakes, something that often helps her when wrestling with a case. Brown hair, cut very short, hazel eyes, good skin. She's attractive, Judy realises, but in a way that isn't immediately apparent. Chloe seems to be single now but, aged eighteen, she had had an affair with a man twenty years her senior. It hadn't been illegal, as Choe had pointed out, rather defensively, but the relationship was definitely inappropriate, in Judy's opinion. Neil Thomas had been Chloe's teacher; there was a power – as well as an age – disparity. Maddie had a similar affair at a similar age and Judy thinks that it still affects her to this day.

Judy gets out her notebook and flicks back to her last interview with Chloe. She doesn't turn on the overhead light but uses her phone torch to see the page.

He was so different from my other boyfriends. They were schoolboys, all spotty and jealous. Neil was cool. Or so he seemed to me.

Why does this ring a faint bell? What is she remembering? It's something the boss said, she's sure of it. She'll give him a ring. Nelson never minds being contacted at home.

But Nelson's phone is switched off.

33

Ruth is floating on a black sea. She is being carried inland on an inexorable tide. The beach comes up to meet her, the rocks jagged and threatening, gleaming with moisture. She opens her eyes. She's in a white room, with a smell that makes her think of hospitals. Ruth moves her head.

And sees Nelson lying dead in front of her.

Ruth opens her eyes again. She is in a sitting room, old-fashioned and dreary, green curtains and brocade sofas. The sound she heard earlier is in the background. A clanking noise. Jacob Marley's chain. The Black Shuck dragging its shackles behind it. Ruth sits up and realises that she's staring into the eyes of the devil dog. He is watching her intently and, as he moves his head, his collar clinks gently.

'Don't move,' says a woman's voice.

'Michelle?'

It seems incredible but no more incredible than anything else that has happened to her. Nelson's wife is sitting next to her on the sofa. Nelson!

'I saw him,' says Ruth. 'He looked like he was dead.'

'Harry?' says Michelle. There's never any doubt which 'him' they would both mean.

'I saw him. Lying on some sort of table,' says Ruth. 'Maybe it was a dream.'

'His car's outside,' says Michelle.

The dog growls in the back of its throat. Is it the animal that Ruth saw in the barn that day? She can't be sure. It's black with a narrow head and a brown muzzle, lying in front of the door, paws stretched out in front, obviously on guard.

'What happened?' she says to Michelle.

'I don't know,' says Michelle. 'I got a text from Harry asking me to come to the farm. When I got here his car was outside. And yours. The front door was open so I came in and I saw a man with a dog. He said Harry was in this room but there was only you, lying on the sofa. The man told the dog to guard us and then he locked us in.'

'A man? What was he like?'

'Tall and thin,' says Michelle. 'I didn't recognise him.'

Tall and thin. Could it be David Brown? But why would David lure her and Michelle to Black Dog Farm? How does he even know Michelle? Ruth shakes her head, trying to clear it.

'I got a text too,' she says. 'It said to meet him – Nelson – at Black Dog Farm because he'd discovered something important. I assumed it was about the case.' She can almost *feel* Michelle disbelieving this.

Then Michelle says, 'I might have known it wasn't from him. He never puts a kiss on the ends of his texts.'

Ruth says nothing. Nelson never usually puts kisses on her texts either. Why hadn't she noticed this earlier? Perhaps, subconsciously, she had thought it was a sign that he was softening in his old age.

'Someone else must have sent them,' says Michelle. 'Someone who has Harry's phone.'

'But why?' says Ruth. She stands up and realises that she's very unsteady on her feet. She sits down again. The dog makes a warning noise in the back of its throat.

'Don't make any sudden movements,' says Michelle. 'The dog's trained to spring at any time. I remember Jan telling me that's how they train police dogs.'

Michelle sounds admirably calm. Ruth had never imagined Michelle being like this in a crisis. If she'd thought about it at all, she would have expected her to start crying and having hysterics. Instead, Nelson's wife is sitting up very straight, keeping one eye on the dog without making direct eye contact. She's wearing leggings and trainers, Ruth notices. She's suddenly aware of her head hurting a great deal.

'I think he hit me on the head,' she says.

'Yes,' says Michelle. 'You were out cold when I came in.'

Instinctively, Ruth puts her hand in her pocket for her phone. She was sure that she was holding it when she came in.

'He took our phones,' says Michelle. 'At least, he took mine. I assume he took yours too.'

'Why?' says Ruth, hearing her voice shaking. 'What's going on?'

'I don't know,' says Michelle. 'This is the house where those people were killed, isn't it?'

'Yes,' says Ruth. 'I excavated the garden here. And I saw that dog too, when I was here with . . .'

She stops. Michelle is looking at her. It's hard to tell what she's thinking. That's the problem with symmetrically beautiful faces. They can look very blank.

'Do you really think you saw Harry earlier?' says Michelle.

'I don't know,' says Ruth. 'I could have been dreaming. He was in a room like a hospital ward.'

There's nothing hospital-like about this room. It's full of fringed lamps, antimacassars, gloomy oil paintings. On a table near the fireplace there's a china vase, a photograph of a graduate in a gold frame and an old-fashioned Bakelite object.

'Look, Michelle,' says Ruth. 'A landline.'

They lock eyes.

'I'll distract the dog,' says Michelle. 'You phone.'

Without waiting for an answer, Michelle clicks her fingers. 'Here, boy.'

The dog turns its snake-like head towards her. Ruth makes a lunge for the phone. She's half expecting it to be disconnected but a comforting whirr fills her ear. Shakily she presses nine, nine, nine. The dog comes towards Michelle, hackles up.

'What service do you require?' says a woman's voice.

'Police,' says Ruth. 'Police!'

The door opens and a man enters the room.

'Mum! Why haven't you turned the lights on?' Miranda comes dancing into the kitchen.

'It's very restful to sit in the dark,' says Cathbad, following her in, laden with book bags and piano music.

'How was your lesson?' says Judy to Michael.

'OK,' says Michael. 'Mrs Mazzini gave me two new pieces to learn.'

'She says he's getting on really well,' says Cathbad. It was Judy who wanted Michael to have piano lessons but it's Cathbad – himself opposed to formal music tuition – who gets to sit in on the sessions. Judy tries not to resent this.

'Put the lights on, Mirry,' she says. 'I was just thinking.'

'There's a beautiful full moon over the sea,' says Cathbad. 'A ghostly galleon.'

'Dad was telling us about the Norfolk Sea Serpent,' says Miranda. 'I wish I could see it.'

'It's a good story,' says Judy. 'I'm not sure I'd like to meet a sea monster though.'

'I would,' says Miranda.

'Shall we just have scrambled eggs for supper?' says Cathbad. 'It's nearly seven o'clock.'

'Good idea,' says Judy. She feels a bit guilty for not starting supper herself but luckily Cathbad doesn't think like that. The eggs are in a ceramic hen on the counter, fresh from the farm shop, free-range, some still with straw attached. Judy gets out a bowl and a whisk. Cathbad starts to cut the bread. Thing barks from the hall a second before there's a knock on the door.

'Shall I go?' says Michael.

'No,' says Judy quickly. 'I will.'

Cathbad is by her side as she approaches the front door. A tall shape is visible through the glass.

'Who is it?' says Michael, picking up on his parents' nervousness.

'Probably just one of the neighbours wanting to borrow something,' says Cathbad.

But, when Judy opens the door, she sees, not a friendly neighbour, but the man she interviewed at the police station that afternoon.

David Brown.

'What are you doing?' says the man. 'Get away from the phone.'

Ruth drops the receiver. She can hear a voice asking, 'Are you there?' She hopes that the operator can hear what's going on, that someone will rescue them.

The man crosses the room and replaces the phone onto its cradle. He's very tall, with thinning brown hair. He also looks vaguely familiar. She tries to remember where she might have seen him but her brain refuses to cooperate.

'Sit down.' The man gestures at her and it's only then that Ruth realises that he's carrying a gun, a long one like a rifle.

The dog has resumed its position in the doorway. Ruth sees Michelle looking at it, assessing her chances of escape. The man must have seen her too because he swings round.

'Sit on the sofa,' he says. 'Both of you.'

Ruth and Michelle sit on the sofa.

Michelle says, 'Where's my husband? DCI Nelson?'

My husband. Even here, even now, the words have the power to hurt Ruth.

'He's in the surgery,' says the man.

The surgery? What's he talking about?

'Is he OK?' says Michelle. There's a note of panic in her voice that Ruth recognises as echoed in her own when she says, 'Why have you brought us here?'

'DCI Nelson has to let Chloe go,' says the man. 'I thought, if anyone could make him, it would be you two. You're his wife,' he says to Michelle. 'And you.' He turns to Ruth. 'Everyone knows about you and Nelson. Chloe saw you here together.'

Ruth can feel Michelle staring at her. Once again, she's amazed at the way she's still able to feel everyday emotions. In this instance, shame and embarrassment. Don't think about it, she tells herself. Concentrate on getting yourself out of this mess. Getting all three of them out of it: Ruth, Nelson and Michelle.

Why is the man talking about Chloe? Then she gets it. Paul and Chloe Noakes, the children of the murdered parents.

'It's Paul, isn't it?' she says. 'We met on the beach that day.' Maybe if Paul remembers that he knows her, that she's a real person with a life and people who love her, maybe then he'll let her go. 'I'm a friend of Cathbad's,' she says. 'Do you know Cathbad?'

'The druid?' says Paul. Is it Ruth's imagination or does he lower the gun a fraction?

'That's right,' says Ruth. 'His son's a friend of my daughter.

I've got a ten-year-old daughter. Kate.' Her voice breaks when she says Kate's name. Ruth has always thought that, if anything happened to her, Nelson and Michelle would look after Kate. But what if all three of them die here together, in an awful parody of their love triangle? Who will look after Ruth's daughter? Cathbad and Judy? Her father and Gloria?

Michelle's voice cuts through Ruth's thoughts.

'Where's Harry?' she says. 'Where's DCI Nelson?'

Michelle's tone, or maybe her use of Nelson's rank, makes the man raise his gun again.

'He's in the surgery,' repeats the man, impatiently.

Then Ruth hears something. A noise that's almost a groan. The dog hears it too. He tilts his head, listening.

'Is he in this house?' says Michelle.

'I'm sorry to disturb you at home,' says David.

'You should be,' says Cathbad. 'This is an invasion of my wife's privacy.'

Judy has never heard Cathbad sound so angry. Also, she's not his wife.

'What do you want?' she says.

'I'm worried about Ruth,' says David. 'I went round to her cottage just now and she wasn't home. I know she was planning to go straight home after work. Her daughter was at a sleepover.'

It occurs to Judy that David knows rather a lot about Ruth's movements.

'She's probably just out with a friend,' says Judy. But

even as she says this, she feels a twinge of unease. She and Cathbad are probably Ruth's closest friends in Norfolk. If she's not with them, where could she be, on a school night? With Shona possibly. But Judy thinks this is unlikely. Ruth and Shona don't seem particularly close these days.

'Do you have any idea where she could be?' says David.

Judy's first thought is to ring the boss. Ruth often complains about Nelson wanting to know where she is and what she's doing. 'It's like being electronically tagged,' she says. But Judy knows that Kate, being a bright tech-savvy child, has linked her parents' phones so Nelson can keep track of Ruth, if he so wishes. But Nelson hadn't been answering his phone earlier. A thought occurs to her.

'Excuse me,' she says to David. She goes back into the kitchen and picks up her work phone. If Nelson has kept his radio on, she will be able to track his GPS location. She clicks on 'DCI Nelson' and a pulsating red dot appears.

'That's strange,' she says aloud.

'What is?' Cathbad appears in the doorway.

'Nelson is at Black Dog Farm.'

34

'Is he here?' repeats Michelle. 'What have you done to him?'

'Don't worry,' says Paul. 'I've patched him up. I know how to do first aid.'

'You've patched him up?' says Michelle. 'What happened?'

'He'll be all right,' says Paul. 'The bullet didn't hit any vital organs.'

'The bullet?' Michelle almost shrieks. 'Did you shoot him?'

Paul looks down at the gun almost as if he's surprised to find himself holding it. Can Ruth charge at him while his attention is distracted? She moves, very slightly, tensing herself for action, but Paul notices. He points the gun at her. He looks like someone who's used to handling a firearm.

'Don't move,' he says.

'I won't,' says Ruth. 'But can we see Nelson? Please?'

Paul looks at her. His face is perfectly pleasant. If Ruth saw this man in the street, she probably wouldn't notice him but, if she did, she'd think him a reasonable, respectable member of society.

'We might be able to help,' says Michelle, also adopting a softer tone.

'All right,' says the man. 'But don't try and get away.'

'We won't,' says Ruth. They stand up. Ruth has a ridiculous urge to hold Michelle's hand.

'This way.' The man gestures at the door. 'Heel, Dexter,' he says to the dog. Dexter. Ruth stores the name away for future reference. Just like with the skeleton, having a name makes the creature seem more real. This is not a devil dog, she tells herself, it's just a pet, man's best friend. Good dog, Dexter, she says to herself, remembering the way Nelson had talked to the animal. Oh God, Nelson. Please don't let him be badly hurt.

Using his gun as a pointer, he directs them into a hall. Ruth has a vague impression of faded yellow wallpaper and of a grandfather clock ticking loudly. There's an open door directly in front of them and the light coming from that room seems different, brighter and more ominous.

'In there,' says Paul.

Ruth knows at once that it's the room that she was in earlier. And there is Nelson lying on a bed in front of her.

Michelle gets to him first.

'Harry,' she says. 'Harry. Are you OK?'

He's obviously not OK, thinks Ruth. Nelson is lying on his back with a professional-looking dressing around his shoulder. Blood is seeping through the bandage but what worries Ruth most is Nelson's colour. He's deathly pale and his hair is dark with sweat.

Ruth comes nearer. Nelson opens his eyes. 'Ruth?'

'He's delirious,' says Michelle. She turns on Paul, who is standing against the door, which is now shut. The dog, Dexter, is at his side.

'He needs help,' she says. 'He needs to go to hospital.'

Ruth puts her hand on Nelson's forehead. It's hot and clammy at the same time. Michelle is right; he needs to be in hospital.

'Please,' she says to the man. 'We need to call an ambulance.'

'Not until you let Chloe go,' he says.

'Who's Chloe?' says Michelle.

'Chloe's my sister,' says the man. 'Nelson thinks she killed our parents. That's why I had to do this. To make Nelson let her go.'

'I'm sure this can be sorted out,' says Michelle. Her voice is calm and reasonable, the sort of tone Ruth imagines her using to defuse family quarrels. 'But we need to call an ambulance now.'

'Please,' says Ruth, hearing her voice shaking. 'Nelson needs medical help quickly or he'll die.' She knows that she's crying now.

'Not yet,' says the man. He looks towards the hall as if he hears something.

'Look, Paul,' says Michelle. 'If you call an ambulance, everything will be OK. But if . . . if anything happens to Harry . . . to DCI Nelson . . . you'll be in serious trouble . . . he's a police officer.'

In serious trouble. It doesn't sound threatening enough. If anything happens to Nelson, Ruth will happily kill this

Paul herself. But maybe Michelle is right to take a quieter approach.

'Please,' says Ruth. 'Please, Paul.'

In answer, the man turns and leaves the room. Locking the door behind him.

Judy is driving towards Black Dog Farm, David Brown at her side. She's not quite sure how this happened. One moment she was telling Cathbad that she wouldn't be long, the next she was on the road with David giving her directions.

'I know the way,' she snaps.

Why is he here?

'It's quicker by the A148,' David says now.

Judy ignores him.

'Harry,' says Michelle. 'Harry. Can you hear me?'

Nelson turns his head and mutters something. Ruth thinks it could be 'police'. Is Nelson telling them to call for help or is he such a policeman that he's still working even whilst in delirium?

'The police are on their way,' she says.

Michelle gives her a look. They are standing either side of Nelson's bed, something that – if Ruth had time to think about it – seems like a bad joke. Or a nightmare.

'Do you really think they're coming?' says Michelle.

'I don't know,' says Ruth. 'I hope so. I mean, they can trace the call, can't they?'

'I don't know how these things work,' says Michelle. 'I'm not in the police. I'm just married to one.'

There's a short silence. Nelson says something else, the words ending in a groan. Ruth looks around the room: desk, filing cabinet, sink, window covered by a pleated blind. This must be the room that Nelson mentioned the last time they visited the house. *There's a room in this house that's all done up like a doctor's surgery. Creepiest thing you've ever seen.* Now the place looks as if it's been the scene of a fight, or some other altercation. The metal cabinet is dented and there are papers scattered on the floor. Stranger still, she can see the markers that are used in scene-of-crime investigations. Plastic cones with numbers on them. One on the floor by the desk, another by the door. Well, there's no time to solve that riddle now. Ruth goes to the sink and pours some water into a paper cup. She holds it to Nelson's lips, but he moves his head away, muttering again.

'Do you think the bullet's still in him?' whispers Michelle.

'I don't know,' says Ruth. An image comes to her of a man being forced to drink brandy before a bullet is cut out of him. She sees snow, black top boots, shirt ruffles red with blood, a coach and four. Then she realises that she's thinking about a Georgette Heyer novel. She has no idea what to do for someone who has been shot. Not in the twenty-first century. Not in the real world.

She goes to the door and bangs on it.

'Let us out!'

'Let's try to break it down,' says Michelle.

Ruth remembers Nelson shoulder barging the door of the barn. It didn't look too difficult then. 'Let's do it on three,' she says to Michelle. 'One, two, three.' Together, they charge. Ruth is quite dazed by the impact, but the door doesn't budge. Michelle runs at it again, making a noise like an enraged animal. She's far stronger than she looks. But the door remains locked.

They both look back at Nelson. He seems paler than ever with dark shadows under his eyes. Ruth notices, as she has noticed before, how long Nelson's eyelashes are when his eyes are shut.

'Is he going to die?' says Michelle. It feels almost like the first real thing Michelle has ever said to Ruth, her voice empty of anything except love and fear.

'No,' says Ruth, knowing that she must stay positive for all their sakes. 'The police will come. And the bullet's just in his shoulder. Paul said that it hadn't hit any vital organs.'

She has no idea why either of them should believe Paul but saying it makes her feel slightly better.

'What shall we do?' says Michelle. Up until now, she has been amazingly strong. She was the one who distracted the dog so Ruth could make the phone call. She faced up to Paul, even though he had a gun in his hand, and then she tried to calm him down, using the power of all her years as a mother. But now she is trembling, and tears are running down her face.

Ruth puts her arms round Michelle. 'It'll be OK,' she says.

Some instinct makes Judy park at the end of the drive. As she and David hurry along the gravel path, Judy sees the boss's car. When she gets nearer, she sees Ruth's car parked

next to it. Judy feels awkward all of a sudden. Is this a lovers'
tryst? Will she walk in on Ruth and Nelson together, something she has always dreaded? But then she spots another
car, a smart silver Mazda. Judy can't be sure, but she thinks
this belongs to Michelle. Judy goes closer. Yes, there's a
Redwings sticker in the back. Like Ruth – and Judy herself –
Michelle is a big supporter of the local horse charity. But
why would Ruth, Nelson and Michelle all be here?

'There's a van parked in the barn,' says David, who has
been wandering around the yard.

Judy feels another twinge of fear. 'Stay back,' she says to
David. And she walks towards the house. The front door is
open but, somehow, that feels even more sinister. A security
light comes on as she approaches and she remembers the
first time she saw Black Dog Farm, the dark figures of the
armed officers suddenly illuminated by the glare. *Police! If
you're in there, come out now and no one will get hurt.* Should she
be shouting something similar now? Or should she wait for
back-up? But, then again, maybe Ruth, Nelson and Michelle
are just sitting down to a cosy chat about their three-
cornered love affair.

As she hesitates, she hears a shot coming from the house.

35

Ruth and Michelle hear it too. They look at each other and Ruth sees her own terror reflected in Michelle's wide blue eyes.

'What was that?' says Ruth.

'It sounded like a gunshot.'

Has Paul shot someone? Has he killed himself? Murdered the dog? But before any more thoughts can chase themselves round Ruth's head, the door opens and Paul stands there, still holding the gun. The dog is at his side.

Instinctively, Ruth and Michelle move to stand in front of the injured Nelson. Shielding him.

'We heard a shot,' says Ruth.

'Oh that,' says Paul. 'I was just shooting at a rabbit. My dad used to be able to kill a rabbit from a hundred yards away.'

That's a strange thing to be proud of, in Ruth's opinion. She knows that country people often see rabbits as pests, but she can't help thinking of Kate's Sylvanian Cottontail bunnies. She wonders if Paul is losing track of reality. If so, can they use it to their advantage?

'Paul,' she says. 'We need to get an ambulance. Nelson is really ill.'

Paul comes towards the bed. Michelle moves infinitesimally closer to Ruth. Close enough for Ruth to smell her perfume, a scent she has often detected on Nelson. Michelle's hand brushes against hers.

'Move away.' Paul gestures with the gun.

'No,' says Michelle.

'I didn't mean to hurt him,' says Paul. 'I just needed to get you all here. Nelson must let Chloe go. She didn't kill them.'

'I'm sure everything can be sorted out,' says Ruth, in her most soothing voice, the one she uses for stressed undergraduates. *Of course* you can have an extension on your essay. *Of course* your sister won't be charged with murder.

Paul seems to hesitate. He lowers the gun. At that moment there's a sound from upstairs. A sort of clunk. The dog raises its head and lets out a short, staccato bark. Ruth touches Michelle's hand and dives for the door.

'Did you hear that?' says David. 'It sounded like a gun.'

No shit, Sherlock, thinks Judy.

'We need to stay here,' she says. 'I've called for back-up.' The reckless spirit that is inside her – invisible to everyone except Cathbad – longs to enter the house but she knows that to go in, alone and unarmed, would be madness.

She looks at David to check that he is listening, but he's staring at the roof of the house. She can hear the weathercock turning in the wind. When he speaks, it's almost to himself. 'There's another way in,' he says.

'What?'

'There's another way in. If you get onto the roof of this outhouse, you can get onto the roof. There's an attic window that doesn't close properly.'

'How can you possibly know that?'

'I used to live here.'

Can this be true? Judy doesn't have time to find out. She knows that she should wait for back-up – it should be here any minute – but, in the meantime, Nelson could be in danger. Nelson, Ruth and Michelle.

'How do I get up there?'

There's a flat-roofed outhouse, just a large shed really, near to the gable end of the house. David gives Judy a leg up. It's lucky he's so tall. From this vantage point, Judy is able to scramble onto the sloping roof.

'It's the window at the far end,' says David. 'The latch doesn't close properly.'

Judy isn't expecting it to work. If David has lived in this house, it can't have been recently. People get their broken windows mended. Even the Noakes family, who didn't seem particularly house-proud. Judy edges along the gutter. The roof is tiled but slippery with moss. She can't use her torch because she needs both hands, but David is shining a light on her from below. When she reaches the far window, she sees that it's held by an iron latch, slightly ajar. She's able to wriggle her fingers inside and manipulate the metal bar upwards. It takes a couple of anxious minutes but eventually the window swings inwards and Judy drops inside.

She's in an attic room with sloping ceilings. There are

boxes everywhere, some with the warning 'Hazchem' encased in a sinister chevron. Hazardous chemicals. If Judy gets out of here alive, she'll send a chemical weapons team over in the morning. Judy finds her phone and switches on the torch. The door is in front of her. She's terrified that it'll be locked but it opens easily. She pauses on the landing. Two storeys below she can hear voices and the sudden bark of a dog. Immediately she hears Cathbad's voice in her head. *He said, 'I think I've heard the Black Shuck barking.'*

Not now, Cathbad, says Judy silently. And she starts to descend the stairs.

The hall seems very dark after the overhead light of the hospital room. Ruth hesitates for a moment, feeling dazed. She thought the sitting room was opposite the so-called surgery but, just for a second, she can't see the door in the gloom. Has it disappeared? Is this the house of nightmares where everything rearranges itself as soon as your back is turned, doors becoming walls and staircases sinking into the ground? No, of course not. There it is, closed but she hopes not locked. Ruth turns the handle. Yes, here are the fringed lamps and the depressing sofas. And here is the table with the vase, photograph and telephone.

Ruth grabs the phone and, once again, dials 999.

'Stop!' Paul is at the door, the gun pointing at her.

Ruth doesn't stop. Ridiculously, she closes her eyes as if this will protect her from a bullet.

'Ambulance,' she croaks. 'Black Dog Farm. Near Sheringham. Someone's been shot. Please hurry.'

She opens her eyes. Paul is still aiming at her but, to Ruth's amazement, a figure suddenly appears behind him and fells him to the ground with what looks like a karate chop.

'Judy?' Ruth wonders if she is, after all, dreaming.

'Get the gun,' pants Judy. It's on the carpet by Ruth's feet, the long barrel pointing towards her. She picks it up gingerly just as Michelle appears in the hallway.

'Judy,' she says. 'What are you doing here?'

'I got in from the roof,' says Judy. 'I've called for back-up.'

A wave of relief sweeps over Ruth. It's so strong that she has to sit down, her head swimming. She puts the gun carefully on the sofa cushions.

'What's going on here?' says Judy.

'Harry's been shot,' says Michelle. 'He's in the room across the hallway. Paul left the dog guarding him.'

'The dog,' says Judy. 'I thought I heard a dog.'

She is fitting handcuffs onto Paul who doesn't seem to be resisting. 'Paul Noakes. I'm arresting you on suspicion of attempted murder . . .'

Ruth looks at Michelle and they both hear it at the same time. The unmistakable sound of a car pulling up outside. Ruth exhales. Police? Ambulance? Either way they are saved. And, a few seconds later, a uniformed police officer appears. Ruth feels weak with relief.

Judy has pulled Paul to his feet. 'Get him in the squad car, Mark,' she says to the policeman. 'There's an injured man in the other room. Is the ambulance here?'

'What's going on?' says Mark. He sounds rather dazed.

'DCI Nelson's been shot,' says Judy. 'The gun's over there.'

Mark goes over to the sofa and picks up the gun. He breaks open the barrel with one practised movement. Thank God, thinks Ruth. We're safe from it now.

But Paul says, 'It was you.'

Mark looks up and snaps the gun shut again.

'You killed my parents,' says Paul.

Ruth expects Mark to ignore this. Even to laugh. But instead he says, very seriously, 'I had to do it, Paul. For you and Chloe.'

Judy moves forward but Mark turns the gun in her direction.

'Stay there, Judy,' he says in a polite tone.

'You killed my parents,' says Paul again.

'Yes,' says the policeman in what strikes Ruth as a dangerously offhand tone. 'The world's a safer place without them. That's what Chloe said.'

'Does Chloe know?'

'Of course she does. She let me into the house, she gave me the gun.'

Ruth looks at Michelle, who looks at the door. She knows that they are both thinking about Nelson in the next room, injured, delirious, possibly even dying.

'DCI Nelson's hurt,' she says desperately, to the room in general. 'We need an ambulance.'

Mark ignores her. So does Paul. They are staring at each other.

'Was Chloe there?' says Paul, almost in a whisper. 'When you killed them?'

'Of course. She'd wanted me to kill them for a while, but I couldn't bring myself to do it. But then Nathan died. And that was your dad's fault, Paul. He gave him the wrong dose of a vaccine. It was the same with the other boy, Jem. Well, you know about that, don't you? He died here in this house. You took his body out to sea in the boat.'

'I couldn't save him. He was already dead when I—'

'You just did what your dad told you, didn't you,' says Mark. 'That's all you ever did.'

And then several things happen at the same time. There's a siren outside. Mark raises the gun. There's that scrabbling, slithering sound again and the dog bursts into the room.

'Dexter,' shouts Paul to the dog. 'Seize him!'

But the dog hesitates, looking at Mark, wagging its tail. 'You forget,' says Mark. 'I've bonded with that dog now. I took charge of him this morning. I love animals. Here, boy ...'

While his attention is distracted, Judy throws herself at Mark. The gun falls to the floor. Ruth runs into the hall and shouts 'Help!' Two paramedics appear, looking wonderfully solid in their green uniforms.

'In there,' pants Ruth, pointing to the white room.

Michelle is at her side as they lift Nelson onto the stretcher. Ruth hears voices outside and, when they emerge into the hall, it is full of police officers. Judy is grasping the arm of a handcuffed Mark. Tanya is there too, holding the gun. The new young DC has Paul in custody. They all jump when the grandfather clock chimes. Nine o'clock. It feels like midnight.

'Are you coming with us?' says the paramedic to Michelle. Or Ruth. Or both.

'Yes,' says Michelle. 'I'm his wife.'

Then she turns to Ruth. 'You can come too.'

36

The ambulance driver does his best along the rutted track, but Ruth is worried about Nelson, who is awake and obviously in a lot of pain.

The other paramedic keeps talking to him. 'Hang on in there, mate. What's his name?' he says to Michelle.

'Harry.'

'Hang on in there, Harry.'

But Nelson isn't Harry to anyone but Michelle, thinks Ruth. Don't die, Nelson, she tells him silently, as she has thought once before, in similar circumstances; the ambulance ride, lights shining on the wet road, Nelson's blood seeping into her hands. She looks out of the window and sees David Brown standing outside Black Dog Farm, watching them drive away. She waves feebly but, of course, the windows are opaque from the outside. As she watches she is sure she sees something else, a black shape crossing behind them, its eyes glowing red in the darkness.

The journey takes no time at all, or else it takes hours. The siren must be on but Ruth can't hear it inside the ambulance. She's aware only of Nelson, who seems to be drifting in and out of consciousness. Michelle sits beside him, holding his hand. The countryside slides past, industrial estates, golf courses. At least it's night so the roads will be clear. Then a series of roundabouts and the ambulance is slowing. The paramedics are readying themselves for action. The doors open and Nelson's stretcher is lifted out. Ruth sees a neon sign saying 'A and E'. The paramedics are actually running now, which terrifies her. Michelle follows, loping along easily in her trainers. Ruth pants after them.

The stretcher-bearers pass through the waiting area, along a corridor and through a set of swing doors. Ruth is only a few metres behind but, when she pushes through, she finds herself in an empty corridor, the next set of doors swinging to and fro. One of the overhead lights is failing and it flickers on and off like a distress signal.

Nelson is somewhere in the hospital, but Ruth has no way of knowing where he is. She can ask but she doubts if anyone will tell her. After all, his wife is at his side.

Judy holds a team meeting as soon as they are all back in the station. It feels wrong to have a briefing without the boss, but Judy is now the senior officer in charge. Nelson has been taken to hospital and, according to the paramedics, he is 'stable'. Judy has to get on with the job in hand. Mark Hammond and Paul Noakes are both in custody.

'Did you guess?' says Tanya. 'Did you guess about Mark?'

Her voice is devoid of its usual undertone of snark. Judy knows that they are all stunned by Mark's arrest. He's a much-liked officer, a local boy, the object of everyone's sympathy after Nathan's death. Coming only a few years after the murder of Tim, another valued colleague, it's a blow.

'No,' says Judy. 'But just this evening I suddenly thought about him. When Chloe was talking about her teenage boyfriends, she said they were all "spotty and intense". I remembered the boss telling me about Mark's speech at Nathan's funeral. They had known each other since they were spotty schoolboys, he said.'

'All schoolboys are spotty,' says Tony. 'It's not much to go on.' He's the only one who seems to be revelling in the drama though, to his credit, he keeps trying to look serious and solemn. But Tony didn't know Mark. Or Nathan. Or Tim.

'So Mark was having an affair with Chloe Noakes,' says Jo. She's sitting in on the meeting because Mark's involvement – and Nelson's injury – makes the case high priority. Judy believes that Jo is actually quite shocked. She hasn't mentioned press conferences once.

'The teacher at Greenhill said that Mark and Paul had fought over a girl,' says Tanya. 'I suppose that was Chloe.'

'I think so,' says Judy. 'Paul is very protective of his sister. As she is of him.'

'But Chloe had an affair with Neil Thomas,' says Tanya.

'Yes, and that's when she split up with Mark,' says Judy. 'But I think they got together again recently. Chloe wanted her parents dead and she thought Mark was the man to do it.'

They have arrested Chloe too. She's in an interview room downstairs, separated from her brother and her lover.

'I can't believe it,' says Jo. 'I mean, he was a copper. A good one, by all accounts.'

'I don't think he would have done it if Nathan hadn't died,' says Judy. 'But that sent him over the edge. Nathan died on Thursday the nineteenth. Mark knew that he'd been taking part in illegal drugs trials at Black Dog Farm, saving up to get married. Mark went to the farm that evening and shot Douglas and Linda dead. Chloe arranged it all. She was in the house when it happened. They set it up to look like suicide except that Mark made a mistake with the finger-prints. He wasn't to know that Douglas was left-handed.'

'What about the suicide note?' says Tanya.

'Mark did that,' says Judy. 'It wouldn't have been hard to send it to Douglas's printer. Mark was good at IT. Neil Thomas taught him.'

'And Alan White?' says Tanya. 'Did Mark kill him too?'

'I think so,' says Judy. 'I think Alan saw Mark leaving the farm that night. He recognised him because he was another of his ex-pupils. And Alan said something to Cathbad about going to the police. He must have said it to others too.'

'Poor old Alan,' says Tanya. 'He was looking forward to his retirement.'

It's an unusually empathetic statement from Tanya. But Judy feels sorry for Alan too. She remembers him telling Cathbad that he was scared and that he needed protection. If she'd followed this up, maybe Alan would still be alive. But there's nothing to be gained from this line of thought. She is in charge of the investigation now and their priority must be to make sure that the guilty people are charged and that the charges stick. She starts to outline the interview strategy when Tony interrupts to say, 'What about the dog that was buried in the garden? Did Mark know about that? Is that why he put it in the suicide note?'

'I don't know,' says Judy. 'One person who probably did know is David Brown, the lecturer at UNN. Apparently, he used to live at Black Dog Farm.'

'David Brown?' says Tony, his smooth brow wrinkling. 'Oh, he must be the son of the Manning-Browns. You know, the woman who fell into the combine harvester?'

If Tony is going to continue being so cheery, thinks Judy, it'll be a long night.

'This is an interview under caution,' says Judy. 'Present: DI Judy Johnson and DC Tony Zhang.'

'I know how it goes,' says Mark Hammond.

'You have a right to a solicitor at any time while in police custody. Do you want us to contact a duty solicitor for you?'

Mark shakes his head, but Judy needs him to say the words.

'You would like this interview to go ahead without a solicitor?'

'Yes.'

'OK. Can you tell us what happened on the night of Thursday the nineteenth of September and morning of Friday the twentieth, at Black Dog Farm?'

'I drove there on my moped, left it in the bushes by the lane. I walked up to the farm. Chloe let me in and gave me the gun. I don't know where she got it from. Paul had the dog – he often looked after him in the week – so there was no danger of him barking. Douglas was in the kitchen reading the paper. He stood up when I came in and I shot him. Linda was there too, I hadn't seen her at first. She screamed and ran past me so I followed her and shot her as she was running up the stairs. Afterwards I put Douglas's hand around the gun so that his prints would be on it. I left it beside him, then Chloe and I left the house. I gave her a lift back to Lynn on the moped.'

'Did you write the suicide note that was found in Dr Noakes's study?'

'Yes, I did that when I got home. It was easy to link my computer to Douglas's printer. I tried to make it sound like Chloe's father – she said he was a pompous bastard – but I wanted to say sorry too, especially for the story about the body in the garden. Chloe said that used to terrify her as a child.'

Judy notices that Mark's face changes when he mentions Chloe. He really does love her.

'Let's get back to the night of the nineteenth,' she says. 'Did you see anyone when you left the farm?'

'I didn't think so at the time. We went by the back roads and everything was very quiet. But Mr White must have seen us leaving the house. And he told Paul.'

'Alan White told Paul Noakes that he'd seen you leaving the house?'

'Not exactly. Alan told Paul that he knew something about the murders but that he didn't want to tell the police because he didn't trust them. That must have meant that he saw me and recognised me. He knew I was in the police. I'd even given a careers talk at the school. Paul told Chloe.'

'And Chloe told you?'

'Of course.' Mark sounds almost smug but Judy is willing to bet that there were many things that Chloe didn't tell her boyfriend.

'So you killed Alan?'

'I had to. I felt bad about it. Really. He was a decent bloke. I always liked him at school, even though some of the other kids took the piss out of him.'

'How did you kill Alan?'

'I arranged to meet him at the dig. He was there early. I saw Alan leaning over, looking into the trench. I'd picked up a big stone earlier and I hit him over the head with it. Then I pushed him into the hole.'

'Did you know that he was dead?'

'Yeah. I was pretty sure he was.'

'What did you do next?'

'Went home. I was on compassionate leave after . . . after Nathan died. His funeral was that morning.' His face changes and, for the first time, Mark looks moved. He pinches the bridge of his nose as though he might cry.

'Did you stage a break-in at Black Dog Farm this morning?' asks Judy.

'Yes, I wanted you to find out about the drugs trials. That's why I put the thing about Noakes's scientific work in the note. I made it look like a break-in because I knew that meant that you'd have to do a proper search of the place. But then Paul turned up at just the wrong time. Typical.'

'Did Paul know that you killed Alan?'

'No,' says Mark. 'He never knows what's going on. Chloe's

always had to look after him. He's just an idiot. I mean, look what he did today, getting Nelson's wife and mistress over to the farm, trying to force Nelson to let Chloe go. But Chloe wasn't even under arrest, for God's sake.'

He sounds genuinely exasperated.

In Interview Room B, Tanya and DC Bradley Linwood are questioning Paul Noakes.

'Did you shoot DCI Nelson with intent to kill?' asks Tanya, getting to the nitty-gritty.

'I didn't mean to kill him,' says Paul. 'It was only a shotgun, pellets not bullets. I just wanted him to agree to let Chloe go. I knew DCI Nelson would come if he heard there was a break-in at the farm. He doesn't seem to be able to keep away from the place. I got the incident sign from Mark's car.'

Tanya, who often resents the boss's hands-on attitude, now feels offended on his behalf. And how was shooting him meant to change Nelson's mind? She hopes that Paul won't get off with an insanity plea.

'What happened after you shot him?' asks Tanya.

'I put him in the back of the van and drove him up to the house. I cleaned up the wound and dressed it. I looked after him,' he says, with a pleading look. 'My dad taught me about first aid.'

It seems his dad taught Paul more than he originally let on, thinks Tanya. It strikes her that Paul has been seeking approval all his life, from his parents, his teachers and now from the police. Well, that might work to their advantage.

'You must have a lot of medical knowledge,' she says. 'Did

you help your father with the drugs trials?' Bradley looks at her admiringly.

'Yes,' says Paul. 'I helped him administer the drugs and I sat with the volunteers afterwards, monitoring their reactions.'

Volunteers. It's technically true but it seems a loose way to describe people putting their lives in the hands of doctor and son.

'What happened to Jem Taylor?' she asks.

'He had an allergic reaction,' says Paul. 'It couldn't have been predicted. He died before I could use the EpiPen.'

'What did you do next?'

'We couldn't leave him at the farm. I took his body out in the boat and put it in the sea. After all, he had that sea serpent tattoo. I thought it was quite fitting.' Again, that hangdog look.

'What happened at Black Dog Farm tonight?' asks Tanya.

'I took DCI Nelson's phone and I texted his wife and Dr Galloway. I knew she and the DCI were having an affair. Mark told me. Apparently, everyone in the police force knows.'

Tanya and Bradley avoid looking at each other.

'I thought they could persuade him to let Chloe go,' says Paul. 'But things just got out of hand.'

'What about the dog?' says Tanya. 'Did you set the dog on them?'

'Dexter? No. I just told him to guard them. That's what he was trained to do. He was Dad's guard dog.'

'I thought your dad didn't like animals,' says Tanya. 'That's what you told us.'

'He liked working dogs,' says Paul, as if this is obvious. 'He just didn't have time for pets.'

'Did he keep the dog to stop anyone coming too close to the house?' asks Bradley. 'So that they wouldn't find out about the illegal drugs trials?'

'That's right,' says Paul. 'He picked a black dog because of the legend. That's why he changed the name of the farm too.'

'You said that your dad used to frighten you with stories about a body buried in the garden,' says Tanya.

'That's right,' says Paul. 'Chloe must have told Mark and he put it in the note. Dad liked to scare us.'

'I'm not sorry,' says Chloe, in Interview Room C. 'I'd do it again.'

She looks at Judy, chin raised, half smiling. Judy wonders if this is the first time that she's seeing the real Chloe, the woman who obeyed her bullying father by becoming a doctor and then calmly set about arranging his death.

Chloe has explained that, on 19 September, she visited her parents 'to discuss finances'. 'I'd had to remortgage my flat and Dad, predictably, told me what a mess I was making of my life. How I should be financially independent at my age.' Chloe had walked from Sheringham so that her car wouldn't be seen outside the house. She pretended to leave at ten but had doubled back and hidden upstairs until Mark arrived at midnight. Apparently her parents kept late hours so she knew they would still be in the kitchen 'putting on the dishwasher and preparing to go to bed'. She'd given the gun to Mark and he had used it to kill her parents.

'Mark would do anything for me,' she says now. 'When I was young, I thought it was a pain how possessive he was. He would go mad if he thought any other man was looking at me. He even got into a fight with Paul at school because he thought that Paul should protect me more at home. Mark knew about the abuse. Well, some of it. He says that's why he became a policemen, to protect children like me.'

'But you split up with Mark and went out with Neil Thomas,' says Judy.

'Yes,' says Chloe. 'At the time Neil seemed so much more exciting. An older man, married and all that. Mark was devastated. He hated Neil. That's why he left that badge in Dad's office. To try and frame Neil. It was Alan's badge but they all had them, all the Night Hawks. That was stupid. I told him. No need to complicate things with break-ins and cryptic clues. We'd nearly got away with it. If it hadn't been for Paul going off the rails like that, shooting DCI Nelson, kidnapping his wife and mistress.'

Would they have got away with it? Judy isn't so sure. She thinks that Mark, at least, would have cracked eventually.

'When did you get back together with Mark?' she asks.

'About a year ago. I finished with Neil when I went to university. I left it all behind me, boyfriends, family, everything. They were the happiest years of my life. But then I came back. God knows why. And it all started again with my parents – not the physical abuse but the mental bullying. Dad going on at me about being a GP. He thought I should be a hospital doctor at the very least. Mum not sticking up for me. She never did. I think she loved her pupils at school

more than she did us. She was in thrall to him. I met Mark
in Lynn one day and it started again.'

'The affair?'

'Yes. Mark was still in love with me.' Chloe even allows
herself a smile of self-satisfaction at this. 'I was fond of him
too. It was nice to be with someone who adored me like that.
But then I started to realise that Mark was the perfect weapon.
He still hated my parents because of what they did to me. He
could handle a gun, he was used to acting under pressure. At
first he was reluctant but, when Nathan died, he suddenly
agreed. He loved Nathan. They were best friends from school.'

The perfect weapon, thinks Judy. Was that all Mark had
been to Chloe?

'I'm not sorry,' Chloe says again. Judy wonders if this can
really be true. She thinks of Chloe describing her parents
'putting on the dishwasher and preparing to go to bed'. Did
she not feel a pang when outlining this familiar domestic
routine? But then Chloe says, 'My dad sexually abused me
for years. My mum knew. Or at least she suspected. And she
never did anything. He used to say that, if I said anything, the
body in the garden would come and get me. That's why Mark
put it in the note. When I told him about the abuse he said,
"shooting's too good for them". And I think he was right.'

Tony Zhang looks as if he almost agrees with this. Judy,
too, feels that any sympathy she might have had for the
dead couple has evaporated in the light of this information.
She thinks of Paul saying to Tanya: 'It was worse for Chloe.'
But Chloe is still an accessory to murder. Judy can only hope
that the jury will be sympathetic too.

37

Ruth walks slowly back to the waiting area with the nailed-down chairs and defeated-looking people. She wonders whether she should ask someone to look at her head, which still aches where she was hit, but she doesn't have the energy. She'll just sit quietly and text goodnight to Kate. It's only when she sinks into an uncomfortable plastic seat and reaches for her phone that she realises that she doesn't have it. Paul took it when she was unconscious and she has no idea where it is now. Then the full force of this hits Ruth. She has no phone. She can't contact Kate and send her a cheery 'Good night xx'. Kate could be hurt or in danger and Tasha's mum would have no way of contacting Ruth. Her lungs start to contract and suddenly she doesn't know how to breathe any more. She gulps at the air but it's as if her throat has closed up. The room tilts and starts to fragment. Wash your hands. Smoking is hazardous to your health. Protective clothing required in this area. X-ray do not enter.

'Ruth! Ruth. Are you OK?'

Ruth opens her eyes. A face is on a level with hers but she

has trouble assembling it into someone she knows. Glasses, dark hair, large nose, angry expression.

'David?' she gasps.

'Breathe,' says David. 'Breathe in through your nose, out through your mouth. In, out. In, out.' Someone else said this to her once. Cathbad. Just thinking of Cathbad's name makes her relax slightly. She manages one breath, then another.

'That's it. Say this to yourself. Total calm. In, total. Out, calm. My therapist taught me that once.'

The room slowly rights itself. Total calm. But she isn't calm. Nelson is seriously injured and she can't contact Kate. She can feel herself hyperventilating again.

'Here.' David is holding out two phones to her. One is in a sparkly pink case, the other has a cracked screen.

She takes the cracked phone.

'Thank you! How did you find it?'

'It was in the house. In the kitchen. The place was swarming with police but, in all the confusion, no one noticed me take them. I recognised yours because your case has a picture of a cat on it.'

It's Flint, of course. The case was a present from Kate. Laura helped her design and order it. A wave of love for her daughter and her half-sister sweeps over her.

Ruth keys in her passcode. 011108. Kate's birthday. It's so obvious, she should really change it. There are no messages, nothing to worry about. She texts good night to Kate although, as it's nearly ten o'clock, she hopes that she's not still awake. The clock over the reception desk is stuck at ten to five. Ruth wonders if she should ring Laura but she doesn't have her mobile number. Kate has it but Ruth doesn't. The sparkly phone must be Michelle's. Should she try to open it, to try to ring Nelson's daughters? She stabs at it but the phone is password protected, of course. What is Michelle's password? Harry? One of the girls' birthdays? Their wedding anniversary? Ruth doesn't attempt to unlock the phone.

She turns to David. 'Thank you for bringing my phone. I'm afraid I was panicking a bit.'

'That's OK,' says David. 'I know I'd be lost without mine.'

'How did you know I was here?'

'I knew this is where they'd bring DCI Nelson. Are you still in a relationship with him?'

Ruth closes her eyes. She's grateful to David but she really doesn't want to have this conversation with him. Besides, is she in a relationship with Nelson? The tense implies something ongoing and active. He's the love of her life but that's not the same thing.

'It's complicated,' she says at last.

'Most things are,' says David, stretching out his long legs in front of him. 'You know,' he says, in a different tone, 'I used to live at Black Dog Farm.'

Ruth turns to look at him. 'Really?'

'Yes. I was born and brought up there. Then, when I was eight, my mum was killed in an accident. A really horrific accident. She was clearing a blockage in the machine and she was dragged into it. She hadn't set the safe stop system properly. I only found that out later.'

'How awful,' says Ruth. 'I'm so sorry.'

'It was horrendous,' says David. 'My dad just didn't talk about it. Never mentioned her name again. Then, two months after Mum died, he announced that he was sending me to West Runton Prep School. They were the worst years of my life.'

'I'm sorry,' says Ruth again.

'I had nightmares for years,' says David. 'The blood. There was so much blood. The ambulance. My father in the sitting room reading the paper. *Reading the paper.* As if nothing had happened. In my dreams the house became a mansion with thousands of rooms, or a tiny cell with barred windows. I went to therapy as an adult and they said I was suffering from PTSD. I learnt techniques to cope with it, but I wondered what would happen when I saw the place again. Would I collapse? Have some sort of fit? But, when I went back there, when you were excavating the garden, it was a shock to see that it was just a house. Bricks and mortar.'

He thought he'd seen someone in the window, Ruth remembers. She wonders who it was that David thought he saw.

'The dog,' she says. 'The dog in the garden . . .'

'That was Rex, our Doberman,' says David. 'My dad loved that dog. I was always a bit scared of him but, that day, when I was watching Mum's body being taken away, Rex came to me and comforted me. I've never forgotten it. He died a few years later and Dad buried him in the garden. I was away at boarding school at the time.'

'So you knew what the bones were,' says Ruth. 'You could have told me.'

'I'm sorry,' says David. 'I just felt so emotional when I saw Rex's remains. And then we saw that dog running into the barn. I thought I was seeing things. I couldn't tell you then. You would have thought I was mad.'

'I wouldn't have thought that,' says Ruth. 'But I think I can understand why you didn't say anything.'

'I didn't want anyone to know. I spent years being The Boy from the House of Death. People saying that Dad killed Mum. Some people even saying that I'd done it. I didn't want all that again. I didn't tell anyone at school. Even Alan didn't know. I almost didn't apply for the job at UNN but, I don't know, the lure of Norfolk was too strong.'

'I know what you mean,' says Ruth. 'I almost got away once but now I'm back. Was that what you were talking to Troy about? The fact that you used to live at Black Dog Farm?'

'Yes. Troy knew because his uncle was one of the policemen who attended the scene.'

The scene. It's very much a police word. Just for a second Ruth tries to imagine exactly what the scene was like. So much blood, David had said.

'It must have been hard going back,' she says.

'I feel better for it,' says David. 'As if I've laid the ghost. And I'm glad that I was there today because I was able to tell DI Johnson how to get into the house.'

'I couldn't believe it when I saw her,' says Ruth. 'I thought I was dreaming.'

'That was the house,' says David. 'It does things to your head.'

Maybe this is true, thinks Ruth. She thinks of Paul today, pointing the gun at them and rambling about Chloe and his parents. Did the policeman – Mark – really kill them? Whatever happened, it's easy to imagine the farmhouse casting a malign spell over them.

'I thought I saw the Black Shuck today,' she says to David.

'Maybe you did,' he replies.

Has he seen it? Ruth wonders. Has she seen it? She remembers the creature loping across the path, the flash of red eyes. Then she thinks of Nelson and nothing else seems to matter. She sits, gripping her phone with its picture of Flint. David stays silently beside her.

It's nearly midnight by the time Judy gets to the hospital. Mark Hammond has been charged with the murders of Douglas Noakes, Linda Noakes and Alan White; Chloe Noakes with conspiracy to murder, and Paul Noakes with attempted murder and false imprisonment. Judy has arranged for Jan Adams to take care of Dexter but there's still a lot of paperwork to get through in the morning, to say nothing of the furore when it gets out that a police officer was involved. But that's for another day. Right now, Judy is thinking about Nelson, her mentor, friend and, though he would hate to hear this, father figure. As she parks in the car park, she's not surprised to see a smart jeep in the space next to hers. When she gets to the main entrance, there he is, checking his phone.

'Hallo, Clough.'

'Judy! I just heard about the boss.'

If Nelson is the father, then Judy and Clough are the

siblings, vying for his attention. When they worked together, this often used to annoy Judy. She felt that Clough was always trying to play the bloke card with Nelson, talking about football and drinking (both things Judy also enjoys, incidentally), excluding her. But now, seeing the concern on Clough's face, Judy feels suddenly very close to him. They are family, after all.

'I rang just now,' she says. 'He's out of surgery and they say he's stable.'

'Was he shot?' says Clough. 'That's what I heard.'

'Yes,' says Judy. 'He just can't seem to stay out of trouble.'

'I saved his life once,' says Clough as they go in through the double doors.

This is one of Clough's favourite stories, starring himself in an impossibly heroic role, pulling Nelson out of the sea, giving him the kiss of life.

'You saved mine once too,' says Judy. 'Remember the mad horse that tried to kill me?'

'Necromancer,' says Clough. 'He won the Grand National the next year.'

The waiting area is almost deserted, but Judy is not surprised to see that Ruth is still there. She is surprised, though, to see that Ruth is asleep with her head on a man's shoulder and that the man is David Brown.

Ruth must have heard them approaching because she opens her eyes.

'Judy! Have you got any news?'

'He's out of surgery,' says Judy. 'And he's stable. That's good news,' she adds, because Ruth has gone very white.

'Don't worry, Ruth.' Clough bends down to give her a quick hug. 'He'll be OK. He's as tough as nails.'

David stands up. 'I'll go and ask at the desk.'

They all look at him and Judy knows that they are all thinking the same thing: who is this man and why is he presuming to ask about Nelson? But, before anyone can speak, the swing doors open and Michelle appears. Her face is pale and set and it's impossible to know, by looking at her, whether she's the bearer of good news or bad.

Clough rushes over to hug her. That seems to be his role here, comforting male friend. Still, he does it rather well.

'How are you, love? How's Nelson?'

'He's going to be OK.' Michelle sits beside Ruth, who turns to her. Ruth passes Michelle a sparkly pink phone. Michelle looks at it for a minute and then her face crumples as if she's about to cry. Judy sees Ruth hesitate and then put her arm round Michelle's shoulder.

Then Michelle says, 'He's OK. They got the bullet out – actually it was a shotgun pellet – and it hadn't touched any vital organs. Seems Loony Paul was right about that.'

Suddenly, both women are laughing. David and Clough hover, both holding paper cups of water. Michelle wipes her eyes and says to Ruth, 'Do you want to see him?'

Nelson is in a recovery ward. His eyes are closed and she thinks he's sleeping but, when she comes closer, he says, 'Hallo, Ruth.'

'Hi, Nelson.' She takes his hand which is lying on top of

the covers. It's his left hand, with the wedding ring. His right arm is bound up.

'Are you OK?' she says.

'Grand,' says Nelson, with a slight smile. He does look better than he did when lying in that horrible room at Black Dog Farm but he's still very pale with dark circles under his eyes.

'Did I dream it?' says Nelson. 'Were you and Michelle both there?'

'Is that your worst nightmare?' says Ruth.

Nelson shakes his head, which looks as if it hurts him. 'My worst nightmare would be losing you.'

'You won't lose me,' says Ruth. She wants to stay holding his hand but she knows Michelle will be there in a minute. She lets go. Nelson seems to be asleep but when she stands up, he says, 'Don't leave me, Ruth.'

38

In the end, it's rather a lovely wedding. Gloria wears a mid-night blue dress and a large hat that prevents Arthur from getting close enough to kiss her. 'Thank God,' Simon whispers to Ruth during the ceremony at the church, clearly not keen to witness his father worshipping Gloria with his body. Kate is a bridesmaid, along with Gloria's three granddaughters, wearing dresses of lighter blue with silk flowers in their hair. They all look beautiful but Kate, as the youngest, gets lots of attention. Ruth watches her daughter skipping around the reception and thinks that Kate will be on a high that will last several days. And, next week, she is playing Scrooge in the school play. Ruth resigns herself to spending Christmas with Sarah Bernhardt.

The reception is held in a hotel in nearby Blackheath. It's family only but Gloria's family is so large that they fill the function room with ease. On Arthur's side there are only Ruth, Simon, Cathy and their children, and Arthur's older sister Phyllis, who seems underwhelmed by the occasion.

'We're outnumbered,' says Phyllis, when Ruth steers her to a table.

'What do you mean?' says Ruth, dreading some reference to being 'the only white people in the room'.

'We're not Christians,' says Phyllis, with a rather sly grin, as if she knew what Ruth was thinking. 'I'd thank God for it, if he existed. Look at that preacher, Father Whatsit. Doesn't he love himself?'

Ruth thinks that Phyllis is referring to the church elder, Brad, rather than the vicar, Father Anthony, an inoffensive man with white hair and a diffident manner. Brad, on the other hand, sports a mahogany suntan and has the brightest teeth Ruth has ever seen. He gave the sermon at the wedding and the gist of it seemed to be, 'Be as much like me and my lovely wife, Poppy, as you can.' Poppy has a matching tan and what looks like a designer outfit. Ruth doesn't think it's worth speculating where the devout couple acquired these things.

Ruth had forgotten that Phyllis wasn't a Christian. Maybe this is why she hasn't been much in evidence over the years. The last time Ruth saw her was at her mother's funeral, a day that now seems dreamlike in its sadness.

'Ruth, darling.' Gloria has appeared at her side, still wearing the hat. 'Have you got something to eat? How's Auntie Phyllis?'

'I'm not your auntie,' says Phyllis but Gloria doesn't seem to hear. Maybe the hat is impeding her hearing.

'I'm just about to go to the carvery,' says Ruth. 'This is a lovely reception.'

'Arthur and I are just so happy to have our nearest and dearest around us.' Gloria reaches out to pat Simon's hand. Simon has softened enough over the last few months not to flinch.

'Your sons are so handsome,' says Gloria to Cathy. George and Jack are both at different awkward stages; George is thin and spotty and Jack large and glowering. But Cathy blushes and smiles. To her, of course, her boys are beautiful. They are to Ruth too, who is a fond aunt – although she's also not fond of being called 'Auntie'.

Kate dances over and Ruth manages to persuade her to sit down and eat some food. Gloria's son Ambrose proposes a toast to the bride and groom.

'To the bride and groom,' echo the guests. Ruth drinks her Prosecco too quickly. At least she isn't driving. She and Kate are spending the night at the Eltham house. Gloria and Arthur will be off on their honeymoon in Torquay.

'Don't know why Arthur wants to get married at his age,' says Phyllis, tucking into her roast beef.

'It's the companionship,' says Cathy. 'Someone to grow old with.'

'They're old already,' says Phyllis.

Ruth will probably never grow old with Nelson. At fifty-one some people would say that they are old already. Will she have to spend the next twenty or thirty years of her life on her own? She remembers her father saying, 'I don't want to spend my final years without sex.' Even though the remark had been desperately embarrassing, Ruth had quite admired him for making it. Her father is eighty-one and he is clearly determined to live a full life with the woman he loves.

It's been more than two months since the events at Black Dog Farm. Nelson is still on sick leave but is well enough to be thoroughly fed up with his own company. How on earth will he cope with retirement? Nelson says that Super Jo is nagging him to call it a day. 'If she thinks that being shot will stop me doing my job, she's got another think coming.'

Nelson's mother Maureen is arriving today. Another one of the strong women in his life: Jo, his daughters, Ruth and Michelle. Perhaps Michelle most of all. Ruth will never forget standing with Michelle in front of the injured Nelson. They would both have died for him and that, in a way, is the strongest bond of all. Maybe, after all this time, she's a little in love with Michelle too.

Ruth has seen Nelson several times over the last few weeks. She even visited him at home, sitting trapped on the sofa with his arm in a sling, Michelle hovering in the background. But last week was the first time that she felt that she'd really spent time with him. Nelson came to help Ruth and Kate put up their Christmas tree. It had been one of those cosy afternoons when Ruth was able to imagine that this was her life now, two adults and their child, putting up their tree, laughing about Cathbad's home-made decorations. But then Nelson had gone home to his wife and other family. She ought to be used to it by now but somehow she isn't.

Ruth was offered counselling after the 'hostage situation'. She doesn't know if Michelle has accepted, but Ruth hasn't taken the police up on their offer. She's too busy, she tells herself. And the end of term was pretty hectic. Ruth has managed to secure a grant to get a facial reconstruction of Stan, the Blakeney Point skeleton. David was delighted and is still enthusiastically pursuing his deadly virus theory. Ruth had thought that she and David had reached a new understanding that day at the hospital but she still finds him incredibly annoying at times, particularly when he's telling her what she should do and how she should do it. David has also teamed up with a rather terrifying Swiss scientist called Claudia. For the first time in ages, Ruth thinks of her ex-boyfriend Max, who had a dog called Claudia. Should she have married Max? Should she have married Frank? Well, it's too late now.

George must have been knocking back the Prosecco too because he suddenly raises his glass: 'To Granddad and Gloria.'

'To Granddad and Gloria,' say Ruth, Kate, Simon, Jack and Cathy.

It sounds almost like a hymn.

Nelson and his mother are walking together. Maureen arrived in King's Lynn at lunchtime, declared herself simultaneously exhausted by the drive – although, in fact, her daughter Grainne had done the actual driving – and in need of fresh air. So, after a hearty lunch cooked by Michelle, Nelson and Maureen take Bruno for a walk in the grounds of the Sandringham estate.

'The Queen's here for Christmas,' says Nelson, 'you might see her.'

'Get on with you,' says Maureen, but Nelson thinks she's keeping a pretty keen eye out all the same.

They are walking through pine trees. Nelson thinks the trees look and smell like Christmas. Two days earlier, Michelle and Laura had collected their Christmas tree and decorated it. They wouldn't let Nelson help. 'I'm fine now,' he'd grumbled, 'stop cossetting me.' 'We can manage,' said Laura. 'Besides, you always put the decorations in the wrong place.' It had been news to Nelson that there was a wrong place for Christmas decorations but he had quite enjoyed watching his wife and daughter hanging the ancient baubles on the slightly off-centre tree (he would have done a better job of securing it in its pot). Earlier that week he had helped Ruth put up her tree and watched as Kate adorned it with frankly bizarre-looking objects donated by Cathbad. How long can he go on living two lives? Not long, is the answer.

'Mum,' he says, 'while you're here I'd like you to meet Katie, Ruth's daughter.'

'I've met her before,' says Maureen. 'In Blackpool. Pretty little thing. Where's Bruno? Has he run off?' Maureen loves Bruno and, as with all her closest relationships, she expresses this in constant nagging.

'He's here,' says Nelson, as the dog comes charging through the bracken, tail wagging. He picks up a stick and throws it for him. 'Let's stop for a minute.'

'Are you tired?' says Maureen. 'I knew this walk was too much for you.'

They didn't tell Maureen about Nelson's accident until he

was home from hospital and, even then, it had been hard to stop her racing down from Blackpool, convinced that only she could nurse her beloved son back to health. Now she looks at him sharply as they sit on a wooden bench inscribed, 'For Joe, who loved walking here'. Bruno brings the stick back and stares at Nelson until he throws it again.

'You've lost weight,' says Maureen.

'A bit,' says Nelson. 'I needed to. The thing is, Mum, about Katie. The thing is . . . she's my daughter.'

He has imagined making this confession a thousand times but, when it comes to it, it's surprisingly easy. The words are said, and the world is still turning. He looks up at the spiky pine branches, dark against the pale winter sky.

Maureen says, 'You had an affair with that Ruth? And she had your baby? Does Michelle know?'

'Yes.'

'Your wife's a saint. Far too good for you.'

'I know.'

'And she lets you see this Katie?'

'Yes. It's been hard for her. But she thinks . . . well, it's not Katie's fault. She shouldn't have to grow up without a father.'

'You should have thought of that before you broke your marriage vows.'

'I know.'

'So Katie's my grandchild.' Nelson had known that this would get to her and it's his main reason for having this conversation. Maureen is Katie's only grandmother. They should get to know each other.

'She's your grandchild. Sometimes she reminds me of you. She's very clever, for one thing.'

Maureen says nothing but he knows that this has struck home.

'Poor little mite,' says Maureen at last. Then she says, 'Do you love this Ruth?'

It's not what Nelson was expecting. He thought his mother would focus on her new grandchild and on Michelle's saint-liness. He's shocked into telling the truth.

'Yes,' he says. 'But I couldn't leave Michelle. Not now that we've got George.'

'But you've got Katie too,' says Maureen.

'I know. It's a mess. And it's all my fault.'

Maureen puts her hand on his arm. Her voice is unex-pectedly soft and very Irish. He'd forgotten she could sound like this.

'It's not all your fault, Harry. You've done wrong though, no doubt about it, but what good does it do anyone if you're unhappy? This way no one's happy. You, Michelle, Laura, Rebecca, George. Even Ruth and this Katie. You know, I was in love once.'

'With Dad. I know.' He assumes that Maureen is about to embark on a lecture about the sanctity of marriage.

'With your father, of course. But, about five years after he died, I met someone else. Do you remember Eddie, who used to coach you at football?'

Nelson dimly remembers his ex-football coach, a large man with a loud laugh. He'd been Irish, like Maureen.

He remembers that his mother had started coming to his matches. Nelson had been touched, thinking that she was trying to replace his father, who'd been a big supporter of the team.

'You were in love with Eddie?' Even saying the words sounds absurd.

'He wanted us to get married,' says Maureen. 'But I thought it was too soon. I thought you and the girls weren't ready. And, well, Eddie couldn't wait for ever. He was still fairly young. I was too, of course.'

'Did you regret it?' asks Nelson.

'Yes,' says Maureen, reaching out to pat Bruno, who has come back with the stick. 'I did regret it.'

'What shall I do, Mum?' Nelson can't remember ever having said these words before. Not wanting to hear the answer, anyway.

'I think you know what to do,' says Maureen. They sit in silence for a while and then they stand up and head for home, Bruno bounding beside them.

ACKNOWLEDGEMENTS

The Night Hawks was written, edited and produced in lockdown. I feel very lucky to have been able to continue to write during this time but I wouldn't have been able to do so without the team at Quercus, particularly my wonderful editor Jane Wood. Thank you, Jane, for everything. Huge thanks also to Hannah Robinson, Ella Patel, Katie Sadler, Bethan Ferguson, David Murphy and Florence Hare. This has definitely been a team effort. Thanks also to Liz Hatherell for her meticulous copy-editing and to Ghost Design for the wonderful cover.

Thanks to Claudia Albertini for taking part in an auction to become a character in this book. All proceeds go to CLIC Sargent, the charity supporting teenage cancer sufferers, so a huge thanks to Claudia and to everyone who took part. Thanks also to my friend David Brown for allowing me to use his name for one of my characters and for making a donation to Shelter. I need hardly say that the real Claudia and David bear no resemblance to their fictional counterparts.

Thanks to the many experts who have helped with this book – any mistakes are mine alone. Thanks to Dr Charlotte Houldcroft for the invaluable information about bio-hacking and viruses, to Linzi Harvey for her continued help on bones and to Graham Bartlett for advice on policing. Thanks to Mary Williams for inside information on the academic life.

Black Dog Farm is imaginary but the Black Shuck is as real as a legend can be. Thanks to the podcast 'Weird Norfolk' for information on this and many other Norfolk tales. Thanks to the *Eastern Daily Press* for articles about the Norfolk Sea Serpent and the Sheringham mermaid. I am also indebted to a wonderful book by the Wells Harbour Master, Robert Smith, called *Crossing the Bar: Tales of Wells Harbour*.

Thanks to my incredible agent, Rebecca Carter, and all at Janklow and Nesbit. Thanks to Naomi Gibbs and the team at my American publishers, HMH. Thanks to Kirby Kim and all at Janklow's US branch. Thanks to all the publishers throughout the world who publish these books with such care. Thanks to all my crime-writing friends who have also helped so much in this scary, isolating time. Special thanks to Lesley Thomson, William Shaw and Colin Scott. Thanks also to David Gilchrist and the UK Crime Book Club for all their support.

This book is dedicated to my niece and nephews, Francesca, William and Robert Lewington, who, many summers ago, listened to my stories about a boy called Sylvester. Love and thanks always to my husband, Andrew, and to our children, Alex and Juliet.

Finally, thanks to you for reading this book. If 2020 has taught us anything it's the value of reading and bookish communities. Thanks to everyone who has bought or borrowed any of my books. I appreciate you more than I can say.

Elly Griffiths, 2021

An excerpt from the next Ruth Galloway
mystery, *The Locked Room*, follows.

PROLOGUE

—

At first, she thinks that he'll be coming back. It's all a mistake, she thinks. He can't mean to leave her locked in the dark for ever. And it is dark. She doesn't have her phone. Where did she leave it? There are blanks in her memory which scare her even more than the locked room.

She tries to pace it out. Eight paces forward, eight paces across. When she reaches a wall, it's cold and clammy. There's no window. The door is metal. She heard it clang behind him. She can't remember entering the room. Did he drug her? She thinks, from the cold and damp, that she must be underground. She imagines earth above her head, fathoms of it. Is she in the basement of a house? Is anyone above her?

What did he say? That he'd be coming back later? Why can't she remember any more than that?

Does he mean to leave her in the dark for ever?

CHAPTER 1

Saturday, 22 February 2020

It feels strange being in the house on her own. When she was growing up here, her mother always seemed to be in possession, even – mysteriously – when she wasn't actually present. Ruth remembers coming home from school and feeling guiltily relieved when the double-locked front door meant that Jean Galloway was out at her part-time job. But, even as Ruth turned on the TV and raided the biscuit tin, there was always the sense that Jean was watching her, not just from the black-and-white wedding photo over the set – Jean in an uncomfortably short sixties dress, Arthur surprisingly dashing in a thin tie and Mod suit – but from every corner of the neat, terraced house. And now, even though Jean has been dead for nearly five years, there's still the same sense that she's hovering somewhere on the edge of Ruth's consciousness.

Maybe Jean is hovering because Ruth is currently in her mother's bedroom going through a shoebox of photographs marked 'Private'. Ruth's father has gone away for the weekend with Gloria, his new wife. When they return, Gloria wants to redecorate so Ruth has offered to go through her mother's belongings. Gloria (however much she likes her, Ruth can't think of her as her stepmother) has been very tactful about the whole thing. She hasn't changed anything in the house since she moved in two years ago, living with Jean's clothes in the spare room wardrobe and Jean's pictures on the walls. It's only natural that she would want to redecorate a little and, frankly, the house could do with it. Now that she doesn't live there, Ruth notices the peeling paintwork, the faded wallpaper, the outdated furnishings. Once these were just part of what made up her home but, looking at the place with Gloria's eyes, Ruth can understand the desire to freshen things up a bit. And, if Gloria has managed to persuade Arthur to get rid of his comb-over, there's no limit to her powers.

Ruth is alone because her sister-in-law Cathy has taken her daughter Kate to the zoo, reluctantly accompanied by Kate's seventeen-year-old cousin Jack. Kate loves animals and has been looking forward to the treat all week. Ruth hasn't been to London Zoo for years but she has a sudden vision of the Penguin House, an art deco marvel of curves and blue water. But didn't she read somewhere that penguins were no longer kept there because it turned out not to be suitable for them? She has the uncomfortable feeling that zoos, especially in the city, aren't suitable for any animals. She braces herself for a debate with Kate on this subject when she returns. Kate is a great one for philosophical debate. Ruth can't think where she gets it from. Kate's father, DCI

Harry Nelson, is allergic to the word philosophy. See also: art, archaeology, spirituality, yoga and vegan.

So far the photographs in the shoebox have not lived up to their intriguing label. There are a few pictures of Jean when she was young, as a schoolgirl in plaits and as a young bank clerk in a dark suit. Ruth peers at the faded prints, trying to detect any resemblance to herself, or to Kate. Ruth has often been described as looking like her mother, but she has always thought this was just because they both had a tendency to put on weight. Now, looking at the young Jean, she thinks she can see a faint likeness to Kate in her direct gaze and defiant stance, even in pigtails. It's a real sadness to Ruth that Kate never really got to know the grandmother whom, she now realises, she rather resembles in character.

A picture of a fluffy dog is a mystery. Jean always refused to have a pet and thought that Ruth's acquisition of two cats in her late thirties was a sign that she had, in her words, 'given up'. Next there's a picture of an older Jean in a long white dress, like a nightdress. What on earth? Then Ruth spots the grim-looking building in the background. Her parents' church. This must have been Jean's second baptism, when she was 'born again'. Ruth doesn't share her parents' faith and, when she was growing up, she had bitterly resented the church's influence on their lives. Finding God seemed to mean that her parents lost touch with everything else. For the truly righteous, religion is a full-time job. But the years have softened Ruth's stance and she was particularly glad that her father had the church's support after her mother died. In fact, the Christian Bereavement Group is where he met Gloria.

She shuffles through several adult baptisms until there's only one photograph left in the box. It shows three cottages surrounded by flat marshland. Ruth looks again. It's her cottage! Her beloved, inconvenient home, miles from everywhere, facing the Saltmarsh, inhabited only by migrating birds and the ghosts of lost children calling from the sea. Jean always disliked the house. 'Why can't you live somewhere more civilised?' she used to say, a south London girl born and bred. 'Somewhere with shops and a proper bus service?' Why on earth would Jean have kept a photograph, a rather scenic one too, of the despised cottage?

But there's something wrong with the picture. The cottages are painted dull pink rather than white and are surrounded by a low hedge rather than a picket fence. The car parked in front of the last house looks boxy and strange. Ruth turns the photo over and sees, in her mother's characteristically loopy handwriting: *Dawn 1963*.

Ruth was born in 1968. She looks again at the picture, taking in the sepia tones and the rounded edges. There's no doubt about it. Her mother had a picture of Ruth's cottage, taken thirty years before Ruth ever saw the place.

Ruth takes the shoebox of photos into her room and puts it by her case. She's sleeping in her old childhood bedroom, barely big enough for a bed, bookcase and wardrobe. Kate has Simon's old room which was bigger because he was older and a boy. 'Boys need more space,' Jean used to say, in answer to Ruth's regular complaints. But Simon, unlike Ruth, was a neat, contained creature and would have fitted comfortably in the box bedroom. Ruth remembers that he never expanded to fill his room in the way that Kate has done over one night, clothes on the floor, open books on the bedside table. Ruth picks up the clothes, though she knows she should make Kate do it herself. Kate is eleven, after all.

Ruth has packaged her mother's clothes into two bin bags, one for charity and one for recycling. There was nothing she wanted to keep. Arthur has already given Ruth her mother's gold watch on a chain and her diamond engagement ring. Ruth keeps these in a wooden box with Kate's pink hospita bracelet from when she was born ('Girl of Ruth Galloway') and a shepherd's crown, a fossilised sea urchin meant to bring good luck. This last was a present from her druid friend Cathbad.

Looking through her mother's belongings has made Ruth feel sad and restless. She needs some fresh air. The house is in a residential part of Eltham, rows and rows of Edwardian terraces and thirties' semis, slightly smarter than in Ruth's day but still presenting a rather grey and forbidding aspect. There's nowhere very exciting to walk, unless you make the trip to the park or the cemetery. Ruth decides to go to the local shops. It's a depressing little parade but it has a Co-op where she can buy a *Guardian* and a cake for tea. As Ruth walks, she thinks of taking this route with her schoolfriend Alison. When they were children, they went to the news-agents every Saturday to buy comics. Later, they both had paper rounds, slogging through the early morning streets delivering the *South London Press*. Later still, they lied about their age to buy alcohol from the sleazy off-licence on the corner. On impulse, as she passes this shop, now a Tesco

Metro, Ruth takes a selfie and texts it to Alison. She's not very adept at doing this and cuts off half her face but Ali will get the message.

When she gets back to the house, Cathy, Kate and Jack have returned from the zoo. Kate is full of information about tigers, sloths and an okapi called Meghan. Jack is quieter but, in between mouthfuls of cake, tells them a quite frightening number of facts about spiders. Cathy shudders but Ruth says that Cathbad apologises if he disturbs a spider's web. 'They are great works of art,' he says.

'Is that your wizard friend?' says Cathy. She has refused cake because 'it's a five hundred calorie day' but she's not a bad sort really.

'He's a druid,' says Kate.

'What's the difference?' says Jack.

'Druids are real,' says Kate. She specialises in unanswerable replies which can sound rude if she's not careful. Ruth is just about to plunge in with more questions about the zoo when her phone pings. It's from Alison.

R U in Eltham?

Ruth types back 'yes' though she knows Kate wants to remind her about the 'no phones at the table' rule.

OMG. It must be a sign! School reunion tonite! U up for it?

Is she?